T0279173

TANGLEROOT

TANGLEROOT

KALELA WILLIAMS

FEIWEL AND FRIENDS
NEW YORK

A Content Warning from the Author:

Tangleroot is a work of fiction, but it's inspired by history, as well as problematic parts of our present-day. So there are disturbing elements in this novel: ideology and language that is racist and otherwise offensive; sexual harassment and assault; and graphic violence. Please take care as you read. For a list of resources that might be helpful as you process this book, please visit my website, **kalelawilliams.com**.

A Feiwel and Friends Book
An imprint of Macmillan Publishing Group, LLC
120 Broadway, New York, NY 10271 • fiercereads.com

Our books may be purchased in bulk for promotional, educational, or business use. Please contact your local bookseller or the Macmillan Corporate and Premium Sales Department at (800) 221-7945 ext. 5442 or by email at MacmillanSpecialMarkets@macmillan.com.

Library of Congress Cataloging-in-Publication Data is available.

First edition, 2024
Book design by Meg Sayre
Feiwel and Friends logo designed by Filomena Tuosto
Printed in the United States of America

ISBN 978-1-250-88066-6
10 9 8 7 6 5 4 3 2

TO MY MOTHER,

ZEBORAH S. WILLIAMS,

WHOSE NAME I SPEAK ALOUD

AS I WRITE IT ON THIS PAGE.

YOU ARE ALWAYS WITH ME.

I WILL ALWAYS TELL YOUR STORY.

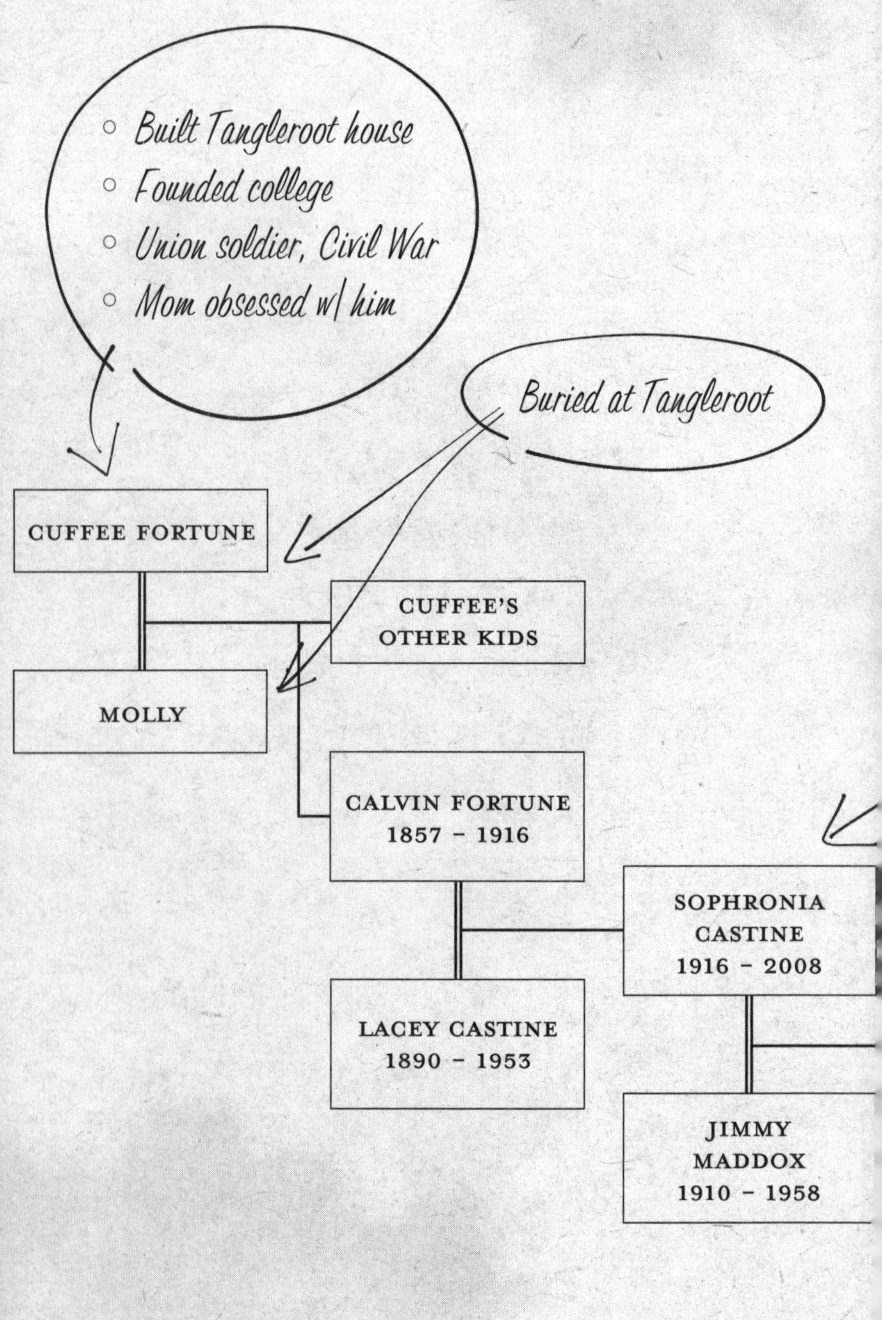

Built Tangleroot house
Founded college
Union soldier, Civil War
Mom obsessed w/ him
Buried at Tangleroot
CUFFEE FORTUNE
CUFFEE'S OTHER KIDS
MOLLY
CALVIN FORTUNE 1857 - 1916
SOPHRONIA CASTINE 1916 - 2008
LACEY CASTINE 1890 - 1953
JIMMY MADDOX 1910 - 1958

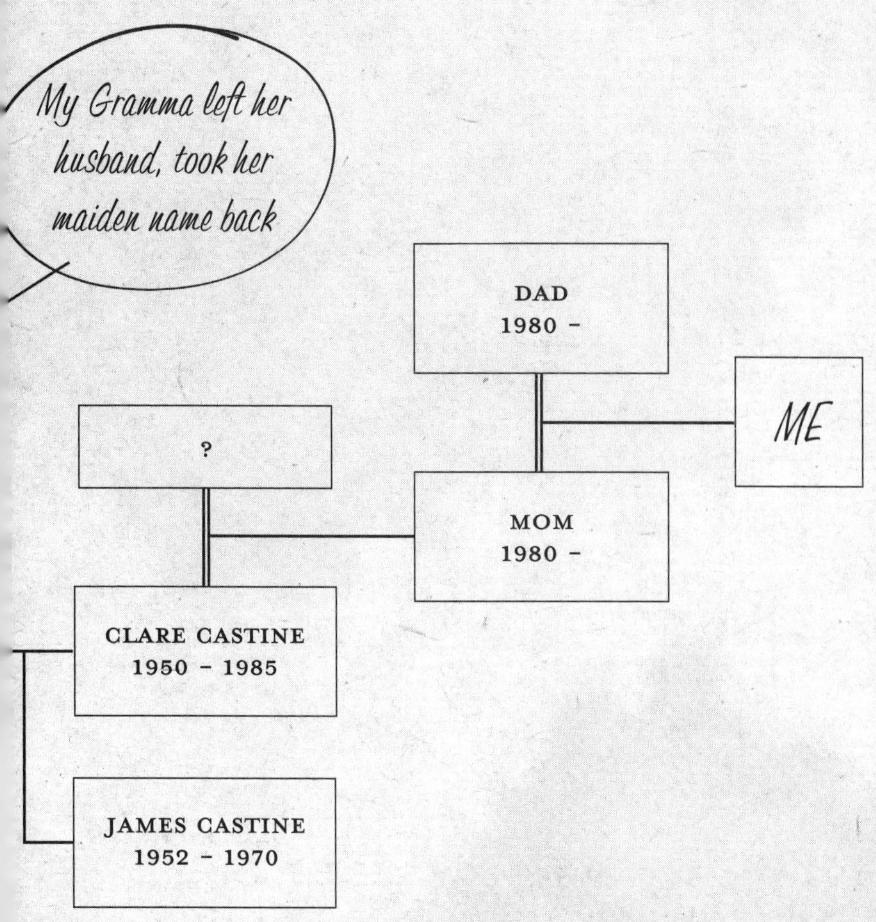
My Gramma left her husband, took her maiden name back
DAD
1980 -
ME
?
MOM
1980 -
CLARE CASTINE
1950 - 1985
JAMES CASTINE
1952 - 1970

CHAPTER 1

Mom wasn't gorgeous, but she carried herself with an understanding that she was, and people tended to take her at her word. They'd indulge in a few extra seconds to watch her when she walked by, or hold the door open for her a minute too long, or they'd ferry her drinks at receptions like this one—especially men. No one ever saw Mom's set, I-told-you-so chin, an inheritance from Gramma, who was gentle and sweet-faced but barbed with the nerve to leave her husband in the 1950s and take her maiden name back. No one saw the severity of Mom's gaze, as if she were glaring at you over a set of invisible glasses, the way her dressmaker great-grandmother would have scrutinized a garment, her mind drafting a pattern of gathers and tucks. With Mom's eyes, hair, and complexion the same auburn shade, it was as if she'd been cast out of bronze, not made of flesh and blood like the rest of us. Perhaps her coloring was the unknown of her, inherited from a nameless father.

What people saw of her were the soft things: her dimples, her curves, the tiny zigzag curls of her voluminous mane. They noted the proud way she owned a room, which she could do, being five foot nine with slim, muscled limbs. And more than anything, they talked about how brilliant she was. How accomplished.

I'd been hearing this my whole life, how wonderful and amazing Mom was. So I hung back from it all, loitering in the rear of the chandeliered hotel ballroom by the cheese-ball station. I'd sampled all the different kinds except a loaf rolled in rainbow sprinkles. The "Birthday Party" flavor looked questionable as hell, but why not? Just as I scooped a big dollop, Mom appeared from the crowd of Stonepost College alumni, who unlike the confetti sprinkles were all one color: white.

"Noni, sweetie." She kissed my forehead while I burned with embarrassment. "The program's about to start. Let's head up front."

"Thanks, but I'm okay right here." Blending in with the wall while snacking on weird cheese was my superpower.

"I'd like for you to go up with me."

"Mom." I sighed. But who could blame me for my annoyance? This felt like the ninetieth reception she'd dragged me to, and her multicity meet and greets were merely stops along the route to where I'd be stuck all summer: Magnolia, Virginia, a town with a smaller population than my high school. Worse, this was my first summer before college and my *last* summer with my best friend. And what was even more awful was that I had to turn down an internship that I was insanely lucky to get. Instead, I'd be trapped in a rural county in the middle of nowhere. The closest I'd get to an eighteenth birthday party would be this blob of cheese squatting on a Chinet plate. Even though said blob was surprisingly delicious, having to be here wasn't fair.

A bristly-bearded guy with a nameplate clipped to his shirt got Mom's attention as I helped myself to more cake-batter-cream-cheesiness. "Dr. Castine, we're going to go ahead and get things rolling if it's okay with you."

"Absolutely. Thank you." Taking my elbow, she led me to the front of the crowded ballroom. "Sweetheart, I need your help."

"With what?"

"With opening the program. The development office wants you to introduce me tonight."

She wanted me to make a public address? Was she kidding? "No thank you," I said emphatically.

"Noni, I know. It's last-minute. They just thought it would underscore the meaning of Stonepost's history. I agree."

"Mom, you know I get nervous about this kind of thing."

"I know, honey. But you can't back out."

"Back out? I never backed in."

"Noni, you'll be fine." She showed me a folded sheet of paper. "I need you to do this. Please, just this once. Your name's already on the program."

Sure enough, there I was, listed in print. "Mom! What the hell!"

"Watch your language." She spoke under her breath. "This'll take five minutes. I know you're anxious, but you'll be fine." Before I could protest again, she guided me behind a set of curtains, then clipped a microphone battery pack to my sash. "Just thread this right through your top," she instructed. I unbuttoned the lace-fronted jumpsuit I'd sewn for my graduation, snaking up the thin cord. Mom clipped the tiny lavalier mic to the collar.

The bearded guy waited outside the draping, instructing, "Just push the lever on the pack to turn it on. The mic won't sound like it's amplifying, but it's working."

"Can you feel the button?" Mom asked. "There's a speech for you on the podium." She wrapped her arm around me. "You'll do fine."

I was nervous. I knew I should take deep, calming breaths. But I was also irritated. How could she put me up to this? Instead of sucking in any kind of zen vibes, I pushed short breaths out, like a pissed-off dragon exhaling smoke.

"About that speech, Dr. Castine," Bristlebeard said. "The version on the podium is ours, with edits."

Now Mom was the pissed-off dragon. "Oh, come on."

"We felt the naming issue . . ." He spoke quietly while I fought every urge to walk away.

She cut him off. "I've omitted the idea from our other receptions, but this is the one event where I feel the audience will be conducive to hearing—"

"The team respects your judgment, but reconsidering . . ."

". . . that I would like to move toward renaming this college after the Black man who founded it?" She spoke in both a whisper and a growl.

"It wasn't my decision. The board . . ."

A slow groan leaked from Mom's parted lips. In theater terms, the "boards" meant the stage. But in college-administration speak, "the board" meant the board of directors, a committee of bigwigs who criticized Mom's every move. The man seemed flustered. "They felt it's important to hear your vision for Stonepost College, yes. But this is a fundraiser . . ."

By now we were in the front of the ballroom, my glob of cheese was in the trash, and Mom looked like she didn't know who was more maddening: me or her staff member. Closing her eyes, she placed her hand on the small of my back, giving me a little push forward. "Just read what's on the podium," she muttered. "*Their* words."

I didn't want to read anyone's words, but what could I do? Walk away? The truth was, I couldn't win against Mom. In the end, she always got her way, with me at least. And that's why I would be stuck in Virginia all summer.

I swear I heard at least one or two old ladies coo "*Awww*" as I stepped onstage. They saw a cute teen with a perpetual, overgrown adoration for her mother. I saw a mother who stood a few feet away with an unmistakable don't-screw-this-up glare.

Just read the speech, I told myself. *Just read it and get it over with.* "'Good evening, everyone. My name is Noni Reid. Not many seventeen-year-olds have the privilege of living in the house their great-great-great grandfather built.'"

I told myself to treat it like a class assignment, not that I was terribly good at those. "'But I do. My ancestor Cuffee Fortune was enslaved most of his life.'" My palms sweated like an Olympic athlete's armpits as

I recited how Cuffee constructed a plantation house in central Virginia, in my mother's janky little hometown.

Okay, maybe I phrased it differently.

"'So he'd be proud to know that today, his descendants call his legacy home.'" It was all a lie, to me, anyway. What he built wasn't my home. Our place in Wellesley with the gray siding and beige shutters was home, with my bedroom Alyssa and I redecorated one weekend, painting the walls an electric shade of purple that would've made Prince jealous.

But I just stood there talking about Cuffee Fortune. Mom was constantly lecturing me about our historic legacy even though tonight, her belief—that the college's creation, not just its construction, was owed to Cuffee—was struck from the printed speech with neat lines in red pen. Sparks flew from her eyes, but how could I care about her disappointment when she didn't care about mine? Presiding over Stonepost College—this was her dream.

Swallowing, I continued. "'My ancestor was a field hand. But he was also a foreman. Because he oversaw the construction of Stonepost College. And only weeks ago, my mother took the helm of this historic institution. My mother and I, by our legacy, are . . .'"

As I took a sharp breath, my anxiety took a back seat to sadness. I missed my best friend, and I needed time at home to make things up after our rift. I wished more than anything that I hadn't been forced to turn down the internship that would've shown off *my* talent, and what *I* worked hard for. All of this meant so much more to me than a man who had been dead way longer than I'd been living. "'My mother and I, by our legacy, are . . .'"

Mom's eyes bored into mine.

"'My mother and I,'" I started again. But I couldn't finish this speech that wasn't mine. The words wouldn't come, not with anger in their way. Tears squirted from the corners of my eyes, and my chin wrinkled like a dirty shirt balled up in a laundry basket. How dare my mom make me say all these lies about how grateful I was to go to Nowheresville, Virginia. I had been so excited about my last summer with my friends before college, and even more about landing such an awesome internship. It wasn't fair that my parents' divorce and Mom's new job had to steal it all away.

The tears kept coming. Reaching behind my back, I fumbled but managed to flip the lever, turning the mic off. As I walked off the platform, speech unfinished, awws and coos wafted from the audience. Fine, let them think I was overcome with emotion from Cuffee's story.

But Mom knew better, and she was furious. Still, she didn't betray a speck of her anger, not to anyone who didn't know her at least. But I knew from the tightness of her shoulders, from the narrowing of her eyes as she stood at the side of the stage. Leaning close, I spoke under my breath. "Mom."

She fidgeted, shaking her head almost imperceptibly, making it clear she wouldn't hear me out. It was maddening. "I told you," I whispered. "I didn't want to do this!"

Sharp gasps and shocked faces accosted me as I walked away. As I realized why, I wished I could sink through the floor. Why hadn't I just thought for two seconds? Of course Mom had turned on her mic—as soon as she'd seen me falter, she'd gotten ready to take the podium at a moment's notice. Sheer embarrassment forced more tears I'd been holding back to drip down my face, and all the snot I'd been snorting up to dribble out. Did I really hot-mic? In front of 150 old people?

But I had a right to be mad! She dragged me to this event, just like she was dragging me to rural Virginia. Pulling me away from my entire life: from my best friend, from my internship, from my very dreams to stand apart from her. Outside the ballroom doors, a couple checking in at the front desk stared at me. So did the clerk, and a bellhop wheeling an empty cart, asking, "Miss. You all right?"

Ignoring him, I pushed open a door to a conference room and slammed it shut. Leaning against the whiteboard, I slid like cake batter on a rubber spatula and ended up on the floor. Why did Mom have to make me stay in the middle of nowhere all summer?

Then I heard her high-pitched voice. Was she here?

She wasn't. I could hear her on the other side of the wall, as clearly as if she were standing next to me.

"My gosh," she said, earning chuckles from the audience. "*That* wasn't supposed to happen." More laughter. "But if you've ever raised teenagers, you know they can be unpredictable."

"Like trained bears!" someone shouted. He was met with the audience's laughter. Because everyone commiserated with my mother, not me.

"Please allow me to introduce myself." She went on as if nothing happened. "I'm Dr. Radiance Castine, and this past May, I had the distinct honor of being inaugurated as the president of one of the most prestigious liberal arts colleges in the . . ."

Scrambling up from the floor, I couldn't escape the sound of her voice fast enough.

CHAPTER 2

This past May, while Mom was having the distinct honor of being inaugurated as the president of a prestigious liberal arts college, I was in our living room in Wellesley, swishing through rows and rows of stage costumes hung up on a portable rack. My hands ran across a touchable kaleidoscope of fabrics: stiff netting, silky satin, plushy velour. I couldn't believe I'd helped design and create so many garments.

But even with the dizzying textures and hues, the room felt stark and empty. Our furniture had been cleared out. Mom's art had been lifted from the walls. It felt bare and bittersweet.

I couldn't wait to leave for Boston University in the fall. And maybe I was prouder of myself for my work on the costumes than anything else I'd ever done. But why was my achievement, and my new beginning, paired with the end of living in the house I'd grown up in? And why did it take away my last summer with my best friend, Alyssa?

"Ta-da!" I brought out her dress for a featured scene.

"Oh my god!" She held it over her jeans and spun around. It was turquoise with a rosette of conch shells arrayed on the shoulder, and a sheer train ruffling behind like sea-foam. "This, like, makes up for me not getting the part as Ariel!" She'd cried about losing that role. That's why I'd made her dress extra-gorgeous.

"This is so awesome! Thank you!" Alyssa Byrne's eyes were bright and grateful. I had invited her over for a sneak peek of the wardrobe, as she was playing Miranda in *The Tempest*. Each spring, the local theater in Wellesley offered a program for high school seniors, called "Bards in the Burbs." Kids were coached by professional actors and crew for a Shakespeare performance. Alyssa was one of the few students picked. So was I.

And so was Kendall Kovak, a whiz on the light board. She grunted as she riffled through the racks. "I'm surprised your mom let the theater have your place." When the wardrobe room at the playhouse flooded, my parents had agreed to use our vacant living room as a temporary space, with our house being only a few blocks away. There, the theater's professional costume designer Mindy and I sewed and stored costumes. Mindy and the show's director said our family saved the whole production.

"I thought your mom hated theater," Kendall said.

"It's not that." Mom had been taking me to plays a few times over the years. "She just wants me to be some big-time academic, just like her."

"Dr. Castine is awesome. But if she had her way, Noni would be starting a PhD right now." Alyssa laughed lightly, adjusting a lavender wig she pulled over her asymmetrical haircut. She'd known Mom for years.

"Exactly. My mom sees this as a hobby. Even though we did it for a grade." The Bards program awarded class credit for show prep and rehearsal. Now that we'd just graduated, the show run would start in a few days, and we'd get a stipend.

"Your mom is such a buzzkill." Kendall suddenly looked imposing, wearing a velvet cloak I'd made with a creepy trim of black feathers and dangling small animal skulls I'd convinced my school's biology teacher to offload from his collection. "Even if you consider school assignments a buzz."

She wasn't entirely wrong, but her bitching about my mother annoyed me. She and I weren't that close. Kendall, who went to private school, met Alyssa and me right before the holidays, during a Bards orientation. I'd been friends with Alyssa forever, if forever meant the sixth grade. But Alyssa glommed on to Kendall, developing a hard-core friend crush. The next thing I knew, Kendall was our third wheel.

Or maybe I was the third wheel.

Still, I loved the Bards program. I was the only student chosen for costuming, and the program was a chance to dust off my sewing skills, which had gotten a little rusty. I was designing and drafting patterns from scratch, something I'd always done for myself but never anyone else.

As someone with an eye for clothing fit and fabrics, Mom feigned enough interest when I talked about this costume or that. But she had also coerced me into applying for a high school program with the Boston Black film festival. And she was plenty miffed when I chose the Bards instead of Black culture.

But these after-school Shakespeare sessions didn't feel like "just an elective," as Mom insisted they were. Within the first week, the costume designer was blown away by my skill and talent. That's exactly what Mindy said, and she was in her twenties and did this for her job. I even overheard the show's director, a self-important man who gave much criticism and little praise to us students, dole out a rare nice word to the other hired professionals. "That Noni Reid? She's *good*," he'd said. Nyles Pompa was the guest director of *The Tempest*. He had landed in Boston from New York, where he was a million-time Tony award winner. There was big buzz in the industry because he would soon open his own theater. So hearing his compliment was almost like borrowing some of what Mom must have felt all the time. A sense of accomplishment. The shine of acclaim.

Instead of creeping in her shadow, I was glowing on my own.

Alyssa held up the turquoise dress again. "Do you think I could have this after the show? I'd wear it to the cast party. Or maybe to Ethan's fireworks bash."

"Too bad you're gonna miss his party," Kendall told me. "That, and everything else."

"Maybe you can come up for the Fourth of July, Noni! We could do something for your birthday the next day."

"But you won't catch our Nantucket trip in August. My brother's taking us all sailing." Kendall was grinding salt into a paper cut. "And you'll miss our trip to the lake house."

It kicked rocks, having to leave. Just because Dad was staying with his brother and my aunt until who knows when. Because my uncle turned a second spare room into his office, so Dad's crashing on an air mattress wouldn't cramp his work-from-home style. I'd moaned and groaned to just about anyone who'd listen.

Vibrations echoed throughout the house's emptiness as the front door opened and closed. Kendall's boyfriend, Laronté Harris, strode in, as if he owned the house free and clear. She must've invited him. I didn't. And there was no hello, only a "Shhiiittt!" as his eyes swept the tall ceilings. "Look at this fancy-ass mansion."

Like Kendall didn't live in an even bigger "mansion," and he'd been to her place plenty. My phone buzzed. Mom, again. She was in Virginia, getting our new house ready and meeting with staff from her new job, even though she hadn't technically started yet.

"I have to get this," I mumbled. In my old bedroom, I wrinkled my nose from the chemical smell of fresh paint. The real-estate agent changed the sexy purple walls to bland gray because she had insisted they would "show better." Not that Mom seemed to care. She was enamored with our new place in Virginia, saying that buying the house was taking back what was ours, because our ancestor built it.

As my mother prattled on about a shift in her fundraising tour schedule, I didn't pay attention. Last fall, I got used to her traveling all over the country when her book made the *New York Times* bestseller list. For years, Mom had published niche scholarly texts that only hardcore academics cracked open. This one was different. Like, it had made a small splash in the news.

But when she said, "So you'll drive down with me this Wednesday instead of mid-June," I stopped her.

"Wait. Mom, what?"

"But don't worry. The theater can continue using our living room until the new owners move in next month. Your aunt will manage the adjustments the new homeowners negotiated, so it works perfectly."

"You said *Wednesday*?"

"Yes. This week," she said breezily. "Of course, you'll miss *The Tempest*, but it's a good thing you're doing costumes so you won't be needed for the actual show."

"I'll miss the performance run?" I couldn't believe what she was saying.

"It's being live streamed, so you'll see it."

But I wouldn't hug Alyssa before her first professional performance. I wouldn't watch my costumes come to life on the actors. I wouldn't celebrate our efforts at the cast party. "No, Mom. I'll miss it. I'll miss it all. Please . . ."

"I know it's disappointing, but once I start the tour, I'll be in a city-to-city frenzy, and I won't have time to—oh. I've got to board my plane. I can't wait to see you. Love you, sweetie."

She was making me miss everything? Woozy with disbelief, I was greeted by Laronté's smug smirk in the living room. I hated that he was cute. "So Noni, you're trading one Big House for another, huh? Only the next one will be on a genuine plantation." He laughed, as if anything was funny, when nothing was. "That's some 'moving on up' nigger shit."

"What does *that* mean?" Kendall giggled, leaning against his chest. "'Nigger shit'?"

I got fierce. "Hey, you don't get to say that!"

Her face flamed red. "I'm repeating him!"

"Yeah, Nones, chill the fuck out." Laronté wrapped his arm around her. "She's saying it in context."

"I don't like hearing that word, either." Alyssa nervously glanced between me and Laronté.

"What, you don't listen to music?" Laronté prodded. "You don't watch TV?" His mouth split into a grin, loose and easy. The fucking nerve. "I was playing, Noni." He enunciated, as if to mock the way I spoke. He smacked my hip with the back of his hand. Reflexively, I jumped away.

"What the fuck!" Kendall barked. "Don't flirt with my friends."

"C'mon, Kendy." Laronté kissed her nose. "You know I don't date Black girls. They ain't cute and sweet like you."

Alyssa's mouth gaped open. But instead of defending me, she faked a laugh. "Noni's not really Black. Not with how she talks, so properly."

"No, no, no, none of this modifying with an adverb. It's 'talking proper,'" Laronté emphasized. "That's how real Black folk say it. Right, Noni?" He lifted his hand as if for a high five, then snatched it away. "Wait. You wouldn't know."

On top of Mom's news, this was too much. "What is your deal? All of you!"

"Come on. I didn't even touch you." Laronté shrugged.

"Seriously, what crawled up your ass?" Kendall snapped.

"I just made a joke!" said Alyssa. Her tone softened. "What's wrong? Did your mom drop something else on you?" She reached for me, but I turned my shoulder away.

Kendall grabbed Laronté's arm. "Let's hang at my place." She motioned to Alyssa. "You coming?"

My best friend looked between both of us. Before she could speak, my phone buzzed again. It was Nyles Pompa, the show director. He hardly ever spoke two words to me. Why was *he* calling?

The next morning, I was so charged with excitement I didn't need coffee. "Hey, Dad!" I poked my head into the open bathroom door, where he was knotting a tie around his neck.

"Hey, Noni-Pony." He smiled at me in the mirror. We looked alike, but at the same time, we didn't. If it weren't for the tightly scrunched waves of his hair, you could almost mistake my dad for a white man. I was light-skinned, too, but the color of a bulletin board. My hair was less of Dad's texture and more of Mom's. But while my mother wore hers out and soft, I spent hours each week using every heated device known to humankind to force mine straight. If I ever chemically relaxed my hair, Mom would either kill me, or she'd shave it off herself.

Unlike either of my parents, I was short and "curvy," as clothing brands called it. My classmates used to call me chubby, at least until high school. That's when boys started throwing the word *thicc* at me, like it was both a compliment and a slur. Either way, jeans that fit my waist barely went over my calves, and they felt too snug around my thighs. I would never have the long, lithe frame of my mother.

"So I have this amazing opportunity. For the summer." I followed him to the guest room doorway.

"I'm listening." He slid a blazer from his closet. It sported leather elbow patches, the kind professors wore—although Mom, who *was* a professor, wouldn't catch herself in a look like that if her life depended on it.

"So you know the Bards program?"

"That's all you talk about now. You're in your zone." His smile turned lovey-dovey in that mushy-father way. "I'm really proud of you."

"Oh, Dad." And in a rush, I told him that the guest director was starting a brand-new theater, The Chasma, in downtown Boston.

"Your mom and I went to some black-tie fundraiser, remember? He invited us. It's supposed to be 'edgy,' right?" Dad made air quotes. "What do they call it, 'fringe'?" More air quotes.

"Yeah! Fringe is kind of like, weird plays." I dumbed it down a bit. Dad worked in tech, so he didn't get into theater terms. "And guess what? They're hiring a summer intern to work with the costume designer. And they want me!"

He stopped in the middle of buckling the messenger bag I'd made for him last Christmas. "Where are you gonna stay?"

"Well, that's the best part. For both of us! There's housing for actors and crew. You have to pay rent, but it's subsidized. Some big donor owns the building, so it's way below market rate. This means I could get an apartment. An awesome two-bedroom downtown!"

"They offer housing to minors?" His eyebrows lifted.

"Yeah! As long as I live with an adult relative. So you can move in! You could stay the whole summer, long enough to spend plenty of time looking for your own place. It's not forever; you just have to be there until I'm eighteen. An adult."

"Only technically," he countered. He was getting annoyed as he searched his top drawer. I plucked out a tie pin for him. Dad wore jeans with his shirt untucked, but he spiffed up with a jacket and tie, unlike the other supercasual guys he worked with. He always said to dress for the job you want, not the job you have—at least, if you're Black.

"So you'll do it?" I asked.

"Sorry, kiddo." He ruffled my hair like I was a little girl. I flushed with annoyance. "I don't have time for a move. Remember how I got a new boss? Dumbass can't even code. So now I'm dealing with his job because he has no idea what the hell he's doing, while I'm stuck in middle management. Passed over every damned time."

"But living downtown would mean you'd be less pressed for time.

The apartment is right on the T. You'll get to work in fifteen minutes." I stood at my full height, which wasn't much. "Dad. This makes the most sense for both of us."

"This internship sounds great. But you'll have other chances when you get to college. BU's got a drama department."

"But I have this, now. A chance to do theater with artists from around the world. Please. It's my one chance to do something for myself." Why wouldn't he get it? "If I don't do this internship, I'll never get out of Mom's shadow."

Reaching over to the rack in the foyer, he grabbed the keys to his Lexus. "Your mother wants you to stay with her this summer. She makes the big bucks. What she says goes. Always has."

Dad saying Mom made "the big bucks" was always how he *passed* the buck. How he copped out, as if he couldn't make a decision on his own. I wouldn't let him this time. "Dad, you're divorced. You don't have to be stuck in Mom's shadow, either."

His eyes darkened as he slipped out the door. And he got rid of all my pleading just as easily as washing his hands.

CHAPTER 3

For what seemed like the entire drive down I-66 and then I-81, Mom reamed me out for what I'd done at the reception. "Your behavior was absolutely unacceptable. Unacceptable!"

"I'm sorry, Mom." I'd said it a million times, but it wasn't enough. And it was her fault! She shouldn't have put me up to making that speech. And she shouldn't have made me give up everything to come with her to Virginia. It wasn't fair.

"There will be repercussions for this, Noni. You are going to find a full-time job in Magnolia, and that is how you'll spend the next three months," Mom said. "Working. You need to learn responsibility, and diligence, and—I don't think I've ever been more angry!"

I slouched in my seat. We'd been on the road for hours when Mom finally took an exit, going from a major interstate into the middle of nowhere. She drove us down an incredibly steep road surrounded by thick woods—it felt like we were driving down a mountain. Pasture and farmland spread out for what seemed like miles, and more mountains sprawled in the distance. One winding road after another took us past barns, country churches, roadkill galore, and old houses. Some were ramshackle, but others were mansions looking straight out of *Gone with the Wind*, tucked way far back down long, earthen paths. You could see them if you peeked through the trees. They were so fancy, signs staked along their driveways boasted names and the dates they were established: GILDED PINES, 1817. BRAUNSTON, 1806. TWENTY PACES, 1799.

Finally, we reached our own burgundy-and-gold sign: TANGLEROOT, 1822. "We're home," she said, her voice gentle, as if the word meant something. As if the sight of Tangleroot calmed her down. Or shored her up.

"I thought this place was built in 1838," I muttered. It was amazing how much I remembered from that speech she put me up to. And from what she'd said my whole life.

"The house was." My mother explained that it wasn't the homes that were named, but rather, the plantations. The property. She drove up an impossibly long gravel driveway lined with thick-trunked magnolia trees. The redbrick house Cuffee built was smaller than some of the others I'd seen, maybe even smaller than our place in Wellesley. But it made a stronger statement, with tall columns, arched windows, and soaring chimneys.

"It's fortunate the president's house at Stonepost is being renovated. I'm glad to be starting off here." Mom parked the car behind a row of hedges.

"So when the renovations are done, we'll have two houses?" I hefted my suitcase from the trunk and followed her.

"That won't happen for a year. And I don't own the house at Stonepost College." She searched inside her purse. "College presidents usually don't own campus property. So it's common for us to have two residences."

She handed me a set of keys, attached to a glittering *S* key chain. Not even an *N* for the nickname I'd been called pretty much my entire life. An *S* for the given name I'd always rejected because it was the worst ever. I wanted to toss the keys into the hedge.

Instead I followed her into a hallway so large, it could have been a hangar for a small plane. I looked up at the crystal chandelier suspended above us as Mom, like a real-estate agent, immediately began pointing out various features. "The parquet flooring is original to the house. So is the carved walnut trim. Don't you love the Palladian windows?"

"Uh-huh." I followed her around as she showed me the piano room, which housed her vintage Chute & Butler; a library with floor-to-ceiling bookcases built into the walls; and a formal dining room. From the outside, the house looked modestly sized, but it was a deception. Our place in Wellesley was all high ceilings and millions of windows. This house offered genuine space.

The furniture was all Mom's taste—floral prints, delicate paisleys and swirls. The soft feminine colors and patterns were at odds with her African art: masks grimacing from the walls, pointy-boobed statues standing proudly near doorways.

Downstairs was what I guessed was the only comfy space: an expansive kitchen and den with a huge TV and overstuffed couches.

Mom's bedroom was on the top floor in the east wing. It was her style, the wallpaper striped ivory and gold. She showed me the narrow closet. "They were uncommon back then. They were actually taxed as separate rooms." She'd converted a smaller room into a walk-in for her countless suits and dresses.

"Where's my bedroom?" I asked as we stood inside one of the guest rooms. It had a pencil-post bed with a gauzy canopy. The wallpaper was dappled with tiny clusters of green leaves. A prissy ten-year-old girl would kill for this room. There was even a wooden chair with some kind of doll sitting on it.

Mom adjusted the lace curtains. "Isn't the view gorgeous?" Outside, a backyard sloped down into a steep hill. A creek shimmered near the wood's edge.

"Yeah, whoever visits will love it." Not that anyone would drive out to our no-man's-land. "What's this?" I picked up what was on the chair: a faceless figure made of brown cloth with braided black yarn for hair. Stubby arms poked from a faded bluish-greenish dress.

"I saw her at an antique shop in Daventry," Mom said. "I felt like she just belonged here."

"This?" Holding it up, I realized there was another side to it. I flipped the skirt over, and another faceless doll half greeted me—an ivory-clothed one with yellow yarn hair in a pink dress. It was weird and baffling. "Mom, what *is* this?"

"She's called a topsy-turvy doll. They were popular in the nineteenth century, and it's likely that Black and white girls played with them."

I turned the doll upside down again, revealing the Black doll. "There's, like, no face." I thought of my mother's old Raggedy Anns with their glassy eyes and painted-on smiles.

"Many enslaved women were never taught to embroider."

"You think an enslaved woman made this Freaky Friday craziness?" I flipped the skirt over to reveal the white doll again.

"Look carefully."

And then I saw. The Black-girl half of the doll was worn, with frayed hair and dingy cloth. The white side was nearly pristine. It was as if one side had been loved more, played with more. "I felt like she belonged here," my mother said. "I wanted you to have her. *Her.*"

I knew she meant the Black side. Then something occurred to me. "Wait. Is this supposed to be my room?"

"Of course it is."

"Then where's my stuff?" I plunked down the doll.

"Your belongings are all in storage. You can bring them with you to BU. Look, I want you to see something." She opened the closet. All I noticed was how tiny it was, how inconsequential, but Mom regarded the inside of the paneled door. At first I thought there were paper dolls glued there, but then I realized they were drawings of white women in big, old-fashioned dresses bedecked with huge bows and flowers. Gowns with enough fabric to tent a village. Gowns wide enough to double as parachutes. The color was faded and the papers peeled at the ends, including the printed descriptions someone had pasted on the corners of each sheet.

"'Latest style of walking-dress,'" I read aloud. "'Rich gray silk, double skirt, postilion jacket. Sleeve gathered into a cap of velvet tartan, and cuff of the same.' What the hell is a 'walking dress'? Mom, what are these?"

"Fashion plates. Pictures from nineteenth-century fashion magazines. *Godey's Lady's Book, Peterson's*. The *Vogue* of their day."

I sneered at one of the drawings. "Oh, look, here's a riding dress. Is that different from a sitting dress? Or a standing dress? Is there a pooping dress?"

She folded her arms. "You're into fashion. I thought you would like this room. And a teenaged girl lived here, you know. A white girl. She pasted those pictures. And you know who else may have slept here?"

I shrugged.

"A Black girl. A girl her age. *Your* age. We know the white people here had a young maid, and sometimes servants slept on their enslaver's bedroom floor. Like dogs." Mom shut the closet door hard, as if something evil were inside. "So you're taking this room, you're sleeping in this antique bed, and everything this white girl had is yours. It is *yours*."

I rolled my eyes. She tossed me a sharp glare. "You can't appreciate anything, can you? Not even reclaiming what was taken from you."

The only things I wanted to reclaim were my suede curtains, my satin leopard-print sheets, my black lights strung along the walls. Maybe I sounded a bit like a jerk, so I tried to dial it back. "This isn't really my style, and I'd just like my stuff back."

"Your bedroom in Wellesley looked like the champagne room of a strip club," Mom snapped. "Do you think I'd decorate a historic home with lava lamps? Grow up, Noni, will you?"

She stalked out of the room, leaving me there.

As if the old room wasn't providing enough history, I had to help Mom clean up an old cemetery. While we drove down Union Road, she chattered about how it was once the thoroughfare of a Black community called The Gather, another legacy of Cuffee Fortune. "After the Civil War, his former enslaver gave him land instead of payment for staying on: some here, and some in Daventry. Of course, the Daventry acres were rocky and unfarmable."

"Um-hmm." I thought about texting Alyssa. Something like: *Greetings from Pokesville VA, pop. 6.* But we hadn't spoken since that disastrous day at my house. And in spite of what had happened, I missed her.

"When Gramma was growing up, we had our own general store, our own bakery." Mom narrated our ride through wilderness. I loved how she said "we" and "our," even though she wasn't alive back then. "We had our own church, of course. And Cuffee's first school, before he opened the college. The schoolhouse is still here, on the other end of the road."

"I'm surprised you're not taking me there."

"It's private property now." Either way, there wasn't anything else left of The Gather now, from what I could see. Just scrubby forest and brush surrounded the road.

"Do you own any land here?" I asked.

"Gramma did. But she sold it to the city."

"If Cuffee's land was so precious, why would she part with it?"

"She had to, like most everyone else." Mom explained that in the 1950s, the town pushed almost all The Gather residents out using something called eminent domain, when the government forces people to sell their private property. But the town paid unfairly, according to Mom. And while they were supposed to build a park and make way for power lines, that didn't happen. Everyone was kicked out for nothing. "Cuffee's schoolhouse was on the edges, so it wasn't torn down," Mom said. "And we got a lawyer to protect the cemetery. But the rest was razed."

I spent the afternoon tromping around the graveyard, picking up beer bottles with rubber-gloved hands, struggling not to complain. Teens sometimes drank here on weekends, but the grass was cropped short, and there wasn't a weed in sight. "Does the town take care of this place?" I asked.

"It's a private cemetery. Someone has to come out here and mow."

"Who?"

Mom didn't answer. Instead, she went on and on about Cuffee Fortune and his son Calvin, my great-great-grandfather, her one-sided conversation punctuated by the clank of bottles tumbling into a black trash bag.

"Hey, why isn't Cuffee buried here?" I asked, picking at a cluster of cigarette butts. "Is he in a Civil War veteran's cemetery or something?"

Mom smiled, as if pleased I'd remembered a fact about him. "It's true that he ran away from Tangleroot to join the Union Army. He even lied about his age to be admitted, since he was too old. But no, he wanted to be buried on the plantation."

"Why? He was free when he died, wasn't he?"

"He outlived many of his children, and they were buried there. So was his wife, Molly. The owner of Tangleroot considered Cuffee to be a 'trusted servant.' It made sense that he might've given him permission to be buried with his family one day."

"So I guess we're going to that cemetery next."

"I don't know where the enslaved community's burial ground is. I'd like to find it, though." Mom bagged more trash. "We're Cuffee's only living descendants, you know. His few surviving children never married." She explained the fate of his other kids, including a son who was killed during the Civil War and a young daughter mysteriously scratched out on the plantation records. "Just a line drawn though her name. I have no idea why."

There were also farm accidents and illnesses, that kind of thing. Sadly, most of the Fortune kids didn't inherit the meaning of their last name.

"How do you know this, anyway?"

"It hasn't been easy to find out. Cuffee left a memoir, detailing his life up to a month before he died. But when my mother was in a car accident, Gramma sold the manuscript to a collector, to pay for her hospital bills. It means that memoir is likely out there somewhere." Mom blotted sweat on her forehead with the inside of her elbow. "But for now, much of what I have is what Gramma told me from reading it."

As we tackled more graves, I listened to even more family history. Cuffee's son Calvin Fortune had a child with my great-great-grandma Lacey Castine. "Lacey was a dressmaker, though she never got credit for her designs. She worked for a boutique that clothed the rich grand dames around here."

"I know. Of *course*." Lacey was my middle name, but for me, her story ran deeper. When I was eleven, my mother sat down with me at the dining room table. She taught me how to thread a bobbin on her old 1990s sewing machine, how to snap close the presser foot, how to guide the cloth, and how to stitch a straight line. When I mastered that quickly, she praised me for inheriting my great-great-grandmother's skill. Then she taught me how to read a pattern, how to cut it out and pin it to fabric. We made a pair of drawstring pants. We stopped there. And when I began to inhale YouTube videos and online tutorials, when I later bought a new Singer with years of stashed Christmas money, she seemed caught off guard. In hindsight, my focus might have scared her. Maybe even my skill, the way I could draw a pattern and turn out a whole new outfit over a weekend, if I wanted to.

She said she appreciated my hobby, but for Lacey, dressmaking was one of her only avenues to earn a living. I, on the other hand, would go to college. And if I studied harder, if I directed my energy to my schoolwork, I could earn a PhD. Maybe even two. Like her.

She's said that again and again over the years.

Lacey's child with Cal Fortune was Gramma: Sophronia Castine, my great-grandmother and namesake, though everyone called her Fawnie for her cutesy look and doeskin complexion, Mom had said before. Gramma raised my mother, because Mom's mom, Clare Castine, died in a car accident when Mom was six. Clare was also buried here, as well as her brother, killed in the Vietnam War. It was the kind of lucklessness that plagued Cuffee Fortune's family.

Mom's dad was a married doctor. Clare Castine had hopes of him leaving his wife, but Mom never learned her father's name. And she never even wanted to know, which I didn't understand. I pictured a family tree, one with a blank spot for Mom's father. One that looked like this:

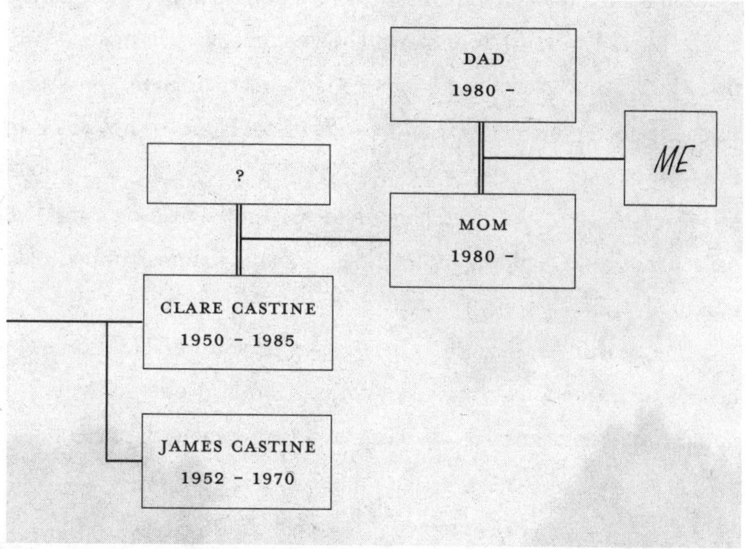

Lacey scrimped and saved to send Gramma to Hampton University, but she dropped out when she became pregnant. My great-grandfather abused her—not physically, Mom said, but emotionally. He belittled her. "Women were supposed to just deal with that back then. Even now we are," my mother said. Her grandmother divorced while her kids were in diapers, then took back her maiden name, which hardly anyone did back in the 1950s.

"There just weren't that many opportunities for Black women with two kids. She had to clean houses while she raised my mom and uncle. And while she raised me." Mom swatted away a bee. "The school bus used to drop me off at the library. And that's where I stayed, until Gramma, or the neighborhood woman who used to watch me, could pick me up."

She smiled mischievously. "In high school, a friend and I sometimes went to guest lectures and author talks at Stonepost. We'd sneak across an old railroad bridge. The trestle was condemned and it was honestly illegal, but we did it anyway."

I imagined my studious mother as a child, finding a sunlit library corner to read and do her homework. Or as a teenager risking a dilapidated bridge, not to get to a party or concert, but to listen to a professor. "Of course, everyone knew what we were up to. There are no secrets in this town."

"Doesn't seem like it." I followed her toward the tall iron gates. She paused, her hand alighting on the ridge of another stone, but her body obscured its inscription.

"I hope living in Magnolia can tell you who you are." The sadness in her voice gave me pause. But there was hope, too. Both emotions seemed mingled, co-conspiratorial—as if one could bring about the other.

During the rest of the week, Mom went to work, and I spent most of my time lounging around in my PJs, watching TV in the den on the bottom floor. I thought again about texting Alyssa, but I couldn't think of what to say. Besides, she didn't text me, either.

It pinched, her silence. I followed her online, and I knew she was hanging out with Kendall and Laronté. They were always together. It was still tough to tell who was the third wheel. That hurt, too.

Whenever Mom got home, she'd bitch and whine that I should do something.

"Do what?" I'd ask her. "There's nothing to do."

"Read a book," she'd say. "Read what?" I'd ask. I didn't feel like reading anything. "Go for a walk," she'd say. "Walk where?" I'd ask her. "Into a cow pasture?"

Finally, she got to me, and I decided to go for a damned stroll. I trudged across the bridge leading over the creek, past a small whitewashed brick building at the bottom of the hill, one with a pointed red roof topped by a weather vane. Mom had mentioned someone rented the former stables, which the Haneys, the couple she bought the house from, had refurbished. "Apparently, he's a quiet, elderly man," she had said of our tenant.

But I wasn't out here to run into some weird old guy living in a horse barn. I just wanted to be alone.

I walked the ribbon of trail that reached into the bristly woods. You could get lost along these snaky paths. Rounding a curve, I saw what looked like a rock garden. But it was a tiny cemetery enclosed by a short, iron gate. A few gravestones pointed upward from clumps of weeds.

Somewhere on the Tangleroot property, there had to be a cemetery for enslaved people, but Mom hadn't been able to find it. The graves in most enslaved folks' cemeteries were only marked with rocks, easily lost in brush, she said, or with wooden crosses that would have long since rotted away. The enslaved people's burying ground at Tangleroot might be too overgrown with trees and shrubs to locate, or the uncarved stones might've sunken into the earth altogether.

I never thought of the white family being buried here, too. But it made sense. I knew rural families often buried their dead on their property, not in a churchyard. Still, it seemed strange that a cemetery was basically in our backyard.

As I studied each burial, a crude family tree emerged. A tall, pointed gravestone signaled Thomas Dearborn as the family patriarch. He was born in 1808 and died almost seventy years later. Beside him was Martha Dearborn, born in 1817 and dying in her fifties. Her tombstone read *Beloved Wife and Mother*. Flanking them were two small stones. One simply read *Infant, 1840*. The other child was named after his father. He died when he was four years old.

From the dates on their graves, I knew that Thomas and Martha Dearborn were the enslavers of Cuffee Fortune, our family ancestor. And Mom knew all this, of course. She had found rosters with Cuffee's name. She even found, in old letters, references to him constructing the house. But she had never called this white family by their names. To her, they were Cuffee's enslavers. It sounded harsh, but I could see how it made sense to her. They denied Cuffee his humanity. Maybe she felt no point in giving them something they would have never given her, a Black woman.

But just like Mom's and my ancestors, these people had lived, they had married, they had died.

And they had buried loved ones. I knelt to better read another stone. It seemed like a century of dead leaves were jammed up against it. With a flat rock, I dredged them away. The engraving was weathered, but I made out the words.

HERE LIES

SOPHRONIA DEARBORN

BORN JULY 5, 1841

DIED AUGUST 18, 1859

AND INFANT SON

BORN AND DIED AUGUST 18, 1859

REST WELL, BELOVED DAUGHTER AND SWEET BABE

So eerie. Sophronia was my given name. July 5 was my birthday. This girl had died when she was just about my age. It must have been childbirth that killed her, and her poor son, too. That happened to a lot of women and their babies back then. The girl couldn't have been Thomas and Martha Dearborn's daughter, because she would have had a married name. So she was their daughter-in-law, then. And her husband? He had probably moved on, to a different town maybe, and found himself another teen bride.

I thought about that lonely graveyard for days. And for the rest of the week, when Mom again harped at me about finding a job.

"You know, this isn't exactly the place where I can do that," I said. "I don't have any experience driving a tractor."

"Please, Noni. You didn't think you were going to spend your whole summer playing games on your phone."

I had thought about unpacking my Singer, but I didn't even feel like sewing. "What else am I supposed to do? Go cow-tipping?" Even though I was focusing on my game of *Zombie Worldz* and didn't see her, I knew she was rolling her eyes. Right back at you, Mom.

"You can start with some chores around here. Then you're going to have to get a job. It's nonnegotiable."

"I told you, I don't know how to bale hay. Seriously, where am I supposed to work?"

"You have two choices. My friend Blondell needs a server at her restaurant."

"No way. I'm not waiting tables at some dive for hicks."

"That's offensive. Don't ever use that word again."

"Sorry."

Mom riffled through a stack of mail. "If not Blondell's, you can work at the college. My office needs help, since our intern's getting surgery. So you'll start tomorrow?"

I sighed.

"Well, you're going to have to, because we have a board meeting and I already promised you'd help for at least the day."

"What?" I tossed my phone on the couch. She was screwing up my game, anyway.

"And if you don't find a job by Monday, you'll either be at Stonepost all summer or Blondell's. That's it."

"Trust me, I'll snag something."

"Fine." Mom lifted her chin.

"Fine," I shot back.

CHAPTER 4

My mother kept her favorite necklace in the velvet-lined top case of her tall, narrow lingerie chest. She wore it sparingly, and always on days that mattered—when she interviewed with Stonepost College, for instance. Or when she was up for tenure at Harvard twelve years ago, and she'd stooped in her narrow-skirted dress, letting me fasten the clasp.

The necklace was made of black beads that lowered a pendant. That itself was a large square, fitted with teeny-tiny shapes of glass, each vari-colored piece etched with eensy-weensy zigzags of color. It was hand-made.

Today, her necklace glittered between the jut of her collarbones. While I hastily set out cardboard coffee dispensers and arranged a tray of breakfast sweets, she stood at the head of an oval-shaped table, surrounded by gray-haired, suit-wearing white people in padded leather chairs.

No one spoke. Instead, the recording of a woman's voice: slow, high-pitched and melodic, distinctly Southern and unmistakably Black, filled the room.

"Cuffee Fortune visited the most well-to-do colored families in Philadelphia to raise money for his college. He appealed to the Stills, the Whites, and the Heskys—the Heskys were especially generous."

A pair of tongs clattered to the floor, resoundingly loud. My fault. Everything had been a disaster from the start. I was supposed to grab coffee from the shop on campus, but their equipment had broken. Cursing the butt-crack-of-dawn meeting, I had to hop in Mom's car and drive to Starbucks, then barge into the conference room, lugging everything in while the meeting was underway. And it was an important meeting, because Stonepost College's board of directors was basically my mom's boss.

"We can stop the recording here," Mom told her assistant. She addressed the room. "My grandmother Sophronia Castine was extraordinarily detailed in describing how Cuffee Fortune came to not only supervise the construction of this college but source funding for it. To found it."

"What have you proven with documented evidence?" a rotund man asked.

"Thank you for this question. Slides, please?"

An image of an old document appeared as the lights flicked off. Sepia-toned pictures of Black men flashed on-screen. I hastily birthed a stack of disposable cups from a plastic sheath.

"What did that woman say about the Hesky family?" a board member asked.

"Her name was Sophronia Castine." Mom spoke pointedly. "And I have not found evidence of a Hesky family, despite extensive research. But the other families are very well-documented."

A woman with a helmet of graying blond hair shook her head. "Radiance. You are aware this isn't evidence of anything."

A murmur rose around the table. My mother's lips thinned. "I'm asking that we present this historical record to the student body and faculty, and let them decide if a vote is warranted." She touched her necklace, as if it gifted her with her superpower.

The older woman spoke sharply. "You're serving as president because of overwhelming support from faculty and other stakeholders. *They* wanted you in this position." She didn't add, "not us," but she very well could have. Instead, the woman faked a little laugh. "We never realized you'd be a battering ram about changing the very name of this institution based on some story your nana told."

My mother's coppery eyes blazed. I knew what reeled through her mind—the same thing that pissed me off when my classmates suggested I only got something because of my race. When my teachers implied I was given a good grade as a favor, when I knew I had earned it. It bewildered me that she dealt with the same thing when she had two PhDs and was a former professor and Harvard dean with an award-winning book on the shelves. Unlike the alums at Stonepost College's receptions, these stony-faced people seemed to think she Blacked her way into all her credentials.

"I motion we adjourn," the woman said. "And re-discuss this at our March meeting. If there's enough information then to warrant an end-of-the-fiscal-year vote, we shall. I say we would need irrefutable evidence by June. Can you supply that?"

"I can," Mom pledged.

The motion was seconded, the meeting concluded. Mom, with a withering look, stalked out of the room. No one seemed to care. Instead, the board members herded around me, since I stood near the coffee. I hastily glided away, my arm brushing a stack of napkins. They fluttered to the floor, somehow reminding me of falling handkerchiefs.

The round-bellied man whispered to the stiff-haired woman, "A child doing a grown-up's job." For a moment my ears burned, until I realized he wasn't talking about me.

"I need your help," Mom said as I filed papers in a tall cabinet.

"But I need to finish—"

"Walk with me." She touched my shoulder.

I followed her out of Harper Hall, the administrative building. Here and there she smiled and greeted students as they crisscrossed the walkways, some whizzing by on bikes or skateboards. She knew many by name, white face after white face at Cuffee Fortune's formerly all-Black college.

"Romanesque style with elements of Gothic," Mom said as I craned my neck at a long-throated gargoyle stretching several stories above me. The campus was beautiful and naturey, with pretty ponds and willow trees. The buildings were gray stone and redbrick with steep roofs and pointy turrets. "Cuffee adhered to the height of architectural fashion."

"It's a beautiful college."

"That's why it was stolen."

I didn't know what she meant. In the library, students read on couches or browsed the stacks. How did a historically Black college become all white? She must have told me once. Or twice. Or eight times. The difference now was that I wanted to know.

A heavy book lay on a coffee table. Mom picked it up, wincing like it was bad produce at a supermarket. "All lies." She set it down.

While she chatted with a librarian at the reference desk, I flipped through *An Eminent History of Stonepost College* by Vermilion P. Harper. Written in 1938, it seemed to be full of pompous language: "Our county, in the very heart of Old Dominion, lacked a college worthy of educating its venerable descendants of planter families, blah blah blah."

The last part I made up, because a black-and-white photograph distracted me from the text. An elderly Black man in overalls stood with his hands on his hips, his white-bearded face raised as he surveyed the tall scaffolding. He stood as straight as a skyscraper.

Cuffee Fortune was a trusted servant of planter Thomas Dearborn. Despite being lured into the Yankee army as a younger man, this faithful Negro devoted the last years of his life to supervising the construction of Stonepost College, furthering the dream of Stonepost's first president, Vermilion P. Harper.

A pair of bronze hands firmly pulled the book from my light brown ones. Mom placed it on the library counter. "Come with me," she said.

In a dim, high-ceilinged hallway hung a beautiful tapestry. It was a quilt unlike any I'd ever seen. The fabric was all shades of blues, reds, and whites, some pieces patterned with stripes or a star. Instead of uniform squares or triangles, these were varying shapes randomly pieced together. I admired how the scraps were stitched together with bold, bright yellow zigzags of thread.

A placard read:

THE PRESIDENT'S QUILT
CIRCA 1900

THIS "CRAZY QUILT," CREATED IN A POPULAR STYLE OF ITS TIME, IS ATTRIBUTED AS A GIFT TO THE FIRST PRESIDENT OF STONEPOST COLLEGE, DR. VERMILION P. HARPER. ALL THAT IS KNOWN OF THE ARTIST IS FROM THE INITIALS "TA" EMBROIDERED ON THE QUILT BACK. THIS QUILT IS BELIEVED TO HAVE BEEN CREATED FROM CIVIL WAR MILITARY FLAGS.

I felt drawn to the tapestry. I could've looked at it all day. So when my mother lifted a tall wooden stool from a seating area and brought it over, then slipped off her magenta high heels and climbed up, I asked, even as I held the wobbly legs steady, "What are you doing?" A few students passing by stopped, watching us.

She spoke only to me. "Being that Senator Vermilion Harper was an avowed racist, this is likely made from Confederate regimental flags. I would dispose of it if I could. But it belongs to the college. All I can do is put it away."

She pulled at the quilt. "For now, I want the pleasure of taking it down myself."

One quilt corner slumped down as she unfastened it. Then the other. The tapestry sagged to the floor. I couldn't forget how a whole passage of the speech she'd written for me at the fundraising event was "edited" out. Guilt surged through me for humiliating her that night. How frustrating it must be to fight so hard just so history can be seen for what it is: true.

Gone with the Wind Chimes sold useless, overpriced yard decorations, including what had to be the world's largest collection of grinning, pink-lipped mammy figurines. The owner, Glenda Dorsey, said *of course* Radiance Castine was *unforgettable*, and she was just so *fascinated* to meet her daughter, but she just didn't need *any* help in her shop. Maybe when the school season started and her shop assistant went back . . .

"I'll be in college," I said quickly. I didn't want to work there anyway.

I tried Southern Accents Homeware. Lovey Catlett told me the same thing. So did the ladies who owned the antique stores in town: Bayonets & Bonnets, and Buried Silver. They all sold mammy paraphernalia; they all studied me like I was some kind of specimen.

But Mrs. Dorsey came out of her shop as I was heading to Mom's car. "You know, Trianon would be just the place for *you*." She gave me quick directions to whatever that was. Go up the main drag, Senator Vermilion P. Harper Street. Veer right onto June Bug Drive. Cross the bridge over the creek and go a few miles down Confederate Dead Road.

Jeez, these Southerners and their names. Senator Harper Street formed a long U off the main highway and was your typical Main Street, U.S.A., but with magnolia trees planted in perfect rows. It had your Farmer's & Life Insurance, your Magnolia Bank & Trust, your Southern Charm Beauty Parlor, your Bait & Tackle, and your array of churches. At the curve in the U stood the town courthouse. Its tall dome presided over everything, including the grassy oval of fairgrounds in the middle.

The courthouse seemed to turn its back on a steep, stony gorge. The cliff was probably hundreds of feet deep, crossed only by a rickety old wooden railroad bridge, one blocked off with tall metal gates and Trespass at Your Peril signs worthy of a haunted house. It was the same bridge Mom used to sneak across, and I recognized her bravery and, yeah—foolhardiness. But I could see why you'd want to cross—because from here, the roofs and steeples of Daventry's buildings, and the turret of its clock tower, seemed touchably close. Daventry was a small city, but a city nevertheless, one with art galleries and good restaurants, an art-film house and live-music venues, Mom told me. She commuted there each day, a forty-minute drive. "Two miles away but a world apart," she once said. She'd convened a committee charged with restoring the bridge into a biking and running trail.

Once, she said, both Magnolia and Daventry were nameless little parishes. When the railroad line was built, folks in Magnolia soon raised a fit about smoky engines sullying their town, and the influential Harper family pushed for the trains to be diverted. No one wanted change. Meanwhile in Daventry, factories fed by the railroad sprang up. Businesses bunched around. That little city prospered.

But Magnolia remained trapped in a bubble of time, like a little village in a snow globe. The town leaned into being stuck in the past and nowadays attracted people who liked to spend their weekends "antiquing" or whacking balls around the golf course. But otherwise, there was nothing here. There wasn't a single place to get a latte. You couldn't order Thai or Chinese food, or pizza. You couldn't even buy a pair of jeans.

Trianon had to be more than a mile down Confederate Dead Road. The street seemed to meander forever, shadowed by thick-trunked trees.

Finally, the road opened up to a long, tree-lined driveway like the ones leading into the other plantations. And that's what Trianon was—a plantation, circa 1784, according to a fancy sign outside. It was far bigger and more imposing than the Tangleroot house. What kind of job could I even find there? I decided to knock on the back door. Something about knocking on the front door scared the daylights out of me.

The woman who answered was the first other Black person I'd seen in Magnolia. Light-skinned and slender, she wore khaki pants, a crisp pinstriped shirt, and her long, silvery hair wound up in a bun. Her face broke into a smile. "My word! It's you!"

Immediately, she enfolded me in a hug. I didn't mind, not at all. "Come in, come in, come in!"

She introduced herself as Valerie Golden. "I recognized you as soon as I saw you. I *knew*." She stared at me with a soft and wondrous smile, as if my face were the answer to some long-unknown riddle. "You hungry, darling?"

She checked some scones in the oven, talking and talking. "I took care of your mama after her mother died, while Ms. Castine worked all day cleaning houses. Your mama and my oldest son were best friends, and I'd always wanted a daughter. So I took Radiance under my wing. I watched her ballet recitals, her spelling bees, everything. So you're like . . ." She played with the edges of her pot holder. "Well, you're like a granddaughter to me."

She absolutely felt like family to me, too—but the kind of family you want, not the kind you end up with.

As she busied herself at the stove, I asked, "So you—do you—"

"Do I own this place?" Valerie threw back her head in laughter. "Far from it. In fact, the people who used to own this place also owned my kin. Here, eat this while it's hot."

She passed me a scone and a cup of tea. "I'm supposed to be the manager, but everybody pitches in as we can and somehow, even with three girls serving today, we're still considered short-staffed. Guests here have to be attended hand and foot, just like the old days. And when I say old days, I mean 1822." She shook her head. "I better watch my mouth."

My own mouth was full of scone, melty and soft. It was one of the best baked anythings I'd ever eaten. The tea was just as heavenly, and I wasn't even a tea drinker. "That's a raspberry rosemary scone. And a jasmine green tea with dried cucumber, melon rind, and lemongrass," Valerie said. "I bake everything here, and I blend my own loose leaves."

"Wow, this is all so delicious. Thank you." Valerie set another scone on my plate as I asked, "So this is an Airbnb?"

She sipped from her own cup. "No, this is an old-fashioned inn, and the owner calls herself the 'proprietress.' What in the world brought you here, sweetheart?"

"I was hoping for a job."

Her frown dipped deep. "Your mama's gonna have a fit if she knows you set foot in this place."

"Why?"

"Doesn't matter, she just will. And listen, you don't want to work here."

"But you work here."

"I don't have options at my age, sweetheart. But a smart girl like you with so much promise? I don't want this for you."

"There's nowhere else I can get a job." Mom wanted me to work, so why would she be mad at me? And serving coffee and cookies seemed a lot easier than hauling trays around in some diner. "Please, let me talk to the 'proprietress' or whatever."

"Baby, you don't want to do that."

"No, I do."

"Honey, trust me."

"Trust *me*. Please. I'm basically an adult. May I see the proprietress?"

She groaned. "You are a hardheaded person's child. Sit tight, baby doll. I'll get her. After you see more of this place you'll understand."

A few minutes later, I waited in a stuffy parlor with enormous portraits of dead, rich-looking white people glaring at me. This place felt oppressively fancy. I heard footsteps, but the person who bustled in was not much older than me. She wore some kind of old-fashioned English peasant costume: a long, navy dress and a checked apron, with a flowered cloth wrapped around most of her ash-blond hair.

"Mrs. Chilton will be here in a moment." She spoke formally, but she had a country twang, eyeing me with a who-the-hell-are-you look.

"Thanks." I gave her a who-the-hell-are-*you* glare back.

After a while, I wandered out into the enormous, opulent central hallway toward voices and laughter across the hall. In another parlor, four middle-aged women sat around a table holding fans of cards. They wore pearls and pastel cardigans, even though it was a million degrees outside. Another woman dressed like a peasant served them tea from a silver pitcher.

"You have to tell me about Crystal's engagement party," one of them drawled. "I'm sure it was a disaster."

"She's just one generation above white trash," another said.

"One generation?" Her friend scoffed. She noticed me. Immediately remembering my jeans and ponytail, I slunk back into the parlor, passing the time by glancing at the dour-faced portraits on the walls.

"I see you're getting acquainted with my ancestors." A slim woman in tight, pink satiny pants minced into the room on high heels. She had a slow, Southern drawl that gave life to the Old South, stretching "I" into a breathy "*Ah*" and "ancestors" into "*aancestuhs.*" She seemed to be in her sixties, with a blond pixie cut gone awry, pieces curling upward every which way: a hairstyle of a thousand cowlicks. She smiled, though something seemed to tug at her expression as she looked at me. It was something like worry, or even sorrow.

She took both of my hands. Her skin felt cool and she smelled of gardenias. "I'm Mrs. Elaine Eugenia Harper Chilton, though folks call me Lana Jean. You must be Noni. Looking at you is like looking at your great-grandmother. She cleaned my family's home for years, you know."

"Oh."

"And you do favor your mother as well, though perhaps you've a more agreeable expression. I was her high school principal, you know."

"Okay."

"There's so much history here in Magnolia. Especially with Senator Vermilion Harper hailing from our town. You might know he was my grandfather."

"Of course." Actually, I didn't quite have a handle on who this senator dude was in the first place.

"Born and raised in this home. His father was George Harper III, a great statesman and patriarch of Trianon. His great-grandfather had been a lowly tavern keeper who rose to become a wealthy tobacco planter."

What was I supposed to do, applaud?

"The Harpers were the founding family of Magnolia, but others followed suit," Lana Jean Chilton bragged. "Like the family who lived at Tangleroot. The Dearborns."

The same people who enslaved Cuffee Fortune. The family of the mysterious girl whose grave lay nestled in the woods.

She went on. "The Dearborns were of new money, but respectable stock. However, it was the Harper family who owned most of our county's land. Trianon wasn't our only plantation, not with all the Harper cousins. Perhaps you've passed by our family's other surviving plantations: Hollis Hall, Gilded Pines. I myself live at Twenty Paces."

"Um, yeah."

She smiled. "So what brought you to my lovely inn, darling?"

"Someone told me about a job. A Mrs. Dorsey?"

"Oh, Glenda. Of course she did. Sweetheart, let me show you around." She took my hand—a Momlike gesture—and led me out. In the wide hallway, a gold-framed portrait very different from the others caught my eye. It was an oil painting of a blond woman wearing a white satin dress, one with petal-shaped skirts that belled out just like a magnolia flower.

"My grandmother, Priscilla Lavigne Harper," Mrs. Chilton explained. "She wore this gown at Magnolia's very first Founding Families celebration. This spring will mark Founding Families' one-hundred-year anniversary."

"It's a beautiful portrait." Honestly, it was striking, the painter capturing details down to the sheen of silk. More wow-worthy was the skill of the dressmaker. She would've had to make the fabric splay and lift like an opening blossom.

"The senator's smoking room," she announced at the doorway of a wood-paneled parlor. A gigantic oil painting almost as tall as me hung above the fireplace, surrounded on either side by lit candelabras. Mounted above the portrait was a long gun with a scary-looking bayonet poking from the end. On the mantel lay a single, long-stemmed rose. And on either side of the fireplace stood two flags—not just the state flag of Virginia, but the Confederate stars and bars. I cringed hard, but what was I supposed to do? Tear it down and light it on fire with the candle flame?

"That is Senator Vermilion Harper." Mrs. Chilton spoke reverently of the portrait.

"Uh, wow."

"He was a great man. A great, great man."

Uh-huh, I got that from the whole shrine situation. The square-jawed senator glowered at me with a stern expression.

"The very founder of the college where your mother works." She nodded up at him admirably.

"Right." That's not how Mom would phrase any of this.

"Well. I should show you the rest of the inn." It was as if nothing else at Trianon mattered. Upstairs, she opened the door to a monstrosity of a bedroom. Everything was embroidered and festooned with lace and/or ruffles. "Our Savannah Chamber."

"Um . . . oh."

She showed me another equally appalling bedroom of decorative horrors. "Our Charleston Chamber's guests will be checking in soon. We're always full, often with returning visitors. There remains a dedicated clientele that longs for the experience of living in the *real* South, a feeling that's all but vanished with today's"—she airily waved a hand around—"agitation."

At the stair landing, she stopped at a framed photograph of the senator posed beside an American flag. "It's troubling, Noni. If the new high school principal gets her way, we'll have a radical school board and a curriculum that sullies my grandfather's legacy. But the senator was a product of his time." She added, "Even your mother's book that paints slavery in such a slanted perspective—it just might suggest hate for people like me."

I wanted to protest. Mom's book didn't paint anything. Formerly enslaved people described their lives, and they were terrible.

But Lana Jean Chilton smiled gently. "I shouldn't burden you with such. You're here about a position, after all." She ushered me downstairs. "And I might have something. But your mother would throw a fit."

"She wouldn't. I'm here all summer and she says I have to work." I followed her into one of the parlors.

"Oh, does she now." Lana Jean Chilton meandered over to the baby grand in the corner and stroked it with her fingers, like a game-show model advertising a prize. "Since you're Radiance's daughter, you must know how to sight-read." She straightened a page of sheet music. "Play this, darling. And sing to it."

Plunking myself down on the bench, I gave the music a once-over. It looked pretty simple, but I hadn't played in months. Mom used to make me practice, but lately it had become one of the only battles she lost. Positioning my fingers, I played and sang an unfamiliar song with weird and drippy lyrics: "Furl that banner, softly, slowly / Treat it gently, it is holy / For it droops above the dead." It seemed like something Mom would complain about. But Mom complained about everything—for instance, she'd say I was a little sharp.

Lana Jean Chilton pressed her hands to her chest. "That was beautiful!" She sat beside me with her Southerner's sense of personal space. I resisted the urge to scoot way over.

"You are a splendid girl. But Radiance would be furious if you worked for me." She gently cleared her throat. "Excuse me. Dr. Castine. She can be rather particular about her title, can't she? She can be particular about a lot of things."

I kept my mouth shut. Zipped. Hadn't Mom mentioned she used to clash with her high school principal?

"She's always been that way. Forcefully opinionated. It must be like walking a tightrope a mile high, being her daughter."

I wasn't going to say a word.

"You must feel like you have to be perfect. Just like her."

I studied the piano keyboard. The grandfather clock in the corner ticked quietly. A trace of soft laughter wafted in from across the hall.

"Well." Mrs. Chilton patted my arm. "My guests, four nights a week, dally here in the music parlor for wine and cheese. Thursdays through Sundays. Just from two until five or so—or longer, if there's a wedding." She absentmindedly keyed a few bars on the piano. "They'd find songs like 'The Conquered Banner' to be a diversion from their cares."

I looked up.

"My guests are gracious. They'd tip well, on top of what I'd pay. For an accomplished pianist, I would think fifty dollars sounds fair. An hour."

I did the math.

"It's just too bad it wouldn't work out . . ."

"No," I interrupted her. "No, it would work out fine. I'd love to do it."

"But your mother . . ."

"I told you, Mom wants me to work. And she loves when I play the piano. She'd be thrilled."

"Well, then." Mrs. Chilton pressed her hands together. "You seem so confident. I would like to offer you a position. Can you start this Thursday?"

I hesitated, thinking about the peasant look of the other girls. I hated that costume. As if reading my mind, Mrs. Chilton said, "I'd ask that you wear something nice. Something appropriate for church."

"Yes, I can do that. You'll see me later this week!"

For the first time since I'd been in Magnolia, I was excited. It wasn't my costume design internship, and I didn't love playing the piano. And I definitely didn't love Lana Jean. But this was a wild amount of cash.

My phone died on my way home, but I cranked up the radio and couldn't stop grinning. Never mind I could only get a country station. Six hundred dollars! For a few hours a week, to basically do something Mom tried to make me do anyway!

It almost felt like something good was finally happening in this crummy town.

CHAPTER 5

"Absolutely not. *Absolutely not!*" Mom was livid. "You will not work in that woman's house. Never!"

"Mom, it's not her *house*! It's an inn, and besides, what's your deal? You wanted me to work."

"Not *there*!" Still dressed from work, she stomped toward the library, giving me no choice but to trot after her.

"For God's sake, it's playing the piano, Mom! You're always telling me to practice, and now I get a *job* playing, and you have a problem?"

Mom slammed her purse down on the desk. Everything in the room rattled. "I am absolutely appalled that you laid eyes on that house, and you still want to work there!"

"It's better than waiting tables!"

"Waiting tables is an honor compared to working in *that* place."

"Mom, you act like it's some seedy motel. It's a fancy inn."

"I know exactly what it is. I just can't believe you want to work for her. Haven't you heard a thing about Founding Families? And that abhorrent statue? Have you listened to a word I've said?"

Not really, because Mom had railed about a lot of things.

"Lana Jean was the very engine behind it all. She . . ."

"Mom, I don't know what you're talking about!"

"Stop it, Noni. Just stop it. I can't hear this anymore." Mom rubbed her temples. "That woman is one of the most despicably racist people on earth. Her grandfather was Vermilion Harper, for god's sake. The man who stole *our* college!"

It wasn't our college. "Mom, Valerie Golden is Trianon's manager, and she's Black. She said she took care of you when you were a kid."

“That was a long time ago. I have no respect for Valerie at all. It’s clear she has no respect for herself, either.”

I felt defensive. “How can you say that about her?”

“Easily, since she’s willing to lower herself to work for Lana Jean Chilton! A woman who has her servers dress up like slaves!”

I blinked, both because Mom used that word and because it just occurred to me. “Slaves?” I repeated. Mom always stressed, “*en*slaved.” Because people were born their own, free persons and forced into slavery, she said. It was an act done to them. Her saying “slaves” felt like a slap on the face.

“Didn’t you see them?” Mom demanded. “The aprons, the head-scarves?”

I didn’t answer, embarrassed it didn’t occur to me before. Because what would English peasants be doing in a Southern plantation home? “Mom, they’re white, so it doesn’t matter, right? And she’s asking me to play the piano. She said I could wear a church dress . . .”

Shutting her eyes, Mom shook her head. “I cannot speak to you right now. This discussion is finished!”

Later, I googled Vermilion Harper. I remembered that Mom had bitched about him plenty during the impromptu history lessons she pushed on me. He was some old codger who lived to be over one hundred, born during the Civil War. He was the first president of Stonepost College, and he served in the senate for seventy-six years, fighting tooth and nail for segregation. He was infamous for a vicious segregation speech he gave in May 1955.

I clicked on a link to the grainy, black-and-white video clip. An unsteady camera panned over downtown Magnolia. There was a creepy festival-like atmosphere, with tents sprung up along the fairgrounds, as if vendors had set up shop. People crowded the green space and crammed the main street. Then the camera focused on the senator, who was much changed from the giant portrait in the Trianon house. In the painting, he'd been handsome for a dude in his forties, if you liked the stern principal-looking type. In the clip, he was massively old, stooped and liver-spotted. He stood on the courthouse steps before the enormous audience.

Trembling and shaking, maybe from age, maybe from anger, or maybe both, he leaned onto a cane. "People of Virginia," he spoke into a microphone. "We must stand for what we believe in!"

His words were met with ringing applause. "We must stand alone!" His voice was strong for such an old man, although he seemed to hold on to that cane for dear life. "Because the radicals, and the commies, and the Yankees, and the damned Negroes want to take away everything we hold dear. Our way of life!"

Rabid cheers filled the air.

"We will not let them! I would rather burn down this courthouse. I would rather burn down this town. I would rather burn down the state of Virginia, before I allow Negroes to take away our schools, our jobs, our churches, our history, our heritage, our *women*!"

The audience roared, whipped to a crescendo as slowly, the old man lifted his cane, standing on his own two feet.

The thunderous shouts, blending with the static of the video, were overwhelming. "Burn it down!" The senator thrust his cane high into the air. "Burn it down!"

As soon as Mom rounded a bend on the highway, I saw it, even though it was way down the road. Really, you could probably see it from space. A huge barn, just like the dozens of other barns I'd seen in Virginia, except it was painted an obscenely bright, migraine-inducing lilac. As we got closer, I could read the ginormous, hot-pink sign with pictures of smiling cows, chickens, and ducks.

"Charm on the Farm? Are you kidding me? What the hell is this?"

"Young lady, don't use that kind of language." She glided her Volvo into the lot. Mom had finally bought me my own car, a 2017 Toyota Corolla with a dented side, but she still insisted on escorting me to my first day of work, as if she didn't trust me to arrive on my own.

As I stepped out of the car, a strange, deep moan filled the air. "What is that noise?" On the other side of the parking lot, behind a wooden fence, stood the answer. "Mom! Those are cows!"

She sighed. "Yes. Cows." There were three huge reddish-brown ones with sharp, curved horns. One lifted its throat and lowed, loud and long, a sound rising in volume before tapering off: *mmmmAWWWWuuhh.*

"Blondell's house is across the fence," Mom said calmly. "This is her farm." On the other side of the road, a ginormous horse stared at me. Weird-looking speckled chickens pecked around. Fat gray geese, straight out of a nursery rhyme, waddled into a pond.

It was unreal. The giant purple barn had a wide front porch and wind chimes singing all over the place. The double doors swung open and a woman came flying out.

"Oh my goodness! Radiance!" She grabbed Mom in a big hug.

"Look at you! Wow, you look beautiful!" Mom gushed.

"Please, I'm a sack of potatoes. Did I miss the time warp? You look like you're still in college."

Mom motioned me forward. "Blondell, here's Noni! Noni, this is Blondell Pankey."

Blondell was Mom's age and plump, heavy in the hips, wearing tight jeans and a plaid top. She had loads of shiny brown hair in a loose ponytail down her back. I reached out a hand, but she grabbed me in a tight hug instead. I should've figured.

"Great day, you're all grown up!" she exclaimed. "And looking just like Fawnie Castine. Just as pretty as she ever was!"

She showed us around inside. "So whimsical!" Mom glanced around at the cow-print cushions on the chairs and brightly colored quilts hanging on the walls. Four girls and a guy who looked around my age were busy rolling forks and knives into checkered cloth napkins or setting the wooden booths and tables with bottles of ketchup and steak sauce.

"You'll love it here," Blondell told me. "We work hard but we're all a friendly bunch. Right, Kara?" She spoke to a girl who refilled salt shakers.

Kara flashed a cheerleader smile and nodded. With her girl-next-door freckles, brightly colored overalls, and a ribbon in her red hair, she looked like something you'd buy in a store. I didn't like her already.

"Business is booming," Blondell said proudly. "Our food's tasty and guests love our animals. All heritage breeds."

"Really?" Mom tilted her head. "Fascinating!"

"They're the kind of livestock farmers bred back in the day," Blondell told me, as if I cared. "Hardly anyone raises them anymore, but they're part of history. So I do."

This all made me nervous. "Am I going to have to . . . muck poop?"

Mom looked pissed, but Blondell just laughed. "Of course not, sweetie. We've got a farmhand who feeds the animals, so you just have to worry about feeding our customers. We offer fantastic service. Don't you think, Amy?" Blondell moseyed over to a girl with short hair tied back in a pink bandana. She filled plastic squeezy bottles with ketchup. "Our customers like bright smiles and lots of 'em."

"Can do!" She gave a thumbs-up. Was this a cult?

Mom gave me a worried look, like she was afraid I wouldn't make it through initiation. "I imagine your customers tip well if you're friendly."

"Oh, they do. And I pay a good wage." In the kitchen, we watched four guys around my age dredge raw chicken in buttermilk or chop up cabbage for coleslaw. The one who seemed to direct the others was Black, with flour-streaked dark brown arms. Mom immediately asked if he was related to someone named Clay Nichols.

"That's my dad," he said.

Mom beamed. "My gosh! You favor him so much! Clay was my date to the Hay Bale Ball during our sophomore year." I was humiliated, but he seemed to take it in stride. "Please tell him Radiance Castine said hello."

"Dr. Castine?" He peeled off his glove to shake her hand. "I'm really pleased to meet you. I'm Jabari Nichols. I read your book, *The Remembered.*"

Mom's eyes widened with delight. "Did you?"

"For a Black Studies class I took at community college. I'm hoping to transfer to a four-year college."

"That's excellent!" Mom looked like he just made her week. "Oh, and you should meet my daughter. She'll be here this summer before she leaves for college." She practically pushed me forward.

"Our newest farm girl," Blondell said happily. He shook my hand. His deep-set eyes were curious and kind.

"Noni Reid."

He smiled. "It'll be nice to see you around."

I kind of wanted to know a little more about him. But still, I was relieved when the exchange was over. But then, Blondell turned my way. "All right, Noni, we got us a busy day. You ready to fill out some paperwork and put on your uniform?"

If I thought the day was going downhill before, it really started flying down the express lane to hell after Mom left. My uniform turned out to be a gingham shirt the exact shade of loud, screaming purple as the barn and denim overalls, the cuffs rolled up right below my knees. And to finish it off, tacky bubble-gum-pink Keds. A poster in the staff dressing room advertised the dress code: *DO wear long hair in pigtails, braids, or a ponytail. Creative hair colors are cool, but DO wear a hair accessory like a scarf or ribbon. We farm folk keep it cute!*

Gag. And this was the *one* day I'd worn my freshly pressed hair down, thinking Mom would find it more professional. And there wasn't a hair tie to be found in my jumbled backpack.

I rummaged around. In a set of drawers, beneath a blow-dryer and straightening irons, I spied a pair of barrettes. They were studded with red, blue, and clear rhinestones in the shape of an American flag. I pinned my hair back. The stars-and-stripes were as farmy as you could get.

By the time I filled out all my hiring paperwork, it was almost lunchtime. Blondell told me that Mom would pick me up around eight, an eternity away. "Which is perfect, 'cause we can get a full day of training in," Blondell said.

By now, it seemed like customers were streaming in every minute. "I'm going to pair you with Fluvanna Fluharty. Her family owns the farm across the field from mine, and they raise the best sausage you've ever eaten."

I was confused. Raise sausage? How do you raise sausage?

"Fluvie's been here since we opened, and she waitressed at the Maggie Café two years before that. Lots of experience." She tapped a girl in a mint-green gingham shirt wearing yellow sneakers. It was instantly depressing, because this Flu girl must have been working since the ninth grade. She didn't look a second older than nineteen. And—she wore a mullet. It was some variation of a hairstyle I'd seen on white men in old eighties movies: feathered bangs—hers accentuated with a neon-green bow—close-cropped sides, and a spillway of layers down her neck. That wasn't the most glaring thing about her, because her hair was pink. Bright, blazing pink, the kind of shade you need shades for.

"So I hear you're from Boston." She spoke with a thick twang. She walked and talked, so I had to follow her.

"Yeah." I glanced at the colorful designs spreading down her forearm. A farmer with a sleeve tattoo and pink hair?

"I've never been. Not a lot of hog shows in Boston."

Hog shows? Was *that* how the sausage was raised?

Fluvanna whisked to the window where the kitchen staff set out steaming plates under a warming light. She checked the number on a ticket. "Grab these. Hold one in your hand and prop the other on your wrist, just like that. Follow me. We're heading to table nineteen."

I tried to keep up as she rattled stuff off. "The restaurant's in a grid pattern with table one closest to the door. Then you just count up counterclockwise. Except for table twenty-two, that one's after table twenty-three 'cause it's in the corner. Same with table thirteen, it's where table fifteen should be."

That didn't make any sense. She smiled as she handed two customers their plates. Somehow she knew they weren't from around here. "Where y'all traveling from?"

"We're passing through, visiting family in Greensboro," one said. "From Maryland."

"Really? Do y'all live anywhere near St. Mary's? I went there with my 4-H club for a livestock fair. It was beautiful, over by the water. I really want to go to Annapolis, because they've got the naval academy, and I hear the boys are really cute."

"We live in Silver Spring," the middle-aged man said. "Nothing romantic about that, it's just a giant strip mall. But you're right, Annapolis is wonderful."

His wife added, "And those young men sure are handsome."

"I can't wait to visit," Fluvanna said. "Y'all enjoy everything, now. If there's anything else I can get you, you just holler."

She offered up another smile as she refilled glasses at another table. "How y'all doing?" she asked the two customers. "Everything delicious?"

"Always is, Fluvie," a bald, burly man said. "Who's this little jewel you got with you? I ain't seen her around."

"This is Noni. She just moved here." She talked about me like I wasn't there.

"Moved here?" the other guy said. "Nobody moves here. They just move away."

"Or die," his friend said. They both burst out laughing.

"Her family hails from here." Somehow Fluvie knew my whole history.

"Do they!" the burly man boomed. "Who are your folks, Noni?"

I didn't smile or even answer. Fluvie cleared her throat. "Her mom is Radiance Castine." Jeez, what didn't she know about me?

The man smiled, a big, spreading curl of his lips. "So *you're* the daughter." He and his friend exchanged surprised expressions.

The friend spoke soberly. "Don't bring up any business, Bill."

I didn't know what he meant, but I was annoyed anyway. Especially when the burly guy said, "I saw your mama at Schuler's other day. I bet she's still got men fighting over her."

I tried not to scowl at both of them, but I must've failed. As we went to the next table, Fluvie said, "We're supposed to be friendly to our customers. That's what we're known for at Charm."

"Those guys are gross."

"Blondell says to come get her if we get a problem we can't handle. But that's just Bill and Arthur. They work at the golf course."

"How my mom looks is none of their business."

"Around here, everything's everyone's business," she said. "You'll get used to it, I reckon."

Despite what Fluvie told me, I didn't *reckon* I'd get used to anything. The lunch rush seemed to last forever. I felt my head would explode from all I had to learn. Where the drink stations were. The "sweet tea" everyone asked for versus the "unsweet tea" with the rag tied around the pitcher handle. I mixed the two up at one point. One of my customers took a sip of what was supposed to be sweet tea and sprayed it out all over the table.

"Sweet tea's a big thing," Fluvie warned as she taught me how to refund a whole dinner. "You gotta get that right. You'll learn, though. You're doing good."

But the table numbers were still a mystery, even though she explained them two or three times. I didn't know any of the items on the menu, so when people said vague things like, "I'll have the chicken," I didn't know if they meant fried chicken, rotisserie chicken, chicken pot pie, or chicken and dumplings. Worse, I didn't know to ask right then—so when I went to punch in the order, I was bewildered by the different selections. And then I had to go back to the table to ask. And the customer would say, "You know, the chicken."

There were too many things to remember. Customers would grab me as I rushed past them and ask for random things, like extra napkins or salad dressing. Anything I didn't write down, I forgot. So when I swept by on my way somewhere else, they'd ask, "Where's my ranch?"

When the lunch rush finally ended, I wanted to sink down on the sofa upstairs in the break room. "Do we get to chill a bit? Until dinner?" I asked Fluvie.

"Grab a bite if you need it. Take five minutes. We've got side work to do."

The slow hours between lunch and dinner were spent mixing

buttermilk and herbs for homemade ranch dressing, or whirring heavy cream into whipped peaks. Most of the servers were nice, if a bit rushed and standoffish, but they seemed to joke with one another and with the kitchen guys. Still, I had zero interest in making friends. Not even with Jabari, who passed me a smile and a "How're you holding up?" every time he slid a plate underneath the warming light. I'd hit a wall and had no idea how I would make it through the evening. Before I was anywhere near ready, the dinner crowd came flooding in.

The next day, I followed Fluvie again. Somehow, I managed to endure both her perkiness and the exhausting job. On Wednesday, Blondell paired me with Madge, a thin-faced woman in her mid-twenties who chewed gum incessantly and talked about her kids even more.

"It's Nicorette." Madge smacked her gum. "I'm trying to quit. Smoking's bad when you got kids. I got four." She whipped her phone from her pocket, flashing pictures. "Jason, Jackson, Jacob, and Jonathan. They're a handful. This morning, I was getting Johnny dressed for day care, and he said, 'Mommy, I want to wear boots like Daddy!' Ain't that funny? My husband does construction; he wears boots every day. You married? You got kids?"

"I just graduated from high school."

"What are you waiting for? Clock's ticking."

Somehow, the only clock that wasn't ticking fast enough was the one on the wall. Especially when I turned a corner fast and clumsy, bumping smack into another server, Darlie. My tray crashed against my chest. I yelped from the cold sting of iced tea soaking my shirt, and the burn of hot coffee, *owwing* when the glass pitcher crash-landed on my foot.

"Oh shit!" But my Keds-clad toe broke the pitcher's fall, and it didn't shatter.

Thankfully, Darlie was only holding clean dish towels. She was unscathed. But her tone was scalding. "There are children in here!" She bustled away.

"Corner!" someone announced, just like I was supposed to have done a few seconds ago. Fluvie wheeled around. "Oh no!" She looked down at my sodden shirt and overall bib. Her eyes moved to the pitcher, glass, and mug, arrayed at my feet like offerings at an altar. "You okay?"

"I feel stupid."

"Don't. It happens to everyone. Do you have a spare uniform upstairs?"

I shook my head.

She grabbed my tray and picked up the dishes. "Let's find Darlie, and see if she has another set. Y'all are about the same size."

"No, no, that's okay," I said quickly.

"Well, let's at least get you some towels."

It didn't miss me that Darlie had been carrying a stack of them.

After work that week, I went straight to bed. Mom would knock on my bedroom door, asking how my day was. Evening after evening, I repeated that I was too tired to talk. I didn't tell her my days had been terrible and soul-sucking, and that I was relieved not to see Darlie on my shifts after I had collided with her.

On Saturday, Darlie was back on the floor. We passed each other without speaking. After closing, I hesitated as I walked into the staff room, where she was brushing her hair.

"You got through your first week!" cheered Fluvie. She shared the mirror with Darlie, buffing on blue and purple eye shadow.

"Yay!" cheered Amy. I looked away, because she was changing into shorts. She wore big grandma panties.

I wasn't feeling any of the hurrahs. Not with my tired shoulders and aching feet, with my sore arms and legs and everywhere. And not with Darlie standing there, gliding the pink-tipped brush through her long hair. I unclipped my overalls and changed prudishly, middle-school-gym-style.

"Darlie, are you free tonight?" Amy asked.

"I think so! I'll see if my little sis can watch the kids awhile longer." She fished around in a dresser drawer.

"Noni, you should come!" Fluvie's wide blue eyes reminded me of Alyssa's. "We're going to catch a movie. There's a drive-in right outside town."

"Hey, where are my barrettes?" Darlie rummaged more. "My flag barrettes."

Oh no. My first day of work felt like ages ago, but I remembered using those red-white-and-blue barrettes. What had I done with them? I was so tired that night, I couldn't remember. They were probably at home, on top of my dresser. Or on my bathroom counter. Or somewhere on the floor. I felt ashamed for just assuming I could use them. And for not putting them right back. "I'm sorry," I spoke up. "I borrowed them on Monday, because we're supposed to wear ribbons and stuff, and . . ."

"Did you ask anyone? Because that's not borrowing, that is taking something that's not yours. That's stealing. Maybe that's what you're used to, but that's not what *we* do. Even my four-year-old knows better."

"I think I just brought them home by accident."

"By accident?"

"It's no big deal, Darlie! She'll bring them back," Fluvie said.

"My boyfriend gave me those. We both work hard to buy what we own. Not everyone has a rich mom like *she* does." Darlie yanked on a tight Blue Lives Matter T-shirt. White stripes crossed big boobs.

"My mother isn't rich," I said.

Everyone turned and looked at me. And no one spoke a word, not at first. Not even Darlie, who quietly clasped on a gold necklace. The bulky pendant was in the shape of a studded circle that didn't quite close. Then she muttered, "Your mom is a lot of things you don't know."

"What does that even mean?"

"Maybe it means you shouldn't snatch things from people, things that are special to them."

The other girls swapped looks.

"So bring my barrettes back," Darlie snapped. "Find something else to put in your weave."

I should have snapped right back, called her out right away on what she said. But I was at a loss for words. The silence in the room, the complete stop from the others as if some force froze them mid-action, mid-breath—it grated against my brain like a deafening noise. Like a fire alarm blaring or an ambulance siren blasting into my eardrums. The kind of sound that hurts.

Finally, Fluvie spoke up. She sounded nervous, but firm. "Darlie. I don't think what you said was okay." It was tentative, as if she didn't even *know* why Darlie's statement was so awful. But her intervention, as wavering as it was, gave me a second to take a breath.

"It *wasn't* okay. And I'm not wearing a weave." I grabbed my book bag. "But if I were, that would be my business, and my choice of style." I added, "So stay out of my hair."

Jabari caught me as I was getting into my car. He'd started to smile, but it melted when he saw my face. "You okay?"

I thought of telling him about Darlie. But what good would that do?

"I'm good." I lied to him instead.

He didn't seem to believe me. "Hey. The first week of any job is always hard, especially this one. You should've seen me. I almost burned the place down. But here's the good news." He patted the side of my car. "For the most part, everyone here is really cool, and they'll help you out when you mess up."

I thought of Fluvie, for all I didn't get her mullet, her accent, and her hogs.

"There's a couple of folks you might watch out for, but overall, it's a good job to have." He smiled. "Who knows, you might even like this place."

I couldn't help but smile back—a little.

CHAPTER 6

"Why are you baking?" It was ten in the morning. I'd just woken up, and the whole kitchen smelled like cinnamon. I had Sunday off, which I needed. I was exhausted to the point that my whole body was sore.

Dressed as Susie Q. Homemaker in a plaid sundress, my mother looked up as if she was absolutely puzzled by such a question. As if she baked every Sunday. On the table was a wicker basket lined with a gingham napkin and stuffed with homemade muffins and cinnamon rolls. There was also a bag of coffee and a tin of expensive tea.

"I'm making a gift basket for our tenant." She fitted in a bottle of whiskey, which more or less ruined the whole breakfast theme.

"The weird old guy?" I remembered passing the run-down stables with a weather vane twirling in the wind, the day I found that girl's grave in the fenced-in cemetery. "Have you met him yet?"

"Not yet. But the Haneys said he's really nice. And I saw a Jeep out there this morning, so I guess he's home."

She wanted me to go with her to greet him, but I wouldn't. "Bring pepper spray," I warned her. "I don't feel like finding your body."

She rolled her eyes and stepped out the back door.

A half hour later, she returned, her face glowing.

"I was starting to worry." I was in the kitchen making more coffee. I missed Starbucks. The nearest one was a forty-minute drive away.

"Oh, he wasn't home. As I was walking down, the Jeep was driving away."

"So you left a picnic for the ants?" I held up the French press. "Coffee?"

Mom shook her head. "I'm okay." She hung a set of keys on the wall rack. "I have a key to the cottage. And I figured he wouldn't mind if I left the basket. Those old stables are beautiful. The Haneys must have spent a pretty penny in restorations. New flooring, skylights."

"How long did you spend poking around?"

Mom looked a little sheepish. "Longer than I should have. He's a very interesting man."

"Find any porn?"

She rolled her eyes again. "No, Noni. He's very neat and spartan. It seems he's really outdoorsy. It's great that he's staying active in his older years. There was a mountain bike on the porch. One of his closets was open and filled with camping equipment. And he's one of those old men who works out. Retired military, maybe? He has a very nice home gym. Fully equipped."

She sighed. "But then I saw a cat. A big calico, sitting right there, watching me. She did not approach, but I left immediately." Mom was deathly afraid of cats.

"So he's a retired military hippie. With a killer cat." I flicked a clawed hand. Mom tried to smile. She knew her fear was irrational—a phobia. It was a point of shame for her. But still, I knew in her mind, she was fleeing for her life.

For the first time ever, I resorted to crossing off each passing day on a calendar. I couldn't get to BU fast enough. It would be strange reconnecting with Alyssa, since we hadn't spoken since those two days after we graduated when she just fake-laughed as Kendall and Laronté said those shitty things. But she'd apologize—right? And maybe then, things would go on as they always had.

At work, most everyone warmed up to me. Kara invited me bowling in Daventry. Madge invited me out for appetizers at the County Seat. One night Jabari went to the drive-in with Fluvie and Amy, and was disappointed that I wasn't coming. I gave a half-hearted excuse.

I decided not to say anything to Blondell about Darlie's weave comment, and I certainly wasn't going to tell Mom. I didn't want her to get fired. I just wanted her to understand why what she said was hurtful, but I couldn't find the words to tell her, and it wasn't my job to educate her, anyway. I picked up a shift for her when her baby got sick, but hurt hung in the air between us. We related to each other like the pendant on the necklace she'd clasp on after work: a circle that didn't quite close in the middle.

But what was the point in reconciling, or making friends, when I was moving five hundred miles away in a few weeks? Besides, the Charm servers weren't people I would hang out with. They listened to country music. Some of them had kids. Fluvie was even a farmer.

And I had a rich mom.

On the Fourth of July, I got home late, expecting Mom to drag me out to see fireworks on the fairgrounds, with plans of staying out past midnight and catching the first moments of my birthday on the fifth. But the ping of music greeted me instead: a medley to a Tracy Chapman song Mom streamed often but never played on the piano. Wearing a chenille duster over her nightgown and teal satin wrapping her hair, she focused on a sheet of music, her fingers methodically moving along the keyboard.

I could have gone to my room, unnoticed. But instead, I stood beside the piano, listening as she finished the song. "What happened?" I knew something had.

"Oh, nothing." But she pivoted around on the smooth bench, removing her reading glasses. They were new, white with varicolored flecks. I thought of cupcake sprinkles, of the night at her reception when I'd mortified her.

"Nothing happened, really." She reconsidered. "Well, something. Slight."

"What?"

"Just . . . I was in Lynchburg for a meeting. Afterward I thought I'd get a glass of wine at the riverfront and finish a book I'm reviewing. Some boys were clustered beside me at the bar. College-age kids."

"White kids?" I guessed.

She nodded. "It was crowded. Happy hour. And I was the only Black person there. One of the boys knocked into my shoulder as I read on my phone. So I scooched over a bit. And I heard his friend caution him. 'Watch yourself,' he said. 'Someone's behind you.'"

My mother shook her head. "The kid just looked at me. And he bumped me again, really hard this time. Like a shark bumping a boat. Enough so that my drink spilled all over my lap."

"Well, what'd he say when you cussed him out?" I wanted to know.

"I said nothing, sweetheart. I gave the bartender a twenty and left."

Why did I feel ashamed of her? "You didn't say anything? You just let him do that?"

My mother's gaze was an inquiring one, as if she were reviewing my face like the book she'd tried to read.

Maybe she was searching for the resemblance of herself.

"He scared me." Her eyes were wide and luminous.

Even though I hadn't posted anything on social in weeks, I took a peek at my accounts on July fifth. There were tons of messages, just like every year. Notes from old classmates. From my aunt Nichelle, my uncle Brian, my cousin Kadeem. And there were HBDs from folks at Charm: Fluvie, Amy, Madge, Kara, and of course, Blondell. Jabari sent a gif of a guy slurping ramen noodles. *Hope your birthday is soup-perb.* Leaning over the railing on the back porch, I actually giggled, even though it was dumb. Soup? Like, why soup? We never talked about soup. Soup wasn't a traditional birthday food. We didn't even serve it at Charm. Why was I still cackling from the randomness of it?

As I scrolled, a text popped up. Another happy birthday with a flurry of celebratory emojis. It was from Alyssa.

But there was no apology. No acknowledgment of what happened.

Alyssa had been the new girl in my sixth-grade class. The other kids teased her because she'd had a slight Southern accent, having moved from Tennessee, an accent she worked to change over the years. But that day, I told her I liked her unicorn socks. Later, she'd been the first girl I hosted for a sleepover. Mom made us deep-dish pizza, along with gooey brownies.

Remembering the history of our friendship felt sharp and hurtful, as if my mind had a cramp. I needed to walk, to think. Should I ask for an apology? But maybe the adult thing to do wasn't to dwell on how you messed up. Maybe it was to move on. After all, when my parents argued, Mom was tense and aloof with Dad afterward, but they otherwise pretended as if nothing had happened. If apologies were given, I never heard them.

I stopped on the porch steps, sending a text. *Thanks! How are things?*

Great, she wrote back. *Hope your birthday's fun.*

Two deer wandered out of the woods fringing our sloping backyard just as I made it to the trail. The larger doe stamped her foot twice, staring warily as I passed. I took a snapshot and, without thinking, sent it to Alyssa.

Wow, she responded.

I saw deer outside almost every morning, sometimes the whole herd that roamed the woods. And there were other animals I caught sight of: a fox, skulking off into the darkness. A skunk waddling toward the creek. A pair of red-tailed hawks that nested in a tall pine and lurked on the wing. Mom even swore she saw a black bear one morning as she jogged through the woods, which thoroughly freaked me out. "It was more afraid of me than I was of it," she'd said. How she could be blithe about a four-hundred-pound bear and terrified of a twelve-pound tabby was a mystery. As I walked, I told myself it must have been a friendly black Labrador.

I wished I could describe to Alyssa the wildlife park that was my new backyard. How the landscape seemed to proffer a birthday gift, every step I took along the trail showing me a different vista of mountains. I could never access nature this way back in Boston, just by leaving my back door.

But as long as I stayed in Virginia, I would have to walk my mother's path. I couldn't veer away, not one step.

I couldn't even tell my best friend about finding the cemetery. It was too much to describe over text messages. So was the topsy-turvy doll on my bedroom chair and the fashion sketches on my closet door. We'd been disconnected like a phone line.

If I had remained in Boston, we could have talked about what happened at my house—or not, since we were rounding adulthood and maybe adults just dealt with things differently. But our friendship would've been intact. And now? Alyssa was probably texting with Kendall, gossiping about the fireworks party the previous night.

Why did Mom make me come here? I picked up a rock, imagining it was a pebble I could toss and ping Alyssa's window, the way friends in movies did.

I surprised myself by throwing it with everything I had.

"Owww!" A white man appeared from out of nowhere, rubbing his face. "I think I lost an eye!" The man was very tall, and very outdoorsy-looking in cargos and hiking boots, with a camera strapped around his chest. And his hair was very white. But he wasn't old at all. Younger than Mom even. He wasn't smiling, but there was mirth in his shining eyes—both of them.

"I'm sorry." I guessed who he was. "You must be our tenant in the horse house? But my mom said you were like, ninety."

"Ninety?" he questioned. "Oh, right, that would be because of Mrs. Haney, the lady who moved out of Tangleroot. Always describing me as 'a nice, white-haired gentleman.' No, I'm still in my thirties. I'm Will Taylor, by the way." He stuck out a hand. "So what's got you frustrated?"

"Who says I am?" I was intrigued at his guesswork.

"I do. When I was your age and I couldn't get through to my dad, I'd hurl a stone at a tree. Break a stick and toss it into the creek. Scream, knowing no one could hear me."

I hadn't thought of that one.

"So I'm guessing you can't be from around here," I said. He definitely didn't sound like a Southerner. Then I remembered how Alyssa said I wasn't Black because I spoke "properly." And how she had been born in the South, herself.

"Born and raised in Magnolia," he said. "So was my dad, and his dad, on down the line. At Braunston. The family plantation. I was the kid who left."

"But you're here." I stated the obvious.

"I came back a few years ago when my dad got sick. I stayed after he died."

"I'm sorry for that." Then I asked, "What made you leave before?"

His face hardened. "Something happened my senior year. I knew I had to leave the second I graduated."

"What was it? What happened?"

He just shrugged in a way that closed that topic but suggested an offer of another. Falling into step, I asked, "So what did you do when you left?"

He'd gone to a state college in Fredericksburg, studying biology. While he was there, he got his helicopter pilot's license, and he interned with a wildlife organization. "I was annoyed when that job brought me right back to Magnolia over the holiday break. Angry, really. It was fraught here. I stayed in a hotel in Daventry. I refused to talk to my dad."

"Why was it fraught?"

"The trial?" He said it as if I would know. "Your mom . . ."

Mom *had* once mentioned being in court in Virginia years ago, but she clamped up pretty quickly, as if she couldn't manage to say more. Now, I guessed why. "Did she get arrested for crossing the old railroad bridge?"

"Hmm." He seemed to consider something. "I don't know anything about her crossing that bridge. I was only here because of bear sightings near the courthouse."

I gasped. "Another one? Are bears something I need to plan for?"

"They pass through from the mountains sometimes, but this one set up shop. So our group rigged motion-activated cameras and an outdoor mic. It was cutting-edge technology back then." He said a sow, or lady bear, had been injured by a hunter's bullet and was denning her cub near the gully. "We were able to relocate them to a sanctuary."

"You saved lives."

"Those two, at least." There was a hint of sadness in his tone. Had there been another bear that didn't make it?

After college, Will went out west, flying wildlife biologists for population counts and radio tagging. Then his dad got him a job in DC flying politicians. He hated every minute of it. Now, he sold wildlife photography, and he owned an outdoor gear shop. "It's in Daventry. Right near your mom's college."

"It's not her college, she just pretends it is," I grumbled. "Just like she pretends the Tangleroot house is meant to be ours."

"Maybe it is yours. Just like how Braunston *isn't* my home. A sprawling mansion built from a community's pain. But I don't know what to do with it. I could sell it, but some family like Lana Jean Chilton's would move in, and that's the last thing Magnolia needs." He sighed. "I want Magnolia to evolve. I feel like maybe one day I can do something to change this place?"

We walked farther. Will knew the forest paths like Mom *thought* she knew what I should do with my life. But unlike my mother, he seemed to care what I had to say. I talked about my last couple of years in Boston. When I described my experience with the theater's costume department, he asked, "Why does it mean so much, design?"

For a moment, I couldn't articulate an answer. And then: "My mom just writes it all off as 'fashion.' As if she doesn't care about style. When her closet contains multitudes."

He laughed at my Walt Whitman reference.

"But it's not about fashion; it's choices. I ask, *What would this person wear?* But really I'm asking, *What would this person* do?" Remembering the fashion illustrations glued to my closet door, I murmured, more to myself than him, "Like Sophronia Dearborn."

"Sophronia Dearborn?"

"A girl who lived here once. She's got my first name. And my birthday. Today."

"Oh, awesome! Happy birthday!"

"Thanks. I'm eighteen. The same age Sophronia was when she died and was buried with her baby. Their grave is on our property."

"Well, that got dark."

By now the trail circled back to the cemetery gates. "I'll show you."

Will studied her marker. "Maybe you can find out more about her.

If she's got your name and your birthday, she deserves your attention, right? Here, let's get pictures of the gravestones, so you can write down the names and dates later."

He took shot after shot in silence, but I felt listened to. He didn't act like I was some emo teen who just belched up all her feelings. I even confided, "I'll definitely keep all these photos from my mom."

"Why's that?"

"She would hate if I researched the family that owned this house, when I've never cared about all the Black history she throws at me. She's fight-the-power like that. She wouldn't like your family, either."

Will's green eyes flicked away. Something I said was a needle poking under his skin. "Maybe ask her how she feels? But regardless, you're an adult. You have every right to research what you want. So that's your real name? Sophronia?"

"Yeah. Sophronia Lacey Reid. I was named after my Gramma, Sophronia Castine, but she was really my great-grandmother. Sophronia was common back in the day. I hate it. I've *never* answered to it."

Will tested the word aloud. "Sophronia. I like it. I'm with your mom. She named you well."

Back inside, Mom was in the library, staring hard at her laptop screen. She'd come home from work early, though she didn't notice me until I said her name.

"Mom?"

She slid off her reading glasses. "Sweetheart! Happy birthday! I'm sorry I've been so absent today."

She hadn't been. She'd left a card for me, along with chocolate-banana muffins on the kitchen table. "Eighteen." She smiled as if at some wondrous thought. "I'm the mother of an adult. Wow. We'll go out tonight to Charlottesville and celebrate."

"Actually, Mom, could you make pizza?" I remembered the first time Alyssa came over to our house back in Wellesley.

"Pizza? Of course. And you know what? My assistant gave us tomatoes from her garden, so it's extra perfect. I'll pick some basil." Closing her laptop, she stood up. "Hmm . . . I'm not sure where I can buy fresh mozzarella, but the Prices make goat cheese. And I'll swing by the Fluhartys' for sausage. Oh!" She snapped her fingers. "Blondell's wife went foraging yesterday and bragged about a whole basket of oyster mushrooms."

It sounded so good, this stone soup of pizza toppings. "How was your walk?" she asked as I accompanied her on the back porch.

"It was nice. I met our tenant. He's cool, actually. Outdoorsy, just like you guessed, but not exactly old. Yeah, we went by the old cemetery." I decided to take Will's advice. Sort of. "Hey, what do you know about the white family who lived here at Tangleroot? The Dearborns."

"I had to look through their papers to learn about Cuffee, since he was their property. But really. Who cares about them?" Mom yanked basil from one of the terra-cotta pots on the porch.

"Who cares?"

She attacked the green onions. "We pay far too much attention to society's aristocrats. White aristocrats. But I have a much more important use of my time, my skill, and my intellect. So do you." She pointed at me with a batch of scallions. "It's an imperative, uncovering our stories. We *have* to, especially your generation of scholars and researchers. There's enough people digging up theirs."

Scholar or researcher? Like that described me at all. "So you've never been to the graveyard out back? Where they're buried?"

"I've walked right on past it. The only cemetery I'd like to see is the enslaved folks' burial ground. If I can ever find it." She looked out past the porch rail, toward the land spreading beyond. "Where our people rest is unmarked, Noni. Just like our history. Those white enslavers? Let them be dust. We have to ensure that our ancestors are remembered."

While Mom stretched dough in the kitchen, chatting with my aunt Nichelle on speakerphone, I went upstairs and opened my closet, studying the fashion plates pasted to the inside of the door. Who *was* she, Sophronia Dearborn? What were *her* choices?

On the top corner, near the door hinge, was something I had never noticed before: a ripped scrap of paper pierced by a metal thumbtack. It was a torn drawing of some sort, with turquoise shading along the paper's jagged edge. How many decades had that scrap been there, and what had been torn away?

Using the pictures Will sent me, I wrote out the names and dates in the family plot, drawing lines to make a short family tree.

That's when I got stuck.

Why was Sophronia Dearborn called "beloved daughter," not "beloved daughter and wife"? Maybe the Dearborns didn't pay the extra money for two additional words carved into their daughter-in-law's gravestone. Because Sophronia Dearborn had to be married. Right?

The surname Castine was passed through a line of mothers: from my great-great-grandmother Lacey, to her daughter, my Gramma, because they were both single moms. Maybe Lacey and Calvin Fortune had plans to get married, but Cal died while she was pregnant with his child. And Gramma left her husband because he was abusive, even though it meant she had to abandon the middle-class life he afforded her. And then there was my grandmother, Clare, who didn't change her name since she was having an affair with my granddad—and I would never even know his name, since Mom didn't want to find out. My mother, of course, like a lot of my friends' moms, simply kept her last name when she married.

But aristocrats, as Mom put it? From back then? I'd watched period movies. You could ruin your life just by strolling a garden alone with a guy. You did what it took to avoid casting shame on your family. Still, could it be possible that Sophronia Dearborn, the daughter of a wealthy planter, was a single mom, too?

During dinner, the back of my mind hummed with the idea of finding out Sophronia's story before I left for Boston. If nothing else, it would give me something to do while I was stuck in Virginia all summer. When Mom went to bed, I went through her genealogy research files, all neatly organized and labeled. The original documents were photocopied in their spidery, nineteenth-century penmanship. Mom had also typed them—transcribed them, as she called it—making everything easier to read.

There were notes about hog-killing, barn-repairing, and ill-fated crops. But I didn't find anything useful. In fact, all of Mom's research pertained to Cuffee. Then I noticed Sophronia's name on a will dated February 1858:

> *I, Thomas Dearborn, do publish and declare this to be my last will and testament. It is my will and desire that my beloved wife, Martha L. Dearborn, receive all my personal property of every kind and description, to be managed and controlled by my executor Lemuel Paulding.*
>
> *Upon the death of my beloved wife, my property shall be divided among my daughters Sophronia C.*

Dearborn and Daphne H. Dearborn. To my eldest daughter Sophie I give Negroes Cuff, Effie, Harriet, and Joe. To my youngest daughter Daphne I give Negroes Molly, Lottie, Isaac, and Foster. It is my will that the remainder of my personal property be sold and the proceeds thereof equally divided among my daughters.

So Sophronia Dearborn, or Sophie, was the girl buried in the cemetery. There was no Dearborn son, and no maiden name mentioned. So could it be possible? That she *wasn't* married? Maybe she was raped. But maybe she was rebellious, a badass who slept with a guy, marriage be damned. Or maybe she was in love with a man she couldn't marry.

Either way, if she did find a lover outside of marriage, she must have had her own mind. And if she was a woman before her time—did she even agree with slavery?

Her father, Thomas Dearborn, was certainly all-in, the way he nonchalantly listed human beings as items to be passed along. Splitting up Cuffee and Molly as if their marriage meant nothing. Willing everyone beyond the few "Negroes" he named to the auction block. That was almost 150 people, according to his inventory list.

And—I took a look at our family tree for this one—Cuffee and Molly had a boatload of little kids. My ancestor Calvin? He wasn't born until 1857. That means at the time the will was written, he was only a year old.

What would have become of Cuffee's children if Tom Dearborn died? Did he seriously mean he wanted *all* the rest of his personal property sold? All of it—even a one-year-old baby?

Tom Dearborn died of "apoplexy" while his wife, Martha, was done in by "ague." I didn't know what those things were, but neither sounded like much fun. Nor did dropsy, fits, consumption, croup, brain fever, lockjaw, spasms, grippe, and flux, or any of the other weird-sounding ways there were to bump off.

"Any luck?" Ming asked when she stopped by again. She had suggested I check death records when we weren't able to find a marriage record for Sophronia Dearborn. We had also looked for an obituary, but the only one I found was for her father, Tom Dearborn, who died in 1877. I scanned a copy, even though it didn't provide any new information about Sophie. His obituary actually mentioned that Cuffee attended his funeral. Of course, Mom had also droned on about Cuffee's enslaver giving him land after the Civil War as payment for work, so his presence at the white man's service made sense.

None of this got me any closer to Sophie Dearborn. Ming said some marriage records had been lost over time, but the death registers were marked with an *m* if the deceased was married, with a *w* if the person was widowed, and *s* if they were single.

"I haven't found her yet," I said, not taking my eyes off the microfilm reel.

"Keep looking. She's got to be there somewhere." Ming Xiàng was a librarian at the Library of Virginia, where I'd gone to dig up information about Sophie Dearborn. I had to swap hours with Madge, then drive two hours to Richmond. I had gone by the county archives, but a 1960s flood destroyed most of their records. The Magnolia Historical Museum was open by appointment only. When I was finally able to go, they didn't have anything useful, either, unless you wanted to look at an entire family tree of Senator Vermilion Harper plastered on the wall, showing his roots all the way back to England. Still, the ancient docent lent me a few books about the nineteenth century, which I figured couldn't hurt.

I'd also looked through Mom's stuff, but she was just as obsessed with Cuffee Fortune as the town was with the old senator. I'd even peeked into the family history site Mom used. She'd shared the password with me a long time ago in an effort to get me interested in learning about Cuffee. They mostly had census reports. Of course, it was cool seeing Sophie's name pop up on an 1850 document. Her grave proved she existed, but seeing her name recorded on paper made her seem more real. But ultimately, those records didn't tell me much.

At the Library of Virginia, Ming got the ball rolling. When I told her about Sophie Dearborn's presumed love child, she seemed invested in finding the answer, too. She showed me how to use a microfilm reader, a huge, clunky machine that looked like a circa 1982 computer. You'd spool rolls of film—long, dark, translucent ribbons like I'd seen in my parents' old photo collection—into something like the slide of a microscope, with a glass plate that clamped the reel down. Flick a switch, turn a crank, and a grainy image evolved on the dark, slanted screen.

After nearly going blind reading nineteenth-century handwriting, I finally found Sophronia Dearborn. Cause of death was listed as childbirth, which was what I had suspected. Then I ran my finger along the screen, tracing her row. And I found it: the "married" column.

Sophronia Dearborn was not.

CHAPTER 7

So how long are we supposed to be here?" I asked after complaining about the heat again. Okay, I was bitching excessively, but I was dying. The sun was a fierce, evil little ball. Only the stingiest of breezes blew. Sweat pooled beneath my bonnet.

Yeah, about that. I'd been forced to work the Magnolia Cattle Festival, and Blondell thought it would be cute if her staff wore costumes, so she enlisted my help. It was Darlie who was meant to be a milkmaid, though in a little fit of revenge, I made her dress aggressively girly: floral-printed cotton with tucks and flounces everywhere, the opposite of what seemed like her blue-jeans and American flag T-shirt style. I even sewed a crinoline, an underskirt made of layers of stiff netting, to pouf it out.

But when Darlie's kid got sick, the dress ended up on me. Once Blondell shortened the hem for me and laced the corset-style bodice tighter on my smaller frame, the fit was perfect, even if the look was far from it.

I fanned myself with a paper menu. I was hot, and not in a good way. Fluvie was way cooler (literally and figuratively) in a flared mini, a cowboy hat, and boots.

We staffed a table spread with a gingham cloth and cheese balls. I'd mentioned the cheese balls at Mom's reception to Blondell, and she actually loved the idea, tasking Jabari with recipes. With so much dairy, we basically had a constipation station.

"You've only gotta last till five. That's all!" Fluvie was downright upbeat, shamelessly admiring her cow-print skirt. "And you said I can keep this?"

"If you don't want to block today out of your memory," I muttered.

A few yards away, a bluegrass band strummed awful tunes on a stage decked out with American flag bunting.

Jabari came over with a platter of more cheese-ball blobs in mini-cupcake wrappers, each with a cracker thrust in it like an axe through a pumpkin. "Staying cool?" he asked us.

"Today's great. And it's nothing like Founding Families," Fluvie said. "That used to last three days."

"What exactly *was* Founding Families?" I remembered Mom yelling at me about it when I'd told her I'd work for Lana Jean Chilton.

"*That.*" Jabari's brows lowered. "So Mrs. Chilton and her cronies used to host this weekend-long event every year. It was supposed to celebrate Magnolia as a perfect Southern town by puffing up the 'founding families.'" He air-quoted. "But it was really about how great enslavers were."

"Oh, but there were garden tours and formal balls . . . ," Fluvie argued.

"Where people dressed up like enslavers," Jabari added.

"Oh, but . . ." Fluvie was interrupted by a customer she knew. While she chatted, Jabari looked at my costume. "Blondell told me you made all these getups. Like, you sew."

"It was a favor . . . ," I started off, embarrassed. Sewing was so old-school. Like, home-ec old-school. Ironically, it felt unfashionable.

"That's really awesome. And you're—your dress is really pretty." He almost seemed nervous as he smiled. "How're you liking the festival?"

"It's—" I tried to think of a word. "Cowy." I looked around at the crowd. It was also white. Really, really white.

It's like he read my mind. "There's a few of us." He nodded to his left. "That's Pastor Price and his wife, Andrea."

"Yeah, Mom and I went to a service once," I said. "We've never been a churchy family, but Mom goes sometimes to keep up with folks."

"I'm about the same. And you met the Goldens? Valerie and Reggie?"

"I met Valerie almost as soon as I got here. And I just met Reggie today." They'd both stopped by the Charm table, with Reggie joking that he saw a ghost: my great-grandmother Fawnie Castine's. He was a light-skinned man with Santa Claus–blue eyes and as much warmth and personality as Valerie.

Jabari pointed out Regina Chapel, the new high school principal, who was waiting in line at the face-painting booth with her family. She'd come over for dinner once, and she and Mom fumed about how some members of the school board were ransacking school library shelves, and even wanted to ban teachers from showing videos of the senator screaming. Dr. Chapel had said, "Of course they want to ban your book."

Mom had crossed her arms, let-'em-at-me-style. "I'm ready for it."

I told Jabari about all this. "The school board's a big deal," he said as a cow mooed in the distance. "With Dr. Castine in town, there's a push to get progressives elected this fall. There's talk of a national curriculum project that uses literature to teach history. Whoever chairs the committee gets to pilot the project in their home school district, if the district allows it. Your mom's name has been mentioned. So Dr. Chapel wants Magnolia High School to be prepared."

I was a little embarrassed that I had barely paid attention during Mom's talk of local elections. "Progressives on the school board? Here?"

"Andrea Price is running." He nodded again at her and her husband, Pastor Price. "So is Blondell's mother-in-law. And Dr. Derry. She's a retired Stonepost professor who lives here in town."

"The Founding Families committee must be reaching for their smelling salts."

Fluvie turned her attention back to us, just as Jabari's brows lowered over his deep-set eyes. "Founding Families fell out of the picture six years ago. There was a huge protest, because of the statue."

"The statue?" I helped myself to the birthday cake flavor. This one was made of chocolate cake batter, with a hint of funk from something fancy like Brie or Camembert. With a square of graham cracker, it was deliciousness.

"You don't know about the statue?" Fluvie looked at me with surprise.

Jabari explained. "There was going to be a twenty-foot-tall bronze statue of Senator Harper holding his cane in the air. Installed right there on the courthouse steps, where the senator made that racist speech in the fifties."

Looking at the domed courthouse looming ahead, I remembered his chilling voice thundering *Burn it down!* It made no sense to ban the video from schools, because that speech *happened*. Why not show it, and talk about it? What was the school board afraid of? Tarnishing his memory, as if that memory itself were a monument?

Fluvie shrugged. "I was a kid, but even now when I look back, I don't understand why so many folks came out to protest the statue. I mean, it wasn't okay, but it also wasn't going to hurt anybody."

"Statues are symbols, and symbols are lightning rods," Jabari told her.

"Like flags." Fluvie seemed to be talking to herself. "Like when—" She rubbed her sleeve tattoo.

Jabari looked down at me with soft eyes. It almost seemed like he wanted to put his arms around me to protect me from something. "The statue was going to be unveiled during Founding Families' opening ceremony. Your mom was there. She and Valerie Golden got lawyers involved."

I remembered how Mom had spent almost a full summer "back home." I was in middle school.

"The courts ruled the statue wasn't legal, because of an old law that was never taken off the books," he said. "And that opening ceremony was shouted down by protestors. With all the negative publicity, Founding Families never happened again. Your mom's a badass. Of course, you already know that."

"It's hard to believe Mrs. Golden protested," Fluvie pointed out. "She works for Mrs. Chilton."

"But she didn't then," Jabari said. "She was a floor manager at the candy factory." He handed out two cheese balls to customers before telling me, "Until it closed down."

Mrs. Chilton's husband, Mayor Dr. Conway Chilton, strode onto the platform as the band took a break. A big, ruddy man in a tan suit, he grabbed the microphone and opened his mouth like he was belting a sonata. But I could barely hear a word.

"Mic's out!" people yelled. Jabari jogged over to a couple of guys puzzling over a speaker system.

After almost ten minutes of troubleshooting, Doctor Mayor boomed into the microphone, "Good job, Jabari. Let's thank Borton Brothers A/V Incorporated! And y'all give it up for the Bang Diddlies! Now let's applaud the real stars: the cows of Magnolia!"

"You saved the day," I said quietly as Jabari returned to our table. "For the cows."

He smiled back. "I used to do A/V for my friend's company in Daventry. I know all the tricks. And you have to with the speakers they're using."

"They look pretty new and shiny."

"Yeah, the town signed the Borton Bros as the exclusive contractor for municipal events and even helped subsidize all that fancy A/V equipment. But this model's got too many bells and whistles. Someone can hack into the whole system's Wi-Fi if they know what they're doing. And there's a kill-switch to prevent hot-mics, but if you accidently trip it, it's not easy to reset."

My face burned, thinking of my own hot-mic at the hotel ballroom when Mom put me up to making a speech. If she'd had a kill-switch, she might've used it on me.

Grabbing an empty tray, Jabari headed back over to the Charm truck just as Blondell came by. She dismissed me and Fluvie. "Y'all go enjoy the rest of the fair. Amy'll be here in a bit."

I was already untying my ruffled apron as Fluvie asked, "You sure?"

"Of course, sweetheart. Go have some fun." She asked me, "Your mom coming?"

"She's got work to catch up on," I said as Doctor Mayor congratulated the newly crowned Miss Moo Magnolia, who was tied to the stage. Draped over her neck was a glittery white sash, the kind beauty queens wore.

Blondell pouted. Her cow, Devonth Heifer, lost to the beefy Bette Midler. "Well, *this* is a good time for a bathroom break." My boss stalked off toward the porta-potties. I guessed Fluvie and I were stuck for a few more minutes.

"Bette's a good gal. I delivered her twins this past spring," Doctor Mayor said. "Was her first time calving: breached birth, uterine torsion, and she handled it like any good mama would. Let's hear it for the Bovine Miss M!" He quipped, "And speaking of good mamas . . . let's welcome my lovely wife, Lana Jean Chilton."

Mrs. Chilton, wearing an awful pink outfit with her boobs looking like they'd take flight from its plunging neckline, minced onto the stage.

"And my beautiful children," he said as three blond men and three blond women paraded up. They had a Duggar-family age range: The oldest must have been past forty. The youngest, who, like the cow, wore a beauty queen sash, looked around my age. All of them wore big TV grins. "Y'all, say hello to my kids: Brigade, Palmetta, Planter, DixieStar, Stonewall-Jackson, and Cicada."

"I'm going home," I mumbled when Blondell returned.

"Is your name Debbie?" She grinned when I gave her a *huh* look. "'Cause you sure are a downer!" I groaned. She shooed me away. "Go walk around with Fluvie. It's okay to have fun."

The Chiltons' oldest son, now brandishing a shiny guitar with his red shirt unbuttoned to his hairy navel, sauntered back up to the platform with a couple of band members. The crowd went nuts. If "fun" meant listening to him, I wanted out. But Fluvie insisted I join her. "Let's go see the show animals!"

I'd just seen a cow win a beauty contest. Now I was picturing some sort of bovine chorus line. "The show animals?"

"The livestock show! It's a judging event. Like in *Charlotte's Web*?"

I nodded blankly.

"I'm hoping my Berkshire barrow gets breed champion. He's headed to the state fair this fall! And then he's off to market."

This little piggy went to market. I had the faintest memory of Mom wiggling my toes. Only—I always thought the pig went grocery shopping? Jeez, maybe he should've stayed home like his brother. I asked, "What's a barrow?"

"A castrated boy hog."

Definitely should've stayed home.

"Come see him!"

I found myself following her to the pens on the other side of the fairgrounds, away from the crowd's crazed screams over the country song "Jesus Was a Good Ol' Boy." Once I got the slightest whiff of livestock, I couldn't bring myself to get any closer than ten feet. From here, the enormous pig looked like a bear in a wooden stall.

"His name is Paint It Black." Fluvie had to shout a little over Brigade Chilton's baritone twang. "I've been part of 4-H my whole life, and I want to train as a vet tech one day, but it's hard to save up, with helping my family and all. You're so lucky, going to college this fall."

Her longing made me feel uncomfortable. I had always known in theory that there were kids who didn't go to college. And a few of my classmates planned on taking a gap year. But it seemed no one who graduated from my high school intended to stop there. Fluvie was nineteen. Like me, she'd just turned her tassel.

Onstage, Brigade Chilton ripped off his shirt, tossing it into the crowd. Women practically fainted. Fluvie projected above the noise. "The money I make from Charm helps a lot, especially since Blondell pays better than any other waitressing job. But if I could work in an office, I'd have my weekends free to volunteer with 4-H more, and I could save up faster."

Now Brigade was announcing that the band would take a break. His fans were audibly disappointed, but it meant I didn't have go too hoarse when I asked, "So if vet tech school doesn't work out, you're going to—what?"

"Just keep on Charming and farming." Her eyes sparkled at her little joke.

"But—" I was interrupted by a gushing sound behind me, like someone turned on a bath faucet. The giant hog was relieving himself, a stream of pee like a garden hose going at full blast, drilling a puddle into the dirt. It was disgusting. "There's gotta be some way to get to college,

Fluvie!" I was almost shrill. "You can't live here and raise pigs your whole life like some inbred hillbilly. You can't stay stuck in Magnolia."

Her eyes widened. Without a word, Fluvie turned and left.

I peeled off in the opposite direction, as if to run away from my own mistake. Why did I *say* that? It should've been: *Fluvie, you're too cool for Magnolia*. And she kind of was! She'd stood up for me even, that horrible day when Darlie was so racist.

"Well, hello!" Mrs. Chilton's honey-sweet drawl stopped me as I wove through a tented village of vendors. Her hair, grown out a bit, was streaked an almost white blond along the center part. She looked like a badger.

"Oh, hi." I couldn't meet her eyes. I'd never actually called her to turn down the piano gig. I just didn't show up when I was supposed to. "I'm sorry I couldn't take the job."

"Oh, don't fret one little bit. It was your mother, wasn't it? She wouldn't let you work for me." She patted my arm. Her son was back onstage, this time crooning a slow jam, prompting more feminine shrieks. Mrs. Chilton asked, "I suppose Radiance is too busy to make it to today's event? I'm sure our festival isn't as important as her career."

Her daughter Cicada bounced up beside her. "You must be Mrs. Castine's daughter! Oh my gosh. You're so beautiful!" I smiled back as a thank-you. "Look at that scrumptious dress! Mama, doesn't it remind you of the ball gown Lilette Delacorte wore for Miss Cotton Boll?" She grabbed my wrist as if we were friends. "Where'd you get it?"

"Oh, I made it."

"Really?" Cicada said breathlessly. "You *made* that? Mama, look at how gorgeous it is!"

Lana Jean's chilly blue gaze pried at the various gathers of my gown. "I myself am exceptional with a needle, but that pattern must have been tricky to sew."

"It wasn't all that hard because I drafted it."

Her already-arched eyebrows rounded even further in surprise, McDonald's-like. "You created the pattern from scratch?" She half circled around me, examining the vast skirting. "Isn't inheritance marvelous. I suppose you know your great-great-grandmother . . ."

"Was a dressmaker," I finished.

"My grandmother—the senator's wife, Priscilla Lavigne Harper—was her client. One year, she was unforgettable in a confection of your great-great-grandmother's making. People talked about Nana's dress for months. Cicada, of course, you know this history."

"Oh, Mama," she said reverently. "The magnolia gown."

I remembered the portrait in Trianon of a woman in a white dress, one like a blossom. I had no idea my ancestor had made it.

Cicada seemed lost in dreamland as she blew a kiss at one of her brother's bandmates. Lana Jean waxed on. "My grandmother was positively captivating. Of course, Nana couldn't tell *anyone* the seamstress was—" She stopped, but my mind filled in the blank.

Colored.

Lana Jean seemed to examine my face. Closely. Her smile tilted down at the corners, but then she simply patted my shoulder. "Oh, but I've taken enough of your time. Run along now."

Cicada also skipped ahead of her mother, calling back, "We should get tea sometime, Noni!" As if that were a thing girls our age did.

I felt almost dazed from Lana Jean's anecdote. But it also occurred to me that with her encyclopedic knowledge of Magnolia history, she might know something else. "Mrs. Chilton?" She turned. "Remember how you mentioned the people who lived at Tangleroot? The Dearborn family? Do you know anything about them?"

"Is this for a class project? Before school starts? Ambitious, aren't you?" She said it like it was a bad trait. "Well, I have papers from all the planter families in Magnolia. My father collected them before his death. But more than that, when I was just a little thing, my grandmother sat me down on her knee and shared stories about our planter families that were passed down to her. You see, *her* grandmother was a belle."

"Any interesting stories?" I asked. Across the fairgrounds, a cow bellowed. A character dressed in a gray Confederate army uniform waded around on stilts. Children pointed up at him, screaming with delight. I wanted to scream at him, too.

"Oh, everything Nana told me over the years was fascinating. It was a glorious time, all the parties and balls." Mrs. Chilton smiled dreamily, as if she'd been there. "As for the Dearborns, let's see . . . there were two daughters, and one died young. Still but a girl. It was terribly tragic."

"How did she die?" I asked suddenly.

"I have no idea. Southern ladies were delicate flowers. But my grandmother never talked of death. She spoke of the elegant silks, and the dancing . . ."

"What about scandals?" I broke in. "Were there any scandals?"

Mrs. Chilton looked appalled. "Why on earth would you ask?" She lowered her voice and gripped my shoulder. "Now, I know others may have told you about our upstanding Southern men keeping women of a certain ilk as their paramours."

"No, I . . ." I shook my head.

"Why, perhaps even your mother has told you stories of plantation men carousing among the servant class. It is a myth, you understand."

"I was just trying to find out . . ."

"Overseers," Lana Jean said plainly. "They were the ones cavorting in the slave quarters. They were nothing more than trash, see. Our gentlemen upheld the utmost virtue, and it is a travesty to know such falsehoods have been spread about them. So many lies about our men. Like my dear son."

Confused, I was taken aback by her ferocity, matched by what seemed like sadness. Her eyes were like fierce blue flames hissing from a gas stove. "You tell whoever put this idea in your head that not a drop of it is true. When I think of the senator's forefathers who built Trianon into a great empire, accused of such moral turpitude, it's enough to make me swoon."

"No, no, no, there's no need to swoon, I'm sorry I brought this up . . ."

I was relieved when someone called her name. It was Glenda Dorsey with Lovey Catlett. They gave me a dismissive hello, though I could feel them watching me as I hiked up my long dress and tromped through the grass.

Heading toward Harper Street, I realized I was leaving just in time. Mom had made it here after all. Hoping she wouldn't see me, I turned in another direction. She was talking to Blondell and a Charm regular, and I could tell from their gestures that they were both gushing over her outfit.

They were not the only people who noticed Mom. Among a sea of jeans and camo, she stood out like a celebrity. To be fair, she was wearing denim—but it was her foil-printed sheath with its skinny fit and dipping neckline. And she wore her imitation snakeskin wedges and a Swarovski crystal necklace, its iridescent beads catching the light like a thousand tiny prisms.

People noticed. Men looked at her too long. So did women. Even kids stared. They'd played that game before. You know the one, when you look at a picture, picking out the one thing that's not like the others? Why did Mom have to doll herself up so much? This was a cattle festival, not a cocktail reception. The only thing the two events had in common were cheese balls.

I ducked through a knot of people, trying to disappear. Not that I didn't stand out myself, dressed as I was like Anne of Green Gables.

"Hey, Noni!" It was Will.

"Oh! Hey!" I was jumpy, still tingling with embarrassment over insulting Fluvanna. And I had definitely insulted Lana Jean Chilton, too. That mostly bothered me because now that I'd asked her to dust off the family skeletons once, I couldn't do it again.

"You having fun?" Will asked. "Wait—lemme guess—no."

Smiling wryly, I shook my head.

"And lemme see—Blondell Pankey had you wear this getup and let you out early to enjoy the festival? And now you're wishing you brought a change of clothes?"

"Are you psychic?"

"I just know Blondell really well. She and Valerie both took me under their wings when I was growing up." He scanned the fairgrounds. "Either of them here?"

For some reason, I didn't want Will to see Mom. And I knew that's exactly who Blondell was with. "They're somewhere."

Onstage, someone announced a wife-carrying contest. The winner got his wife's weight in beer.

Will shrugged. "I'll find her. Hey, how are things with you?" The man onstage hollered for husbands to round up their wives.

"I'm ready to pack up and ship out. If I could leave right now . . ." I trailed off. Because striding up with long, leggy steps was Mom. She paused to pet someone's German shepherd, like a politician making nice-nice with a random baby. Then she smiled and waved at me in that fluttery way of hers. Coming over, she squished me against her as if she hadn't seen me in weeks. "My goodness, look at you!"

I just stood there with my arms at my sides, not hugging back.

She was transfixed. "You're so pretty in your little dress!"

"Mom, quit."

She fussed with my skirt. I smacked her hands away. Ignoring me, she tugged at the lacing on the bodice. "Turn around so I can see you. What an adorable bonnet! Gosh, you're just like that little doll in your bedroom!"

"Mom, stop it!" Humiliated, I whirled to face Will, as if to say, *See what she's like?*

But Will stared at Mom like she was something rare and mythical and enchanting. He stepped forward to shake her hand, reaching right past me, as if I were made of air.

"Hi. I'm Will."

"Oh! Nice to meet you. I'm Radiance." Mom finally noticed him, exuding her usual charm.

"Radiance. What a beautiful name. It's really good to finally meet you, too."

"Finally meet me?"

"Yes. After the card, and that awesome gift basket . . ."

Recognition flashed on her face, and her other hand reached up to enclose his. "Are you our Will Taylor? At Tangleroot?"

He nodded. "That's me."

"It *is* good to meet you! My daughter told me how great you are."

I said one whole sentence to Mom about him. And I wanted to kick him when he said, "She's an awesome kid." An awesome kid? And why was he being all puppy-dog eyed? He knew how she really was.

"I think she's pretty special." Mom gave me a soppy look as she tweaked my French braid. I flinched and blushed.

"The gift basket you made me was really amazing," Will said. "Was that all homemade?"

Mom gave him an aw-shucks look. "Oh, just something I whipped up."

"And I'd never had Japanese whiskey. So clean with that hint of smoke."

"Hakushu is decidedly my favorite. So where are you from, Will?"

"Right here."

"Oh! Here! Who are your people?"

He shuffled his feet. "My mom . . . left when I was a child. My dad's name was Hudd Taylor."

It was like someone dumped a bucket of ice water over Mom's congeniality. "Hudd? You're Hudd's son?"

"Yeah."

"So you're related to . . ." It was like she was struck speechless.

"My cousin."

I didn't understand what was being said here. Or rather, what was not being said. And no one bothered catching me up.

"Taylor's such a common last name. I didn't imagine you'd be any relation, much less Hudd's . . ."

"We're not alike." Will interrupted her. He pushed his hands into his pockets. "I never agreed with my father about anything. And my cousin was so much older. I barely knew him."

"That's good." She stammered. "I don't mean . . ."

"I understand. But since we're neighbors, maybe I could take you both to lunch one day."

"Perhaps." Then it was as if she remembered her manners. "Of course."

I spoke up. "I should get going."

"Oh, I was hoping we could walk around together."

"No thanks. I've seen everything." And I had. Now I just needed to forget all of it.

CHAPTER 8

At work the next day, I was as glum as ever. Halfway through the day, Blondell tried to cheer me up. "Honey, why the sad face? Your mama's sending you to college this fall! Lots of us here would give anything to go! Even me, even at my age."

This only made me recall what I'd said to Fluvie. I stung with shame. That morning, she asked me if I could bring a bowl of butter to table eighteen. She didn't smile or joke around, not with me at least. Or maybe not with anyone. Kara even asked, "Hey, do you think Fluvie's okay? She's like a zombie."

Blondell's soft blue eyes were solemn, too, as she walked with me to the dining room. "Maybe you don't think your mom cares about you, but she does, with everything she has. My parents disowned me years ago. They died without a word for me."

This stopped me. "Why?"

"Because I left my husband to be with someone I've loved my whole life."

I thought of Jessica Suarez, lanky with a goofy demeanor and frizzy, flyaway hair that looked at odds with the well-tailored men's suits she always wore. Mom was technically her boss, since she taught biology at Stonepost, even though all three of them went to bars together some nights. Occasionally Jessica came into Charm, and she'd duck down and kiss Blondell's cheek. They'd ignore the unkind stares from some of the customers.

What was it like to be a real adult and for your parents to stop talking to you forever?

*

That night at dinner, Mom asked, "Honey, is there anything bothering you?"

Pick a number, I could've said. One, there was Sophie Dearborn. Uncovering her mystery before I left for Boston seemed like a faraway dream. Her story would remain buried, like she was.

Two, it felt so hard to find common ground here. Over and over again, I replayed hurting Fluvie's feelings.

And last, even what I thought was solid ground shifted like quicksand. Will was supposed to be on my side. Instead, he practically flirted with Mom.

I shrugged when she asked again if I was all right. I'd made us chana masala, and she had generously complimented the dish, although it came out bland and blah. Maybe I should've done the adult thing and at least told her about Fluvie. Also, I should have used more turmeric.

Instead, I listened to Mom update me on the renovations of the old railroad bridge, that unusable crossing. ". . . access to shops and restaurants in Daventry . . . ," she went on. "You'll have your Starbucks!"

"I'll be in Boston by then," I reminded her.

"I should post this on Rallyround." Darlie hopped from the truck to unlock the barred metal fence, scowling at the school board–election signs in front and all along Charm's lawn.

"What's Rallyround?" I asked.

"A social site that calls out stuff like this. This *activism* at my workplace." She hissed the word. "The site's got security glitches, and I know how to hack into people's live streams," she bragged. "I could post on a page with lots of followers, so everyone'll see how I have to work surrounded by protest signs."

"And you'll probably get banned," I told her. "Also, these are campaign signs, and this is Blondell's business and her farm. She's entitled to endorse whomever. Especially her own mother-in-law." Signs urged votes for Mary Suarez; the pastor's wife, Andrea Price; and a retired Stonepost professor, Gertie Derry. Lana Jean had written an op-ed in the town paper and funded a billboard featuring her own face (even though she wasn't running) with the slogan VOTE NO ON SCHOOL BOARD RADICALS. But Mom thought these "radicals" had decent chances of winning, because of their deep ties to the community.

"You know these people have an agenda." Darlie swung open the gate. The three cows trotted over like board members to a coffee station. Despite Blondell's promise that I wouldn't have to feed the animals, here I was, easing her old Chevy into the open pen. Charm's livestock hand had quit. So we all had to pitch in for now, and I had to listen to Darlie talk like she was some cyber genius.

Leaving the keys in the ignition, I opened the tailgate and flaked a hay bale the way Blondell had shown me, tossing sheaths onto the ground. At least I wasn't working with Fluvie. We hadn't spoken since the day she asked me to bring butter to a table.

Only yards away, the cows chowed down, ignoring me as much as they unnerved me. But I stood firm. I didn't want to be like Mom, with her baseless fear of cats. Yesterday, Blondell told me the cows' model or brand or whatever was "Milking Devons," and they'd once been bred as milk, draft, and beef livestock. Then she explained her animals' bovine family tree, naming sires and dams—basically cow mamas and daddies—telling me about heifers in heat and artificial insemination with purchased semen, as if there would *ever* be a quiz.

Darlie stooped at the shed, pouring water from a spigot into a five-gallon bucket. The hose was busted, so we had to refill the water by hand. "If these people win, my little sister's gonna be made to feel like she's the reason there was slavery."

"Why's that?"

"They want our students to follow some national bandwagon, to read books that make them hate themselves. Books about segregation, and slavery."

"What's wrong with discussing what happened?"

"My ancestors could've had slaves. You think I want to talk about this stuff? You think my little sister does?"

"You think *I* do? It's uncomfortable for me, too. Talking about history isn't about piling blame on you for what your ancestors did way down the line. It's thinking about *our* actions and *our* choices, in *our* own times."

"I heard your mom's part of this whole thing."

Mom was officially under consideration to chair the Courageous Curriculums Initiative, she'd reported.

"Maybe she could add *her* own history into it," Darlie grumbled.

"What is that supposed to mean?"

"You know, *you* could have ancestors who owned slaves." This time, she looked me in the eyes. "You're light-skinned. Where do you think that comes from? Zimbabwe?" She grunted as she threw more water into the trough.

"Does this ever get old to you?"

"Does *what* ever get old."

"Saying racist BS?"

For a moment, I thought Darlie stepped in actual cow poop. She looked that shocked, and that disgusted. "What did you say? What did you call me? You called me a racist!" A snarl marred her face. "Blondell is going to hear about this!"

"I hope she does."

Her mouth roared open, as if to scream at me. And then it shut. Maybe she thought about what it would mean to tell Blondell. Maybe she thought about her children. Her little sister. Her dreams for herself. Her own choices that could get in the way.

I practically snatched the bucket to fetch the next round. I was furious with her and clumsy in my borrowed mud boots, but I would help haul water.

I had been typing the week's specials until an Instagram message from Cicada Chilton of all people threw me way off. *Let's have tea at Trianon soon!!! OMG, I'm ADDICTED to Valerie's strawberry rooibos.*

Jabari Nichols came into Blondell's office. "Hey! I just talked with your mom." He grabbed a clipboard from the wall. "Told her about a political science paper I'm writing. She had some suggestions about how I can tighten my thesis."

"You just talked to her?"

"Yeah. Now she's gabbing away with Darlie."

"With Darlie?"

"Yeah. With *her*." So he knew what she was like. But what was Mom doing here in the middle of her workday?

Quickly, I responded to Cicada with a noncommittal *Sure!* Which really meant *Never!* I wasn't about to risk Mom's rage for a cup of Earl Grey.

But when I saw Mom chatting it up at the hostess stand, just as Jabari had said, I knew her rage had come calling. Maybe everyone else was fooled by her smile, but not me. She was red-hot poker mad. With one ice-cold look in my direction, I knew 100 percent of her wrath was blasted at me.

But what had I done?

She sought me out like a missile. "Let's go."

My stomach lurched. "Go where? I can't just walk out of work."

"Your shift is covered. We're leaving."

My heart pounded. At this moment, I was as terrified of my mom as she was of tabbies. She grabbed my arm in a death grip. "Go get in the car."

"Mom, I'm not—"

"Get in the car!"

I scrounged up enough attitude to grumble, but one look from Mom shut me up. She was silent until we got on the main highway. Once there, she lit me up like a firecracker. "Sophronia Reid! I do not have time for this!"

I gulped, wide-eyed. She never called me that unless she was furious.

"Blondell called me. You're not the only one at Charm who's been out of sorts. Fluvanna Fluharty?"

My heart seized at the name.

"She's been quiet, and Blondell found out why. You insulted her! You said—I won't repeat it. You used a slur! Is that what you think of people around here?"

I was silent, flooded with guilt, a feeling greater than my disgust at that giant hog peeing. Now, it was as if someone turned on a faucet of shame inside me and left it running.

"Is that how you feel?" Mom repeated.

"No." Did I mean that? My chin quivered.

Mom's eyes were pinned to the road, but she knew. "Don't you dare cry. This isn't about *your* feelings."

"Does she forgive me? Fluvie?"

"She owes you nothing."

The dial on that faucet of shame twisted further. Where *was* my mom taking me? She seemed mad enough to murder me and leave me in the woods.

"I'll tell her I'm sorry."

"I spoke with her. I went to school with her parents, so we have a rapport. She doesn't care to speak with you at all. I asked if she wanted you fired—which is her prerogative seeing as to how you insulted her—and she declined. She's leaving Charm, in fact. For an office job."

A bend in the road revealed a tall wooden church. I felt enough guilt and shame for a whole congregation.

"You will not be going to Boston," Mom said.

I stared at her. "What?"

"You're not going to Boston University."

"What? No! Mom, please!"

"You were pulled from the wait-list, anyway. And *that's* only because the stage director—that Nyles Pompa—has contacts at BU. He intervened on your behalf. Otherwise . . ."

I was both blindsided and flattered. "He did?"

She sniffed, as if she never meant to tell me. "He thought you'd do well in their theater program. But you can unpack your suitcase as soon as you get home."

"Mom, no! I said I'd apologize to Fluvie."

"*I* said she doesn't want to hear from you!"

"But please, Mom. Let me go back home. You're not serious!"

"There are thirty-two thousand students enrolled at Boston University. It's an enormous school that you're not ready to attend. Mark is not in a place to be the parent you need. We've both decided that you'll stay home this fall." She spared the briefest of glares in my direction. "Home is *here*."

"Mom, no. You can't make me go to Stonepost."

"I would never force my colleagues in admission to accept you, and the curriculum at Stonepost is too research-intensive and rigorous for a student of your level."

That hurt. It was like her students were smarter than her own daughter.

"So I won't go to college at all?"

"Of course you will. You'll attend college in central Virginia. Near Magnolia."

A college near Magnolia? Near Mom? I looked at the fields and farms we passed, the ramshackle barns and roadkill-splattered road, which seemed to represent the entirety of the state. I'd never get away from her. I'd spend the next four years under her thumb.

"What college, Mom?"

"It's called . . ." Clutching the wheel, she drew herself up, as if preparing to say something she was loath to. "Prudence Cocke Community College."

"Prudence who? *Cocke?*"

"Cocke with an *e*."

"A college called Cocke?" I wasn't sure whether to giggle or scream. "Is this a joke?"

"The Cockes are a very old family of Virginia." She turned down yet another highway.

Finally, she stopped hard to park. "Get out."

There it was. Prudence Cocke Community College. A banner advertised fall registration.

"Mom, no."

She came to my side and gripped my arm. "Is this what you want?" Mom tugged at me. "To humiliate yourself in front of your future classmates? Because you're enrolling here, Noni. You don't have a choice."

I got out of the car, but not without protest. "Mom. Why are you doing this to me!" Why couldn't she understand me? And why *had* I told

Fluvie how I felt about Magnolia? Why couldn't I have kept my mouth shut? Now I was going to community college. Community colleges didn't have dorms. I would have to live with my mother.

"Mom, just let me stay with Dad and my aunt and uncle. I'll go to community college there. Please, listen to me!"

"You're going *here*," Mom muttered as we went into the building, her fingers tight around my arm.

We reached the registration counter. "Are you going to talk, or am I?" she hissed in my ear as if she were holding me hostage, which wasn't far from the truth.

I was too close to tears to talk. Wearing pigtails and overalls, with the laces of one of my Keds dragging all over the floor, I looked like a fool. The registrar stared at me like I was some alien life-form. The last thing I needed to do was cry.

"My daughter is enrolling." Mom was as calm as ever. She showed her phone screen to the registrar. "I've already gone online and selected her courses."

Around me, students my age were talking to the registrars themselves, without their parents. They seemed to be dealing with snags, not signing up for classes, which they'd undoubtedly done online. I felt stares on my back.

Glancing at the screen, the registrar said, "There's pre-reqs for these."

"I've already spoken to the dean. My daughter is perfectly capable of excelling in these courses, and"—she scrolled on her phone—"you'll see the override form he signed."

The registrar gave me another weird look, typing away at her computer. She printed something out and handed it to Mom.

Mom thanked her, giving the sheet to me. Reading the list of classes, I felt like I'd throw up. "Mom, I can't do these!" I was signed up for Multivariable Calculus. For Cellular Biology, plus a three-hour lab. Advanced

French Conversation, and something called Special Topics in History: The US Civil War. And of course, Introduction to Black American Studies.

I followed her down the hall toward the exit while she snapped, "If you think going to community college means you're going to fool around on your phone all day, you can forget it. If there's a single C on that first semester transcript, I'm cutting you off, Noni, and I mean it. You'll be on your own, down to putting a roof over your head."

"But Mom, I can't . . . this is Cell Bio!" I rattled the paper at her, as if to convince her. "Multivariable, and I haven't even done Calc BC!"

"You'll enroll in the tutoring program. And you won't have time to do anything but chores, study, and work. That's it. I told you, I'm done with your attitude."

"But, Mom. Mom, listen to me. This once. Mom!"

She tuned out my complaints, walking fast down the corridor, as if she were trying to catch a plane. She was so much taller, her strides so much longer. I couldn't keep up.

"I'd like to hear your reactions to our reading from Castine's *The Remembered*. Who would like to discuss their thoughts?"

Professor Corn, who taught my Black Studies class, was a big woman with a soft, calming voice and a coily 'fro. With her smooth, dark skin and full, perfect features, she was more beautiful than a person had a right to be. She wore loose, flowy dresses, always in some exotic design: African kente, jewel-toned Indian prints, bright kimono patterns. When someone complimented her, she'd give them a mini-lecture on the historic origins of the fabric.

I glanced at the assignment I hadn't bothered reading, a narrative by a formerly enslaved woman named Euphemia Sterling. Maybe I'd just been too annoyed that we were using Mom's latest book for class. Flipping back a few pages, I skimmed the introduction.

In 1889, two Harvard University graduate students traveled around the rural U.S. South. Their goal was to compile narratives that captured the antebellum nostalgia so prevalent among the former planter class. However, the men did not interview former enslavers—they interviewed the formerly enslaved, intending to find those who remembered their lives before the Civil War with affection and endearment. Instead, they heard stories of cruelty, deprivation, and loss. The two students never published their work, but in 2018, these narratives were rediscovered.

Mom had stumbled across that old manuscript, which turned out to be a historian's holy grail. She spent the next few years researching and writing annotations—basically explanations and context—and essays about what these stories said about the institution of slavery as a whole. The book came out last fall, and she was off on a whirlwind book-signing and lecture circuit.

Professor Corn prompted us. "Let's explore the sasha and the zamani, and how they connect to Sterling's short memoir. Who will begin our discussion?"

Wait, who was Sasha? I turned the page.

In some East and Central African beliefs, the dead are part of dimensions of the past. The sasha are those who exist in the recollections of their loved ones. As long as one is remembered, one lives. When a sasha's last surviving loved one passes away, they become part of the zamani, the true dead.

But when our names are spoken and when our stories are

told, we are always here, abiding in the minds of our descendants, whether they are kin by blood, or by belonging . . .

"Class?" Professor Corn brushed past my desk, stopping within the silence. "Noni. Perhaps you might share. How do they speak to you?"

They? I realized she meant the sasha and the zamani. But these weren't concepts: the sasha and the zamani were *people*. The dead.

My ancestors.

"How do they speak to you?" she repeated.

"I don't know."

Her eyes were as dark as a midnight sky and yet as reflective as the moon. It was as if she could see right down to the living cells of my lineage. Like she *knew* my past kin spoke, not in words but in mysteries. Not in resonant tones but in quiet whispers. I thought of Tangleroot's wooded acres, that lockbox of secrets. Of weathered rocks that might mark Fortune graves. My mother and I had no knowledge of where our ancestors' graves lay on the very property where we lived, and yet the Dearborn family's carved stones stood behind an iron fence, meant to last forever. My gaze fell from hers to the page.

. . . there is power in the breath that invokes a name, that calls forth a story . . .

"I'm sorry," I told her.

She only smiled. "You'll come to know." It was like she'd promised a future—or foretold one.

All us chillen had to wear was a coarse homespun shirt. No shoes, even with the ground frosted hard

as lead. At night we huddled like kittens, else we'd freeze to death . . .

They made us slave girls bear babies when we was yet children, sometimes not more than twelve years old. Forced us up with grown men . . .

That lash hiss like cold water on red hot metal. Bust your hide wide open, lay bare your back. Then they pour down the brine. Make you pray hard to die.

Kin by blood, or by belonging. I sat in the hallway outside the food court, *The Remembered* open on my lap. It was lunchtime, but I wasn't hungry. Not after reading this testimony. No. I felt chilled to my DNA.

"Ira Giles." I spoke a name beneath my breath. "Flora Woodsall. Roscoe Freeman."

The din of the dining hall overpowered my voice. And yet, in that tinny sound, I felt I could hear their ringing intonations.

A few students in my Black Studies class ate together, their texts flipped open. They weren't eating, either, just talking. I could ask to sit with them, to join their conversation. With them, I could process the hurt of reading these narratives.

But why connect with anyone when I'd be leaving next year?

After two weeks of community college, I was at least getting used to some kind of cycle. I worked at Charm on the Farm Monday and Friday, ten to six, and a five-hour shift on Saturday morning. On Wednesdays I had a three-hour lab. Before that was my marathon session with my tutor. With my other classes crammed on Tuesdays and Thursdays, those days seemed endless, especially since the college was an hour away from Tangleroot. So there wasn't much time for socializing anyway, which suited me. I had no need to be anything but alone.

At my locker, I stuffed my fat, heavy lit book inside. That text? *The Knudson Anthology of Black American Literature,* also edited by Mom. With Professor Corn's "Dr. Castine's contention is this," and "Dr. Castine posits that," I was thankful for my different last name. Because unless I wanted to be seen as some kid who could never live up to "Dr. Castine's" accomplishments, I couldn't let my professor find out that I was my mother's daughter.

CHAPTER 9

The Schuler's Market parking lot was getting resurfaced. Another time, that would've been a good thing. The asphalt was as pock-marked as the moon, ruts deep enough to take out a tire.

Today I was just annoyed. I would've gladly pretended to off-road it just to get this chore done sooner. "Damn it, Mom," I muttered to myself, slamming my Corolla's door. She'd texted me on my way home from work, asking me to pick up two lemons. I had to park down the street by the Second Presbyterian Church and hoof it up the sidewalk.

"Hey, Noni." Will Taylor seemed to be going the same direction. "Noni."

I pretended to ignore him.

He was right beside me. "Boo!" He spoke right into my ear.

"Can you *not* treat me like I'm twelve?" I tried to make it out like I was half joking. But my chuckle came out like a dry cough.

"You all right?" Will asked.

"No, actually. I'm stuck here in Podunk, Virginia. For a year. Mom's not letting me leave."

The supermarket's sliding double doors jolted open. I grabbed one of those handbasket things—as if I needed one for a couple of lemons—but the metal was rusted and the handle broken.

"I know. Your mom mentioned . . ."

Mom mentioned what? And when? "I ran into her earlier," Will explained.

"I'm sure that was a pleasant surprise."

Will shot me a confused look.

"The way you were falling all over her at the cow festival. I thought you'd break your nose, you face-planted so hard." The lemons were all squishy and overripe. I picked the two worst-looking ones.

Will's laugh was just as dry. "I made eye contact, like a human with reasonable social skills. What was I supposed to do, stare directly at the sun because your mom's really pretty?"

So because she wasn't just pretty to him, but "really pretty," he had to fawn over her. When he knew what she was like.

"These all look terrible." I set the basket on the scuffed white floor and started to walk out. Then I remembered a grocery store clerk would have to pick up after me, so I put the lemons back on the stack and the basket back on the rack while Will watched, trying to look concerned and—I could tell—trying not to snicker.

"You're here!" Mom called out. She was all sugar and sunshine, completely ignoring that I shut the front door a bit too hard.

I didn't respond. Something was happening in the kitchen, and I hated that it smelled delicious.

She stood at the bottom of the stairs. "Did you get the lemons?"

"No, and that was a favor. That store has shitty produce."

"Noni! Your language!"

"Guess I should've said it in French."

The doorbell rang.

"Can you grab that, please?" The skirt of her sundress swung as she spun back to the kitchen.

When I opened the door, I wanted to shut it then and there. It was Will. One arm cradled a bottle of wine. And in his other hand? Two lemons, and not the same ones I'd picked out.

⁂

They were for the citrus sweet potatoes Mom made, which she served as a side to locally raised glazed pork chops. I wondered if they were from Fluvanna Fluharty's pig farm, which sent a coil of shame from my brain to my heart. She was the reason I was stuck at college in Magnolia.

No. I had to rephrase it in my mind. *I* was the reason.

As I helped Mom carry the dishes upstairs to the dining room, I whispered, "You didn't mention Will was coming."

"We were running this morning, and I thought I'd invite him over."

"You go running together?"

"We were both running and we saw each other. So we finished our mile together. I'm his landlady. I should invite him over."

"It's not like that's part of the lease."

"It is in this town."

We ate in the dining room, me staring morosely at my food, Will with a dinner compliment every five seconds, and Mom talking it up about Stonepost College.

Will mentioned, "We actually work near each other. I own a shop on Graybrook Drive. It's called Nothing Ventured."

"Oh, yes! I've seen it. An outdoor shop, right?"

I endured their conversation. Mom pretended to be interested in kayaks. Then Will tried to turn the conversation to me, asking how work was going.

"It's work."

"Noni's also been really busy at school." Mom proceeded to describe my exact schedule, counting out the classes on her fingers.

"Mom, nobody cares."

"That's not true." Will put down his fork. "I care. Radiance, you said Multivariable Calculus?"

"That, and a Black American Studies class. Oh, Noni, I read an essay in *Callaloo* that your professor wrote." She told Will, "It's a literary magazine. Denise Corn referenced my book!" She clasped her hands, genuinely flattered. I think Mom sometimes forgot *The Remembered* was a bestseller. Lots of people read it.

When she started gabbing on to Will about how well I practiced my French, I couldn't stand it. "I should go now." I pushed back my chair. "Homework."

"We haven't finished dinner, but . . ."

"I've got another full plate of calculus waiting upstairs."

"Of course." As I left, I heard her boast, "I'm so proud of her. She's never been this focused before."

It wasn't true. During my apprenticeship, I worked tons of extra hours. I had long planning sessions with the costume designer Mindy. I read anything I could get my hands on about *The Tempest*, including the play itself a billion times. I filled the walls with taped-up costume sketches, and sewed until my needle-stabbed fingers felt like they'd fall on the floor. Then sometimes, I'd have to rip out all the seams and redo everything, until the vision in my mind revealed itself in a muslin mock-up on a mannequin.

Mom was the one who came by the vacant house to check on last-minute repairs. She'd see me draft and stitch and fit right there in our otherwise empty living room. She just never had the eyes to appreciate my work.

"Happy birthday, Dad." I couldn't manage much enthusiasm, but at least I was giving him a call.

"Hey! Thanks! How are things?"

"They're fine." I walked toward the post office, a paper gift bag draped over my wrist. I'd bought him a candle in a scent called "Saddle Sweat," which smelled leathery and musky. It wouldn't make it to Boston for another week, but at least I had tried.

"School's good?"

"It's okay. Math's kicking my butt. And my Black Studies professor is all over the place. Nothing we do is chronological. We jump around, one era in history to another. It's confusing."

"Sounds like she's comparing different periods," Dad said, which annoyed me. Who the hell was he, Mom?

"I guess." I wasn't going to reveal my actual gripe: that I was put-a-fork-in-me done at having to read Mom's books and hear about Mom, Mom, Mom.

As if the universe wouldn't give me a break, Dad wanted to know, "So how's your mother?" He asked in that too-casual tone he always used when the conversation came around to her. And I got the feeling that he didn't *actually* want the truth—that yeah, while Mom worked a ton and was frustrated with her college's board of directors, she was spending her free time playing the piano or fooling around in the flower garden. She was also thrilled that her favored candidates for the school board won. "It shows our messaging was heard. And maybe this town is finally changing!" she'd exclaimed.

Plus, she was having chatty dinners with Will Taylor.

I just gave Dad the verbal equivalent of shrugging my shoulders. "Same old, same old." Then I took a deep breath. "Hey, Dad. I was thinking how MassBay Community College is right near Uncle Brian's and Aunt Nichelle's. Next semester, I could take classes there and live with you all."

"Don't start this shit, Noni."

"Hear me out, Dad. Maybe I could find a part-time job at the theater in Wellesley. Because I finally have something . . ."

"Noni . . ."

I had to finish my sentence. "I finally have something *I'm* recognized for."

"I'm not talking about this."

"You don't have to talk. Please, just listen."

"What does your mother think?" He played the same tired game.

"She thinks I should be ecstatic because I'm living in some house a dead dude built. But I'm very much alive, and I *had* something of my own in Boston . . ."

"This is up to her. Our conversation ends right here."

"Dad. You're as much my parent as she is!"

The line went silent. I looked at my phone as if it had slapped me. That's how much it hurt.

The courthouse dome towered ahead. I thought of the senator clutching his cane at the top of the stairs, screaming of fire. Above me loomed the town's namesake trees, each studded with tapered cones peeking between clusters of broad leaves. Bright seed pods, as red as Skittles, emerged from the cones' many, many crevices. I found myself wondering when their cotton-white flowers would blossom, and if those seeds would one day fall like drops of blood.

The next week when I came home from class, Mom sent me a text in the nick of time. *I left a key for Jabari Nichols. He's making dinner for us! Will's coming, too.* If she hadn't told me before I heard someone with heavy footsteps rooting around in the kitchen, I might've grabbed one of her vases and pitched it like an MLB All-Star.

Dinner was a thank-you, Jabari said. He was the president of the Black Student Association, and Mom made a "really, really generous gift" to their scholarship fundraiser.

"Oh, I remember you mentioning you were in school. My first day at Charm."

"Yeah. I'm saving some money for a four year." He pulled out a bag of flour. "We're at the same college."

"Prudence Cocke?"

"I refuse to say the name out loud. It's undignified." He snickered. "I think you're in class on the days I'm not."

"Well, you're definitely not taking my Mom-worship class."

"Dr. Corn's?" He laughed. "I had her last year. She must teach with stars in her eyes, since you're Dr. Castine's kid."

"She has no idea. And the stars-in-the-eyes is why."

Jabari set a heavy hardback on my mom's cookbook stand. He opened to a page with hand-scribbled notes all across the margins. "Well, I'm around if you need *another* set of eyes," he said. "Like on your capstone paper."

"Thanks." Outside, I heard Mom's car pull in. "Can I help you cook?"

"Take one of these Sanpellegrinos for yourself and pour a couple of glasses for your mom and Will," he said. "That's all the help I need."

With her long legs stretched out in the Adirondack, my mother was as breezy as the fall day itself. It was "Our applications are expected to be up a little this year," and "Oh! The announcement date for Courageous Curriculums Initiative has been set! Let's hope I'm selected to chair." And "The engineering firm gave us a timeline for the railroad trestle!" Her smile waned. "Of course, there's talk of the town council reserving the right to name it." Then the mood fully shifted with a deeper sigh: "And Stonepost's board is giving me hell about finding 'evidence' that Cuffee Fortune founded us."

I sipped my Italian soda while Mom and Will puzzled through potential scenarios of how to deal with the board. He thought of getting the press involved, but the discussions were under a confidentiality agreement. "If word gets out, the board will think I leaked it." She rubbed her eyes as if the thought made her tired. "I've chased every lead, but beyond oral history, I can't prove that Cuffee founded us. If I only had that memoir he wrote!"

Dinner was five stars. Jabari served homemade udon noodles with lamb from the Prices' farm. He'd bought the ginger, eggs, and kale at a farmer's market as well. The seaweed and sauces came from an Asian grocery store he visited when he was last in Richmond. His mother owned a fancy restaurant in the Fan District, and cooking was definitely his inheritance.

Mom insisted on cleaning the kitchen and wouldn't back down. This time, she put on an audiobook and sent Jabari, Will, and me outside. "How's your research going?" Will asked me.

"Research?" Jabari looked interested. When I filled him in on finding Sophronia Dearborn's grave, his eyes grew eager, though my story ended with a groan. "Everything's stalled. All I've found are birth records, death records. They don't tell you stories."

Jabari seemed to hesitate before he asked, "Have you—have you talked to your mom? Does she have any ideas of what to look for next?" He was verbally tiptoeing.

"My mother is a live wire when it comes to history." When I told him about her rant on "society's aristocrats," he nodded as if it all made sense. Then he asked, "Have you talked to Valerie?"

"About something that happened in 1859?"

"Yeah. Back in the early aughts, she started interviewing older people who once lived in The Gather. She even recorded my grandpops. And around here, folks who knew the most about white people were

Black folk. They were serving and gardening, cleaning and nannying. They heard all the secrets."

I still didn't think Valerie's knowledge would help. And besides, I had to bring up my mother. "Talking to Valerie is one way to get on Mom's bad side."

Jabari nodded. "It's too bad Dr. Castine isn't on speaking terms with her."

"Yeah. I don't know what's up with that."

"Your mom thinks Valerie is a sellout." Will filled me in. "We talked about it. Radiance said she'd rather eat dirt for sustenance than work for Lana Jean Chilton. I think those were her exact words."

"Sounds on-brand," I said.

"Radiance knows we don't see eye to eye," Will said. "Valerie works for Lana Jean because she was a manager at a factory that closed down. And her husband couldn't find a full-time job after he was disabled in an accident there."

"It's fucked up," Jabari said. "After that, the Goldens got ousted from their house and had to buy it back."

"What?"

"It's a long story," Will said. "But Lana Jean Chilton pays Valerie more than she'd ever make anywhere else around here. It's worth it to Lana Jean, not that she isn't rich as hell anyway. It's like buying her pride back."

"Buying her pride back? Are you talking about the Senator Harper statue?"

"It was a big deal. The statue debate—or debacle, really, made the national news," Jabari said. "It was less than a year after another huge rally in Charlottesville. Lana Jean got a whole contingent of white-rights groups from all over the country to see the senator's monument installed."

When Mom had traveled to Virginia for the senator's statue protests,

I'd been in middle school, but I recognized the worry in my dad, as well as my aunt and uncle, for her safety.

"Radiance never understood the necessity of Valerie's decision to work for Lana Jean. But I do. I owe a lot to Valerie," Will said. "She reached out to me when my dad got sick. Even though he was a die-hard racist, even after everything he'd done, she encouraged me to come home."

"Everything he'd done?" I asked.

He ran right through the stoplight of my question. "She's the kindest person I know. But by that point, Dad and I hadn't talked in years."

Stretching, Will stood. "I should go inside and check on your mom. She was pretty feral about not wanting help." Mom had all but chased us out of the kitchen. "I'll see if I can coax her into drinking another glass with me while we finish up."

With Will back inside, I asked Jabari if he grew up in Magnolia. "I grew up in Richmond, but I spent summers here because that's where my dad was raised. It made sense for me to stay here in the family house and save up." Around us, the light slowly crept from the sky. "I don't mind it. The friend sitch could use improvement, though. Seems like everyone in town's over forty, with that many kids."

I laughed, thinking of Lana Jean Chilton.

"Sometimes my buddies from Richmond will spend a weekend. Or the guys I used to do A/V with, out in Daventry. It's like a country retreat to them."

"What about folks at Charm?"

"The other kitchen guys are into hunting, stuff that's not my thing. I hang with the servers sometimes. But not all of us click."

"You mean Darlie."

"Exactly Darlie. Whenever she gets invited along, I'm out."

Maybe Fluvie would've talked about me the same way. As I

considered sharing with Jabari that I insulted her, words somehow came out before I was ready for them. "I, um, I hurt Fluvie's feelings."

Jabari nodded as if he knew.

"I guess word got around Charm?" I asked nervously.

"Everyone saw she was out of sorts. She kept quiet about why. But yeah. She told me."

"I didn't know you were close." The sense of shame returned. I kept my gaze on the foggy distance ahead, the mountains smudged like eye shadow.

"I ran into her outside Town Hall. That's where she's working now. She opened up. I guess she wanted to talk to someone, and she knew I wouldn't gossip."

I wondered if she had forgiven me. "What did she say about me?"

Jabari shook his head. "I promised I'd keep her confidence."

CHAPTER 10

How about we get some Starbucks?" Dad suggested as he drove down I-90.

It was eight in the morning. I'd been up since 2:00 A.M., and I couldn't sleep on the plane since my seatmate was mercilessly talkative. Plus, I was flat-out exhausted from the brutal semester that wasn't quite over. "Actually, Dad? I just want to get to Uncle Brian's and crash."

"But you love Starbucks." He seemed a little disappointed. "We can sit down and catch up."

I still smarted from that day Dad hung up on me. But Dad was Dad. Like Alyssa, he pretended nothing was wrong. And it honestly felt good to be around him again. He was comfortable, easy, uncomplicated. Not like Mom with her perfectionist "be me or be no one" standards. And I did want to catch up, especially to find out why he was driving a rental. Knowing my father, he'd tailgated someone a smidgeon too closely and took out their bumper.

But my eyelids wouldn't stay open. I dozed off in the car.

I woke up when we stopped in front of Uncle Brian and Aunt Nichelle's house. Opening the trunk, Dad lifted out my black suitcase with the red scarf I kept tied around the handle.

Then he hefted out a gray hard-sided suitcase. It was familiar, but it wasn't mine.

"You found a new place?" I couldn't help but feel miffed that he was also just visiting for the holiday. That he'd moved out of my aunt and uncle's without even telling me.

He grinned. "So this is good stuff, Noni. I'm out near Forest Park."

"Where's that?" I'd never heard of that neighborhood. Grabbing my suitcase, I rolled it ahead of him.

"Portland."

"You're in Maine?" Incredulous, I stopped in my tracks.

"Oregon."

Oregon?

"I took a new job. I'm not making the same coin your mom does, but it's still a big deal and a big raise."

"Dad, that's across the country! I'll never see you."

"Of course you will." He was almost giddy as he rattled on about a new tech startup. "There's a satellite office in Philly, so I'll be there a few times a year. You can't get rid of me that easily." He punched the keypad. "When you're back in Boston, I can drop by."

"Drop by? After a six-hour drive?" My cousin Kadeem lived in Philadelphia, and he always complained about the travel time. But that was beside the point. I fumed as I set down my suitcase inside of the quiet house. Dad left the entire state, and he didn't say a word to me. He left this entire region of the country! And he was moving—no, he'd already moved—three thousand miles away!

"When we talked on my birthday, I was gonna tell you I'd moved. But you were pretty upset."

"You were already gone? That was weeks ago! And *you* hung up on me, Dad!"

"I couldn't get through to you." His hand hovered over my shoulder, but stopped. "Hey, I know it doesn't feel like it, but this is good news! You've got a brand-new city to spend time in. You'll love Portland. It feels like the right place for another go at life."

"Yyyooo, you're almost as tall as Ma." Kadeem scraped his shoes on the mudroom mat, then strode in, giving me a bear hug.

"And she's gotten so pretty!" Aunt Nichelle stretched to take a pie plate from the cabinet. I looked the same, though, and I was stuck at five foot two like I'd been since the eighth grade.

"How's college life?" Kadeem asked. In the living room, my dad and uncle screamed a flurry of expletives, and my cousin's eyes darted to the game on TV. "Ohhh shiiit!" He strayed from the kitchen.

Aunt Nichelle took the opportunity to continue our conversation. How did Mom like her job? Was she working too hard?

"She's busy, but she's doing great." I shimmied sugar into a pot of cranberries.

"That's good. When we talk, she sounds challenged but happy. I wanted to make sure." Grabbing a long fork, she poked the curved turkey neck that simmered in a broth of its own making. I could almost taste the oniony gravy it would become, spooned on top of cornbread dressing, even as I myself stewed about Dad moving to the other end of the country and not telling me. After a moment, my aunt asked, "How are *you* feeling? With your dad's news. I take it he finally told you."

"He just threw that at me today."

She sighed. "I'm sorry. I should've told you myself, but he asked everyone to keep it quiet and we respected his wishes. Adults don't always know best." She stabbed at the turkey, as if she blamed the bird. "Mark's been wanting to leave for a minute. To come to terms with things, I guess."

"The divorce? I thought that decision was mutual." I hastily scraped a lemon across a zester.

"Mutual or not, there's always someone who wants a split more than the other."

I sensed my aunt was hanging on to another part of the story. "There's something else, isn't there?" Bits of citrus peel rained into the bubbling pot as the tight-skinned cranberries popped open.

Aunt Nichelle sighed. "Your father did something a few years ago. He hid it at first, but Radiance found out. It was cataclysmic. The beginning of the end of their marriage."

Cataclysmic? Where had I been? Could it have been the same summer when Mom traveled to Magnolia for the protest?

"He had an affair?" I whispered. How could he *do* that? And how could I have been so out-of-touch with my parents?

"An affair might not have been so complicated." My aunt pushed a rolling pin over pie dough. "Your father, he—well—" She struggled to explain. "He gave away something. Your parents got therapy, but Mark always felt justified. Radiance saw it as a betrayal."

"Was it money?" I guessed. "Did he invest in something shady?" I gasped. "Did it have something to do with this 'upstart company' he's working for?"

"Nothing like that. He—"

"Got a little tense in there!" Dad announced as the men paraded in, interrupting us. It must've been halftime. Uncle Brian grabbed a beer and snagged an apple slice from a bowl of pie filling, while Kadeem poured my aunt a glass of wine, asking if he could help with anything. Dad peered over my shoulder. "That smells delicious."

"It's the same recipe Mom makes," I said acidly.

The very mention of her cleared the room like a fart. Dad and my uncle casually slipped into the living room. "You got this, right?" Kadeem left without waiting for a response. I looked at my aunt, expecting an answer, but I knew from her troubled eyes that she regretted saying anything at all.

And I understood. Whatever secret she held wasn't hers to share.

"Who's Ethan?" I asked, or more like, shouted from the back seat, trying to be heard above my best friends' voices and the hip-hop music blasting from the speakers.

"Another guy from BU," Alyssa called back. "Hayley's boyfriend. Oh, wait, you don't know Hayley . . . oh my god, Kendall! You're going to totally hit that truck behind you."

"I got it." Kendall pressed her lips together in concentration as she parallel parked.

"You claimed that last time," Alyssa said.

"What happened last time?" I asked.

"Kendall practically totaled this Prius—"

"I just nudged it."

"Wrecked it."

"Tapped it."

"It was wild, Noni."

"It was *fine*. But my stepmom still made Dad get me driving lessons." Kendall edged up closer to the car in front. Just like how Dad sprang the news on me that he had moved, Alyssa surprised me with a group text. She and Kendall were going to a party. Kendall had chimed in: *Hope you can come with!* There it was, the adult thing: Just move forward. Don't get stuck in the mud of who did what wrong.

Cutting off the Audi, Kendall asked Alyssa, "What about that time you almost ran over Pete?"

"Pete Hassan? From our theater program?" I asked.

"Another Pete," Kendall said as we walked up the front steps. "This geeky guy who lives in our dorm. Oh my god, you would totally laugh your butt off, Noni."

"He's the biggest dork ever," Alyssa told me. In funny, nasal voices, they both said, "Hall Council time!" Then they dissolved into giggles.

Inside, techno music blared, and a few people drunkenly danced in the living room, but most just hung out. The place smelled of weed, booze, incense, and sweat, your typical eau de partay. Kendall and Alyssa immediately connected with other partygoers. They all seemed to know one another either from college or from Kendall's private school. The lights were dim, but the turnout seemed Magnolia-white. Alyssa tried to introduce me to a couple of her friends, but it was impossible over the noise.

I poured a beer, more of a prop than a beverage, then went outside. Being tipsy always meant I'd get either silly or philosophical, and that wasn't my mood.

"Hey, what up, Noni!" Emma McConnell was outside on the rickety back porch, smoking in the wintry air. She'd played Ariel in *The Tempest*, the role Alyssa had desperately wanted. "We missed you at the cast party. Too bad you couldn't see your costumes in the show run!" She stubbed out her cigarette. "I hear you're still living out in the country. That sucks! And getting that really awesome internship and having to turn it down? That's so awful! How are you, by the way?"

Not good, that was for sure.

I told her I was fine.

"That's great. Brrr, it is so colllddd!" Emma shivered. She and Alyssa crossed paths as one went inside and the other came out.

"Ugh, I still hate her for getting that part," Alyssa complained. "I would've done it so much better."

Emma was tactless, but she'd been awesome in rehearsals, so I wasn't sure if my best friend was right. I reminded Alyssa, "But you got the pretty dress, remember?"

"That's true." It felt like old times when we could just be there for each other. As if she felt the same way, Alyssa said, "I guess we haven't been in touch much. How's Virginia?"

"It's, you know. Okay, I guess." I told her a little about community college and Charm, though I left out a lot about my new life. Most of it, really. Darlie. Fluvie. The fact that Cicada Chilton, Lana Jean's daughter, messaged me *again* about having tea together.

And I left out Jabari, though what was there to say? He was just another friend. A handsome friend. But just a friend.

I also didn't tell Alyssa about Sophie Dearborn. She wouldn't understand why I was so drawn to her. I didn't understand it, either.

Tightening her thin duster around her arms, Alyssa talked about her classes. She was taking voice lessons. They didn't work, she muttered, because she didn't get a role in the musical *Cabaret*. "I cried for two days. I really thought I nailed my audition. I'm doing props, though. And I got a look at the costume sketches! You'd love them, Noni, though I feel like you'd have even better designs. Oh, and guess who did a guest workshop for the theater department. Nyles Pompa! From the Shakespeare program. He's got his own theater now. He didn't remember my name, but he asked about you."

That felt both flattering and saddening. It really sucked I had to turn down the internship. Alyssa talked about some clubs she was in and a guy she had dated. I read between the lines that she'd lost her virginity. I was curious about what *that* had been like, but Alyssa didn't seem interested in divulging. It felt like a sliding door closing between us. If our friendship was the same as it once had been, she would've told all like a tabloid.

She and the guy were on-again, off-again. "Emphasis on *off*," she clarified. "We had a little tiff. I mean, we're still talking, but we're also not." She sighed a long one. "Kind of like us. I'm sorry I ignored everything that happened at your house. With Laronté. And Kendall. I should have stood up for you."

I didn't know how to respond. *Should I say I forgave her? Did I?*

I asked myself the question before I told her, "I forgive you." I thought of Fluvie. *Did she forgive me?*

Still, I had to bring up, "What's made it hard is that you and Kendall are still friends. Like, close friends."

"We have to be. We're roommates. At least, until I move to the honors dorm next semester. They have a spot for me now!"

"Oh, that's great!" And I was happy for Alyssa, even though her grade-consciousness was always something that separated the two of us. Her parents expected all As, and she gave them everything on their wish list, happily. My mom expected perfection, too, but I never met it. Part of it was because I struggled a bit with some of my math and science classes. But much of it was because I just got bored in social studies and literature, the subjects of Mom's expertise. I almost felt like being good at that stuff would make me more like her. And I wanted to be myself.

Alyssa rubbed her hands together. "I'm frostbitten. Wanna go back inside?"

"I don't mind it out here, but you should. I'll go in in a minute, okay?" It was frigid, but I didn't want to crowd into the stuffy, smoky house, nor huddle around at the firepit with some of the others. What Alyssa didn't say directly was that on matters of race, Kendall was going to follow Laronté's lead, not Alyssa's. As she should. Right?

But Laronté was the one who'd laughed when Kendall blurted out a slur. Why had he done that? Why did he undermine us?

Us. I was thinking like Mom. When Laronté had moved from Dorchester during our junior year, of course I noticed him. There were hardly any Black kids at our school, and he was cute. I wondered if I had a chance. Even after I saw how he distanced himself from me and the other Black students, I wanted him to like me.

The screen door popped open. Laronté strode out, followed by

Kendall. Grinning at me, he did a silly little jig, swinging his bent arms. "How go de plantation? Massa treatin' ya right?"

"You are so stupid!" Kendall giggled hard as she shivered in her short sleeves.

"He feedin' you dem gooood chitlins?"

Complaining about the cold, Kendall disappeared inside before reappearing at the window as Laronté strutted in a circle around me, chickening his arms at his sides. Everyone clustered around the dying firepit pointed and guffawed.

"You know you're just demeaning yourself," I snapped.

"What's de meaning of dat?" He pretended to swing a cane, a realistic pantomime. Fury and pity and shame swelled inside me, and I didn't know who I felt it for the most: Laronté or me.

"You's always been a house slave." He clicked his heels and landed in an exaggerated bow. "Now you's *in* de big house!"

House slave? Me? As he "shucked and jived," as Dad called it? The fuck. I hissed, "You don't have to *be* this way, to be with her!"

Stopping mid-shuffle, Laronté looked up from his stooped-back pose with burning eyes and an icy expression while slowly lifting an imaginary hat.

CHAPTER 11

Mom passed the ride down I-66 with aimless chatter. She'd spent Thanksgiving at Blondell's, where the two of them had cooked together for Jessica and her mom. And the high school principal, Regina Chapel, plus her family. And Will. "Then we went to the drive-in after dinner, and then into Daventry for drinks," she said happily.

"Wow, that must have been a heck of a caravan."

"Actually, everyone was tired," Mom said. "So it was just Will and me."

"Oh." There was a pause. "Did you have a good time?" I asked.

"Sure. It was fine."

We'd escaped the interstate traffic and were in hill country, among rolling pasture and fields, with steep gullies on either side of the curvy road. Mom glanced at me. "Are you thinking about flying out to Portland during spring break?"

I was thankful she brought it up. I had wanted to the whole time, but didn't know how.

She added softly, "I'm sorry I never told you. Mark asked that I not. I almost went against his wishes. I knew you'd feel so hurt, I couldn't say it. I should have, but I just couldn't manage—"

She broke off as a doe darted in front of the car. Quickly, she veered, avoiding her, then spun the steering wheel, trying to right the car's direction. A steep drop loomed close. I sucked in a breath, grabbing around me, searching for something to hold on to. The baritone of a semi-trailer's horn blared low, loud, and terrifying. Mom jerked the wheel and straightened the car. The deer trotted into the woods, white tail wagging.

Her gasp was one of deep relief. She slowed down. "I overcorrected," she said between shallow breaths. "The wheel. I overcorrected. I'm sorry."

"It's okay. I wasn't that scared." I touched my mother's shoulder, realizing she was who I'd been reaching for.

Somehow, for the first time in my life, my final grades were all As. I stared at my screen in disbelief. It had started out so rough in all my classes—I was pulling a C average or worse my first six weeks.

But then I got the hang of things. One thing I learned from my tutoring sessions was how to study. In high school I had never really *studied*; I just did my homework. Sometimes. But in Multi-V, you didn't get much homework. You had to practice problems on your own, over and over again.

And lab reports in Bio had been a struggle. I started off making Ds. It was Will who suggested I sit down with the professor. I did, and she told me I wasn't being concise or specific. We looked at some of my old reports, and she showed me where I was being vague. From then on, she was so impressed with my improvement, she agreed to regrade any reports I rewrote.

Plus my final exam grades were sky-high. They hauled my grades up in all my classes.

And sure, sometimes Mom and I spoke French at dinner, which helped me on my tests, but I also lucked out. A Moroccan poet was giving a reading in Richmond *en français,* and if you went and wrote a short paper about it (also *en français*), Madame Holladay averaged in massive points. It was on a Saturday, but Madge covered my shift at Charm and I drove over.

Then, my Multi-V instructor gave the whole class a chance to do another exam, to make up for what he called a disappointing set of midterms. His tests were so grueling, no one else took him up on it. I did, and scored mid-90s on both the new midterm and the final.

At the start of the semester, Mom had practically strong-armed me into signing over permission for her to view my records. When she came home that night, I heard her hurried footsteps on the hallway floor. She was talking on the phone, knocking on my door, flinging it open once I told her to come in.

Mom's phone was pressed to her ear. "Yes, all As. Can you believe it! I'm so excited. Oh, sure thing. I'll pass along your regards."

She was grinning as she set her phone down. "That was Blondell. She's so proud of you." Her cell buzzed again. "Oh, it's your dad calling me back."

She spoke into the phone. "Mark. Guess what. Noni got all As!" A pause. "That's right, every single one of her classes. Oh, absolutely, I'll put her on."

I shook my head, silently mouthing no. Mom nodded quickly. "You know what, Mark? She's exhausted. Maybe later? Of course I will. Okay, bye-bye."

My phone pinged several times that night. Dad, my aunt and uncle, as well as Kadeem, sent me cash and congrats. Over the next week, Blondell gave me a big hug, a fifty-dollar bill, and kind words. "Honey, I'm so proud of you!" Will took Mom and me to a really cool Thai place in Daventry and gave me a gift card to their local bookstore. It was kind of fun to be fussed over.

One night after dinner, Mom knocked on my bedroom door.

"Just a minute!" I hastily put away the nineteenth-century books I had been stacking up to return to the Magnolia Historical Museum. I hadn't made any new Sophie Dearborn discoveries, and I needed to come to terms that there'd be no more breakthroughs. It was really, really disappointing. Still, after Mom's "society's aristocrats" rant, I didn't want her knowing I'd ever undertaken this research at all.

"I hope I'm not interrupting you too much," Mom said.

"No, not at all."

She sat on my bed, hugging me, then set a gift bag on my lap. Inside was a necklace that looked like her favorite piece, the one with a big square pendant with little pieces of glass creating a mosaic design. While Mom's was in all different colors, this one was in shades of blues and reds with snatches of white and little etchings of yellow marked here and there.

I was flabbergasted. "This is for me?"

"Just a gift of congratulations."

"Thank you! Wow, where'd you get this? I thought you said yours was specially handmade."

"They both are. I've had them for years." She relaxed against my pillows. "Someone made them for me once, but I've been saving this one for you. For sometime special."

"Yeah?" She'd kept this stashed away, just for me. I couldn't imagine the care it must have taken to create the pendant by hand. "Did Gramma make it?"

"Oh no." She chortled a bit. "My grandmother wasn't one to hunch over a worktable with a pair of tweezers."

"Who did?"

She held the piece up, admiring the pendant. "I've always liked this one the best, which is why I wanted you to have it. Think I could borrow it sometime?"

"Oh my god, Mom. Of course." Tiny shards of glass glinted in the lamplight.

Christmas break whizzed by. I brought out my heavy-duty Singer and sewed up a storm. My parents both got corduroy blazers in a rich paprika hue: Dad's had elbow patches from a length of African mudcloth Dr. Corn had given me. Mom's sported mudcloth lapels. Halfway through sewing, it occurred to me that I was essentially making my divorced parents corresponding jackets, but I just went with it.

Alyssa and Blondell each got a bunch of cute silk hairbands. The sage silk of Valerie's fringed shawl would set off her eyes. For Will, there was a maroon canvas messenger bag, like a tan one I'd given my dad once. I reconsidered the rest of the mudcloth. Should I make a second messenger bag for Jabari? But we were just casual friends. Why would I make him a present? Instead, I used some of it to make myself a belt with leather closures. I even got crafty, hand-painting cowrie shells with flecks of gold, and stitching them on.

Sewing scratched an itch. But I was making rote things, things I could sew with my eyes closed. I craved a big project, something that would challenge me. In an apprenticeship at The Chasma, that kind of challenge would have been a day's work.

Mom and I had Christmas dinner at Blondell's huge farmhouse, joining her wife, Jessica, and her mom, plus Will. Everyone but me had a little bit too much wine, though I had a little. We got silly, until a sudden shriek interrupted our banter.

A huge tabby, a basement escapee, wandered in. With a cry, Mom leapt onto her chair with both feet, catlike herself. The table became a circle of confusion. Mom had always explained it away. "Oh, I'd rather not be around cats," she'd say, as if she was allergic. But really, she was ashamed of her genuine fear.

As she teetered on the chair, I could almost read everyone's thoughts. Was this a performance? A joke? A metaphor?

I gathered the cat in my arms. "It's okay, Mom." The twenty-pounder slumped against me, purring. Sweat glossed my mother's forehead. Will got it: She was scared. He clasped her hands and coaxed her down as I returned the big orange tom to his holding pen.

"Hey! Noni!" Cicada Chilton caught up with me on the sidewalk.

"Oh, hey." I tried to match her exuberant friendliness, but couldn't quite get there. Lana Jean's youngest daughter strolled alongside me, as if we were headed to that tea date she'd texted me about a few times—the one that would never happen. Even if Mom happened by right now, she'd be furious that I was within even a generational degree of Lana Jean Chilton.

"So I hear you're at Prudence!"

"Oh, yeah, I am."

"I'm doing a gap. Mama wants me to focus on scholarship pageants. But I'm really excited about college next fall. What classes are you taking?"

"Oh, um." I reviewed most of my grueling spring semester schedule. When I told her I was starting second round of Cell Bio and doing Linear Algebra, she wowed like I was going to the moon. She was fascinated by the Special Topics in History I registered for: this one was American Theater. When I mentioned French, she giggled. "Mon française c'est merde." She reminded me of Alyssa, with the same people-pleasing energy. "Four classes and a lab? That's a lot, right?" she asked.

"It's about average. I have one other class."

"What is it?"

"Um, Intro Black Studies."

"What's that?"

I didn't want to elaborate, but there wasn't really an option. "It's a field that combines different disciplines. Our class is mostly literature and history, but we also study art, music, and film." I judged her face. She was nodding intently. "All on, um, the Black diaspora. That's basically the ways people of African descent have moved throughout the world."

"That's really cool! I bet you get into some really good music. Jazz, funk, hip-hop."

"Yeah, that." I was surprised she had anything to add.

She stopped in front of the Magnolia Historical Museum. "Oh, is this where you're going? Mama mentioned you're doing a research project."

"Sure, it's a project, sort of." One I had given up on. I was only there to return books, but had to schedule with the docent since the place was only open, like, never.

I was about to make my excuses and say goodbye, but Cicada followed me in.

Inside, I shelved the books for the gazillion-year-old docent, who fussed over Cicada. "Oh, our lovely Miss Chilton! I was just talking to your mother. She said you won Miss Whoopie Pie."

"I did, with a very nice stipend from the American Whoopie Pie Association." Cicada smiled demurely. She joined me at the bookshelf opposite a wall covered by a mural of the Harper family tree, complete with painted-on portraits of her dead relatives centuries deep. "So it's great I ran into you, Noni. I've got another pageant coming up, and I was hoping you'd be up for a little fashion design."

"Oh yeah?" I faked interest.

"For an extra-special pageant gown." She touched a copy of a Trianon house portrait: one of Cicada's great-grandmother, Priscilla Lavigne Harper. "One just like this."

When I first saw the original, I had admired the then unknown-to-me dressmaker's skill. Now I knew my great-great-grandmother Lacey Castine had created it.

"I've always dreamed of wearing one just like it." Cicada traced her finger along the painted gown. "When my sister DixieStar was my age, Mama hired a dressmaker to re-create Great-Nana's dress for the same pageant I'm doing this May. But it was awful. It looked like a toilet paper roll that someone's cat had its way with."

It should've been funny, but she didn't laugh. Her light brown eyes were pleading. "Could you design a magnolia dress? Would you make it? You have so much talent."

Could I? Studying the oil painting copy, I wasn't sure. How would someone even construct such a garment, one with structured layers? The petal-shaped layers had to splay out grandly, so far from the wearer's body that they didn't touch the floor.

And as for the *would*—I wasn't sure there, either. Cicada was nice enough, but she was Lana Jean's daughter. Mom would be incensed.

Cicada lowered her voice. "Mama invested four grand for a Giambattista Valli gown I wore for Miss Kudzu last year. For something like this? A replica of this gown that we can't get anywhere else? She'll double that."

Double that? That was *so* much. The amount of money people spent on beauty contests! "I know, it's a lot," Cicada said. "But we're a pageant family. Mama did them, and so did my sisters. My parents have always worked, but we've been so fortunate to have family money. So Mama spares no expense."

But eight thousand dollars? It was a ton of money, and honestly, cash I didn't need. I myself was hugely lucky to have a "rich mom" who could afford my tuition and expenses next year when I went to BU. Plus, I'd saved up my own funds from Charm. "It's great that you like pageants so much," I said.

"Oh, I adore them. I mean, sure, sometimes I wish I could do something else. Like, I don't know, open a record store in Daventry or somewhere. Vinyls, CDs. Vintage stuff."

I empathized with her a little. And hadn't I wanted a challenging sewing project? Plus, wouldn't it be good to have a connection with a girl my age, one who *didn't* repose underground, like Sophronia Dearborn? Alyssa was five hundred miles away. Darlie created a barrier between me and the other servers at Charm. And I had botched any would-be friendship with Fluvie. She didn't even work at Charm anymore. As it stood, my only friend in town had been dead since 1859.

But maybe we could connect over a dream, not a dress. "Would your mom give you start-up money for a record store? The amount she's spending on gowns could set you up."

Cicada breathed an airy laugh. "Oh, the vinyls thing is just a silly thought. After college, I'll work in TV journalism. Then I'll marry and stay home with my children, and then go into politics. Pageants are a perfect preparation for what Mama wants for me."

So there it was. Her life all planned out and stamped with her mother's approval. "So will you think about it?" she pressed. "You're the only person in the world who could make this dress. Mama says it's in your genes. That Grannie's dressmaker, your great-great-grandma, was named—what was it—Velveteen? Silky?"

"Lacey. Lacey Castine."

Speaking her name brought a kind of confidence. Power, even. I could make this gown if I wanted to. I could figure it out.

But the "if I wanted to" part? Mom would dismember me if she knew, and I couldn't exactly hide a giant white gown in my bedroom. Cicada touched my arm. "Hey, I know our moms aren't exactly best friends. But Mama promises ultimate discretion. We even have a workspace for you."

None of it was enough of an incentive. I started to tell Cicada thanks, but that I was really busy.

The door chimed. It was Lana Jean. "Noni!" She fluttered in. "How lovely to run into you! I was just stopping by to tell Barbara"—she nodded at the docent—"about more papers I cataloged in Trianon's cache. My father collected documents from all the plantations in Magnolia."

I felt a spark of hope for Sophie's story. "Did you find anything . . ."

"From Tangleroot? Of course." Turning to her daughter, she asked, "Cicada, did you mention the gown?"

"I did!"

"Splendid." She clapped her hands together. "I await your thoughts with bated breath, Noni." She beamed.

My smile back was as stiff as a hoopskirt, as brittle as a crinoline. Because this, I realized, was how Lana Jean made a deal.

CHAPTER 12

The last face I thought I'd see in a Charlottesville fabric store was Jabari Nichols's. But there he was, stooping to look at buttons.

"Jabari! Hey. What are you up to?"

He was extra handsome in a dress-for-the-job-you-want look: a twill blazer and dark jeans. I looked different, too, because I wasn't in jeans for a change. I'd made a burgundy jumper with mudcloth pockets as a back-to-school gift for myself.

He looked a little chagrined. "One of my buttons fell off somewhere. I have something going on at UVA, so I kinda wanted to match." He pulled at the sides of his blazer.

"I can help if you need me."

"If you don't mind, yeah. So what are you up to? Is that—are you making a wedding dress?"

My face fell as I realized I held a bundle of various half-yard lengths of ivory silks and satins.

"Who's getting married?" Jabari looked down at my cache of fabrics. "Not you, hopefully."

"Oh, no, no, no. I'm making a costume." I mean, what was a beauty contest if not theater?

Outside, we found a bench in Market Street Park. Like most store-bought jackets, Jabari's had a spare button attached to the inside, which blew his mind. But I liked the tortoiseshell ones I'd picked out, and it would only take ten minutes to replace them all. As I stitched, we drank hot chai, one of Valerie's blends. Passing his industrial thermos back and forth and sharing swigs felt intimate, especially with our thighs almost touching.

Jabari thanked me again. "I'm meeting with an admissions dean, so I wanted to look put-together. I'm applying to UVA, Stonepost, and William & Mary as a transfer."

"Those are some tough schools to get into." I pulled a line of thread.

"Yeah. I've gotten straight As two years running, though. And I'm working on a research project for my Poli-Sci class. That's what I'm gonna major in."

"Political science? What's your first-choice school?"

"Stonepost. I like that the classes are almost all seminar-style. Going there as an undergrad is like being a grad student with all the research you have to do."

Yeah, it was freaking Utopia. The streets were paved in gold and free textbooks. "But I get that's not where you'd want to be," Jabari said quickly. "With your mom there, maybe it feels too close to home."

The way he got me almost made me self-conscious, because I had to admit to myself how much Mom outdid me in almost every way. Not that it wasn't as obvious as the sun itself. How could I be known as myself in college if she was its president?

"What's your project about?" I changed the subject.

"Monuments. How the legal landscape coincides and conflicts with the 'mythology of history,' as your mother calls it."

Her again.

"I'm using central Virginia as a case study."

In the center of the park, an empty blot of dirt marked where, in the decades before, a bronze statue of Confederate General Robert E. Lee and his horse Traveller had ridden through the park's sunlight, and finally under tarp-covered darkness before their memorialized journey ended for good. The statue was covered after white supremacists descended into town, rallying around it with tiki torches. The courts battled it out before it was finally removed. It mattered to me that the sculpture was gone, even if I had nothing against the horse.

"How's your research?" Jabari asked. "On Sophie Dearborn? Have you talked to Valerie?"

"Not yet." I still couldn't get how interviews of Black Magnolia residents could lead me to a 150-year-old white girl mystery. As far as I was concerned, the case was cold until Lana Jean turned on the stove. "It's been busy. I went home over Thanksgiving." Boston *was* still home, even though Dad wasn't there and our place in Wellesley housed new owners, people who probably liked gray walls. I told Jabari about Kendall, Alyssa, and Laronté, including his house-party performance—plus about him hitting my hip and *that* whole exchange.

Jabari's brows lowered. "Fuck that kid."

"Want to know something funny? He dropped his driver's license once. His real name is Lawrence."

Jabari shook his head, laughing in disbelief. "What the hell! This guy! He's got some issues."

"What do you think they are?"

Jabari shrugged, producing a baggie of cookies from his knapsack. "Sounds like he's trying to fit in, by any means necessary. Goes to show you, not all skinfolk are kinfolk."

"Yeah." But then, here I was, on some deep dive, researching some white girl because—what? We had the same name and birthday? But it was more than that. It was like she was a friend from another generation. Some way-far-back generation on the other side of a great divide.

It was all confusing. I helped myself to another cookie. "Hey, what are these? They're amazing."

"Chocolate cherry with sea salt. I stew the cherries in a little rum." He offered me a third. "Maybe I could make dinner for you one day."

"Mom would love if you came over again," I told him.

"Actually, I was thinking of dinner with just you."

Heat leapt under my cheeks in spite of the chilled air. I didn't know how to respond, except to hand him back his blazer. Jabari was quick to add, "You know, just you and some other friends. A study session or whatnot."

"I mean, yeah, that would be cool." So Jabari saw me as a study partner. It was fine. I'd be leaving Virginia soon, anyway. Why start what I couldn't finish?

My mind still reeled the next day as I went to Town Hall to file some paperwork for Blondell. It felt strange to walk into the old courthouse building of so much infamy. I took the stairway, finding myself wandering a bit. Each floor offered a different viewing space of the marble stair landing where the senator had once spoken. On the second floor, it was a whole ballroom with a deck. On the top floor, it was a tiny lounge with a little balcony.

In the Permits & Licenses Office, I waited in line, lost in thought. Something felt icky about agreeing to make Cicada's gown. It was just for a silly beauty contest, but it was still a replica of the dress Priscilla Lavigne Harper once wore. Even though Priscilla didn't exactly raise cane atop the courthouse stairs like her husband, she had to be complicit in what the senator said because she was married to him. If she was so morally opposed to his views, she had options. I mean, my great-grandmother Fawnie Castine, a Black woman with few resources, managed to divorce her husband in the 1950s. Surely Priscilla could have figured it out, too.

"Judy, I'm back from break!" a familiar twang sang out behind the counter. I froze. A privacy partition separated the customer line and the clerks, but I knew that voice anywhere.

"Next!" she said cheerily. I was up. But I couldn't move.

"Are you going or not?" the woman behind me asked. Maybe I could wait for the next clerk, but she was re-explaining the difference between a compliance and a recertification application to a customer. The man was practically shouting, and Judy wouldn't be outmatched.

"Who's next, y'all?" Fluvie called out. "Step right up!" She imitated a circus ringmaster.

"Honey, go!" The hoarse voice behind me was like an elephant prod. I lurched forward.

Fluvie's eyes widened just a bit, but then her expression arranged itself into something blandly professional. "May I help you?"

"I'm sorry." It was all I could think of. I slid the permit application into the window slot with shaky hands. "I've been meaning to tell you."

Fluvie examined the application. She flipped a page, and something like interest flickered in her eyes. Maybe she was a little excited that Charm would get an outdoor pavilion. I wanted to tell her that Blondell would paint it highlighter yellow.

Fluvie swiveled away and slid everything through the Xerox. It was strange to see her in a skirt and blouse. She'd grown out her mullet and dyed the pink to black. She returned to the window.

"Fluvie? I know you didn't want an apology, but . . ."

She only stamped the original application, stapling the remaining pages. "The applicant should keep this copy for their records. If the town approves the application, the permit will arrive by mail within sixty days."

I knew it was wrong to apologize here. But my rational brain refused to connect with my stammering mouth. "Do you—can you forgive me?"

"The permit will arrive within sixty days if the application is approved." It was as if she were a bot.

"Fluvie?"

"Is there a problem?" The older clerk side-eyed me.

"Not at all, Judy." Fluvie's voice rang out. "Next!"

Hot with humiliation, I hurried down the courthouse stairs. My mother would be furious if she knew I'd dumped my feelings on Fluvie, especially while she was at work. And Jabari might find out, too, since Fluvie had confided in him after the festival. What would he think of me then? It was so, so wrong, what I did. But now I couldn't apologize for the apology. What could I do?

My feet sped me across the fairgrounds. Lana Jean owned an apartment above Buried Silver, one she planned to redecorate as a rental for vacationers. In the meantime, it was vacant. The cloth was still in my backpack. So were some sketches I had made at home. But I still hadn't dived in.

As Lana Jean described, there was a private entrance behind the store. I walked up a set of interior stairs and keyed in the code she'd written down for me. Inside, the space was bare of any froufrou, nothing like Trianon's tacky decor. It even had gray walls. There was a dining room table and a cracked leather couch and tons of vinyl records on what must have been custom shelving. A skylight cast a pane of gold onto the hardwood floor, brightening the place. Lana Jean had set up adjustable worktables against the wall, along with a whole sewing cabinet. Inside was an arsenal of accoutrements and, even better, a top-of-the-line machine. I wouldn't need so much as a needle from home.

I flicked on the lights to the main bedroom. The walls were dark blue, reminding me of my cousin Kadeem's room from his teen years, the same room my uncle had turned into the office I'd crashed in before we moved to Virginia. But Kadeem never had posters everywhere of Lynyrd Skynyrd, Kid Rock, Led Zeppelin, or Ted Nugent. Those weren't guys my cousin listened to.

And Kadeem didn't have a Confederate flag, one as tall as me. Furled loosely, it leaned into a corner.

I closed the door. Back in the living room, I unrolled a length of drafting paper and began drawing a miniature mock-up of pieces and sections I thought might form a dress. The shame I felt from my interaction with Fluvie still vibrated in my brain.

I caressed the half yards of fabric, feeling for the right weight, the right pliability. The dialogue between my hands and my mind, what a sewing project required, would be what I needed as I bided my time in Virginia. Maybe it would help me forget the chasm that split me from most everyone else in Magnolia. There weren't enough yardsticks in the world to measure the width of that rift.

Valerie lived in the old schoolhouse, out past the cemetery where Gramma was buried. It was a long, neat white clapboard building with a cute bell tower set atop the roof like a steeple.

She read on her front porch with her blanket-shrouded feet propped on a plant stand. I hesitated for a second. She wasn't expecting me, as I'd driven out on a whim.

I had just been at the apartment above Buried Silver, stymied as I worked on the magnolia gown. A finished bodice lay spread out on a worktable, one with eight, five-eighth-inch buttonholes that Lana Jean had specified. She would supply the buttons: She insisted they must be vintage, from her great-grandmother's era. "My nana held on to the originals. She stored them in a red Miller & Rhoads jewelry box." Lana Jean had bemoaned, "I've looked and looked, but they've been lost to time, I'm afraid."

She was confounded as to where her grandmother had put away the box of buttons. And I was equally mystified as to how *my* ancestor had constructed the magnolia gown's voluminous skirt. I made a few sample petals, sewing a backing of canvas onto one and quilting interfacing onto another. Neither worked. The petals drooped with a lining of thin wire. I bought fabric stiffener, but every fabric I used became too shape-shifty, too easy to scrunch. And with the petals of varying length, a hoop or crinoline wouldn't work.

Switching gears would get me out of my funk of frustration. Jabari had long encouraged me to talk to Valerie, to metaphorically dig up some dirt covering Sophie Dearborn's grave. But now I had a paper to write for class, and those recordings Valerie had could really come in handy.

With the Courageous Curriculums Initiative gaining buzz in the news, Dr. Corn, my Black Studies professor, was inspired to add a twist to the syllabus. Our capstone paper had to thematically link readings from Mom's book, *The Remembered,* with narratives by local elders. After chatting with Jabari one day at work, I decided to center my paper on the themes of the sasha and the zamani—the dead who still lived in our memories and those who were gone from remembrances' view. But now, I needed to collect some stories.

And besides, Valerie was the only person in Magnolia who was there for me.

"Hey, sweetie!" She put down her Colson Whitehead novel. Without asking why I was there, she waved a hand. "Come in!"

Like Mom had when I first saw Tangleroot, Valerie wasted no time in giving me an energetic tour. Her home had an open floor plan and a high, beamed ceiling. The space was bright with colorful things, alive with a sense of vibrancy. She'd reupholstered antique chairs with bold African fabrics. Lamps were skirted with funky, colorful shades.

"Wow." I touched the glass-inlaid designs topping an old sewing table, the mosaic reminding me of my mom's treasured necklace. There were others like it. This piece was definitely old, with intricate cast-iron legs and a treadle like a fireplace grate.

"My son would collect antique bottles and china, and make these,"

Valerie explained, saying the furniture itself had been in The Gather families for generations. "That table was your great-grandmother's. She never used it; she just kept it in storage. It originally belonged to Fawnie's mother, Lacey."

"Is there a sewing machine in the inner compartment?"

"I'm guessing so. Of course, with the mosaic, it's painted shut." She traced her finger along a seam of gold surrounding the glass pattern. "Know what else was Lacey's?" Valerie showed me a quilt hanging from her wall. It looked like a collage of silky and velvety fabrics, each cut into randomly sized shapes, and sewn together with bold X-shaped stitches. "This is a crazy quilt I sourced two years ago. I paid a pretty penny for it from a dealer, but I had to reclaim it."

I remembered the tapestry Mom had taken down from the Stonepost library. "Gorgeous. How do you know it's hers?"

Valerie flipped it around and showed me the bottom corner. A little square attached to the backing was embroidered: *Lacey Castine, 1914.*

"Wow."

"Crazy quilts weren't the big style by that decade, but she always favored them, it seems," Valerie informed me. "She made a few for people in town."

A glossy black cat emerged from beneath a plant stand. "Don't be nervous. That's just Sheena, she's frien—" Stopping short, Valerie watched me with amazement as I rubbed the cat's arched back. She seemed to marvel. "I have to also wonder if Radiance is your mother."

"Also wonder?" I asked.

"I just spit out my thoughts wrong. I'm so surprised you're not climbing the walls like she'd be doing."

"I love cats."

I spied an expensive espresso machine on the kitchen counter. "My youngest got me this for Christmas," Valerie said. "I'll make you a cup. You want it plain-old-plain-old, or one of my little concoctions?"

"I'll try something new." I looked at a bank of photographs on the wall. Babies and toddlers smiled and drooled.

"My grands," Valerie said. Two handsome men grinned at me from pictures. "And my sons. Grown now. Almost your mother's age."

One eight-by-ten showed a young man in the very same hallway where I stood, holding a big, fluffy cat. He was very light-skinned, even paler than Valerie. He wore glasses, but his high forehead and generous smile reminded me of my dad.

"Weldon. He was my oldest," Valerie said. "You remind me of him. He was always eager. Curious. Brilliant as all get-out."

Brilliant? I don't think anyone had ever called me that. But the "was" saddened me, as did Valerie's face, because the corners of her full mouth didn't quite lift up all the way, a smile weighted with pain. Turning around, she busied herself on the machine. The cat urgently head-butted my leg. I set her on my lap. Valerie's eyes softened as she watched Sheena nuzzle my nose.

"Didn't you once tell me your oldest son was my mom's friend?" I asked.

"They were best friends."

Sensing she didn't want to talk about her son any longer, I brought up something else. "Valerie, how much do you know about the history of Magnolia?"

"Oh, lots. About twenty years ago, I had this idea of writing a book about the history of this town. The Black history, at least." She'd interviewed people, including Gramma Fawnie. Jabari had converted the audio into MP3s.

"Your mom must have her own CD copies somewhere, but I'll send you the computer files. This place was something, Noni. Homes up and down this street. They called it The Gather because folks were always having little get-togethers: garden parties, book talks, bible study groups."

"Really? That sounds like it was really cool."

"Know how all of it came to be? Cuffee Fortune. After slavery, the white man who'd owned him couldn't pay him cash for his work. So he gave the Fortunes a square mile of land out here instead, and another in Daventry. 'Course, it wasn't even Daventry back then, just a rocky piece of no-man's-land, worthless." The steamer hissed, frothing a tumbler of milk. "But the parcel here? It was farmable. Cuffee convinced other folks to help him clear this land and farm with him, instead of sharecrop for white folks. They raised barns and livestock, then built their own businesses."

She tilted her chin. "Look in that cabinet there. The folder labeled 'Nichols.' There's pictures of The Gather. I got them from Jabari's grandfather. He grew up in town, and *his* father took a bunch of photographs in the early 1920s."

A plastic-sheathed black-and-white image showed rows of wood-frame buildings lining both sides of the street. There were at least two dozen people out doing everyday business, a couple of horses and buggies, and an old-fashioned automobile blurring down the street.

"Magnolia was a lot busier and a lot Blacker than it is today," Valerie commented.

"What happened?" As far as Black people went now, Magnolia was a ghost town.

Lines curved around her mouth. "Fires. White folks would burn down the church one night. We would rebuild. Then they'd burn down a business. We rebuilt again. This happened for years. They didn't come through and burn the whole town out at once like they did in Tulsa and Wilmington. They wore us down. And just like those buildings fell, one by one, our families packed up and moved north."

She told me what Mom once did. In the mid-1950s, the town forced out those who remained, demolishing their homes. "This schoolhouse was left alone until 2002," Valerie said. "Then the city swooped in, eminent domain again. Paid me pennies but said I could rent it until they developed the land. Can you believe it? Renting my own land that I had owned!"

"That's so unfair!"

"It's not the half of it." The town put the property up for sale, because they decided not to build power lines after all, Valerie said. She bought the schoolhouse back, though the cost had gone up, and she'd whittled down her savings. With the factory she'd long managed closed, working for Lana Jean was the only way she could afford her mortgage. "I know it's selling my soul. And worse, the souls of my very kin." She sounded weary. "But Lana Jean pays. Generously even. But that's not generosity. With Lana Jean, it never is."

"What do you mean?"

"It almost doesn't matter. What matters is this: I can be The Gather's caretaker. I can hold this place's memory. If no one's here, all of what we have left would be gone. Do you understand?"

"I think I do." I tasted my coffee. Then I took another sip. "Valerie?"

"Yes, baby doll."

"This is really, really good." It was almost alarming, how good it tasted. The latte had a spicy, deep, and rich flavor.

"You like it?"

"Oh my god. Yes." With the thyme-pecan shortbreads she placed in front of me, I felt like I was in some kind of coffee heaven.

"I make my own flavorings. Reggie likes his lemon and elderflower coffee. That's citrus, cinnamon, and cacao, my favorite." Nodding at my mug, she flicked on the burner beneath the kettle. "I'm making myself a new tea blend I came up with: coconut and ginger."

“That sounds delish.”

She smiled. “Maybe I’m channeling your ancestor’s energy by trying something different. It seems like Lacey Castine was the talk of the town then. Coming down here from up north, when everyone back then was clamoring to go up.”

“Up north? She wasn’t born here?” Mom had always talked about our family like it evolved from the very sands of central Virginia.

“If you believe Jabari’s grandpa—and we can’t ask him because he’s passed on—but his father who took the pictures? He told his son a story.”

“What’s the story?”

“The elder Nichols was working at the depot in 1910, and this woman is standing on the platform, just come off the southbound train. She has a hand-me-down look to her, like she came here without much more than the coat on her back, although she claims she’s a dressmaker who’d clothed grand dames in Philadelphia. Says her name is Lacey Castine, and she has a bit of land, fifteen acres near Magnolia. She asks for a ride, handing him a piece of paper with the place she’s headed.”

Valerie furnished another manila folder. “Turns out the elder Nichols kept that note. And his son gave it to me.”

She handed me a piece of paper folded four ways. On one square was written:

SPLIT OAK LN-15 AC WEST/CREEKBED. C.F.

C.F.? Could Lacey have meant Calvin Fortune? How would she even have known him before she moved to town? And also, how did a Philadelphia girl come to get land in Virginia, anyway?

Aiming my phone, I took a picture. “Seems pack-ratty for Mr. Nichols to hang on to a random piece of paper,” I muttered.

Valerie unfolded it. I changed my mind. “Oh, that’s pretty!” Inside was a hand-drawn sketch of a vague feminine figure, drawn in motion as if dancing. The figure wore a short white dress with a circular skirt that flared like the roof of a carousel, tied with a turquoise sash. It was a beautiful drawing, even with the paper yellowed along the creases. Notes were scribbled along the margins. It reminded me a little of the vague sketches *I* made when I was thinking out a costume.

"Gorgeous, isn't it."

"It looks like a stage costume. Only an actress would wear a knee-length dress like that in 1910." Squinting, I read the notes on the margins: *sil taf,* along with something that looked like a craft recipe: *1T cornstarch, bottle white glue, blg water*. And something else: *corst bon.*

"Huh." I flipped to another photograph of a lithe young woman amid the early 1920s streetscape, holding a child's hand. She wore a pale dress that fell just past her knees and a fringed satchel looped over one shoulder. Her hair was hidden beneath a small, rounded hat.

"I'm certain that's her, your great-great-grandmother Lacey," Valerie told me. "With Fawnie."

The woman's light-skinned child carried a little doll and stared at a passing automobile. I thought of the half-black, half-white doll in my bedroom.

"What does my mom think of all this?"

"I only talked to Mr. Nichols three years ago. He and Jabari's dad had been estranged for years, that's why. But by then, your mother and I weren't speaking. I reached out to Radiance since then, but—no. She doesn't know."

The teakettle shrieked, interrupting the quiet.

"You know what, Valerie? You should open a shop. Coffee and tea, right in downtown Magnolia. With all your botanical blends and sweets."

"A coffee shop?"

"Yes!"

She chuckled. "Baby, that sounds all well and good, but a few things you got to keep in mind. First of all, around here, folks be too slow for espresso. And second, I would have no idea how to run anything like that."

"But you manage Trianon."

She ignored me. "Well, I don't have coffee-shop money, and even if I did, I'm sixty-six. Too old to start a business."

"That's too bad," I said. "Because it could honor what was here. You could call it The Gather: a Coffee and Teahouse." I described to her what floated into my imagination: a shop with the antiques crowding Valerie's home, and flowers growing everywhere. It could host book clubs, poetry readings, anything! Everything I dreamed up rolled out like the hot water she poured for me.

"Oh, honey." She paused, looking up, kettle in hand. Her eyes seemed to flicker with hope, but it was a trick of the light. "That's cute." She didn't sound amused at all, though. She sounded bummed, really bummed.

CHAPTER 13

FAWNIE: So what you want me to tell you, baby? What's this all about?

VALERIE: I'm collecting stories. About The Gather.

FAWNIE: Stories about The Gather? Sounds like something Radiance would do.

VALERIE: Doesn't it? [*laughter*] I just have a few questions. This is being recorded, okay?

FAWNIE: That's all right.

Jabari had sent the audio files a few days after my talk with Valerie, but he'd done one better and typed transcripts. Still, I decided to play the interview. There was a Sophronia who I never knew. She was buried out back, beyond the view of my window. I felt connected to her.

And there was this Sophronia. I had no memory of her but we'd met eighteen years ago. It was so strange hearing her voice, although I'd heard her before, on the day I helped Mom at Stonepost. Gramma's tone matched Mom's in its high, fluty pitch. But Mom's diction was crisp and sharp, and my great-grandmother spoke in a long, drawn-out drawl, distinctly Southern.

Valerie's next question was lost to static, but then Gramma's voice rang out again, clear and slow.

FAWNIE: My full name is Sophronia Fortune Castine. I was born right here in The Gather on Christmas Eve, 1916. Mama said I was a little bitty thing, just four pounds. I came almost two months early and almost didn't make it. Lived up to my middle name.

VALERIE: Tell me where that came from. Who are your people?

FAWNIE: Well, my mama was Lacey Castine. My father was Calvin Fortune. They never did marry, but I suppose they never had the chance, because my daddy died before I was born. He was much, much older, see. You know who his father was, right?

VALERIE: I do, but can you tell the tape, Ms. Castine?

FAWNIE: My granddaddy's name was Cuffee Fortune. He founded The Gather, and he founded the college. He was born a slave, and he took the last name Fortune after freedom came. Cuffee was an African name from his father. It means born on Friday.

VALERIE: How did you find this all out?

FAWNIE: Well, he left a memoir to his son Calvin, my father. And those pages wound their way to me. I no longer have them, as things go, but I've read every word.

Gramma described how Cuffee's Magnolia parcel of land, given to him by Tom Dearborn, became The Gather. Years later, with The Gather's schoolhouse swelling to its rafters, Cuffee boarded a train to shake hands and raise money, like Mom did at the beginning of her college presidency. Now the recording sounded familiar—I'd heard this part at that awful Stonepost board meeting. How Cuffee had visited the homes of well-resourced Black families in Philadelphia. I imagined him sitting in meticulously furnished parlors, a felt hat upon his lap.

It wasn't until 1902, after a very significant gift, that he pulled together enough cash to open the Colored Teacher's College on what was then a lonely outpost of overgrown land with nothing left but the crumbling walls of the long-gone Harper Inn. Cuffee had the ruins torn down. He hired Black builders and contractors, and he supervised the construction of the campus. But more than that, he decided on a collaborative model of study.

Fawnie Castine was detailed in her retelling, offering dates and names. When the railroad came through that same year, up sprang the worth of Cuffee's property. Whites began to both resent and desire the school that would soon open on newly valuable land.

One student arrived early. He boarded with a nearby family, eagerly anticipating the first day. My great-grandmother drew in a breath. I could hear it, deep and raspy.

FAWNIE: He was Milliard Walker—smart-looking boy. Spectacles and all, my granddaddy described him. He was—it was almost the same—oh, I'm so sorry.

VALERIE: You can talk about it, Ms. Castine.

FAWNIE: It was a lynching. Just like—I've said enough.

There was a long stillness before the melody of her story resumed. Local whites promised more violence to students, and Cuffee had no choice but to abandon his dream. The Colored Teacher's College would not open. Vermilion P. Harper swooped in, backed by others. They took the land, the buildings. They drew up bogus deeds. And they opened a new college, named after a feature at Harper's great-grandfather's tavern that brought it the most patronage: a stone post jutting from the ground like a tombstone. A slave auction block. A place where white men once clustered around, drinking beer, casting bids and spending cash on human flesh. The college remained whites-only until 1969.

There was another silence, this time from me as I paused the recording. Whatever was said or wasn't in that deep, ragged breath Gramma took felt heavy and tragic.

I needed a break. Stretching, I went downstairs and made some tea from the new blend Valerie had given me. I pulled on a rain jacket and stepped outside for a walk around the property. The air was as soggy as cereal. The rain had dissuaded me from visiting the apartment above Buried Silver this morning to put in an hour of work. I was grateful. As it was, all I thought of now was a Confederate flag, coiled like a snake behind a doorway.

Mom had come home and made herself tea from the same tin. I found her settled in the library, clacking away on her laptop.

"Where'd you get this tea?" she asked. "It's amazing."

"Valerie." I threw out her name like a grenade. Mom frowned at her cup.

"And you know what? Gramma's mom, Lacey Castine? Valerie said she was born up north."

Mom put down her mug. "She's absolutely wrong. Lacey was born here in central Virginia."

"Do you have her birth certificate?"

Mom turned back to her laptop. "Many county records were damaged by a flood in 1969. That's why there's no birth record for her."

"Have you checked records up north?"

"There's no reason. I've never heard anything about Lacey living anywhere other than Magnolia."

"But Valerie found something else. Evidence. She tried to call you three years ago but . . ."

"Noni, this isn't a court case."

But might have well been to me. "Valerie interviewed an older resident of The Gather, and he said that his father said Lacey Castine . . ."

Mom yanked off her glasses. "If this *were* a court of law, you'd lose. That is hearsay. Not history." Though she glared up at me, she didn't miss a beat as she typed.

"But in Afro American lit, they always talk about how important oral tradition is," I pointed out. "*You* talk about it in your book."

She kept her sharp eyes fastened on me. "Valerie Golden's not a reliable source of anything. She relies on Lana Jean Chilton for her income. I wouldn't trust a thing she says. And sometimes oral history has to be corroborated by written sources, anyway. If you would excuse me, that's what I'm trying to do. I need documentation when I present the name-change to the board again in two weeks."

I knew she didn't want another belittling board meeting. I should have left it alone. But I couldn't. "What's your deal with Valerie? It's not just that she works for Lana Jean, is it?"

"Did you not hear me?"

"Seriously, what is it?"

"Get out of my office, Noni."

"Just tell me . . ."

"Get out!" My mother banged on her desk. The sound seemed to startle us both.

Back in my room, I heard the back door shut hard, and I turned to the window. Mom strode downhill, the hood of her rain jacket too small to cover her volume of hair. An awning of tight curls pushed out above her forehead. I went downstairs. She'd left her hot tea on her desk.

She didn't want to hear anything about Lacey living up north because Valerie said it. Maybe if I could prove Valerie right, I could also prove Mom's anger at her was just emotion that clouded her reason. I finished Mom's tea and pawed through her genealogy records, pausing at a few photographs. There was one of Cal Fortune, the man who passed down the memoir that Gramma had been forced to sell to pay for her daughter's medical bills. In the picture, Cal was middle-aged with creases around his mouth, deepened by smoking a pipe. There was an image of Cuffee Fortune, too. He was trim like he was in the other picture I'd seen of him wearing overalls. But here, he was younger, posed in his Union Army uniform, a resolute expression on his face.

There were plenty of pictures of Gramma, but I now studied some from her younger days. People said the two of us looked alike because she had the same babyish face. She carried hers her whole life, wrinkles and all. Her eyes were hazel, her hair reddish brown.

And there were pictures of Mom and Dad during their simple courthouse wedding. Dad was slimmer then and wore a flowered tie. Mom had a short 'fro and a poufing tummy because I was lodged in there.

Then I located the old birth roster that listed Gramma's: the date, and her parents' names, Lacey Castine and Calvin Fortune. But there wasn't any line for Lacey's birthplace.

Mom's research on a family history website mostly zeroed in on Cuffee's ancestry. She had never even done one of those genetic tests, although looking back, I felt bad I'd ever asked about it. It was shortly after my parents had told me they were splitting. This was something we could all do together, I had said.

Of course it was a last-ditch attempt at bonding, a splash of water tossed on a bonfire, putting nothing out. My father had ignored me. My mother had sighed. "Noni. No."

That's when I had remembered. She didn't know who her father was. And she never wanted to find out. I had friends at school who'd been adopted. Some didn't care to know about their birth parents, but others had gone on sleuthing missions to find them. If I didn't know who my dad was, maybe I'd become Sherlock Holmes, too.

Or rather, Sherlock *Homes*. Trying to find my way to wherever I belonged.

Maybe Lacey had wanted to find a sense of home, too. But on Mom's family history website, I found no records before 1910, even after two hours of searching when I felt cross-eyed. After I typed in every alternate spelling of "Lacey" and "Castine" I could think of, I wondered if Lacey was a nickname and keyed in every possible way to reach Leticia, Alice, Cecile. Everyone was born in the wrong decade, or spent their entire life in Nebraska, or was white, or all the above. It was like my maternal lineage sprang from nowhere.

VALERIE: Can you tell me about your mama's people?

FAWNIE: I never knew much about Mama's father. He was born in Virginia, I believe. Her mother was from Florida, but not near the water, I remember that.

VALERIE: Do you have any good memories of your grandparents?

FAWNIE: I never met them, and all Mama would say was, "They were gone long before you were here." But I've got some good memories of my mother, Lacey Castine. She dressed fashionable enough to make the white girls jealous. And she was beautiful, couldn't no one forget that.

VALERIE: What did she do? For work?

FAWNIE: She was a dressmaker. She'd been a fine seamstress since she was a girl. Oh, our house was papered with drawings of her designs. Mama never went nowhere without a beautiful satchel she made herself. It was always full of pieces she was working on, of sketches and her set of Dixon colored pencils.

VALERIE: She enjoyed her work, then?

FAWNIE: It frustrated her. Wasn't no shop that would hire her under their roof. The white boutique owner in town only paid Mama for piecework, even though she made the whole dress, pattern and all. Mama only had one exclusive client to herself—the white woman took the rest of the well-to-do ladies, passing off my mother's work for her own.

BUT that's what she needed to do, to provide. We ate good food, and we always had new shoes, warm coats, and yards of pretty fabric for dresses. None of that scraping and scrapping others did when the Depression got going.

VALERIE: Where did y'all live?

FAWNIE: She owned a little house on Split Oak Lane, just me and her. With a big yard and a garden.

Our house was set apart from everything else in The Gather, real private. But if you went across the dry creek bed you'd be right at the old senator's hunting cabin, so I never roamed far.

VALERIE: I can see why. You like to get shot.

FAWNIE: [*laughter*] I know that's right. There was nothing that ol' senator hated more than a colored person. We hated him right back.

AND child, I'll never forget that gown Mama made for that wretched man's wife, for some fancy ball. Mama had ordered mother-of-pearl buttons for some ivory satin. I was eight years old, and I begged and begged to get them from the store. She was in such a rush, she let me.

MY play uncle drove me into town. Well, I was supposed to run across the fairgrounds to the fabric shop at 155 Main Street. That's what it was called then. I'll never forget that address, never. I was to go in and ask for those buttons. Then I was to run back to my uncle.

I was so excited. The Gather had a little dry-goods store, and a bakery and things, but Main Street had specialty stores with shiny display windows and white folks from all walks of life. So I was gawking at everything. FINALLY I buy those buttons, and they were so pretty, I took them right out of the packet to watch them roll in my palm. Then a lady comes out of the shop next door. She's wearing a feathered hat and a lace dress. She drops this handkerchief, and it's embroidered with her initials: *PLH*, I'll never forget that. And she's walking down the street, not even noticing. So I pick up the handkerchief, run up to her and say, "Excuse me, ma'am, you dropped this." SHE took one look at my Black face, then reached out her gloved hand and slapped me with all her might. Slapped me hard enough to send me spinning, sent those buttons flying clean out of my hand. I tumbled to the ground, and oh—I hurt—inside and out. I lay crumpled on that dirt road like a rag, watching her walk away. Because that's all she did after she hit me. Just walked away like nothing happened.

VALERIE: Ms. Castine, I'm sorry.

FAWNIE: I cannot forget. Especially after I found out who she was.

VALERIE: Who?

FAWNIE: Priscilla Harper. Senator Harper's wife. My mama's only exclusive client. The woman she was making the dress for.

VALERIE: [*an audible breath*]

FAWNIE: I still feel it sometimes. That slap. Like how they say you can feel your arm even if it's amputated. What do they call it? Ghost pain. I've never seen that kind of hate in a person's eyes. It was a special kind. And the mark she left? It flowered on my cheek, big as a hibiscus bloom.

'COURSE, I came home and told stories. Said I fell while running. Mama didn't believe me, but she never did pry from me what I wouldn't tell. That's another thing about Lacey Castine. She respected secrets. Sometimes I almost wonder if she kept some from me.

The next morning, I readied my backpack for a lengthy day. I would pick up a breakfast shift at Charm for Darlie, whose babysitter had bailed. I would go to the apartment above Buried Silver to try again to figure out how to re-create the dress Lacey Castine made a century ago.

But as I picked up a folder of sketches and notes—another attempt at creating a pattern I had worked on only two days ago—I reconsidered. My great-grandmother would have been eight years old in 1924. After she bought the buttons for a gown her mother was sewing for Priscilla Lavigne Harper, a gown shaped like a magnolia blossom, this "exclusive client" struck Gramma across the face for the mere transgression of existing.

Thoomp. The folder landed in the recycling bin. I had taken on sewing this replica with the hope of discovering the secrets of another young white woman, Sophie Dearborn. But I felt white-womaned out.

Instead, I thought about Gramma. And Lacey. Black women, my kinswomen. Was there more to their stories?

I would tell Cicada and Lana Jean Chilton that I would not make the dress. I had my own family secrets to uncover.

"The sweet, white-haired gentleman!" Bernice Haney was Tangleroot's owner before Mom had moved in. She was delighted that Will had given me her number and peppered me with questions: How was he? How was his store? My mother must be thrilled to be here—how had she decorated the Tangleroot house?

I swear it was twenty minutes before I could get to what I'd called about. "Will thought maybe you'd know a little about the history of the house."

"I don't know much, even though you'd think I would. I was born at Tangleroot, and I'm seventy-eight years old. You must be in the girl's room. With those cunning fashion plates. Must have belonged to a real-life Scarlett O'Hara. That was my room growing up!"

Pacing the old floorboards, I winced. I had watched *Gone with the Wind* once when Mom wasn't home. I thought of the scene when Scarlett struck Prissy, an enslaved woman. How had I ever considered making a gown for Cicada Chilton?

Yesterday, I had decided so resolutely that I would break the news to her that I wouldn't sew it. But now my fingers froze above my phone keyboard. I couldn't find the words. How would I tell Cicada I'd changed my mind—and how would I tell Lana Jean?

I glanced up at the door. "That's actually what I'm calling about." I described the ripped scrap of paper tacked to the upper corner to Mrs. Haney. There was a little shading of turquoise near the rip: the same shade of turquoise as the sash in the dress sketch my great-great-grandma Lacey Castine made notes on. So I thought about what Gramma said about Lacey always carrying sketches and colored pencils around.

It was a long shot, a shot from miles away—but was it possible that somehow Lacey had scribbled on both pages with the same turquoise pencil? That she had once been in this very room?

"Oh, yes, that!" Mrs. Haney was excitable. "When I grew up, there was a whole bunch of papers attached to the closet door. Will you believe it, they were sketches."

I perked up. "What kind of sketches?"

"Of dresses! Like some other teenaged girl had lived there and drawn them, like she'd wanted to be a fashion designer."

"Really?"

"Oh yes. If I remember right, my grandmother found those papers in a pretty bag when *she* moved in after the house had been vacant for some years. That was 1912. I know that, because it was the same day the *Titanic* sank. She assumed the satchel belonged to the girl who'd pasted the fashion plates onto the doors, so she just tacked the sketches up there. Of course, I knew better, because the fashions were from different eras. I don't know what became of the tote. I'm guessing my grandma kept it for herself."

"What about the sketches?"

"Well, one of my children ripped the whole batch down! That was fifty years ago. I figured they were old and valuable, so I sent them to the historical society in Philadelphia."

"Why there?"

"Because 'Philadelphia' was written on one of those pictures. The girl signed her name, too, but heck if I could make it out."

CHAPTER 14

In the dim and lamp-lit reading room, I spread the papers across the long table. There were a dozen hand-drawn sketches of gowns. Rather than the bell-shaped skirts pasted on my closet door, these dresses boasted slimmer silhouettes and graceful trains. But unlike those fully formed figures, these were vague, and seemed to be dynamic. Women were drawn striding, moving, waltzing. You could make a flip-book out of all the papers.

"The artist sketched dresses from the Edwardian era, the early 1900s." Hershel Ashe, the Historical Society of Pennsylvania's senior curator, was a tall, large man who spoke in a low, slow voice. He sounded disinterested, even grumpy, but he knew what I was looking for even when I struggled to describe it. I hadn't called in advance, I'd just shown up blabbering about dresses at the front desk.

The trip to Philadelphia was a surprise, even for me. Spring break had snuck up on me, and Mom reminded me she was leaving town again, which meant I could secretly travel. I was able to get my Charm shifts covered for a couple of days, and thankful not to have the chunky commitment of Cicada Chilton's magnolia gown—not that Cicada knew. Yet. Telling her no seemed more difficult than figuring out how to make the dress. I would text Cicada, I just needed to think of a way to say why I changed my mind.

Because how could I sew the dress, after what I learned about the woman my great-great-grandmother created it for? The woman who slapped Fawnie Castine, my gramma?

But I had to figure out what was up with the scrap tacked to my closet door, the one shaded with turquoise pencil. If somehow, my great-great-grandmother Lacey had been in the bedroom belonging to a dead white slaveholding girl. Maybe I could prove to Mom that Valerie was right—that our maternal line originated up north.

And then maybe, Mom would learn to trust Valerie again.

Hershel set out a sketched blue-green dress on a figure with her undefined arms outstretched, a gown with a flurry of sheer panels, like ruffles on the ocean. I breathed in deeply, because it looked so much like the dress I'd designed and sewn as the character Miranda's wedding gown in *The Tempest*.

And because the bottom corner of the page was torn off. "Wow. There it is," I said.

"Fits perfectly." Hershel watched as I puzzle-pieced the ripped scrap of paper from my closet. "When I started work here twelve years ago, the retiring senior curator told me of a tradition: Every new senior curator was challenged with finding the source of a random package that arrived in 1966. It was just this packet of sketches. The envelope didn't even list a return address or name: just 'Tangleroot.'"

The staff couldn't find Tangleroot on a map, Hershel said, nor did it make sense in any other context. All they could do was file the contents.

"This is history happening right now." Hershel surveyed the sketches. "So these belong to your great-great-grandmother?"

This was my great, great disappointment. "They can't," I said glumly. "*Her* name was Lacey Castine. Not whatever this is." I pointed to the signatures on all the sketches, the long name scrawled in an unreadable hand—a capital *T* and a scramble of other letters I couldn't make out. But the name definitely wasn't Lacey. The only legible word was *Philadelphia*, written clearly at the bottom corner of the turquoise dress picture, opposite the page's rip.

Hershel gently smoothed the folded sheet I'd borrowed from Valerie, the one with notes scrawled on the back. He said what I was thinking: "But this 1910 sketch"—he gestured to Lacey Castine's creased sheet—"is the same artistic style as the Tangleroot sketches. Of course, this dress must be a costume, since—"

"Since only an actress would wear something so short in 1910." I finished his sentence. He looked surprised. "I basically, like, study stage costumes," I said. "And I'm taking a theater history class."

"Are you?"

I nodded. With his index finger, Hershel underlined *Philadelphia* on the Tangleroot sketches. "Look at the handwriting. The same as in the 1910 notes. Was your great-great-grandmother an actress?"

"No. She was a seamstress, but this signature, whatever it is, definitely isn't 'Lacey.'" I pointed out the long *T*-word.

"Could Lacey be a diminutive?"

"Maybe. But for what?"

We were wordless. If Lacey was a nickname, we faced a dead end in finding any trace of her without knowing the whole of it.

Carefully, he put away the papers. "I'll show you a project I'm working on," he finally said. "So maybe this trip can be of some use."

His dejection reminded me of Ming Xiàng's, the Virginia archivist's, when we couldn't find enough traces of Sophie Dearborn to complete her story. It was the same letdown all over again. So even though I wasn't all that curious about whatever Hershel was working on, I followed him into another room full of wide worktables. Each was topped with large art prints in stunning, bold colors. "What are these?"

"I'm curating a theater exhibition. They're old posters for plays and performances," Hershel said. "Late 1800s, early 1900s."

"Wow." They reminded me a little of the fashion prints glued to Sophie Dearborn's door, but these images were huge, the colors as vibrant as wet nail polish. And the posters told a story. There were illustrations of desperate women begging husbands for forgiveness, or swooning as swashbucklers rescued them, in melodramas with titles like

The Wages of Sin or *Only a Farmer's Daughter*. A quintet of women wearing short, tight dresses jumped rope in *Skiptomania*. Limber men scaled colorful ladders for a showcase of Russian athletes. There were cowboys and Indians, pirates, and—

Minstrels. Atop a corner table, a black face with wild hair and a broad mouth outlined in bright pink gaped up at me. I regarded the bony nose, the ring of pale skin around the eyes. This was a white man who'd been painted like a wall. "Spectacular Minstrel Show!" the poster crowed.

"We have our share of these kinds of materials. An intern compiled these, but I'm not including them in the exhibition," Hershel remarked.

"You're not? Why?"

"They're putridly offensive, in case you haven't noticed."

"You could display a content warning. I mean, this all *happened*. People should know about it." I had heard of minstrel shows, and besides, I'd read several chapters ahead in my American Theater textbook. Way back when, white performers would use makeup to color their faces black, then sing and dance and act like what they considered stereotypical slaves. Blackface. And yeah, it *was* hurtful. I remembered Laronté's hands smoothly conjuring an imaginary cane in the chilled night air. Of course, it's not as if Black folks ever actually performed in minstrel theater, or even watched it.

Then I noticed a photograph of two men with slick, painted-on black faces. One had a thin nose and lips, but the other man's features were broad and supple. "Who is he?" My finger hovered above his face.

"He's an African American performer," Hershel told me.

"But . . ." This didn't make sense. A Black minstrel performer?

"In the late nineteenth and early twentieth century, minstrel theater began attracting Black audiences, and even Black performers."

As he explained more, my mind spun. I had no idea.

Hershel then showed me a handbill:

Smiles! Laughter! Screams!
An Evening of Fun
McCabe & Young's
The Leaders of All the Colored Minstrels
Each Member an Educated Gentleman as
Well as a Performer

"Did anyone . . . complain about this?" I asked.

Hershel produced a newspaper article from 1909. "I would call this opinion piece a complaint."

"Hoyt Askew." I murmured the author's name. It nagged at me, like I'd seen it before.

"He was an African American teacher," Hershel informed me. "Quite a voice in Philadelphia. We have a file of his papers and ephemera."

"'Minstrels No More!'" I read the headline aloud. "'We must forever draw the curtains upon minstrel theater. It is a scourge, a flagrant affront! How can we find levity in these belittling farces? With every laugh, there dies a hope of our people, fading into the raucous hall . . .'" Wow, where was this when I'd studied for my SATs?

And more relevant to now, was Hershel right not to include the minstrel theater pieces in his exhibition, out of concern for offending people? Or was *I* right that it should be displayed and rediscovered? I wished I could tell Mom about my visit to Philly. I wished we could talk through this together.

And I wished I could show her the sketch of that gown, the figure's shape almost like the signature below—a tall letter *T* and a tousle of others, a long word. The flounced and fluffy train like sea-foam. Now my great-grandmother's words sounded in my head: *Her mother was from Florida, but not near the water.*

Not near the water.

Tallahassee.

"Holy shit." Everything clicked. I turned to Hershel. "Tallahassee! She's the girl. The one who sketched the Tangleroot papers."

The men would've gathered in the parlor of a narrow brick row home, one not far from where I now sat with my laptop open and "ephemera"—as Hershel called materials like newspaper clippings and pamphlets—spread around me. A handbill told me this, part of the cache of records the historical society had filed in a box simply labeled *Miscl. Ephemera.* It was a square of ivory paper with delicate edges that flaked away. I read and reread every astonishing word.

MR. C.F. OF VIRGINIA

IS NOW IN THE CITY (823 WAVERLY ST.) SOLICITING FUNDS FOR THE FOUNDING OF A COLLEGE FOR COLORED STUDENTS

FINANCE COMMITTEE

MR. HOYT ASKEW, CHAIR

MR. NIGEL ASKEW

MR. WILLIAM STILL SR.

MR. JACOB C. WHITE JR.

Hoyt Askew, who lived on 823 Waverly according to the records, wasn't just a teacher and an opinionated writer. He was family. His daughter Tallahassee was named for his mother's hometown in "Florida, but not near the water," as Gramma once recalled.

Later, she would be called Lacey, and she would become my great-great-grandmother.

The Askews were stars in Philadelphia's thriving Black community. People didn't just sit around at home darning socks back then. By the way the "ephemera" told it, middle-class Black folks were busy with receptions, concerts, meetings, alumni events, or fundraising efforts: like raising money for a new college.

Could "C.F." have been Cuffee Fortune? Maybe, just maybe, I had stumbled upon the very documentation my mother needed, just by prying a little into the slender records that Tallahassee Askew, aka Lacey Castine, had left behind.

I opened another folder. A newspaper clipping like a snake's tongue slipped out onto the table. The 1902 article recorded:

> . . . Miss A., while serving coffee to her father and his guests, asked the committee if she might set about raising a store of money for the College. She then wrote to the U.S. War Department, humbly requesting flags flown by United States Colored Troops of the Civil War. The Department, with little storage space for such relics, obliged. Miss A. created a "crazy quilt" from these tattered colors. In a bidding, a Negro millionaire pledged the highest amount. Rather than keep the prize for himself, he gifted it to the institution.

Frustratingly, there were no full names. Just initials. But it could be that my great-great-grandmother, the inspiration for my middle name, sewed the very quilt Mom took down from Stonepost College's wall with Union flags, not remnants of the Confederacy. This could be the documentation my mom needed to at least get a name-change vote considered at Stonepost. But how could I tell her?

Also, what *was* Lacey, a girl born and raised in Philadelphia, doing in my bedroom five hundred miles away? I needed to find out everything I could about her so I could—

And that's where I drew a blank. There was no record of Tallahassee Askew ever marrying. But why else would she claim another last name? Or another first name, for that matter.

And, Tallahassee disappeared from the records after 1910, when she was present on a Philadelphia census taken that year. But the name Lacey Castine popped up from nowhere, appearing in the Virginia census report, also in 1910.

What was going on?

I kept digging, finding a 1907 ad in the *Philadelphia Inquirer,* the largest city paper, one with a mostly white readership.

DRESSMAKER, colored. excellent pattern design and drafting. Please call 823 Waverly St.

That was the Askew address. Lacey, aka Tallahassee, would've been seventeen, living with her parents and working. There was no record of her attending college like her parents and her brother.

I searched further, finding a few more dressmaker ads from the Askew house. But at twenty, Tallahassee was living on her own on the eighth block of Minister Street. Meanwhile, her older brother was still residing with their folks.

Minister Street was in a rough part of town, according to an old map. She would've lived in a cramped, crowded boardinghouse. She took out one ad from that address and then stopped, as if realizing none of the clients she was seeking would ever call on her there.

So why had she ever left her parents' place at all?

"Minstrel shows?" My father sipped his foamy beer. Good thing Hershel, the curator, had shown me his theater exhibition in progress, because it was a convenient excuse I could hand to Dad about why I was in Philadelphia. I was staying with my cousin Kadeem, who hadn't asked many questions. But he *had* blabbed to Dad that I was visiting, since my father was due to check in with his company's Philly office. So Dad extended his trip to have dinner with me.

"That must be a tough thing to study in class," he remarked.

"It's okay to talk about difficult stuff, Dad." Like moving across the country, I should have added, and not telling your kid until you'd already left. Instead, I explained, "Minstrel theater was a big part of show business starting in, like, the 1830s. Next thing you knew, Black audiences started watching it. Black actors even performed in blackface."

"Huh." We sat outside a German restaurant in an open stall that reminded me of the cowshed at Charm. Propane heaters radiated warmth into the chilly March air.

"So yeah, some people in the African American community complained about minstrel theater, but a bunch of us just thought it was entertaining." There I was, saying "us" again like Mom, when I wasn't even a glimmer in my grandparents' eyes back then. Ugh. Also, yuck.

"How could we *not* be offended?" Kadeem seemed surprised. I described what Hershel had told me: By the time we got into minstrel theater in the late 1800s, white folks had been getting rich on it for decades. Every individual had different motivations, but for some Black people it could've been a reclamation: comedy by us, for us, with *our* spin, the way we did everything.

Intellectuals like Frederick Douglass and W. E. B. DuBois did not agree, I explained. I left out my own ancestor, Hoyt Askew.

"But you know of course that blackface isn't okay now," Dad said cautiously. "Like when frat boys do it."

"Hell no, it's racist," I agreed. He nodded approvingly. That's what I liked about Dad. He didn't flinch over mild cursing.

"I guess it's kinda like how some of us can laugh at Black comedians slinging the n-word, and others of us are offended," Kadeem brought up.

"The same kind of shit my parents gave me about N.W.A. and Tupac when I was your age," Dad told me. "Violence, the n-word, drugs, misogyny. But their music was the bomb. Still is."

I didn't even giggle at his oldfangled slang. "And maybe your parents had a point. And maybe they didn't."

The server came by. Kadeem pointed out a dish on the menu. "How's this sound? Berkshire pork shank with kraut and spaetzle? It's big enough to share."

"Cool," I told him. The word *Berkshire* seemed familiar, just like how *Hoyt* had infused me with that sense of déjà vu. But this time, I also felt a sense of guilt.

Then I realized why. Fluvanna Fluharty raised Berkshire pigs. I remembered the name of her prizewinner: Paint It Black. An old Rolling Stones song that felt different now in light of our conversation.

"So besides racist traditions in theater, how's school?" Dad asked casually.

All three of us sputtered out awkward laughter. I caught Dad up. He traded tech stories with Kadeem, who coded for an online news network. Then my father asked me, "So how's Radiance? She up to anything new?"

There he was again, expecting me to talk about my mother's life, when he'd once hidden some lending scheme or whatever from her, just like he had hidden from me that he left Boston. "Mom's great," I said.

"Yeah? Does she get out at all?"

"Oh yeah. My boss is basically her best friend. She . . ."

"I remember Blondell." Dad cut me off. "Met her when you were a baby." I didn't know that, but it was clear he didn't want to talk about her. "Who else?"

If he wanted to know Mom's business, fine. "She clicked with this high school principal, Dr. Chapel. Oh, and she's really good friends with some guy. He owns an outdoor shop, and he's renting our cottage."

"Huh." Dad faked casual curiosity. My cousin finished his beer and signaled big to the server like it was an SOS, anything to avoid our conversation. Both Dad and my cousin ordered another drink, with Kadeem basically wanting a dissertation on all the beers on the menu. But Dad didn't skip a beat. Once the server left, he commented, "Sounds like Radiance hangs out with this guy a lot."

"Yeah."

Dad took a long sip of his pilsner, as if considering what else to ask. "So, just because I like to picture people, what does Radiance's friend look like?"

"He's tall." I lifted my shoulders. "He's fit."

"Is he . . . you know." Dad shrugged. "You know."

A group of cute white guys jostled by. I looked at them, even with Dad sitting there. Maybe especially with Dad sitting there. One of them grinned at me before immediately poker-facing when he noticed my dad and cousin—but not before I smiled back, my father watching the whole exchange. It was fun to feel pretty. "Is he what?" I asked innocently.

"Is he white or anything?"

"Jesus. Dad. Why are you even asking? I mean, *you* practically look white."

My father paled, then blushed. A loud, guttural whine of engines ripped through the air.

A dozen younger teens roared down South Street on dirt bikes and

ATVs. They reared up into wheelies and gunned past a red light. "The hell's that!" Dad yelled get-off-my-lawn-ishly, but I think he was relieved for the distraction.

"Kids do this all the time." Kadeem went into a whole thing about the eccentricities of South Philly. I loaded my plate up with Berkshire pork, feeling an all-too-familiar sense of guilt, this time for dangling Will around. But Dad deserved for me to fake him out that Mom and Will were dating. He should have told me he'd left Boston from the beginning. He shouldn't have talked about how great Portland was, instead of acknowledging that maybe I would feel a little abandoned with both my parents gone.

Boston was still home. It was where I'd grown up and where I needed to be if I wanted any future outside my mother's shadow. But I never imagined living there alone.

We are pained to announce the sudden death by apoplexy of Mr. THOMAS DEARBORN of TANGLEROOT, early in the forenoon of Sunday last. Mr. DEARBORN was in about his usual health and was at church when friends noticed he suddenly looked pale, even deathly, and was in a dying condition.

He was preceded in death by his beloved wife, Martha, and daughter Sophronia C. Dearborn. A small but loving circle attended his funeral, including Mr. George Harper III and Mr. Lemuel Paulding.

Also there to escort his remains to the grave were Negroes who showed their esteem for him: Foster and Cuffey, as well as young Hoyt who traveled from Philadelphia. Their presence thus too evinced their heartfelt sympathy with the bereaved ones.

⁂

"That's him." She nodded when I showed her the enlarged image of the obituary, printed out from a file I'd emailed her daughter-in-law. "That's my grandfather."

"And *my* great-great-great-grandfather," I said. This was Lacey's father. His name, Hoyt, had nagged at me so much as I rode the train home, I finally looked through all my online records to figure out why. And there he was, mentioned in connection with Sophie's father, Thomas Dearborn.

Mrs. Thelma Askew Tinsley opened a heavy, bible-sized photo album and planted a wrinkled finger right on top of a large eight-by-ten of a sober-looking man in an old-fashioned suit. "Here he is in 1878. Handsome, wasn't he?"

"He was," I said. Hoyt Askew was light-skinned with wavy hair combed back from a high, square forehead. It hadn't been too hard to locate another of his descendants, Mrs. Thelma Askew Tinsley. Online, I was able to find a record of an African American Nigel Askew living in Philadelphia, born in 1881 to Hoyt and Sarah. There weren't a lot of other Black dudes named Hoyt or Nigel in Philadelphia (none), so I figured I was looking at the right people. Searching through the hinterlands of Google yielded Nigel's obituary from the 1940s, which listed his four children. I was only able to find usable contact information for Thelma Tinsley, who lived in Frederick, Maryland. Her daughter-in-law answered my email just before my train stopped in Baltimore.

Cora Tinsley set a glass of lemonade in front of me. Thanking her, I asked the elder Mrs. Tinsley, "Do you remember your grandfather?"

"He died when I was a little girl, so I don't remember much. But my family always talked about him."

"Who were Hoyt's parents?"

"Walt and Maria Askew. But he was adopted, you know."

I hadn't known, but it seemed I was on to something. "Adopted?"

"That's right. They had children of their own, but they raised Hoyt as one of theirs."

Mrs. Tinsley turned the page, showing me an even older portrait of a family. The couple sat in chairs, surrounded by five children. The man was dressed in a Union soldier's uniform and cap like the ones Cuffee Fortune wore in an old picture. The woman was in a dark gown with a ruffled bustle, her hair in a frizzled updo. Hoyt Askew's light skin made him stand out among his darker siblings and parents.

"My great-aunt Carol"—Mrs. Tinsley planted her finger on the face of a little girl. "She was there when he learned who his real family was. Told me all about it."

"What did she say?" My heartbeat sped up.

"He received a letter when he was a young man, about your age. She remembers him clutching that letter, sinking down on the stairway of their home—they had a nice row home; their father worked as an undertaker and made good money—"

"What did the letter say?" I interrupted her.

"Um-hmm." She nodded like she was agreeing with me about something. "The man who wrote it said he was white."

"Yeah?"

"From Virginia."

"Virginia?"

"That's right. The white man was at the end of his life and said he knew Grandpa Hoyt was at the beginning of his, so he wanted to come clean with things."

"Like what?" I scooted my chair closer.

"Bloodlines." She nodded matter-of-factly. "He said he was Grandpa Hoyt's kin."

I almost jumped out of my seat. "What was his name?"

"Oh, child." She looked tired. My heart sank.

"Do you remember his name?" I tried not to seem too eager. "The white man's?"

"Baby, I don't. Aunt Carol must've told me, but I just can't recall." She sounded genuinely regretful. "If I could call her up from the grave, I'd ask. She had a sharp memory, that woman. Said Grandpa Hoyt was quiet as the dead for weeks afterward. Eventually, he wrote something back and the white man replied. They kept up a correspondence. Finally Grandpa Hoyt decided to visit. But the man died of a stroke while my grandfather was on the train, so they never met. Grandpa went to his funeral all the same."

Mrs. Tinsley touched her grandfather's photograph. "It was fitting. It turned out the white man willed Grandpa Hoyt a little land. 'Course, it was down in Virginia, wasn't much he could do with it."

But pass it on to his kids, I thought.

Mrs. Tinsley went on. "And in the early 1900s, Hoyt brought his children to the place he was born."

"He did?" I thought about the scrap of paper tacked to my closet door.

"It was an old plantation. The slave master had willed Grandpa some tokens that his white family refused to give him at the funeral, and Hoyt came to collect. It was while they were on their way to Florida. To Mrs. Askew's hometown on the panhandle."

Of course. The "Florida, but not near the water" business.

Mrs. Tinsley explained, "They stopped through Virginia to see about his land inheritance and to visit a college."

Stonepost!

"Though I'm not sure why. It was whites-only, that school."

But I knew. They wanted to see Lacey's quilt!

"Though they were able to walk right into the plantation master's house. Black folks had been hired to clean out the old place, and they gave Hoyt a crate in the basement, still tagged with his name. My grandfather sure did take those trinkets, useless as they were. He said he was reclaiming every bit of what he was owed."

"What kind of trinkets?"

"A shaving kit. Perfume bottles, I believe. Knickknacks. And something Aunt Carol remembered well: a locked jewelry box Hoyt gave his daughter. The girl's hopes were high. But once she wedged it open, there wasn't nothing in it but papers."

CHAPTER 15

I owe you an apology."

My mother's words nearly made me spit out my coffee. But there she was, standing in the kitchen, her favorite necklace gleaming against her skin. This was the day she was presenting to the board.

It was early. I had barely seen my mother for almost two weeks. After a conference in Houston, other out-of-town obligations came up. She'd texted: She'd be gone longer than expected. Would I be okay without her?

"I'm sorry." Mom met me with level eyes. "You had information about Gramma's mother. If I had listened, I wouldn't have had to scramble." Her face showed immense relief. "As it turns out, Lacey *was* from Philadelphia, and that information changed everything. It's further evidence that Cuffee Fortune founded Stonepost College."

"Really?" I feigned surprise.

Sure enough, Mom described receiving an email from a curator at the Historical Society of Pennsylvania who'd just *happened* to stumble upon some documents he thought that she, the president of a small Virginia college, might be interested in. "I was there eight months ago, and I pored over everything in the William Still and Jacob White collections, but there were files I missed."

I had asked Hershel to send Mom the newspaper article about the quilt, as well as the college fundraising handbill. Because I didn't want to give Mom any hint that I had been trying to uncover Sophie Dearborn's story, mum had to be the word about everything else.

That's why she also couldn't find out that Mrs. Tinsley and I had all but proven that Hoyt Askew, a Black man, was Thomas Dearborn's son.

But of what she did know, Mom was over the moon. In a rush,

she described how she re-listened to Gramma's interview. She always thought Gramma spoke of a "Hesky" family, but it was a misunderstanding of a Southern drawl. After Hershel's email, Mom visited other archives, tracking down purchases and donations. A historian friend flew up from Atlanta and studied the quilt, determining it was indeed likely made from United States Colored Troops flags. Vermilion Harper probably found the quilt in an old trunk. It seemed he was never the wiser.

"The one thing I couldn't figure out is what motivated Lacey Castine to change her name and move here. Inheriting fifteen acres is nice, but it almost seems as if something pushed her to start a whole new life."

"What do you mean?"

Opening her ever-present laptop, Mom flipped between two documents. "She appears as two names in the 1910 census. Tallahassee Askew was counted on January second in a Philadelphia boardinghouse." She toggled. "And Lacey Castine was counted on January twentieth in central Virginia. Between those dates, she reinvented herself. And here's what else I found out." Mom reached for the agave. "When, I, um . . . when I spoke to Valerie."

"You spoke to Valerie?"

"I did."

I almost wanted to give myself a hug. I had gone all the way to Philadelphia to prove Valerie right, in hopes her knowledge would draw Mom back to her.

And that's what had happened. Mom told me about Valerie's folded drawing, which I had returned after my trip. She described what she heard from Jabari's grandfather's interview: how Lacey Castine appeared on the train platform. How Mr. Nichols said she had a "hand-me-down look" to her.

"Perhaps she sold all her nicer garments that she'd made for herself. She needed money to travel. I wonder if there was a major rift between her and her parents. These are all inferences, of course. I don't have documentation of their relationship. But for Tallassee Askew to change her name to Lacey Castine—that's a major reach in starting over."

"Why do you think she chose the name Castine?"

"I always thought it was inherited. I never knew from whom. And when I tried searching some time ago, I hit dead ends. Perhaps it was a long-ago relative she'd heard of. Or some word from the time period—maybe an element of fashion." She looked at me. "Is there? A Castine stitch? A Castine sleeve? Castine lace?"

It flattered me that she leaned on my knowledge, but I had no answers. "I don't know, Mom. I'm sorry."

If she were not on her way to such a crucial meeting, maybe I would've told her about Cicada Chilton's gown. Maybe I would have confided how I had agreed to create it, and had even gotten into the construction of it, but that I couldn't find it in me to finish it—and that I was destined to infuriate Lana Jean.

"Do you think Lacey's parents may have left her on her own?" I asked.

My mother shook her head. "From everything I've seen, from how involved they were in the community as a family, it would surprise me. To never speak to her again? We can't know, but I also can't imagine her parents—" She broke off. "Like all of us, maybe they just needed time."

My mother turned away, placing her mug in the sink. "I should have accepted Valerie's call three years ago." She seemed to say this only to herself.

"Oh my god, Mom. Mom! She's naked!"

Mom leaned against the doorframe, arms folded. "I mean, only half," she said coolly.

The woman was dark-skinned, her short hair waving out from a perfectly oval face. The bodice of her short dress was peeled down, her arms folded around her body. The oil painting was good—the detail of her bent fingers, the beguiling look on her face, and the way the art displayed both side-boob and the dress. The dress was unusual, if a bit familiar: a white skirt that seemed to float in a perfect circle, as if it could spin like a top. An untied teal satin sash slithered across it. On the table beside her was a blue-and-white candleholder, a candle burned down to the nub. Smoldering.

"Mom, this is basically a nude." I was laughing and flipping out at the same time.

I was giddy. When I'd turned in my thesis statement for my capstone paper, Dr. Corn approved it with comment bars reading "Yes!" then "YES!!!!" and finally, "YAAASSS!!!"

A half hour ago, when I shared the statement with Mom, she went on and on about how it could be a "graduate-level" paper. She suggested I look at ephemera from her own collection about The Gather—that's how she came to pull out the flat box from a top shelf in the library. Still, a sense of dread buzzed inside me. I wanted to tell Mom about Cicada Chilton's gown. How I still couldn't bring it to myself to call her, and how I responded to her latest overenthusiastic text with a lie: *The dressmaking is going great!!! I'll be ready for a fitting soon.*

If my brain had an app like cell phones did, it would be called *ANX* for the anxiety I felt from lying. My angst ran constantly in the background of my mind, draining a boatload of battery power.

Soon Cicada would know the truth. So would Lana Jean. No amount of exclamation points in the world could forge their forgiveness then. And would Lana Jean try to get back at me in some way?

Still, it was so rare Mom and I had light moments like this. I couldn't ruin this one, not when she was proud of me.

"Who is this, Mom?" I held up the painting. The beautiful woman's eyes met mine.

"Honey, this is Lacey."

"Whaaa??? Is she? How do you know!" I just about died—with laughter, with excitement, with sheer I-don't-know-what. It's not every day you see your great-great-grandmother naked.

"The dress, sweetie."

For a moment, I cringed, picturing sections of ivory silk taffeta. And then I realized. "Oh my god, you're right, it's the dress she sketched, the one from Valerie's! Did Cuffee's son paint this?" I asked eagerly. The portrait was unsigned.

"Yes. Calvin Fortune. I never knew he was a painter until Gramma and I went through some of her mother's things some years ago." She laughed to herself. "I thought she'd have a stroke."

While Mom pulled through other files, I snapped a picture, and without thinking, sent it to Jabari. Quickly, I followed up with: *This is my great-great-grandma*. As if that helped.

He wrote back, *WTF?*

I'll explain later. But isn't she cool?

No comment.

"Wow." I laughed again. "Cal and Lacey must've had a crazy hot sex life."

"They had a deeply committed relationship."

"You can have both, Mom."

She looked at the ceiling. "Noted."

Holding the canvas against the wall, I asked, "Why don't we hang this? It's freaking awesome."

Mom just sighed, and the good mood between us faltered. I swore I could analyze her brain waves. It would be "inappropriate" and "unseemly" to display the picture.

"Noni." She spoke patiently. "It doesn't match the wallpaper here and would look better in the drawing room."

I grinned. She smiled back winningly. "Go grab the toolbox."

I hurried downstairs, then pulled the heavy 1950s Craftsman box from its shelf above the washing machine. It once belonged to Gramma. Mom wouldn't get rid of it, even though one of the hinges was busted.

That's when something occurred to me. I almost dropped the whole kit and caboodle right on the floor. "Mom!" I yelled as I rushed upstairs. "I just realized—I have to go. A research thing. Can we hang this up when I get back?"

Reggie Golden upturned the rectangular metal jug, stopping the opening with a rag. As he rubbed and circled the cloth along the rim of paint that was the color of his last name, I thought of Aladdin polishing the genie's lamp. The gleaming paint erased to reveal walnut, shined with the resin of the mineral spirits. Only a half hour ago, I had arrived on Valerie's doorstep for another surprise visit. In a rush, I told her how pieces had come together like glass in the mosaicked surface of the sewing table I stared down upon. A teenaged Lacey Castine—then known as Tallahassee Askew—had visited Tangleroot once with her family, to claim her inheritance. And there, in the very bedroom that once belonged to Sophie Dearborn, she accidently left her satchel. All she'd gotten in return was a jewelry box she had to force open.

Perhaps it was a legacy she decided to hold on to, broken though it was. Her father was Thomas Dearborn's son. Sophie Dearborn had therefore been her aunt, one who had passed along to her a love of pretty things to wear. If Lacey had kept the lockbox, she might have stored it inside the sewing table.

Reggie gently opened the sewing table lid. But there was nothing inside but white quilt batting, neatly folded like a comforter.

"Unfold it, honey," Valerie instructed. Words from the song I'd played in Lana Jean Chilton's living room chimed inside my head. "Furl it! For the hands that grasped it / And the hearts that fondly clasped it / Cold and dead are lying low . . ."

I remembered the Confederate flag rolled in a corner of the apartment above Buried Silver. I realized that song, "The Conquered Banner," romanticized those stars-and-bars and the men who fought to keep slavery the law of the land.

And Valerie, I understood, felt there were honors *I* should do. She sensed something other than cotton was nestled in that sewing table. "Carefully," she intoned.

Sure enough, wrapped within was a small wooden box with a keyhole, the lid half lifted, the hinges snapped from moorings as if someone had pried the box open.

And inside, there were papers. Small sheets of paper with ripped edges as if they'd been torn from a book. Handwriting curled across yellowed blankness. Written across the top of the first page was what I'd hoped I'd see: a date, 1858. My eyes took in the word *Tangleroot* in the first line of lacy scrawl.

I made an excitable call to Ming Xiàng at the Library of Virginia as I paced around my bedroom. When I sent her a photo, she surmised they were diary entries. "Maybe they were pages she wanted to keep. Maybe she burned the rest of the diary. Or, the other way around. She could've torn these papers from the binding, intending to destroy them, but dying before she had the chance."

Ming said I could read them at home, but cautioned me to wash my hands before touching the papers, to reduce oils from my skin damaging them. I was to draw the shades and read at the lowest light possible. There would be no drinking tea while I read, nor coffee or even water—I could not risk staining the papers. Then, I could bring the originals to Richmond. It would be my gift to the Library of Virginia, but also to the public. After all, the library would digitize the papers, making them accessible to everyone.

Stretching, I walked around my room, as if seeing it with different eyes. The jewelry box, small and dull, would have once been polished and precious. The topsy-turvy doll would've once been new, the Black doll ever-beloved as she faded like the Velveteen Rabbit. I studied the peeling fashion plates adhered to my closet doors. They too would have once been carefully pasted there, each corner laid down, the way I smoothed my edges when I wore my hair back.

As I had done many times before, I browsed the little squares of descriptions cut out and pasted on each image, those of white women in outsized, convoluted gowns. As much as I knew attire, I didn't understand phrases like *mousquetaire sleeves*; *velvet, set on d'araignée*, and *fauchon of lace*. But this was a language of nineteenth-century fashion that Sophie Dearborn would have read with fluency.

There were other nineteenth-century girls, those shut out from this complicated finery. Girls like Cuffee Fortune's daughters. Like the Black child who would've loved that brown doll, a doll as faceless as the girl herself was to history.

The starkness of that unknown child's world, forgotten. The fancifulness of Sophie's dream-swelled world, preserved. There was the white family's ornate little cemetery on our property. There was another unmarked ground cradling scores of unremembered dead. Where it lay was another mystery, like how an aristocratic Southerner mothered a child out of wedlock. Or how my own mother's last name was only three generations old and fabricated, it seemed, like a design for a lady's gown.

There must be more to Lacey's story, I decided. At my desk, I fired up my laptop, going through the same records I'd already stared at a million times.

And then pieces started coming together again.

By 1910, Tallahassee Askew was broke. For some unknown reason, she'd moved from her parents' lovely row house to a gross boardinghouse. Her ads stopped appearing in the *Inquirer* by then, because the fashion industry was changing. Dressmakers weren't announcing that they were looking for work. Rather, department stores were looking for *workers*. N. Snellenberg & Co. promised a "good salary" for handsewers. Pin fitters at Stewart's on Market Street would enjoy "congenial surroundings."

But Black dressmakers wouldn't find "congenial surroundings" at all. Department stores were calling the shots, and their hiring was whites-only. So it could make sense for Tallahassee Askew to claim a new beginning with a new name.

But could there be some other reason?

My fingers dashed across my keyboard as I looked up the transcripts of Gramma's interview.

VALERIE: Do you have any good memories of your grandparents?

FAWNIE: I never met them, and all Mama would say was, "They were gone long before you were here."

Horseshit! And working at Charm, I knew *exactly* what that smelled like. Lacey's parents lived into the 1930s. Gramma was born in 1916!

With her family being so caught up in Black uplift, and with Lacey just wanting to make pretty dresses for rich white ladies, disagreements were inevitable. But to never speak to them again? To change her whole name?

I read fashion blurb after blurb on my closet door, looking for a bodice in the Castine style, perhaps. A Castine hem. It almost seemed to make sense. As a teenager, Lacey Castine had stood in this very room. She would've looked at the fashion plates and reimagined a birthright.

My eyes drifted to the plain sheet pasted on the very bottom of the door. I had never noticed it, because it was just words in old-timey print: *La Mode Illustrée*. A cover page to a fashion magazine.

Something was handwritten on the corner. I knelt.

Pour vous, Sophronia Castine Dearborn.

CHAPTER 16

My mother left for the airport that morning, heading to a conference. I got my shift covered at Charm and dimmed the lights in my room. Then I set the rosewood box on my desk and tilted up the broken lid. More than a hundred years ago, Sophie likely penned these very diary entries at a desk, or maybe while she reclined in bed with her journal propped upon her gown-shrouded thighs. She would have been within the same four walls where I uncovered her work.

July 18, 1858

I am back to adorning my closet, having returned from School to my dear Tangleroot. My latest plate shows a white dress with star-embroidered blue bretelles criss-crossing the body, uniting at the sash. Sleeves puffed like patisseries. Perhaps due to such, I haven't the slimness such a gown would best flatter. No matter, we have not had new dresses for some time. Not even Daphne, quickly sprouting out of her clothes. Worrisome. I should be turned out.

Walked with Mama to the kitchen house this morning. I hinted: Mama. My school friend Lizzie has had callers.

It was as if I had said nothing. Or everything. The lines between her brows were like the ribbons pulling across that dress.

I can feel what she and Pa will not say. While I worked in the garden yesterday, the negro women clustered in the laundry house told me unwittingly. Muffled cries from the loft. I tried to ignore their weeping while my fingers curled around a clump of bindweed, pulling at those stubborn roots. How they do cling to the soil.

Pa sold hands. Two old men, contagiously surly natures. He says troublesome darkies rot the barrel with their talk, though the slump of his shoulders tells me his ledger is master of us all.

Mama too is cross. As we entered the kitchen, our eyes immediately followed the unshod feet of Cook's pickaninny skimming across the brick floor. Despite her crooked leg she did quite the polka, her doll as partner.

So engrossed was she in her imaginary ball she did not see us.

Quiet, chile! Moll cuffed her before my mother could. I could see the slap forming on Mama's face.

Anger is the bloom of my mother's grief for Aunt, for Aunt's children. No stepmother made plain in deathbed's word and letter. Her own stepmother was as cruel as a fairy tale's. It was a wrath that spared Mama because she married Pa.

My brother-in-law will travel again next week, Mama told me, saying we shall take charge of the children. She talked of our menu to Molly, who softened like pudding when I asked if I might have my favorite sweets. Our cook does so love me.

As we walked to the springhouse, Mama counted off girls on her fingers like goods in a store. Miss S.R. in Richmond, once beautiful, but in her thirties and somehow left on the shelf, could be a good match. There is Miss F.B. in Charlottesville, pretty if you look past that Indian blood clouding her complexion. Or, were he to court the widow Mrs. T. W., he might gain 5,000 acres in exchange for a harelip.

But—<u>no stepmother</u>. How I miss the good times when such heaviness was not mine to hold. Sometimes I read this diary's pages of my years in School, cheered that I ever lived so weightlessly.

August 8, 1858

Caught dancing, the negro girl has been put to work. I am glad for her hands. The children are here, and we have other guests on the way. The Harpers. George must have met so many pretty girls in Philadelphia, he cannot remember me. Would that I belonged in such a category. The pretty part, at least. Philadelphia, I could do without.

I am looking out of my bed-chamber window, watching the slave girl cumbersomely cradle Aunt Hannah's infant, lacking the tenderness with which she cares for her upside-down doll that was once mine. The doll Molly made for me. I used to play with both sides: Sally the Belle and Sully the Darkie. Sally told Sully what to do, end-over-end, before I tired of it all.

Mr. Paulding's four older children cavort under Effie's eye. We have stationed her as a second nursemaid, for the girl Mr. Paulding brought is only Daphne's age.

Have you not someone more fitting to watch them, Mama had asked with some alarm. There is a proper nursemaid, he said, but needed for other work at home. Then he turned to me and spoke of pleasant matters, asking how I enjoyed School. Our talk smoothed Mama's mood.

Ah, the overseer's children just arrived to play. Ruffians, dirty faced. Look at them! They are talking with my cousin's cherubs, wary of one another. The way one might imagine our English ancestors approached the woodland savages.

Oh, no. Cuff's boy is shouting, racing through the field. Something is wrong.

Before I retire I must write what happened. The overseer's wife's dress caught fire. Fortunate the doctor was not on the road, and Olive's grown son rode hard to fetch him. She lives.

I fear to think what happened. No woman of competence torches her skirts over the hearth. And how can the bruises on her arm be explained, or that our overseer is nowhere to be found?

August 16, 1858

I did not think my spirits could be lifted any, but they have risen a floor, like a girl hastening up a flight of stairs to try on a new dress.

George visited with his family last night. He too has risen in height. He is studying medicine, though with such abolitionist hubbub, he withdrew from Pennsylvania in favor of "Mr. Jefferson's University." And he sailed to Europe before returning home, bringing gifts for us all. Belgian chocolates and wine for my parents, while Daphne was presented with ribbon, rosettes, and the smartest-looking braid from Paris. She immediately began tying it all into her brown hair, lamenting that she is too young to wear it up.

And for me: a French fashion magazine! My gasp was so sharp, it startled Isaac as he came to announce supper was served.

What followed to-day! We young people gathered after church. I overheard George's manservant ask my father for permission to marry our Effie. Papa said he would be overjoyed to see a Harper and Dearborn union. I confess, thoughts of another Harper and Dearborn union danced through my mind!

And in spite of myself, I exclaimed: But we should give them a wedding! A little party, for all of us!

We young folks thought it a capital idea, save Effie and her betrothed, who said they wouldn't want "all dat fuss." But Pa approved! We girls launched into plans: We shall wear calicos and muslins, peasant-style gowns. Mama, Daphne, and I shall be industrious and sew ours ourselves, with the help of Moll's girls. It shall be a small and thrifty celebration.

But then! George said he would be delighted for an occasion when we might talk about my School and his travel. I felt like there was nothing else to do but swoon like a tragic heroine.

However, I kept my dreams fastened properly to good sense, and answered him with polite agreement.

I shall be in bed soon. But I perused the French fashion magazine! The gowns, they are each as beautiful as Birds of Paradise. I shall paste the prettiest on my door at this instant. But what is best, is on the frontispiece, George has written it is for me. My heart feels plumed upon seeing my birth-bestowed name in his manful penmanship.

August 21, 1858

To cheer me, Molly sent me little cakes, hobbled to my chamber by her daughter. Immediately I took some to Olive's cabin, but it was Caleb who answered the door as she slept. He shared that she recovers slowly, though a cloudy look upon his face suggested more worry.

And I <u>must</u> confess our talk furthered, though Pa would not approve. Caleb shared his dreams of moving to Oregon territory. Out there, he says in his simple way of talk, "thar's good land and good wark for the takin'." He spoke of broad fields and trees that brush the sky.

Leaving is simply a wish, he said. With his mother invalid and his stepfather absent, he has worked like a "nay-ger" in the yard and a housewife in the kitchen. Thus, I later found Pa in his office and asked if we might loan the Mullers a capable servant. He said we have not *one to spare. His brokering with the traders that roam from one door to another has sent more of our labor to the cotton farms farther south.*

I suggested they might buy one of Molly's older daughters at a very modest price. Papa balked. We cannot afford a "modest price" for a breeding-age girl who is an expert cook and seamstress.

But he consented to sell Molly's smallest. Pa says she is of no use for increase when she comes of age, for he predicts she is not hale enough to withstand childbirth. And I do not believe a man would ever marry her on account of her twisted leg.

Pa said he will fetch her in a day or two. He drew a line through her name in his inventory, closing the leather-bound book and pushing it aside as if the girl were already no longer his concern.

I pray this will do some good, though this child is eight, badly crippled, and small for her age. I fear all is stacked against her, poor Olive Muller.

August 29, 1858

I am unduly vexed. The cause: The sound of Molly's girl screaming early this morning. Mama and I were in the store-house, the sleeves of our work dresses turned up to the elbows, arms plunged in the pickling. My mother: Slave business. Leave it.

But the screams coaxed me to wipe my briny hands upon my apron and rush into the yard.

The child clutched her doll and her mother's dress as other negroes gathered 'round. Molly stood in between Papa and the sobbing girl: Massa, you ain't takin' my baby girl, I'll kill you first.

I was stunned. I have never seen even the most insolent field hand issue a threat. Absent was Cuff. He has been leased out. Would that he were here to restore his wife's usual prudence!

Papa pushed Molly aside as if she were a sheath of cornstalks, though she quickly rooted her small form in front of her child. My sister rushed outside. Go back in, I told her. She did not.

When Pa yanked the girl away, Molly threw herself at him. He shoved her aside, knocking her backward to the ground.

Molly was up in an instant and leapt at my father like a cat. He struck her with a closed fist as he would a man. Her head cracked backward as she fell like a sack of bricks. She lay just as still.

Papa seized the darkie 'neath his arm and brought her down the hill. The doll fell from her hands and she screamed, over and over, kicking at him as he heedlessly trod forward. Daphne too began to cry, though she is too old for tears over "slave business." These matters are as natural to a plantation as trees and water to the earth. Still, I pulled my sister close.

The slave girl would not quiet and neither would my sister. I found myself swooping toward the doll. Holding her made me recall my sweet girlhood, and I turned over the skirt to reveal yellow-haired Sally. I gave her one last *look before returning her to the pickaninny as my father scowled. Even as he carried the girl like a coyote takes a gopher, she flipped the toy over and cradled the darkie side, whimpering for her almost-lost "Promise."*

Such carrying on. For no cause! Pa is only selling the girl to the overseer. Treacherous insolence, when Moll and Cuff are our favorites, along with Effie and Isaac. Our family, black and white.

If only those Yankee abolitionists could have seen this! A caution. This is what would happen should these people live free. Animal instinct, run unchecked.

September 10, 1858

I have put down my embroidery, as I wish to note our preparations for Effie's wedding. Our servant doth protest: no "to-do." But we are having so much fun! Mama gave her dotted muslin and Cook is sewing her a simple dress trimmed with lace, tatted by some Irish girls in town. Mama, Daphne, and I have new frocks as well. I drew the patterns, all in perfect peasant keeping. Mine is of saffron linen cambric, the front breadth arranged en tablier *with bands of Valenciennes lace, and a Marie Antoinette fichu of the same. Because this is a slave wedding, the Mullers are invited. I am sure Olive will enjoy such a diversion.*

After church, I played with my uncle Paulding's children, as they have again arrived for a visit. Then they piled into the carriage with Mama. Isaac drove slowly so that we might walk close behind, as I was invited to accompany Papa and my uncle to enjoy exercise in fair weather. My uncle was most inquisitive about the books I am reading, and how I spend my days. Later, he and Papa talked business for a long time behind closed doors. I feared all was not well, until Papa was gay at supper, as if he had astounding news. I waited and waited but nothing of note was said.

September 19, 1858

News today, all grim. Returned from our stay at the Taylors'. My exercise took me past the overseer's cottage, and I was astonished to find it empty! I asked the darkies. Pa and the overseer had a row, and Henry left in a rage with his wife and their children.

Latching the cabin, I noticed the negro child's doll lying within the wedge of shadow behind the door. I picked it up, giving way to memory, the years ago when Mercy Harper had an Upside-Down doll, and I begged and begged Mama for my own. She tasked Molly with the sewing. Our mulatto said, "You ain't gon' play with her mo' than a minute." Indeed, my envy was greater than my want, and Sally-Sully was soon left in a toy-chest for Daphne to take up and discard to the quarters, back to the very hands that made it.

Holding the doll, it struck me: The child is also gone!

I found Caleb at the tool shed. He said his family moved out west, though he is staying on. I immediately ran for Papa, finding him on horseback. Told him the Mullers are gone and they took our darkie!

He wheeled around, saying she is not our darkie, we sold her.

I insisted: We must buy her back!

We cannot chase the overseer across the country to track a pickaninny, Pa said. Then he softened. She will be taken care of.

But we are not supposed to sell our favorites' children.

The doll is on my desk as I write. I shall keep it with me. What else can I do? I cannot return it to Molly. She might never see her daughter again. Better she have some solace, thinking her child is comforted by her beloved Promise, than know even this was left behind.

September 30, 1858

The negro child will come home. Pa has not reconsidered, but I have made my own designs.

Somewhere in his study, my father keeps the key to a lock-box, some savings he will not consign to the bank. There is enough money, I believe, to purchase the little girl and hire a stagecoach to bring her back.

Finally recovered from punishment, Moll moves about like a ghost. Pa says the sale of a negresses' child is no more to them than the sale of a foal from a mare, but perhaps those living among us whites might absorb some of our tender feelings? I miss the Molly who cared for me, who made me her favorite, and she shall not return until the child does.

I regret I asked we sell her.

I have sought out Caleb. When his family settles, he will tell me where I may send an offer for purchase.

Pa will find out eventually. Perhaps he shall whip me like a darkie. But I convinced him to sell the girl, when she is meant to forever be our property.

October 4, 1858

It is now my lot to move about like a ghost. I believe I shall be married.

For supper this evening, I wore my mauve poplin, as Mama said there would be visitors. As I came down the stairs she tittered most nervously, while my father looked on with the greatest approval. Mama told me my pop is fitting, for Mr. Paulding shall "pop the question."

I laughed, thinking it in jest.

But Papa clapped his hands together. We have talked at length, my dearest Sophie. He will offer you the utmost happiness.

I was incredulous. You have talked? I asked. About me?

Indeed, Papa said. He has asked me for your hand and I have consented.

I felt dumbstruck, recalling the letters my older

friends have pressed to their breasts, adoring words from suitors. This is not how it is done. I whirled to Mama: But Aunt's wishes: No stepmother.

Mama stroked my hair. You could never be a stepmother. You are family. It would lift no greater burden to know you and those darling children shall be cared for.

I protested, But I am too young. I was to turn out.

You are younger than many, Pa said, but you have reached enough age to be a wife. And there is no sense in travels to Charleston for the Season, when a good husband is waiting right here.

Mama added, And we are hosting a party for you, with your friends.

I blinked with confusion.

She provided: Effie's wedding, of course.

I stammered, But Mr. Paulding is my uncle!

The width of Mama's smile was hemmed in by grief for her sister as she said, By marriage he is family, and by marriage he shall remain.

Later, I could scarcely eat. Mr. Paulding said he had heard about my garden, and he wished to see for himself.

I could only stare at him before I noticed Mama's sharp gaze trained upon my face.

I am so ashamed to admit my thoughts as we walked together, my parents tarrying some yards behind us. I could see nothing but the hair blooming from his nostrils, black and thick like a throng of flies. It made me itch. I must have fidgeted.

He asked in his stiff manner, Are you nervous, Miss

Dearborn?

Of course not, said I.

I am quite nervous myself, said he.

Why so? I shrugged in a most nonchalant manner.

He lifted his hat, then, as if unsure of what to do next, placed it back on his head, then doffed it again as he offered a bow.

Because I hope you will marry me, Sophie. I have spoken with your father, and now I am asking you for your hand.

With revulsion I looked at his bent head, the uneven patches of hair. Then I thought of Papa hunched over his ledger, penciling in figures to resolve our dwindling purse. And Mama's grief, how it has grown a new life in her fear for the children. And they—motherless.

I too had made a child motherless.

Behind us, my parents pretended to study the marigolds. It seemed like an epoch passed before I said yes. Another girl may have added some other gracious sentiment, but that single word was all I could utter.

That one word shall fix my fate.

I have taken to writing after turning about in bed, as restless as an apparition. The night has ended with my mother gaily telling Daphne the news. My sister clung to me. Soph, you shall be moving away? To Respite? It is so far. Can I come with you?

Mama glowed like a candle. Sweet daughter, you shall stay with us. But both Effie and Isaac will join Sophie. They are among our most prized possessions, and they shall be her gift.

October 11, 1858

We have endured a bone-rattling visit to what seems like the frontier: Respite, which is indeed far, and down a twisty, forever-long road. However, Mama thought it wise to see Mr. Paulding's plantation with different eyes, those of a soon-to-be wife.

This morning I toured about with Mama and Mr. Paulding's sister, my mother's mouth curving into a frown. For all Mr. Paulding's largesse, the kitchen and dairy and store-houses are in need of upkeep. The darkies have been a year without a mistress.

I feel as stuck as a goldfish in a bowl. Or perhaps removed from myself, as if this is all happening to someone else, and I am merely watching. Somehow I cannot find the words to tell my parents I accepted Mr. Paulding's proposal in haste.

This afternoon, Mr. Paulding and I took a ride about Respite. When we stopped in a field, Isaac brought us a blanket and basket. Mr. Paulding thanked him with a coin.

I strive to be a kind master, and I find a pittance here and there ensures quietude among the negro men, he said as the servant rode away.

It occurred to me the matter of land and slaves has been discussed between my betrothed and my father. He knows he shall own Isaac and Effie both, for a gift to me is a gift to him. Mr. Paulding then reached across me to open the hamper. I shrank away. He blushed and apologized. It was as if he thought me wife already, with he accustomed to such proximity.

That is when it broke upon me that someday soon he will reach in whatever way he wishes. And I will not have the latitude to refuse him.

And to-night. Mama and I worked together in the drawing room, she on a shawl for me, while I made a chemisette, Effie's wedding gift. Mama asked to see the children.

Shortly thereafter, they came marching in, followed by a black negress I can only describe as savagely stately. A child as yellow as a wildflower trailed her, running to accompany Mr. Paulding's children as if they were of one brood, a duckling among baby doves.

I have not come of age in a cave. I have seen mulattos running about Respite during our visits to my aunt. I have seen them on other plantations. Our own Molly is the color of weak tea.

This child is the age of Molly's daughter. For a moment I felt a pang of guilt.

Then I saw this mulatto girl with different eyes. For one, I noticed hers. Mottled green. Downturned at the corners, set beneath a square brow. Like my intended's. Startled, I dropped my linen and she reached to pick it up. I gaped at her yellow face. And I held back my need to slap it.

I cannot live this way, despising my very self for feeling what is only natural.

Thus, if I am to marry Mr. Paulding, if I must—I must also sell her.

October 16, 1858

I am in my bed-chamber taking respite from the wedding festivities. Not mine, for that day has not yet come. But Effie's.

With no orange blossoms to be had, a crown of apple flowers were equally lovely. She and her Chosen shunned the broomstick custom so common among the field hands, and Pa insisted they marry upon the portico. Their wedding demonstrated that he provides for us, his family, in spite of it all. And if those abolitionists stirring up trouble in the North saw this dusky couple, they would throw aside their commiseration upon "poor miserable slaves."

Papa has been quite a host, boasting that he is spoiling our servant. Mama countered that we are merely <u>indulging</u> her for one day, for to-morrow morning we expect her to wait on us with her usual promptness.

We girls are in sprightly cottons, muslins, and organdies, without a thread of silk. As we dressed in my bed-chamber earlier to-day, we heard a ruckus of laughter from Daphne's bed-chamber. Seeking the source, we realized our younger sisters had swiped our slaves' articles from clotheslines and, bedecked in aprons and turbans, were pretending to wed, with Daphne playing the negro bride and Mercy's sister the groom. How funny they were! It was a droll distraction from my impending nuptials.

Were I not betrothed, it would be quite the party.

But Mr. Paulding mostly talks with Papa and the

other fathers and does not care to dance. Thus I must consign myself to the bench and the wall like a widow.

As a laborer, Caleb does not dance with us young ladies and gentlemen but has looked my way many times, as if he is sad for me. George has been whirling about with all the girls but me. All that was between us is spoiled, like custard left out too long.

Well, Mama is calling me. I cannot hide forever.

I am back to these pages, for this day has veered in a wretched direction.

At a moment, George joined me, saying, I believe my well-wishes are in order. He confessed he had failed to realize Mr. Paulding and I had been courting.

I replied, We have been. My parents are happy, and I mean to please them.

Should you not be happy, too, he asked.

I have given my acceptance and I cannot take it back, said I.

George smiled most mischievously: I have heard that the negroes call him Master Balding.

I blanched, for I do not believe it is only the negroes who say this. Such an insult casts shame upon me as well. I reprimanded George: That is an ill-mannered insult to a lady's betrothed. And besides, you might some day lose your hair.

He lifted his hat and grabbed his curls, as if the thought had never occurred to him.

Then Daphne appeared from the French doors, stepping out onto the yard in her new dress. I had been paying so much attention to the making of my gown that I never noticed how she finished her hunter green gingham with quilles of the lush burgundy ribbon George had given her. And beneath her hat, her hair was pinned up with loops of that Marseilles braid! It was as if all the boys saw her with different eyes.

My little sister, who just this morning played pretend like a young girl, had come out. At my party!

Boys flew in her direction like birds to seed. George excused himself immediately.

I found Mr. Paulding within the cluster of men, all prophesizing war with the greatest of conviction.

Then into the yard strode that savage negress, a contradiction of barbarity and grace within her bearing. Mr. Paulding's eyes immediately ripped from my face to her form as she stood, hands on broad hips, and surveyed a table of refreshment.

The children are clamoring for sweets, she said to him, May I tote some to their room, suh? Her diction nearly proper, as if she thought herself white.

Take them a bounty. Mr. Paulding shook his finger with mirth. But don't eat a bite! Then his attention diverted to my astonished face.

I am growing a headache, I complained.

Perhaps it is the music. It is quite boisterous. We shall find somewhere quieter, suggested Mr. Paulding.

We followed the narrow path of the brook. At the water's bend, slave children splashed about with nets while a pair of old aunties watched with sharp eyes as they gossiped under the willows.

Then joy-filled shouts of "Master! Master! Look, Look!" Two mulatto boys raced our way with a bucket, thrusting wiggling minnows at Mr. Paulding while he rubbed their wooly brown heads. Then the girl, that yellow girl with the down-turned eyes came running over, tearful she'd caught none.

A feeling I despise more than the child herself welled up within me.

Mr. Paulding promised he would capture her a gallon of minnows. To me he remarked, I certainly strive to be a kind master.

Then he took my elbow: We shall go fishing, Sophie.

CHAPTER 17

As instructed, I placed the papers back in darkness. They went back into the lockbox, which I rewrapped in batting and placed in an emptied dresser drawer. I still didn't know who had fathered Sophie's child. And why, putting her pages away, did I feel like I'd been betrayed by a friend? Any illusion that she could've been a woman before her time, like a snappy heroine in a historical-fiction novel, had dissolved.

My phone buzzed. Cicada. Again. *Hey, how's the dress? Can't wait to see what you've stitched up!!!*

I froze, trying to think of a way to type that I couldn't make her dress anymore. Because more of my family's history had come to light, and my great-grandmother had carried a painful memory of the original dress for decades.

And after reading about Effie's wedding, a singular happy moment of her life hijacked by white people, the last thing I wanted to think about was an ivory gown.

But how could I say this in a text?

I couldn't. I postponed telling the truth. *Things are going great. I'll be in touch very soon!*

My phone buzzed again. Kendall. *Just checking in. How are things? It'll be fun to see you for Alyssa's b-day.*

It was odd, her text. Not a group text to Alyssa and me, which had happened sporadically after Thanksgiving. A message only for me.

I would see both Kendall and Alyssa soon enough, when I visited Boston. I would also see a show at the new theater, The Chasma. When I'd emailed Nyles that I would be in town, he promised free tickets and a visit to the wardrobe shop.

Call me if you get a moment, Kendall said. The tiny picture of her was one I had snapped more than a year ago during spring break. The Kovaks went to Florida, and Kendall had asked both Alyssa and me to come with. But Alyssa's parents made her visit her grandmother at a Florida retirement home while there, which had left Kendall and me a whole day together.

The two of us had lunch and strolled a street festival. Soon enough, we were chatting like real friends, not just two girls connected through someone else. The anvil hadn't dropped that Mom was taking me to Virginia over the summer, but I told her about my parents' upcoming divorce. Her own home life was far from perfect. She was constantly fighting with her new stepmother.

In one of the shops, Kendall admired the precious stones, while I checked out some vintage crystal necklaces. When we sat at a picnic bench for ice cream, Kendall reached into her shorts pocket and slipped out a brilliant scarlet ring. "Yours," she said. "Genuine ruby. Your birthstone, right?"

I had gasped, pushing it on below my knuckle. It shone like a drop of blood.

"I got it from that antiques place."

"How much did it cost?"

"A grand." Kendall laughed. "So take it off before someone sees you."

Quickly, I'd tried twisting it from my finger, heart pounding. Kendall shoplifted all the time, but never anything so expensive.

The ring was stuck. Kendall giggled at my predicament. "Use soap."

In a porta-potty stall, I managed to loosen it. The jewel gleamed like stained glass in the dim, stinking space. I knew I should give it back to the shop owner, but I was afraid he'd accuse *me* of stealing. So I called Dad.

An undercurrent of anger rode beneath his calm voice. He said he'd call Mr. Kovak, Kendall's father. An hour later, Dad told me that Jim Kovak would return the ring.

But my father made the mistake of telling Mom. She wanted to fly to Orlando to get me. Dad talked her down. She fumed that I could never hang out with Kendall again. Dad talked her down.

I thought Kendall would be grounded. That Mr. Kovak would make her bring back the ring herself and apologize. But she never discovered she'd been found out, because her father never said a word about it.

Research was the one thing Mom and I had in common. The board had agreed that Mom supplied enough documentation for now. They would take the name change referendum to faculty and staff at the end of the semester, but if and only if Mom supplied "irrefutable evidence" that Cuffee founded the college. As tentative as it was, the name-change issue broke on the local news. Even the governor of Virginia provided a statement.

"I'm immensely disappointed this is under consideration," he said in a news clip. "Stonepost College has been a part of our great Commonwealth's legacy for more than a hundred years. And we should hold the strengths of our Southern history proud, just as we hoist high our glorious flag."

Lana Jean wrote another op-ed, this one to the *Richmond Times-Dispatch*. Reading it, I felt wrung out with anxiety. Weeks had passed since I last touched the dress, and I still hadn't told Mom or asked for her help in backing out. I worried not only about Cicada's disappointment, but Lana Jean's potential anger. She seemed like she could be vindictive.

In fact, Lana Jean texted me just that morning. *How is the gown coming along?* I could have told her right then that it wasn't coming anywhere. But all I did was respond with an excuse: I was on it, but I got a little preoccupied with classes. Her response was brief and matter-of-fact.

Do consider this project among your priorities.

⋙ ✳ ⋘

Mom was determined to find the cemetery where Cuffee Fortune and his wife, Molly, were buried. She went out on long treks that lasted hours, sometimes with Will. Twice, a professor helped search. Dr. Derry was a retired professor, an expert on enslaved people's burial practices. But even she couldn't locate the burial ground.

Once—okay, three times—I looked for the cemetery alone. The walking helped quell the never-ending nervousness in the pit of my belly at the thought of Lana Jean's impending fury. I kept an eye out for strange pilings of rocks, for depressions in the earth, the kind of signs Dr. Derry described. I felt drawn to search, because I found myself thinking about Molly.

And I thought about her daughter, whose name I learned was Carrie. Tom Dearborn had indeed scratched her name from his inventory when he sold her to the Mullers. It was crazy—Carrie was long dead—but I worried about her, as if her story had not yet ended. It was almost the way you might worry about a character in a book, even though you know it's fiction? I wished I could save her.

Now that I knew the doll Promise once belonged to Carrie, she almost seemed sacred. Mom would be thrilled, knowing we had a piece of Cuffee's life, a doll belonging to his daughter. But I couldn't share this half without revealing the whole: my mission to uncover Sophie Dearborn. How could I tell my mom how drawn to her story I felt?

But I was also drawn to Carrie, a girl sold from a mother who fought to keep her close. Carrie was only eight when she traveled in a wagon for weeks across wilderness. I imagined all the work she would have been forced to do: hauling buckets of water, made all the more laborious by her disability; hefting heavy cast-iron pots and pans. Shouldering the even heavier weight of loneliness.

All this for a girl described as "small for her age."

As I fell asleep each night, holding Promise, I grieved that Carrie didn't even have her doll. She had no one. Did she survive the trip west? If she did, what happened to her? And how did Molly ever recover from losing her child?

I almost didn't make my plane. After dropping off the papers to a grateful Ming, I went eyeballs-deep into the archives before hauling ass to the Richmond Airport. But I *had* to finish my own sleuthing into Sophie's secrets. Once I broke the news to Lana Jean and Cicada that I wouldn't be making the magnolia gown, I wouldn't get a shred of documents from the Trianon stash.

I tried looking into Caleb, the overseer's son, who seemed to be crushing on Sophie. Tom Dearborn had some records of payment to him, but after November 1859, Caleb's paper trail ended. He wasn't in the 1860 census, though his mom and stepfather showed up in Goliad, Texas.

Caleb Muller finally resurfaced in 1889, after disappearing for decades. He had opened a shoe business in Portland, Oregon. *The right place for another go at life.* I remembered my father's uncontained grin.

But Caleb died the year after his move. Apoplexy.

As for George Harper, he married his cousin (*eew*) in 1863 and became a lawyer. If there were any scandals in the Harper family history, Lana Jean Chilton wasn't telling. Especially now.

I could not find anything of Carrie, Cuffee and Molly's little girl, nor the Black woman Sophie held so much contempt for. Like so many of us, they too were gone from history.

"Multi-futurist." Aria Maldonado was The Chasma's new costume designer. She held up a dress, or robe, or some undefinable garment. It had broad tiers of fabric: an elegant Cameroonian ndop pattern like one Dr. Corn had talked about once, a brightly colored South Asian batik, and the broad diamonds of a Peruvian-style textile. "That's the world I sought to create for this show: a multicultural future."

Last night, I had watched The Chasma's newest performance after I'd grabbed an Uber from the airport. Now, as I toured the costume room with its machines, worktables, and bolts upon bolts of fabric, I wished I could get to work. I wished I could listen to Aria all day.

We talked all afternoon. She shared what she was working on next: costumes for The Chasma's upcoming show, one with a waterscape theme. I even helped her work through a design challenge she had, mocking up a miniature pattern. While I drew, Nyles Pompa buzzed by. "I told you she's good."

"This place is amazing." I gazed up at the light-filled atrium of Boston University's theater building. I wanted to be there as a student, not a guest.

"I just wish I could have a chance. I auditioned for a black box show and no dice." Alyssa sighed, pushing open the door. "How was The Chasma?"

I felt guilty about my glee. I tried to tamp it down but couldn't. "They offered me a job!" I exclaimed as we went out along Commonwealth Avenue. The Chasma would be doing more shows next year, and Aria Maldanado would need an assistant.

"That's awesome!" Alyssa squeezed my hand. "Congratulations!" Around us swirled the noise of traffic and the energy of throngs and throngs of students. There was an excitement at BU, as if there were always somewhere to go and something to do. Alyssa was eager to get to her dorm and get dressed to go out.

Her roommate, Saanvi, had been welcoming when I got in the night before. She even offered to take my sleeping bag and forgo her bottom bunk bed. Really, all of Alyssa's hallmates were super nice. Alyssa's suitemate, Makeba, caught us as we were leaving Kilachand Hall. She freakin' *coveted* my glittery top, she said. "I made it," I told her.

"You *made* that? Girl, that's *talent*!"

The birthday party Alyssa's on-again boyfriend threw at his off-campus apartment was chill and quiet, not at all like the sweat-and-smoke fest we'd gone to over Thanksgiving break. If anything, it was a little pretentious, with everyone sipping wine or expensive beer from curved pilsner glasses.

A few guys, two of whom were cute, struck up conversations with me. But it was the other girls I liked talking to best. All of them were brilliant and cool, and none of them were overtly trying to sleep with me.

Kendall tottered in on impossibly high heels as the party dwindled down. "Where next?" She noticed folks leaving.

"Brexton asked if I'll hang out with him tonight. Would you be okay, Noni, if I did?" Alyssa asked. "I can make sure Saanvi gets you into the dorm."

"Yeah, that's cool," I told her. "I might go grab some food, though. Suggestions?" I was certain the sauv blanc I drank was liquefying my brain cells.

"Let's get tacos!" Kendall linked her arm with mine. Inwardly, I groaned. Just what I wanted: one-on-one time with her.

Outside, she limped along the sidewalk as if her shoes were medieval torture racks. "So I kind of need your advice. About Laronté. He started getting weird."

She bent and adjusted a heel strap, then soldiered on. "I would make a joke, and he wouldn't think it was funny. A few days ago, we talked about—you know. Stuff that's been happening. Those shootings . . . you know the ones."

"Of Black men?" I asked. The news had just reported that another unarmed man had been killed by some neighborhood vigilante. It always felt like a punch to the heart, somewhere vital.

"We've talked about it before. He's always shrugged, but this time he said he worries it could happen to him. I was like, 'You'll never have to deal with that.' Because he's clean-cut, he's smart, he's articulate. Like, compliments! But he just shut down."

Why did she want my advice? I had only ever been friends with her for Alyssa's sake. But even Alyssa seemed to be unlatching herself from Kendall now that they lived in separate dorms. And I wasn't sure if I could ever forgive her for saying the n-word in my house.

"Well, today he broke up with me." She sounded bruised, shocked. "I never expected this. I just want to know—"

She paused. I could hear her next words: *How can I tell him I'm sorry*?

But that wasn't what she asked. "What can I do to get back with him?" She stopped beneath the bright red lights of a late-night Mexican restaurant. "Maybe you should talk to him. Maybe you could convince him . . ."

I disentangled my arm from hers. "We don't have a special way of talking, Kendall. There's no Black code."

"You don't have to get mad. That's not what I meant." She was half snappish, half pleading. And not at all apologetic. I thought of the ring, that stolen red jewel stuck fast to my finger. How Kendall's father never held her accountable.

Maybe she didn't know how to apologize. Maybe she never really learned.

But then, I thought about Fluvie behind the window at Town Hall. Maybe I had never learned, either.

I strode away, turning my head only once to see Kendall watching me as she leaned hard against a pillar. Next year at BU, Alyssa and I would still be friends. Plus, I'd reconnect with classmates from high school and from the Bards program. Aria was older than me but not by much—I'd have her as a mentor. And I'd meet new people, like Saanvi and Makeba.

But just as I'd finally pried off that ring, I decided that my hands were forever washed of Kendall Kovak.

CHAPTER 18

I was nodding. Not in agreement—with exhaustion. My eyes pulsed shut right in the middle of class. I forced them open.

On-screen, in grainy black-and-white footage, a woman in a long, dark gown swung on a trapeze, peeling off stockings and the dress itself to reveal a long white undergarment cinched with a corset. The class had finally reached the textbooks' chapters on vaudeville theater. Any other time, I'd be really interested. But my flight had dumped me off in Richmond a few minutes after eight in the morning, just in time for me to make it to American Theater.

Boston had shaken up my ordinary, but now I was back to my usual worries: namely, telling Cicada—and by extension Lana Jean—that I wasn't making the magnolia gown.

Glitchy old-timey music blared. My professor tapped on the laptop keypad, then tapped again. A banner scrolled across the screen: "An Interview with Madeline Grover, Former Vaudeville Star."

My professor seemed flustered, tearing off a Band-Aid that made her finger useless on the touch pad. She finally stopped the video, but not before a collective sound of dismay filled the classroom.

"I'm so sorry." She addressed the class. "I didn't mean for you to see this. We won't be covering this element of theater in class." She looked around nervously. "Thank you for attending. Next week, we'll . . ."

Ignoring her, my classmates seemed to leave in a huff. I stayed behind in the darkened room. "We're not covering minstrel theater?"

"No. We'll skip that chapter." She hastily shut her laptop and yanked out the adapter.

"Why?"

Professor Seong slid the MacBook into its case. "Didn't you see how it affected everyone?"

"But it's history. It's something that happened, so shouldn't we learn about it?"

My professor only pulled together her things.

"At least," I asked, "can you tell me where I can stream this documentary?"

The train porter might've dispatched a messenger after the famed Madeline Grover appealed to him, frazzled. She'd just discovered that her costumes for a featured act had been left behind in New York.

I'll send word to Grand Central, the porter promised. *But for now, I know a girl who can whip up another in no time.*

At the Lorraine Hotel, Tallahassee Askew would've met a panicked Madeline Grover, star of the touring troupe the Cotton-Toothed Pickaninnies. She must've been starstruck. The way Grover later told it, the teen confessed she spent much of her earnings on tickets to shows at the South Street Theater, the Standard, or even amateur performances in church basements. Her father, Hoyt Askew, had ranted against minstrel shows. But for Tallahassee, they were just fun. She probably reviewed dance steps in her mind, practicing them in her room when her parents weren't home, the way my generation tries out TikTok moves.

But she was there to sew, not dance. She would've gotten to work measuring Grover and her dancing partner, a Black woman named Ginny Sampson, both petite enough to play girls. With a tape measure wound around her slender waist, Grover would've described the lost dresses to Tallahassee.

During her interview, Madeline Grover languidly smoked a cigarette (it was the 1970s when everyone did that indoors) and expressed that she didn't like ragged skirts and exaggerated patches for her minstrel acts. "Slaves were well cared for. Why not show the truth?" She took a long, sumptuous drag. Wide, structured skirts evoked a sense of nostalgia for her, a nod to her mother's hoopskirts on a dreamy plantation, she said. She liked big bows with long tails that bounced as she danced. I listened through earbuds while stationed in the computer lab because my laptop didn't have a disc drive.

She described Tallahassee only as "the young colored seamstress," never by name. But I knew. My great-great-grandmother had sketched a variation of her lost costume, improving upon the original design. She'd scribbled notes on the margins of her sketch.

For the next two winter evenings in 1909, Tallahassee must have sewed through the night. The morning of the show brought another catastrophe. Ginny Sampson was newly pregnant and the nausea had caught up with her. Grover and the troupe's manager watched Tallahassee's lithe form as she made last-minute alterations. Could she dance?

Buoyed by adrenaline, Tallahassee caught on quickly as Madeline Grover taught her the choreography. It would have been a whirlwind. She could've never imagined setting foot into the whites-only Trocadero Theater, much less performing in the magnificent space.

The show would've employed complicated scenery and sets. There may not have been time for a run-through, but Tallahassee's part was only one scene, a scene that only a Black woman could play.

A reviewer detailed the Cotton-Toothed Pickaninnies' debut act. This, I found in an old newspaper database, chafing again at the troupe's name. Two "twins," Topsy and Turvy, cavorted onstage: a Black and a white woman, both playing children, both smeared in blackface. Their dresses were identical, though Tallahassee wore a turquoise sash, while Grover's was pink. A fat mammy character, also a white woman slathered in black paint, chased them with a scrub brush, trying to corral the girls into a tin tub. They danced out of her way, but Mammy finally caught Turvy, who squirmed comically. But with warm water and cold cream on a sponge, Mammy revealed Turvy's bare, white arm. Delighted with her newly white skin, she swung her pale arm in a frenetic, giddy dance. The audience hooted with laughter. Onstage, Turvy's twin now wanted her turn. She shucked and jived Mammy's way, waiting in squeezy-eyed anticipation as Mammy scoured her slender arm. But once washed, a sorrowful wail poured from Topsy's throat like ink from a jar. Dark brown skin remained beneath the black. The audience roared.

As I drove home, I thought of the mammy statues grinning hard, as if with gritted teeth, in Magnolia's antique shops. I thought of the brusque, turbaned white women at Trianon. Of Sophie's sister and her friends parodying enslaved women at her Black maid Effie's wedding. Of the topsy-turvy doll in my bedroom.

I thought of the white blossom dress I couldn't make myself make.

Hoyt Askew might have read the same show review I'd found. Perhaps he slammed the newspaper down on the table, furious and humiliated. He couldn't imagine going to church, to the myriad of functions crammed on his calendar. He couldn't imagine standing behind the lectern at school.

Tallahassee, meanwhile, was memorialized forever. The act was such a hit that it demanded a multicity tour. The next day, my great-great-grandmother posed in a promotional image, one that crowed: "The Famed Madeline Grover with Colored Dancer Tallahassee Askew!" Both women were in blackface, though Grover showed off her bare, white arm. But at the very last second, Tallahassee swept off her wig. She held it away from her body as if it were a dead animal.

Madeline Grover stepped back. Her mouth fell open with shock. The photographer, thinking it a planned stunt, captured the image. The picture was archived, unpublished for decades.

Regret—that's the expression I saw on Tallahassee's face, blackened like a redacted word. That is what I saw in her direct, frank stare, nothing like the grinning, bug-eyed caricature she'd performed. The costume was property of the performing troupe. She would've been required to return it. Instead, she walked away with her painstaking work on her body. I imagined her taking fierce strides down Broad Street, the black of burned cork and Vaseline staining her skin as she defiantly stared back at those who dared look her way. She did not return the costume, I knew, because she wore it years later when my great-great-grandfather Calvin Fortune painted her holding the dress over her half-nude body.

But in 1909, Tallahassee's father, angered and mortified, must have kicked her out of his comfortable Waverly Street row home. All she could afford was a cramped, unheated boardinghouse. She would have felt ridiculed, chased out. And ashamed that her name, Tallahassee Askew, was emblazoned across that newspaper ad, when she wished she'd never had that one frantic night.

But she had land in another state. And a contact: the son of the man for whom she'd raised money by sewing a quilt years before.

And so she changed her name. And she started over.

As soon as I opened the door to the Tangleroot house, Mom swept me up in a hug. She must've been waiting in the foyer. "Sweetie, it's so good to see you! How was Boston?"

"It was fun," I said.

"How's Alyssa? Your aunt was hoping you'd have time to visit, but it seems you were so busy!"

Like we were two friends at a party sharing secrets, she pulled me onto the foyer sofa with her. I wanted to tell her about meeting Aria Maldonado at The Chasma's costume shop. But I also couldn't put off Lana Jean and the dress any longer. I needed my mother's help. I couldn't handle breaking the news to Lana Jean alone.

My mother's face glowed with excitement. "I have something to tell you! Remember how I said my name had been floated to lead the Courageous Curriculums Initiative?"

"Uh-huh." I nodded, but I was really distracted.

"I was officially asked to cochair! Isn't that amazing?" Mom must have sensed I was out of the loop. "It's a national program—one geared toward college readiness curriculums—that teaches how history affects the present, with literature as a tool. Poetry, fiction, memoir."

"And narratives?" I asked. "Like *The Remembered*?"

"Yes. In fact, they wanted authors to chair. Regina Chapel is working toward the pilot this fall, which will be right here in Magnolia! The governor's shaking his fist, but our legal team is poised to handle him."

My mother's eyes shone at the idea of it all, but then dimmed. "I wasn't sure I was the right person for the role. I'm not a K–12 educator. I'll be working with one, but still."

Her confession caught me off guard. She wore confidence like a second skin. This time, her smile seemed at half-power, as if it were dragged by self-doubt.

"Didn't you say it's a college-prep curriculum, though?" I asked.

"Yes, but . . ."

"So wouldn't it make sense they chose someone in higher ed to work with a K–12 teacher?"

"Maybe you're right." She squeezed my hand. "I'm going out to the media announcement in DC at the end of May. I'll be at the same table with the Obamas! Can you believe it? So tell me about Boston. Were you able to sit in on one of Alyssa's classes?"

"No, but I saw a show." I figured I'd get this news out of the way first before going to the magnolia dress. "It was so awesome! It was at The Chasma, the new downtown theater . . ."

"I remember. Your father and I went to their fundraising gala."

"Right." It occurred to me that might've been their last night out together, a thought that kindled a bit of sadness. "The show was incredible, Mom." I surged forward about the designs, making sure to drop the multicultural futurist aspect and the fact that the new costume director, Aria Maldonado, was Afro-Latinx. It was as if to say, *See Mom? I'm not forgetting our culture.* I would need her to know this when I told her about my magnolia dress conundrum.

"That sounds like such a fulfilling experience." Her smile was lips-only, and went nowhere near her eyes.

Still, I tried to keep my enthusiasm up. "And, Mom! They're hiring an assistant costume designer. It's fifteen hours a week."

"Is this something they're considering you for?"

"I've got it, Mom! Starting this June! I know that's soon, but they have cast and crew housing at below-market rent. The fact is, there aren't a lot of kids my age who can sew like I can." I cursed myself for using that word: "kids." "Or draft a pattern from scratch."

"I swear you inherited those skills from Lacey Castine." She seemed irritated with our ancestor. "I know this role is important to you."

It felt like there was a "but" attached, so I used language she liked. "This position is more than a job, it's practical application of a skill. And if you're worried about its impact on my schoolwork, I'll point out that I did so well at community college while working twenty hours a week, and commuting almost two hours to class. I can manage this next chapter with aplomb. And—"

"I wish that Nyles Pompa never deviated you from your path." Mom stalked into the library, plucking her turquoise glasses from her desk. "I've known so many students like you. You're not ready yet—but when you are, you'll be brilliant."

"But Mom, that's what the theater professionals I've worked with are saying. They're saying I *am* brilliant. At design. In fact . . ."

Was this my opportunity to finally kill what had been gnawing at me? To say I was *so* brilliant at garment design that I was commissioned to create an incredibly difficult pageant dress? But now, knowing what that dress was a replica of, it was one I could no longer make?

Could I ask for my mother's help with this mess I had made for myself but could no longer handle?

"You are brilliant in history, in literature." She spoke passionately. "You will be the most outstanding scholar, once you claim that brilliance. Noni, I've been meaning to talk to you. About Boston University this fall."

My heart lurched into my throat. She wasn't going to say what I hoped she wasn't going to say, was she?

"You've been doing so well since we've been here. Things were rocky when you were adjusting. But I thought being in Virginia would be a good thing for you, and it has been."

"Okay." I wasn't sure if I should agree or disagree. Either could work against me.

"You made all As last semester, and you're on track to do the same thing this semester.

"And Blondell tells me how wonderful you are at work. And you've finally taken interest in family history, now that you've been working on this Black Studies project."

"Thank you," I said warily.

"Being here has really changed you. Having the structure of a job. And going to a commuter college. A residence hall arrangement is preferable for most students, of course. But it isn't for students who are ineffective at dealing with distraction."

Her smile was real this time. "And you've been around positive influences. Blondell and Will have been mentors. Even Valerie—" She swallowed, as if it dinged her pride to admit it. "Even Valerie has been like a godmother to you. And the young people you work with have direction and focus. Many of them are balancing families . . ."

"What are you saying?" I asked.

She sighed for the umpteenth time. "You're not going to Boston this fall. I'm sorry, Noni. It would be detrimental to your scholastic well-being, and I cannot permit it."

I couldn't breathe. *Calm down,* I told myself. *Talk to her like an adult.*

"But Mom." I had the croak of a frog. "I've learned time-management and how to prioritize and organizational skills."

"And those skills have served you beautifully," Mom said. "But new strategies must be reinforced and validated by practice. You need another year at home."

The word "home" sounded hollow. But what was rock-solid was the fact that even though Mom couldn't stop eighteen-year-old me from taking a job, she had everything to say about where I went to college. Because I couldn't foot the bill.

"What can I do to convince you I'm ready to be on my own?"

"Oh, sweetheart . . ." She reached for my hand.

But I didn't want to be oh-sweethearted. I shook her away. "When I mess up, you say I need to be here. But when I do well, you say I still need to be here. What *can* I do, Mom? What?"

"Honey, I wish you would see the wisdom in my decision."

But all I could see was my whole future as a marionette, kicking around with strings attached everywhere.

I wanted to yell at her, but instead I found myself breathing deeply and walking out of the room, then outside onto the trail, taking in a view of the mountains and a breath of the honeysuckle-scented air. How could she make me stay here in Virginia?

And how do you know you want to leave?

The question I asked myself was sudden and unwelcome. Of course I wanted to go back to Boston. Jabari would cut me loose once he learned how awful I'd been to Fluvie, and rightfully so. Darlie created a rift between me and the other Charm servers. I couldn't hang out with them with her around. And soon enough, I would have two sworn enemies in the Chilton women.

Will was my only friend here.

But in Boston, I had Alyssa. I had Aria. Even Nyles Pompa gave me every shot he could, because unlike Mom, he recognized talent. And I had the wardrobe room at the theater and the performing arts center at BU . . .

Why does design mean so much? Will had asked. I was intrigued by choices, I'd said. *What would this person wear?* I had asked. But really I'm asking, *What would this person do?*

CHAPTER 19

I would sit at Sophie's grave and talk to her. Tell her how I felt. Ask her what to do. We were so profoundly different and I hated her, but she too had been at impossible odds with her parents.

But when I reached the iron gates, I couldn't bring myself farther. Instead, I looped around to Will's house.

His blinds were open and I could see inside. He was on his couch. A large calico was perched on top of the sofa behind his head. Both man and cat looked the same direction, their attention focused on something.

I was one second away from barging in when I realized it was Mom. Her gestures told me she was distraught. Her body curled near Will in spite of his cat being right there. It stopped me hard. She hadn't wanted to disappoint me. It had hurt her. And her irrational but very real phobia of the animal crouching not a foot away was won over by her desperation to talk it out.

I knew how strong of a need it was, to be heard. And I understood the look on Will's face. I had known he liked Mom. But now, it seemed he loved her.

What it meant was an amendment to my earlier thought. He was now on her side.

I had no friends here.

Will and his new assistant manager were my dinner customers, but I was in a sour mood. First off, I'd almost bumped right into Madge as she carried dirty plates. "You've got your head in the clouds." She set them in a rubber bin. "What's on your mind? Cute boy or something?"

"My mom's not letting me go away to college," I grumbled. "So I'm here for another year."

"Oh, but that's good! Sure, you started off with ruffled feathers, but you've been one of the best waitresses Charm's ever had. Everyone's going to be so happy you're sticking around."

Kara, who was nearby at a handwashing station, asked, "Noni, are you staying in Magnolia?"

"Yeppers, she sure is," Madge answered for me.

"That's so exciting!" She hugged me with wet hands. How did they miss how unfair it was?

While I was in the kitchen garnishing shortcake, Jabari stopped on his way to the walk-in freezer. "Hey! I heard you're sticking with Virginia!" He offered a high five.

I didn't meet his hand. "My mom's making me."

Jabari asked the new kitchen guy to finish up dessert for me.

"I'll make sure it gets to table nineteen, boss," the blond guy assured him before we left through the back door.

Outside, Jabari admitted, "I hate it when he calls me that. At the same time, I don't mind." He sighed. "I knew you were only staying for the year, Noni, but I guess I thought Magnolia was growing on you a bit. Maybe I hoped it was. It's really cool having you around."

But what did it matter? What *I* liked more were the colors and fabrics and designs waiting for me in Boston. I wanted my job in the costume shop. That's where I could be *me*, not my mom's lackluster kid.

"Do you think you could grow to want to stay?" he asked.

Grow to want to stay. As if wanting to leave was kiddish.

The toe of his thick-tread shoes poked a clump of gravel. "Or do you think you might find a way to leave?"

Finishing up Will's table, I couldn't offer service with a smile. Wordlessly, I left his check, not caring if Tricia, his new assistant manager, thought me the greatest bitch of them all. Will handed me some bills. "No change." It was his usual generous tip, even though I was surly as hell. "Your shift's ending?" he asked. I half nodded. "I'll walk you to your car."

As we headed to the farthest end of the parking lot, he said, "You're going to have to be patient with Radiance. She's methodical to a fault. She thinks about things and overthinks them and then overthinks them some more. I'm not sure how she sleeps at night. She's afraid to let stuff go."

"'Stuff' meaning me."

"Especially you. But your mom loves you more than anything. She cares for you so much, sometimes I wonder if there's a little room for anyone else. I hope there is."

I read between the lines. In Sophie's day, a man would ask a woman's father for his blessing of their courtship. Will was asking me.

Behind the fence, a cow lowed as loudly and longingly as if she questioned the universe. I had a question of my own, but for Will. "Did you tell Mom that keeping me here in Virginia wasn't right?"

Did you stand up for me, I wanted to know.

"I told Radiance that you have your own dreams and plans back in Boston. I made a case for you. I know you feel you can't be your own self here."

Above us fluttered a flurry of bats, the colony that roosted in a farm outbuilding. Each night, they took to the wing to feast on mosquitoes and moths. My gaze circled overhead to watch them.

So did Will's. "But here's what I believe. Sometimes in working together, you can set yourself apart. Your mom wants to change Magnolia. You can be a part of that if you let yourself."

Maybe I was half listening. Because maybe there *was* a way to leave. If I finished the magnolia gown, I could earn enough to set myself up in Boston, especially with low-rent housing for staff of The Chasma. I couldn't pay for college, but I could apply for financial aid on my own for the following year. It could work! I already had a part-time job at the theater. I could find a second job.

I could make my own escape hatch. I thought of the skylight on the roof of Lana Jean's apartment. I could leave, but only if I could figure out how Lacey Castine made that dress.

And then it occurred to me. Before she reinvented herself as Lacey Castine, a young woman named Tallahassee Askew left instructions.

Silk taffeta. It was matte, not shiny, a crisp fabric that held its shape, as if it had been starched. That's what *sil taf* meant on Tallahassee's notes, notes she scribbled beside the drawing. My great-great-grandmother must have taken the same techniques she used for her 1910 stage costume, repurposing them almost fifteen years later when her client desired a dress that flared just like a magnolia blossom.

She made her own fabric stiffener with a mixture of boiling water, cornstarch, and white glue. She probably hung it to dry in the cold winter air. Lacking chill, I did have the benefit of days. I set up a clothesline inside the apartment above Buried Silver.

I had carved out hours. I'd gotten the hang of my classes, so it didn't take me as long to write lab reports or finish French recordings for class. I even outgrew my tutoring sessions. And my capstone paper was almost done. It helped that Mom was almost always out of town. With the Courageous Curriculum Initiative's public announcement up ahead, she practically lived in DC. Plus, she was doggedly chasing down leads in her research on Cuffee Fortune. Mom was convinced that if Gramma sold Cuffee's manuscript to a collector in the 1980s, it couldn't have strayed far.

But I *did* have to research how to shape the gown's cloth petals. Tallahassee wrote *corst bon.* I didn't know what that meant, until I read that in the nineteen-teens, women still wore corsets, ones reinforced with a scaffold of steel. I texted Aria Maldonado at The Chasma. While I didn't let on the history of my project, I described my conundrum and asked about corset materials. She'd been trained in period costumes and connected me with an Etsy store that sold reproduction boning from the Edwardian era.

I felt like I had cracked a code. As petals of varying lengths took shape in that blue-and-gray-walled apartment, I wished I could share how I felt with Mom: like a part of my kinswoman's work. And not just hers. I imagined all of us, Black women making, creating ways of being, ways of expression, ways of shaping the lives we wanted for ourselves.

In the fall of our senior year, Alyssa's older sister Kelsey got married in Knoxville, Tennessee. That was where Alyssa grew up, and where Kelsey still lived. Their mother insisted Alyssa attend the bridal shower there a month before. It was the same weekend as our high school homecoming, so Alyssa didn't want to travel. Her only negotiation was that she could bring her best friend: me.

At the bridal shower, the two of us sat on the sidelines as the women experimented with wedding cocktails. We suffered through bawdy jokes that turned Alyssa's face as fuchsia as the lingerie someone got her sister as a gift. We were ignored. One woman asked, "Who's the Black girl?" There was no point in us being there.

That's how I felt at Cicada Chilton's dress fitting. She, her sisters, and her cousins Flouncy and Prancine paraded into the apartment, a wellspring of giggles and squeals. I instantly knew I didn't belong.

The women descended upon the gown that waited on the

mannequin. When Cicada stepped into the dress, it looked like she had stepped inside a magnolia blossom at its fullest glory. The petals radiated outward, three and four feet from her reed-thin legs.

One of Cicada's sisters fastened the rhinestone buttons I'd sewn on as I awaited Lana Jean's antiques. The gown's fit was perfect. I had the benefit of a dress form specially molded from Cicada's body, and not a thing needed to be done. Exclamations of "Oh my god!" filled the room, at such high pitches that it seemed only the bats in Charm's shed would be able to hear them.

No one spoke to me. I wanted to feel proud of my work, of the dress that I had gotten exactly right. But all I felt was crowded out.

And then slowly, the mood changed. DixieStar looked around the apartment. "My gosh, y'all. I haven't been here since I was in elementary school."

"Imagine what he would say if he could see you," Palmetta told her youngest sister. Was she talking about god? She began to weep. "DixieStar, you were so young. But Cicada, you were just a baby! You don't even remember."

"I feel like I know him, though." Cicada placed herself on a tall barstool, the only seat that could accommodate the gown's girth. Tears misted her eyes. She and her sisters knotted together. With her circumference of taffeta, they had to outstretch their arms to hold her shoulders. Flouncy and Prancine huddled around them. Not knowing what to do, I plucked stray threads from a table.

Unexpectedly, Palmetta stood up tall within the cluster of women, like a yellow flower rising from its bulb. Or a golden cobra unfurling from its coil. Because her eyes narrowed. And the room suddenly grew cold, as if inhabited by ghosts.

"This is a family moment. It's best if you leave now." Her tone was as frosty as her highlights. She had none of her mother's civility, as cutting as that was.

I gathered my backpack and left without a word. But I found myself running down the stairs like the token Black character in a horror movie.

The fitting felt too much like a haunting.

Outside, rain fell in fat drops. I hadn't brought an umbrella. Just as I made a dash for my car, the rain began pouring triple time, like pails of water upended by some spiteful god. I thought of the bucket brigade Darlie and I awkwardly formed that long-ago day when we watered Blondell's cattle. As if fated, I heard her voice.

"Noni!" She waved me under the awning of a vacant storefront. "Get out of the rain." Besides answering her occasional frantic group texts about covering shifts, the last time I personally interacted with Darlie was that day in the cow pen. But I was too soaked to hesitate.

"Oh no, you got dumped on." She peeled off her flannel shirt, revealing short sleeves. "Wear this."

"Are you sure?"

"It's not exactly a beach towel, but it's something."

I was grateful for the warm, dry fabric.

"It's the least I can offer," Darlie said. "I know I can't ever make up for the harm I've done, but I'm sorry. For saying racist things. I'm so sorry."

I was thrown entirely off. But I wasn't going to be pushed into forgiving Darlie, not on her terms at least. I couldn't quickly trust this, whatever it was.

"When your mom moved back, my parents had not-nice things to say about her. They went to school with her, you know. They said stuff I won't even go into."

I didn't know what she meant, but there seemed to be something, some secret, one everyone was in on but me. Maybe that's where the sudden chill came from upstairs.

"But whenever your mom's been at Charm, she's been so nice. She's asked about my kids and everything. Just like you. You've taken my shifts when I've needed someone."

Her hand clasped her necklace. "Once, I ran into Dr. Castine after work, and she asked about this. My great-grandma gave it to me years ago. She was the only person in my family who was ever nice to me. Your mom thinks it's made from a Cavan brooch. She said that's an old Irish design, and it's really rare, and—"

She traced the shape of a circle that did not quite close. "Dr. Castine knew so much about who I am, so I went online and read what she wrote. I had to throw away a lot of what my parents taught me. And then I got it. She's right. And so are you."

"I am?"

"Telling the truth about history isn't laying blame. Our ancestors' choices were theirs—and *our* choices are ours. She said—and you've said—that history teaches us to understand the choices *we* make, *now*." She added, "I can do better."

The rain lessened into a pitter-patter. "So can I," I admitted to Darlie. "When I moved here, I had the wrong ideas about everyone at Charm. I have to learn, too."

I thought admitting my own biases would make me feel diminished. But all I felt was that I'd grown somehow. Not become more adult—adults' prejudices could be stuck hard like fried crud on an ungreased skillet. And maybe adults' fears could get gunked on, too. But standing out here with Darlie, I felt like sharing my vulnerability actually made me greater.

CHAPTER 20

"Sweetheart! I ain't seen you in forever. I missed you!" Valerie greeted me at the back door by squeezing me for all I was worth. Leaning into her, I felt like I was worth a lot.

I was glad she was there, at Trianon. "Look at you, all pretty." She fluffed my tight curls. "Your hair is beautiful."

"Thank you." Glancing around, I asked, "Is there a wedding?"

"Not today, though we've had plenty of those. Why folks want to get married on a plantation is beyond me. Misery's in the very dirt." Valerie shielded her eyes against the sun. "Lana Jean's planning some other kind of big function Memorial Day weekend. So she's got a bunch of committee members visiting today, coming from all over. 'Course, she's gonna be in for a rude awakening when she finds herself short-staffed at the end of May."

"Are you thinking about leaving?"

"You thought I was going to stick around here forever?" When I didn't respond, she crossed her arms. "Well, *I* did. Before I made new plans."

A pale, freckled girl in a knee-length flowered dress appeared. "Ms. Golden? Should we put the garland in the drawing room?"

"Sweetie, *always* wait for the event planner. 'Cause whatever you do, she'll change it, so don't waste your time."

The girl nodded and went back in. Valerie told me, "Managing this new crop of servers—whew. They're earnest, but needy."

"Wait—servers? She's not one, is she?"

"She sure is."

My eyes popped. "But what happened to . . . the headscarves? The aprons?"

"Lana Jean ordered new uniforms last week. And she moved all her Senator paraphernalia to her private office—she'll tell you all about how that's his original desk, too. She *tsk-tsked* all dramatic, drawling something like 'the times they are a-changin.'" Valerie did a spot-on imitation. "But the times *been* changed. She just ain't checked her calendar since the 1850s." She pursed her lips. "Now you know, there's something else going on. Some other reason she stashed the shrine and reupholstered those girls."

"What do you think it is?"

"I have all kinds of suspicions."

A blond woman in a silk dupioni suit strode toward the house. She nodded at us before disappearing inside. Valerie *hmmff*ed. Her eyes fixed on me. "So what brings you here, honey?"

I trusted Valerie with everything I had, but the fewer people who knew I was making Cicada's dress, the better. So I stuck with telling her that Lana Jean promised me documents about the Dearborns. In actuality, I didn't expect to receive a single record until the very last stitch on the magnolia gown was done. So I needed to sew on vintage buttons. Lana Jean finally found suitable ones. "I know my mom would be furious that I'm here, but I don't even care. She's not on my side."

Valerie wrapped an arm around me. "Sweetie, I heard you'll be in Magnolia next year. And I know it doesn't make you happy." She squeezed. "But trust your mother. Come on, let's go in."

Valerie had to run to the kitchen, so I waited in the foyer, glancing up at the watercolor portrait of Priscilla Lavigne Harper, Lana Jean's ancestor who slapped my great-grandmother. I wanted to leave a wad of spit on her magnolia-blossom dress, and yet I'd made one just like it. It was so strange, that beveled feeling of pride for accomplishing a piece of work so difficult; of connection with Lacey Castine, one so intimate that

I used her notes—and yet, disdain for the very thing I made. Especially after the Chilton daughters' ungrateful reaction.

The event planner hurtled around the drawing room, furiously bedecking everything with greenery while the servers rushed to keep pace. Lana Jean appeared. "Anya, the dining room presents a shabby welcome. If we can't get a simple planning committee dinner right, how on earth can we host our *very* VIP guest for my crucial announcement next weekend? Those on Capitol Square have uncompromising standards."

"I assure you . . . ," the woman said commandingly, but Lana Jean interrupted her.

"Please. The centerpieces are all wrong and the chair ties are askew."

Askew. I thought of Lacey Castine.

"I'm on it." The event planner charged out, as if handling a national crisis. Sure, this wasn't a wedding, but it felt equally momentous. Maybe Valerie was right: Something seemed up.

"Well, go assist her." Lana Jean shooed away one of the servers. To the other, she demanded, "Make us some tea." Both young women chorused *yes ma'ams*. Some things hadn't changed.

As Valerie rejoined us, Lana Jean turned in my direction. "My goodness, Noni! I didn't see you! Valerie, might you seat her in my private office?" She handed her a set of keys.

Down the hall, Valerie squeezed my shoulder as she let me in. But I now felt distanced from even her. Trust my mother. How could I, when Mom was forcing me to stay here? I had made my own designs for my own future, but they were meaningless to her.

Warily, I sat down on a blue chair beneath the disapproving gaze of the senator's portrait, his bayonet-tipped gun, and the hateful legacy of his flag. Across the room squatted his old desk, where he might have penned his "Burn It Down" speech. A fat candle on a fancy blue-and-white candleholder kindled a thumb-sized flame.

Lana Jean's notebook rested on the desk as well. Its pink girl-boss cover featured big gold letters: *First, Make a Plan.*

Mom and Lana Jean despised each other, but perhaps they were more akin than they knew. My mother liked plans. She made a to-do list every morning. "If you don't plan your day, someone else will plan it for you," she'd say.

That quote fit me. I just had to switch one word.

Day for life.

"I trust dressmaking hasn't taken up too much of your time." Lana Jean took a seat across from me. "And at least you needn't prepare for many changes. I've heard you're staying in Magnolia."

The reminder sank my heart into my gut, like a stone into deep water.

"The word is that you landed a competitive theatrical internship that your mother won't let you pursue. But surely I misheard. No parent would hold a child back from her dreams."

"It's . . ." How could I refute what she said?

"Oh, darling." Lana Jean reached out and touched the coffee table, as if to shorten the distance between us. "You must understand Radiance. Her world is her own spotlight. She was always this way. At Magnolia High School, for instance, my son turned in a thesis paper, which his teacher published in the school gazette. Then unprompted, and unasked for, Radiance took it upon herself to write a rebuttal, and to disseminate it throughout the school! Pages and pages on every student's desk."

"She did that?"

"Yes!"

"What was your son's paper about?"

"Why, it simply was—" Lana Jean stopped, tucking her index finger under her chin. "My, you do ask such investigatory questions. Just like her."

"We're not alike." I spoke quickly. Months ago, Will had said the same thing about his dad.

Lana Jean stood, wandering to the south window overlooking the lawn. "Throughout his tenure in school, my eldest was known as an athlete and a scholar. I've reread his senior paper so many times over the years, I can almost recite it."

Wow, tone it down with the son worship. Was his second-grade artwork still on the fridge, too? I remembered the country singer with the hairy abs, grinding his hips behind an electric guitar. A crack scholar, that guy. What was his name again? I glanced at the wall. Bayonet, maybe? Brigadier? Battalion? Blockade? Beauregard?

"My son was frustrated by the anger directed at our great country. Slavery was a stain in our history. But his research showed that we Harpers, and other founders of Magnolia, like the Dearborns, were kind to their slaves. That the planters of Magnolia operated within a culture of family. Our family, black and white."

I thought of the narratives in my mother's book. There was no Black and white family within those pages.

Mrs. Chilton turned my way. "Tom Dearborn willed your ancestor land, did he not? And Cuffee Fortune learned carpentry and masonry on his plantation."

Wow. So Lana Jean Chilton really believed slavery was a trade school?

"And, he must have learned to read," Lana Jean said. "In order to pen his memoir. And eloquently, I might add, though he did dissemble. Who else could have taught him to write, but his master or mistress?"

I said nothing. Certainly not that learning to read should have been Cuffee's right. It was only remarkable because it was illegal to teach enslaved people. And "dissemble"? What did he lie about, according to Lana Jean?

"When your mother broadcasted her 'alternate history' to her classmates, I suspended her for a week. And do you know what she did? She sent a letter to the editor. Not to our town paper, but the *Washington Post*."

Such a Mom move. I couldn't help but feel a spark of pride. Because there was no culture of family in a town where Priscilla Lavigne Harper slapped a Black child on a public street with no consequence.

"And here you are, an adult. Yet Radiance would be furious if she knew you were within fifty feet of this land." Lana Jean stood beside my chair, resting her hand on the brocade back. "Crossing your mother could be downright dangerous, as my oldest son sadly learned."

"What do you mean?"

She didn't seem to hear me. "Maybe it was that she grew up so poor. Or that she was raised by an ailing grandmother, with no mother of her own. But all eyes must be on Radiance Castine."

From a drawer in the senator's desk, she took out a velvet jewelry box, and placed it on the coffee table. I slipped it into my bag. Vintage buttons, which Lana Jean insisted upon sourcing for her daughter's gown, careened inside like marbles. I hoped they were worth her pained search.

Going back to the window, she opened the curtains to reveal the full might of the sun. "I love Magnolia more than anyone. But this isn't your place, Noni. You need a way out. You glimmer with talent. And yet you'll never get a second glance, as long as you're in her sights."

I was so far in my own world, I almost walked into Jabari.

"Hey." He steadied me. "You feeling okay? I know things are rough right now." His fingers tapped my arm. We were just friends, but I felt tingly. "I really like your company, so of course I'd like if you stayed here. But not if it holds you back."

I wanted to tell him I had a way out, but it meant being in cahoots with Lana Jean. He would like my company so much less if he knew I made a deal with the Devil Wears Prada. But I had to—how else could I leave? Lana Jean was so wrong about so many things, but she was right about one. As long as I stayed in Magnolia, I could never be known as myself.

Still, Jabari was a little like my mother. His pride for Blackness ran river-deep. Mine seemed to gurgle in starts and stops, like a spring. Sometimes I worried it was running dry.

He asked if I wanted to grab lunch. As we headed to the student center, he remarked, "Your hair is really nice, by the way. It's, you know. Pret . . . beautiful."

"Thank you." I'd stopped blow-drying and flat-ironing and hot-combing my hair, thinking it was just fine the way it grew out of my head. But "pret-beautiful" was so much better than "just fine."

We shared a couch at the student center and ate a delicious pasta salad from the same Tupperware dish. Jabari told me he rarely bought lunch when he could both save money and make better food at home. Above us, a bulletin board was shingled with flyers for things like a Studence for Prudence pep club rally, and *Cocke-xanne,* a riff on the Cyrano de Bergerac play.

"School spirit gets a little out of control, right?" Jabari tapped one of the posters. "But the Cocke-a-Doodle Doo Dance could be kind of fun. Some of us BSA members were thinking of crashing it, sorta. Trying to make it cool. It's always really corny, I've heard. Hey, would you—would you think about going with me?"

Was Jabari Nichols asking me on a date? Be chill, I counseled myself. Just be chill about it. But I blurted, "That sounds fun, I'd love to!" Ugh! The enthusiasm! I needed to make a joke. Checking out the date, I snapped my finger in jest. "Guess that means I won't be going to Lana Jean's *very* VIP event."

"Lana Jean's event?"

"I'm kidding." I told Jabari I'd visited Trianon in hopes of Lana Jean providing documents. It was half true, though I knew darned well I wouldn't get so much as a sheet of paper until the dress was done. Besides, something Lana Jean said about Cuffee bothered me—that is, besides *everything* she said about Cuffee. But something in particular tugged at me.

When I described all the event prep at Trianon, Jabari's face tightened into seriousness. "If Lana Jean's suddenly trying to sweep Trianon's racism under the rug, that's actually disconcerting."

"Yeah, Valerie is pretty sus about it, too." I offered, "Lana Jean talked about a special guest, and her 'crucial announcement,' and how people at Capitol Square have high standards . . . but I don't know what she meant."

"I can guess. Lana Jean's running for governor."

"But she hasn't been in politics, besides town council."

"I'm gonna bet that's exactly what she'll tout. She'll bill herself as a 'small business owner' and a 'former principal.' Not to mention she'll crow about being Senator Harper's favorite granddaughter. Think about it—she loves power."

"Who do you think's the VIP guest?"

"Must be none other than Governor Clinch Hallard."

"But is *he* up for reelection?"

"Nah-uh. Virginia is actually the only state where governors can't serve consecutive terms, but word is he's got eyes on the presidency. When you're in politics, you have to keep your friends close and your donors even closer. Everyone knows Lana Jean forks over the maximum allowance for Hallard, and she's the queen of raising even more cash. I bet in exchange, he'll endorse her."

"I don't know much about him."

"His shtick is that parents should determine what schools teach. Of course, he doesn't mean supportive parents of LGBTQ kids. Nor does he mean our parents. *Black* parents. Which he drives home by talking about hoisting Southern history high like the flag."

"And he never says *which* flag." I remembered his press event. "American, or Confederate? You'd think he'd be into Lana Jean's racist rendition of Trianon, then."

"He's gotta care about his broader public image. He can only look *so* racist. Same with Lana Jean."

But I brought up, "At the same time, Lana Jean stood back during the school board elections last fall. She only wrote one op-ed and bought a billboard." I recalled the one with her picture on it, the kind you see for real-estate agents and slip-and-fall lawyers. "But otherwise, she just let it happen."

"All the stuff she did was public. It highlighted her, not the issue," Jabari considered.

"Then maybe she's trying to hold a very public, very media-driven pushback of some issue." I realized, "Maybe she's trying to bring back Founding Families."

But for the din around us, we sat in silence for a second. "But if she *were*, we would've heard about it right now," Jabari surmised. "When she raised the ruckus over the senator's statue, there were thousands of people from all over the country. That's what you need for media attention."

"Maybe for now, she's trying to keep it hush-hush." Behind me, a noisy group of guys sitting around a table laughed loudly, as if to mock the very idea of quiet.

"One way to know is to see if there's a permit on file. When I worked for my friend's A/V company, some of our clients found out the hard way that you need one of those." He took out his phone. "Fluvie would know."

I stiffened. "Fluvanna Fluharty?" As if he could be talking about anyone else.

"She works in the permits office. She probably left work by now, but maybe she can check tomorrow. I'll give her a ring."

I grabbed his hand. "Wait. Don't."

"Hey. I know, things are tense between you both, but." He seemed to be hedging how much he could reassure me without breaking confidence of whatever she'd said about me before. "I'm just gonna ask her what she knows, okay?"

I heard a chirp on the other end as Jabari walked to the opposite wall, sitting inside an old pay phone booth, a vestige of the 1990s that the school kept around because kids took selfies in it. Though it was missing a door, I couldn't hear him at first. But the loud group of guys finally left. So I couldn't help but catch the last of Jabari's sentence: ". . . permit's been filed? Is that something you can tell me?" Then, "Yeah, if you don't mind taking a look before you close out."

I pretended to look at my phone, hoping *all* they would talk about were the permits. It was one thing for Jabari to know how I messed up at the cow festival way back when. But now? The idea of admitting to him that I cornered Fluvie at work?

Why had I done that?

"Oh, yeah, the cattle festival." He laughed a bit. "Gotta expect that every summer. So there's nothing else within the sixty-day deadline?"

Sixty days. I remembered Fluvie's inflectionless voice.

Jabari nodded, chuckling. "We were thinking Lana Jean was trying to do a reboot of Founding Families. Noni overheard some things, so she thought . . ."

My heart beat fast.

"Nuh-uh, she didn't tell me . . ." Jabari stopped. The chill in his eyes when he looked at me shot a current of cold through my veins. He stood up. "Seriously?" He left the phone booth, turning the opposite direction of the food court, down a corridor, walking farther and farther. I watched the broad slope of his shoulders grow more and more rigid until they were right angles with the floor.

CHAPTER 21

Blondell could see something was up when she came into the office. I was taking forever to edit an e-blast. And I needed to finish the magnolia gown, to sew on the buttons that rattled in my backpack like a bottle of Midol, just as my nerves had clattered around when Jabari walked away. After hearing Lana Jean's praise about her son's racist drivel, I'd lost my appetite for sewing. But I'd also lost Jabari. And while I would never choose a guy over my dreams of working in design, his potential interest in me had been the last bit of real sweetness about Virginia left.

I tried focusing my attention on the *Charmer's Almanac*. Blondell reached over and minimized my browser. "Honey, you don't have me fooled. You're not reading; you're just sitting there with a sad look like a puppy dog going to get fixed. What on earth is going on?"

"Nothing."

She studied my face. "No, it's something."

I shrugged. "I guess so. I ran into Lana Jean and we talked for a bit." I didn't tell her I sewed a whole gown for her daughter. "I just want to know, why does my mom hate her so much? Why can't she just get over whatever it is?"

Blondell fidgeted in her chair. "Oh, honey. Let's not open that can of worms."

"See, that's what I'm saying. I didn't know there was a can of worms. What is it, Blondell?"

A frown pressed into her face. "Eighteen years, and your mama's never said a thing." It wasn't a question. It was a statement, one loaded with disappointment. With sadness. With a particular fear shining in her blue eyes, and regret that she'd said anything at all, because now she'd have to say more.

"Ask Radiance to tell you."

I wasn't letting her out of this. "If there's something Mom's been hiding from me my whole life, she'll stonewall more than Jackson."

Blondell groaned. "Fine. Close the door and sit down."

With the score 41–28, the Magnolia High School Secessionists were getting slaughtered by the Buffalo Gap Billies, as if it were the actual Civil War and the field was in Gettysburg. I imagined the scene Blondell set for me: Under the white-bright stadium lights, the men who'd played on Magnolia's football team ten years ago during its most glorious of years—Blondell mentioned three names I'd never heard before: Clayton Taylor, Horace Gore, and Rebel Chilton—escalated into screaming drunkenness as the clock counted down. With their Solo cups making a splash zone of the bleacher seats in front of them, they bellowed at the Seceshes to run to the right, to knock the other guys out, to just fucking pass the ball already.

Blondell and her friend from high school, Jessica Suarez, sat hip to hip. The sparkle of Blondell's engagement ring seemed as blinding as the lights overhead. Her fiancé, a plumber living in another town, had proposed a few days before.

She'd accepted almost happily. Neither she nor Jessica admitted to anyone, not even themselves, that there was something between them more dazzling than that diamond. But my mother could see it, Blondell said. And Radiance was there that night with them, on a visit home during her fall break at Princeton. So was her best friend, Weldon Golden, having driven in from Richmond to see his high school best friend. The four of them sat together on the shaky metal bleachers, eating salt-crusted soft pretzels and staining their fingers Trump-orange with Doritos, drinking Coke spiked with mini-bottles of rum.

At halftime, Blondell and Weldon went to grab more snacks, waiting at the concession stand with overexcited high school students. Rebel and Clayton pushed by, wobbly-drunk. Clayton bumped Blondell's shoulder and shouted, *Guess this dyke finally found a man.*

Weldon stepped out of line. The only team he'd starred in during high school had been academic bowl. He was five foot eight and slim, squaring off against Clayton Taylor, a Chunky Soup can of a man, and Rebel Chilton, still built like the quarterback he once was.

Don't ever use that word again.

The men hurled insults back and forth. Rebel and Clayton called Weldon "street" and "thug," everything that really meant the n-word, Blondell described. During their high school football days, they'd gotten along fine enough with their Black teammates, with the guys who'd played the game. But they'd always nourished a special kind of hate for Weldon and Radiance.

That night, Mrs. Chilton, the former school principal, breezed by: *Boys, what is going* on? She eyed her oldest son, Rebel. The young men peeled apart.

Out with her fiancé the next evening, Blondell ran into Radiance and Weldon at the drive-in. Weldon's trunk was propped open, and a nearly new side table, secured with bungee cords, protruded from the back of his Toyota Camry. He and Radiance had gone for a long drive, and the piece was set out as trash at Twenty Paces. Weldon refurbished discarded pieces like that. And rich people threw out perfectly good things.

Right before the second feature film, heavy tires crunched the gravel road leading to the field. A diesel engine growled. Rebel arrived in his red F-350 pickup with its four-foot-long Confederate flag rippling from the back. He, Clayton, and Horace sat shoulder to broad shoulder in the cab.

Blondell and her fiancé left around then. "So I wasn't there to see what happened next." Her pale eyes fixed on my face. "But Radiance told me everything. At least, I think she did."

Rebel shoved Weldon. *You fucking stole my family's table.*

Weldon staggered backward, popcorn raining on his feet. *Let's just go,* he said to Radiance. The two slid back into his car. He shoved it into drive.

But the boys followed them down the gravel path. On the dark, lonely road, Weldon gunned it. The boys accelerated, their stars-and-bars waving like a threat stitched in fabric.

Their fender was so close, Weldon couldn't see it in his rearview mirror. He suddenly veered his car off the road into a pasture, racing a diagonal path across to connect with Longstreet Street. His rear tire popped. *Go, go, go,* Radiance urged. Her side of the car sank as the wheel rim sliced into mud like a pizza cutter into crust. The car tripped and stopped, trapping them in the middle of the field. Radiance held up her flip phone, trying to get a signal.

Get out. Clayton and Rebel banged on the windows. Maybe they only wanted to scare them. Maybe not. Radiance groped beneath her seat and found the only weapon she could: a long, plastic ice scraper. After yanking the table from the open trunk, Rebel pushed his way into the back seat, grabbing at Radiance's shirt. She and Weldon scrambled from the car. Clayton lunged at her while Rebel held Weldon back. Horace stood by, laughing at it all. But his face must've gone slack when Radiance jabbed Clayton's face with the bladed end of the scraper, stabbing again and again. He screamed.

Rebel was enraged. He punched Weldon, then grabbed Radiance's neck, half dragging, half throwing her into the payload.

Bleeding, Clayton picked up the side table and slammed it into Weldon's back, felling him. Horace stood by as Clayton blindly punched him, kicked him. In the truck bed, Radiance struggled, terrified. She managed to sit up, seeing Weldon lying still. Rebel struck her and she fell back down.

I imagined Molly, our enslaved ancestor, toppling from a blow dealt by Tom Dearborn.

They'd gone too far, Horace shouted. But no one in control listened. Weldon managed to stand one more time, holding on to the tall side of the pickup truck.

As Blondell spoke, the image in my head was of me, age ten, holding on to the sides of an ice-skating rink while Mom swooped up behind me. I remembered the scrape of her blades on ice, the strength of her mitten-clad hands supporting me in the refrigerated air as she pulled me to my feet.

But that night, Rebel picked her up and threw her onto the ground like refuse. She could barely breathe. She watched in horror as Rebel lifted that enormous Confederate flag from its sheath, revealing a gleaming bayonet attached to the end. She saw him raise both arms, saw those crossed stripes illuminated by the headlamps of Weldon's car. In the white light, Weldon's blood gleamed like glass.

Now we did it, Horace said. The others giggled like schoolboys, though Clayton held his eye, his adrenaline failing and the pain setting in. Jumping into the truck, the three fled. A single wounded groan trailed behind them like exhaust fumes.

Let me hold your hand, Mom had said that day at the rink. And I did, and I was unsteady, but we circled the ice.

Almost twenty years ago, my broken-ribbed mother pressed on Weldon's wound, kneeling with the weight of her body. Desperate minutes passed before another car cruised down the road.

Weldon was shuttled into emergency surgery. He lived for days. Four days. But on the fifth morning, after he'd regained consciousness and saw his mother's face hovering above him, pained with a hope she'd dared cling to, he died.

Blondell twisted her hands together. Rebel was convicted of second-degree manslaughter, and Clayton with assault. Will's father and Clayton's uncle, Hudd Taylor, worked their defense.

Standing for the prosecution was Radiance Castine, my mother. She testified.

"That's what broke Valerie," Blondell said. "In all ways. Valerie and Reggie Golden were strapped, having to pay their son's medical bills. Then the town challenged them for their land—and you know who was behind that—Lana Jean. By then, she was on the corrupt town council."

"Whatever happened to Rebel? And his friends?"

She sighed. "Horace never went to jail. He married, moved out to Louisa County, and died of throat cancer a few years ago. Clayton served time, just a little while. But he wouldn't see a doctor about his eye, even with it rotting in his head like a moldy grape. Didn't want it taken out." She shook her head. "He lost his eye anyway, and the infection damned near killed him. He wasn't the same after that. He moved to Alaska, last I ever heard.

"Rebel was supposed to go to Duke for business school, but that was over. He said three years in prison would ruin his life. Someone smuggled him pills, and he died of a drug overdose. Who knows if it was an accident? Either way, Lana Jean blames Radiance for her son's death. And she blames Valerie."

"That doesn't make sense."

"But that's grief. It can pull you right out of your own head, make you become someone else. Lana Jean stayed that person."

Blondell squeezed my hand. "Radiance sees Valerie's job at Trianon—after all this—as something unforgivable. The person she really wants to lash out against is Lana Jean Chilton. But we aim for our closest targets. They're the only ones we can hit in the dark."

A hasty flip of my Linear Algebra textbook page earned me a paper cut. It hurt, but nothing like what I had just learned from Blondell. I looked at the slim, crimson line on my finger. This town's history was anything but linear—it was crooked like crazy, drawn on thick and yet hard to make out. Why couldn't Mom have just told me?

Plugging my finger into my mouth, I knew I needed to switch gears—equations on paper didn't make sense when real life couldn't even add up. I was almost done with the capstone paper for my Black Studies class. I wished I could ask Jabari to take a look. I wished I could have told him what I'd found out about Valerie's son.

I took out a different book: Mom's text, *The Remembered*. There was a strange comfort now about seeing her name on the cover, even though I'd seen it a million times before. I had skimmed Euphemia Sterling's narrative early in the fall semester, but I needed to read it again. And maybe this woman's story would allow me to pull things into perspective. After all, her life had to be far more difficult than mine.

Euphemia Sterling

August 1, 1889

Respite never took to me, and I never did to it. It wasn't easy to find, for one. I remember when the missus had me and my brother ride there to get things settled for our little Miss's visit. Gave us scant directions and sent us not well before dusk. Felt like we was traveling through a ghost story. You take a road what twists around a mountain, and it feels like some road to forever, all 'em woods crowded with hickory and poplar, thick with brush, dark as Egypt. Isaac shone his lantern down, and we see wolf prints in the soft mud, tracks fresh as bakery bread. Plantation itself ain't nothing to holler about, for all that place's master—we called him Master Balding on account of his patchwork scalp—for all he had pots of money. A two-over-two what wasn't well appointed inside, at least not when we saw it.

A brother named Isaac? Master Balding? Could Euphemia Sterling be Effie, the Dearborns' enslaved servant? Holy shit! My fingers tight on the page, I read on.

My miss was his betrothed, see, and Isaac and I was to be her wedding gift. But she ain't want to marry him. Only person wanted a marriage was me. I was newly nineteen, and my intended was Daniel. A more handsome man never walked Virginia, long-limbed and solid shoulders and a sweet, sweet face.

Well, white folks butted in, like they always do. The miss say she want to throw me some wedding and invite her friends. You ever heard of that? Someone say they throwing you a wedding and it's really a party for them? And we still gots to do all the work?

And more than that. Master Balding was a widower, the missus' brother-in-law. Wife's death left four children motherless. And on her deathbed that woman say she ain't never want no mean stepmother for them children. So little Miss, being family, was pressed to marry this man in his forties, with her still a girl.

It stung me like nettles, that proposal. See, Daniel was manservant to a young gentleman whose heart was hung on little Miss, and I felt sure he would ask her to marry him. That would've meant her wedding gift—me, would be my wedding gift, too: I would get a life with my husband. As maidservant and manservant, we couldn't never have no cabin together, but we might have slept together some nights in the same bed. I dreamt of clean ticking stuffed with fresh hay, of wool blankets knitted tight with love.

Little Miss didn't want to share no bed with Master Balding, 'specially when she found out about his passel of yellow children. And about Star. His concubine, that poor woman forced to lay with that man. Wasn't much I could do for her, so I prayed the little Miss would break it off and all would be set right for me again, at least.

Miss must've found her spirit. The day after I was married, I was serving them the afternoon meal, Master Balding and the little Miss out on the verandah.

"Stay heyah should we neeeed sumthin'," she tell me. I knew something heavy would commence and she wanted me close. I was her thing of comfort, a doll for a child.

Sure enough, she say to her intended, "When you asked for my hand you was nuh-vus. Weyel, now it's my tuun fuh anxiety. I must tell you sumthin'."

I do a fair imitation of how the rich white folks talked, all draggy, lazy and slow. Of course, Master Balding look all vexed, and say something like, "Whateeevah could it be, dearest?"

And little Miss says, "I ah-septed yo' proposal in haste, and I have come to reconsiduh what I thought was my affections. I do not wish to marry you."

And he looked like he'd been slapped in the face, but expecting the blow. He mumbled something about wanting the best for her. I was trying to look invisible, but nearly collapsed with relief.

But wasn't nothing to celebrate. Next afternoon, I find her crying in bed, her mama shushing her. Come to find out she couldn't just reject the proposal. My master was in big debt to Balding, see. With the marriage, he'd agreed to forgive it.

It was like a game board, everything set back the way it was. And little Miss got desperate. One day Isaac walked in on her nosing through our master's study like a hog for roots, upturning everything, searching for a key and the store of bills he kept. She bullied my brother into telling her where it was hidden.

Well, Isaac and me, we'd done set up chess boards after white folks played, with all the pieces in place and turned the right way, black against white, even though we ain't know the game.

We'd done arranged the decanters on the shelf to be just so when we'd never took a sip. We'd placed wine in the cellar, whites with whites, when we couldn't hardly see through the glass in the dark. We'd sort books on the shelf in perfect order of the alphabet, even with none of us knowing how to read. That night I helped Isaac put the master's study back to how it was, but we ain't get everything right. So later when that man summoned my brother, his heart dropped to the floor.

Isaac said the master had the coals all hot, and a red-handled poker stuck in the pile like a pitchfork in hay. Told him real calm that a thieving manservant was a waste of a black body. Said only Isaac knew where his lockbox was hidden, and the key besides. And he said—lord this hurts to repeat—but Master said, "Boy, you a smart nigger, but you never been 'ticularly sturdy. So I can't use you for the field, I don't need none of your increase, and I can't honorably sell a thief. Now, use your wits and tell me where my money is, and I'll let you pull off your shirt for a whippin', 'stead of your trousers for something else."

Likely it was meant to scare my brother. But Isaac wasn't about to find out. He fessed right up. I was tidying the little Miss's room when Master busted in with my brother behind him, nearly melted with fear. Master went straight for the jewelry case and demanded I produce the key. There it was, his money. He gathered up everything in that rosewood box and told us to keep our mouths shut.

When Miss found all her jewels missing, she go to her mama, who says they sent her jewelry ahead to Respite for safekeeping. But with her father's money also taken, she knew she'd been caught. That girl came to look at Isaac with narrow, hateful eyes.

Meanwhile my time with my husband grew as bountiful as crops after a good, soaking rain. Daniel's master kept coming around, pretending he was there to talk with Pa but really eyeing baby Miss, who had grown within courting range. I should have known something was wrong, but I was in bliss with my husband. We'd spend time alone before daybreak, while my miss was fit to be tied about that young man coming around for her sister. Each night she'd cuss and fuss, spitting out all kinds of hateful talk.

I was so tired from my early mornings that I slept clean

through my nights. I was so in love with my husband that I couldn't figure something more was wrong. But I was storing up the good times with my beloved, knowing drought was coming fast.

Then, the miss took ill. She filled pot after pot with puke. I thought she ate something strange, and talked to the cook. We was standing by the springhouse, and Moll said, "That girl with child." I remember leaning against the cooling slats, my eyes as wide as pans.

Right then the hired white boy walk by. And I recalled some of the nonsense little Miss would spout at night. Once, she said she'd ruin herself, then no one would marry her.

Well.

By and by, she would lay in her room, humming and sewing and puking, her folks worried up the walls waiting for the doctor to come around from riding the county. When he did, he wrung his hands and whispered what all the slaves knew. Oh, I thought the master would've died of apoplexy right then.

Instead he went on a furious tear down the hill, burst into the hired boy's cabin, shotgun in his arms. That white boy ain't had no idea what for, but he figured it out quick. We never saw him again.

The wedding was postponed for her "illness." The little Miss wanted her parents to send her west, to one of the territories. Said they could get the baby adopted, and she'd become a schoolteacher. Well, that ain't what happened. Me and her was sent out near Martinsville to live with a white family of no name in a real backwoods house. Them was hard days. They ain't never had slaves and like to work me to death.

The little Miss sobbed all the time, and finally she threw a fit and these folks had enough. Put us in a carriage and drove us back.

Master and Missus was disgraced with her showing up all big. You should've seen them scrambling like ants trying to hide her. But there wasn't no secrets around there.

The miss's time came real sudden. Master called in the doctor, but that girl ain't have enough in her. She died in her bed, and so did her baby. The first one, at least.

Wait—the *first* baby? Turning the page, I couldn't read fast enough.

The first come out blue as a ghost. His twin? The only thing blue about him was his eyes. But the cook showed me his fingernails, the little purple half-moon down at the bottom of each, and whispered, "This how you tell he black like us."

The master and missus buried the young Miss with her stillborn child. The missus and master fought, for she wanted to carve that baby's dates on that stone, despite the scandal. Said he deserved to be remembered.

In days, the thriving child darkened like a bruise. Lord, every slave man on that place shook with fear, and every woman's heart stopped for her father, husband, and brothers—and for that black baby. The missus supposedly sent him to a free couple up North. Lord knows if she did; all I know is I never saw that child again.

Now it wasn't scandal no more. Little Miss was a victim. The white men in the county wanted every black man whipped until they found out who raped a white girl, when me and the other slaves knew it was the other way around.

It's why Isaac told on himself. He had to, else some other black man could be blamed. Master threw him in the springhouse. It was dark in there, and damp, and the chill sank into your bones. He stayed in there for five days before they arranged to take him to the county jail to wait for trial.

Isaac told me the full. Little Miss made him, so she'd be unfit to marry. He couldn't do what she needed at first, he couldn't for a while, but he feared for his life and made himself. I remember those nights we talked through those waved slats, his voice then like mine now—breaking.

When they took him from the springhouse, a mob was waiting outside the plantation gates. Then old Master Taylor got riled and tilted his shotgun.

I done moved on from that slavery life. My Daniel died a few years after we married. But he bled clad in blue. He left this earth for my freedom, alls our freedom, and he left me with child to remind me of him each day. I did find another love and had more children.

And I'll never forget their uncle, my baby brother Isaac. I got to remember him, see. Them people wouldn't even give me his body to bury. They threw him in some grave, no stone, meant for him to be gone and forgotten. But as long as I remember Isaac, he's still here. When I pass one day, well then I suppose it'll be his time.

Stunned, I sat with the open book on my lap, looking out of the window at the inky evening sky. "Isaac." I said his name aloud. "Isaac." I felt the weight of it. When the sunrise lifted the dark, I would see the land where he died, where he was buried, that unknowable place.

His sister's story meant the light-skinned man from Philadelphia wasn't Sophie's half brother—he was her son. Sophie's Black son, Hoyt Askew, became Lacey Castine's father. And Sophie, the enslaver buried yards beyond my window, was my great-great-great-great-grandmother. We shared the same birthday, the same name, and the same blood.

Sophie's cache of torn pages ended before Isaac's story began. And Mom had never connected that Euphemia was an enslaved woman living in the very same home as we did. She would have read Euphemia's narrative countless times. In editing her book, she had researched all those who gave testimony. But she was unable to find biographical information for many. Without Sophie Dearborn's papers, she had no way to connect the story.

And I had no way of telling her, just like I couldn't divulge that I knew about that terrible night when she lost her best friend. I couldn't talk to her, because she never found it in herself to share her truth with me.

The next morning, I walked down to the little cemetery behind the iron gates. It was early, the sky white with cloud cover. I sat at Sophie Dearborn's grave.

It didn't feel fair. White plantation girls got such a good rap. It's like they were silk-clad myths, rustling through the halls of history. They were portrayed with no power or agency, as if white womanhood was slavery lite. *Or* there was some fabricated sisterhood between white women and Black servants, of gossip and giggles during hair-brushing and corset-lacing.

Worse, there was a merging of those two untruths: that Black and white women were sisters striding together for freedom from the patriarchy, when our patriarchies were separate and unequal.

Sophie Dearborn was a product of her time, but so was Euphemia

Sterling. So was Isaac. Saying a slaveholder was a product of their time implied there was only one way to be, that the year we were born fixed us in some snow globe of perception.

But people were as prismatic as glitter, falling differently every time you shook the glass. I thought of the heritage breeds clucking and lowing and honking on Charm's Willy Wonka–colored acreage. The past kept alive, even when we no longer needed what it had to give. Those animals, products of their time.

And people? There might've been a hundred ways to be a product of one's time. There must be still.

And too, I thought of the barren flower bed that once held Robert E. Lee riding through an intended forever of all that we raise high on pedestals. There are monuments poured from metals or carved from marble or chiseled into mountains. There are the simpler monuments dedicated to lives on earth, like the one I knelt in front of.

And there are the monuments we create from nothing but the air of our imaginations when we shape the truth of history into a fable. Eras become tales with a story arc. History becomes a story that places the reader at some contrived resolution, the way even the most sobering of museums deposit guests at the gift shop.

"Sophie." I spoke to silence, except for the sounds of squirrels rooting in the brush or the brook rushing over stones. "I learned that we're family. I'm your great-great-great-great-granddaughter."

My voice broke, but I found it again. "And I'm Black. And I'm fucking proud of my people, Sophie. I'm fucking proud of us."

Except for a blue jay screaming overhead, there was nothing. No stream of light flooding from the clouds, no sudden burst of wind, no otherworldly sign that Sophie Dearborn was listening from beyond. And that was fine. I didn't need her anymore.

CHAPTER 22

I had the whole story of Sophie Dearborn. I knew who had fathered her child. I didn't need Lana Jean's documents. But I would finish Cicada's gown because I did need closure, just as each tiny button would secure the bodice. I wanted to be done with it. Done with the dress and done with Magnolia, Virginia.

The early morning sun brushed my shoulders as I walked toward Buried Silver, rays the same pale yellow shade of the formerly vacant building I'd huddled under in the rain. Since then, it had been repainted with a new sign hanging out front. I looked twice at the picture of a steaming mug, the wisps shaped like people clustered together.

Immediately, I tried the door. It was locked. I knocked hard. When Valerie answered, I nearly fell into her arms. "Valerie, I can't believe it!" So this was her secret!

She laughed, sweeping me into a big hug. "I can't believe it, either, baby. But here I am at The Gather Coffee and Teahouse. Proprietress." Making fun of Mrs. Chilton's title, she laughed again, louder this time.

The Gather was the coolest café ever. Besides Valerie's delicious coffees, there would be fresh-baked pastries and cookies every day, plus homemade soups, pot pies, sandwiches, and quiches. And the way she'd decked it out! The sewing table that once held Sophie Dearborn's torn diary pages glinted near the counter. The quilt I knew to be Lacey Castine's made one wall a whole art gallery's worth of colorful. Plus there was a little stage for live music and open mic nights.

I was incredulous. "How did you do this? I thought you were too old, and broke, and—"

Chuckling, Valerie went behind the counter to the commercial-sized coffee machine.

"Seriously, how did this happen?" I looked at the enlarged old photographs of The Gather filling one wall, pausing at the image of Lacey Castine waving with one hand and holding on to a distracted Gramma with another.

"Everything's been a whirlwind." Valerie explained how the space—formerly 155 Main Street, the long-ago fabric shop of pearl button infamy, went up for sale. "I didn't know where I'd get the money to buy it. And I didn't know a thing about running a coffee shop. But ready or not, I'm opening in June."

She explained how she and her husband sank their entire savings into their start-up. Between Will and Blondell, she got consulting, equipment, and supplies. Jabari's mom, a chef, created the menu. Jabari advised her on sound equipment. He and his dad painted the walls and made some building repairs.

"I had to keep this quiet." Valerie placed a mug in front of me. "If Lana Jean got wind I was starting my own business, she'd fire me, and I needed the money."

Nodding, I sipped the drink she'd made. "You like it?" she asked. "It's a cardamom mocha."

"It's so good."

When the roof leaked, Valerie said, the unforeseen expense meant she didn't have enough cash to open, nor enough to see the business through until it turned a profit. "Last week, I got a call from your mama. And I found us sitting at this same table right here. She wrote me a check. It's enough for Reggie and I to make it a whole year without a profit, if it comes to that."

"Mom gave you a loan?" I was flabbergasted.

“Ain’t a loan, baby doll. It’s a gift. Radiance says she’s done a lot of soul-searching.”

So had I. But in my case, I had to make a difficult choice—but it was the only way I could achieve my life’s plans.

Valerie’s hazel eyes were bright with anticipation over her new dream but shadowed with sadness, the way they’d always be in remembrance of her son. He was sasha, the living dead, thriving in her memory but forever gone from her view.

Reaching across, she rested her fingers on my necklace. “Radiance gave you that.” It was a statement, not a question. “Weldon worked in the mailroom at Stonepost College for a time. He always did like that quilt.”

“He did?” I reached up, hand at my throat. “This is a miniature of it?”

“It is. He felt drawn to it like a magnet, and he never knew why. He created this miniature, just like he styled the other necklace after *this* quilt.” She nodded at the tapestry on the wall. “The necklace your mama’s always worn when she’s needed it.”

My fingers encircled my own pendant. On the wall beside me was a photograph of Weldon Golden, forever smiling. He was older in this image, a real adult, mid-twenties. The sun made a halo of his blondish brown hair. A shadow loomed behind him.

Valerie looked at me frankly. “I know you found out what happened to him.”

“Only yesterday. I’m so sorry.”

“Your mother knows that you know, too.”

Blondell fessed up to Mom, then. A quick twinge of anger that she couldn’t let me challenge Mom was replaced by a deeper sense of relief for the very same reason. I didn’t have to confront my mother.

Glancing again at the image of Weldon Golden, I realized the shadow pressed to the wall wasn’t his. It was of someone with a wide berth of hair and slender shoulders. “My mother took that picture.”

"It was the day we lost him." She nodded longingly at the picture, as if she could will him back. "Weldon had been her best friend when they were in school. And years later, when they were both back in Magnolia—well." She stopped, her gaze meeting the floor.

It was enough to inject me with a gut-seizing kind of anxiety. "Valerie, may I ask, when did your son pass away?"

She continued staring at her feet, her hands, his image.

"When?" I spoke gently, but with insistence.

Valerie looked me full in the face. "Nineteen years ago."

"Nineteen years?"

"A few months less than that."

Now I couldn't meet her eyes. "Mom was engaged then." I didn't mean to sound so desperate. "To my dad. Right?"

Valerie twisted her hands. "She and your father argued, honey—over Weldon, since she'd always been sweet on him. Your dad didn't want her to visit Magnolia. They broke things off right before she got on the train."

My stomach roiled as I thought of meeting Valerie for the first time, the look of marvel spreading like light across her face. *I knew*, she'd said.

"And after she returned to Boston?"

"They got back together. She told your father, but he never wanted to find out who was who. It was only a matter of days between your mother being with him and being with Weldon. These things happen when you're young. There's no shame."

My breath caught in my throat. "Does Mom know who is who?"

"How could she, from looking? Think about your father, and look at my son. They're so alike."

"But my dad . . ." I felt I might choke. "He betrayed Mom, too. My aunt said he gave something . . ."

Valerie closed her eyes. "He wanted to help other couples to start their own families. Four years ago."

"*What?* Who?"

"We don't know. It was an anonymous donation. At a clinic."

"But why?" I thought of heritage animals, of sires and dams. The buying and selling of lineage.

"Sometimes people want to leave a piece of themselves in the world, Noni. They want to be certain." She examined my face. "I like to imagine Weldon lives on in you."

My heart felt like it dropped from my body, falling to the very bottom of the earth. Somewhere I could have siblings I would never know, just as the man who had fathered me could be buried in the cemetery at the end of the road.

Valerie reached out, clasping my wrist in her hand, holding it tightly. Have you ever felt time in someone's grasp? I did. I felt my mom's relationship with the Goldens—the years of it, the depth, the durability. The indelible love within.

"I met you when you were only a month old. We all came up to see you: my husband and I, Blondell, and Ms. Castine, who insisted upon the christening in the first place. Your father opened the door with you in his arms. He was beaming. He treated us like family, and he loved you as you are."

Priscilla Lavigne Harper's replica gown hung on the form. Every smooth curve of silk held a static charge of racist legacy, enough to make my hair stand on end. Weldon's death was part of that legacy, a part no one had ever shared with me.

For my entire life, Mom and Dad went along with a fiction that Mark Zavier Reid's DNA made up half of mine, no question. But now someone else could be my father, too?

There were too many secrets here, too few friends, and no dreams for me at all.

A knock at the door startled me. I looked through the peephole. It was Fluvie. What was she doing here? I stayed quiet. But she called out my name. "Noni? It's me. Fluvie."

Did she see me come up here? Looking around the room, I felt cornered. I threw the box of buttons back into my backpack and grabbed the mannequin, waltzing it into the bathroom and shutting the door.

"I was hoping to speak to you about something," she said from the hallway. *Now* she was ready to talk?

"One second." I couldn't do anything about the white taffeta scraps everywhere, nor the sewing machine. I had to open the door.

"I'm sorry to barge in like this." She wore a skirt and a sleeveless blouse, and nervously rubbed up and down her tattooed arm. "I'd erased your number from my phone. But my mom works at the salon across the street, and she saw you come up here."

She eyed the fabric scraps on the sewing table. I cursed myself for not being better at cleaning up as I went along. "Did Mrs. Chilton put you up to making DixieStar's wedding dress? She's always had this point of pride of making all her daughters' wedding gowns with her own two hands. Maybe it's because it's a second wedding . . ."

"Oh. No. I was . . ." I scrambled up an excuse. "Lana Jean has some books, and I was doing a research project for class . . ." I grabbed a history book from my backpack, one I had planned to donate to a Little Free Library box. "I was just bringing this back."

"Well, put it back in the closet, and let's go. You need to see what's happening at the courthouse."

In the closet? I went to the bedroom, pretending I'd seen the walk-in before. A short rod held a few suits and a Confederate reenactor uniform. Otherwise, there were three bookcases. Most of the books were about the Civil War, great big tomes with dramatic titles, and they were alphabetized by author. Who lived here? Was this Brigade's place? I inserted the Catherine Clinton book near at least a half-dozen hardbacks of *Magnolia: A Gracious History*, written by none other than Lana Jean Chilton.

"I'm surprised Mrs. Chilton let you borrow books. Or that she let you in here at all, since only the cleaners have been in. I used to work for them, so I know. She's kept this place as a shrine."

Jeez, how many shrines did Lana Jean have?

"This was her oldest son's apartment. Rebel Chilton's. The one he was living in before . . ." She stopped.

Rebel Chilton. The man who murdered Valerie's son. This is where he lived before he was sent to prison.

A chill filled me, coldness spreading from my heart into every vein of my body.

"C'mon," Fluvie said. I picked up my book bag and hurried out. Lana Jean had stationed me in Rebel's apartment. For all I knew, that flag . . .

"Lana Jean *is* hosting Founding Families," Fluvie said as we crossed the fairgrounds. "But it's permitted as a political rally. For that, you only need to give three-days' notice, and what's more, Lana Jean pressured my boss to keep it quiet. We think she's trying to tamp down counter-protestors."

"We?" The box of buttons rocked around in my backpack.

The Magnolia Historical Museum docent stood outside on the sidewalk, watching us. Fluvie waved. "Me and the guy I'm seeing. He leads security at the courthouse. Turns out, there's no posters or what-all for this thing. Word spread through social media, through groups Darlie used to be a part of. Groups we don't tune in to."

At the courthouse, workers draped red-white-and-blue bunting all along the balustrades. Others unfurled a red carpet down the stairs, as if they were setting up for the worst Oscar ceremony ever. I guessed the men in dark suits were some kind of VIP security detail. There were women who didn't seem to be in any established uniform, though most of them wore flowered blouses and white pants. The Borton Brothers A/V team, whom Jabari had helped out at the cattle festival, loaded in giant speakers. Power-suiting around it all was the event lady from Trianon. She seemed to be everywhere at once.

We watched for a moment.

Then Fluvie gestured down the slope. "There's all these terrible organizations coming to town, like those women in the blouses. They're part of the Bake Sale Moms of America. They seem nice and sweet, but what they do is 'burn' teachers and librarians by sharing their addresses and phone numbers and encouraging their followers to write them hate mail. Even death threats."

"Why would they do that?"

"Because they don't like the way teachers teach, or the books librarians put on shelves." She folded her arms. "There's also the American Cookout Dads, but they 'grill' teachers by following them to work and shouting a bunch of questions: like why they want white kids to hate themselves, or why they're making everyone gay. Then there's the Ladies Who Punch. They go online each week and share a 'menu' of authors they want to hit in the face. They're sort of like the Dean's Fist, but those are college students who . . ."

"How do you know about all this?" It was too chilling to hear.

"Per the permit requirements, Fluvie's boyfriend, Jake got a full rundown of invited guests, and he did some digging himself. These groups don't actually commit violence, but they egg their followers to do it for them."

"And Lana Jean knows these people are coming?"

"She's invited them! And she is a founding member of the Silver Doxes. That's an age sixty-and-up group of stylish people who . . ."

I couldn't stand it a second longer. And I couldn't have anything to do with Lana Jean. Not even the dress for her daughter's pageant this weekend.

Oh god, what if *that* was a part of Founding Families?

"Fluvie, did you see the itinerary and is there a beauty contest scheduled?"

She blinked. "You mean a scholarship pageant?"

"Yeah, the thing where you walk around onstage and show off your legs."

"Around here we call those scholarship pageants."

"Okay. Is one happening tomorrow as part of Founding Families? Do you know?"

"Well, I talked my boss into giving me a copy of the permit . . . It doesn't tell me everything. But Mrs. Chilton checked off the Oratory or Lecture category. Basically speeches. She's invited the governor!"

So Jabari was right.

"And she requested permissions for Pyrotechnics. Fireworks, probably. She also checked off Dramatic and/or Musical Performance and requested a noise-ordinance exception, so that must be Brigade Chilton's band."

"You think that's everything?"

"Founding Families used to do a little skit. I can't imagine they won't do it again this year."

"But there's no way to be sure a beauty contest *isn't* part of the Dramatic Musical category?"

"Scholarship pageants fall under Dance Performance, Chorus Line or Fashion Show, and Mrs. Chilton didn't check that off, and she would've had to install temporary flooring anyway . . ."

So Cicada's beauty contest would be somewhere else. Maybe she was even traveling out of state. With such an expensive dress, it had to be a huge pageant.

But still, something nagged me. "The skit. What's that been like?"

"Oh, they call that a pageant, too, but it's not the Miss America kind. At every Founding Families, they've acted out some kind of play-pretend, and there's always some girl in a white dress. One year they made a whole Confederate cemetery with fake gravestones, and Palmetta put wreaths on all the graves. The last time they painted some old guy in bronze like a living statue of the senator, and DixieStar danced with him. Lana Jean says her grandma began this tradition a hundred years ago."

Oh my god. So that's what Lana Jean wanted: a re-creation of that dress to mark a century of Founding Families. But I was the only one she knew who could make the replica. It didn't hurt that by conniving me, Radiance Castine's daughter, she could symbolically throw up her middle finger at my mother.

"It's almost eight thirty. I have to get to work," Fluvie said.

"Hey, thank you. Really."

"About everything else," she said. "What you said hurt. I want to be a vet tech, or maybe even a veterinarian, because I want to help small farmers raise healthier livestock. My family has bred hogs for four generations, and as long as folks want bacon, we'll keep at it for generations to come. I'm part of that lineage." She rubbed her forearm. "I'm proud of it."

Maybe for the first time, I noticed the actual art of her tattoos. Black Berkshire hogs climbing up a red ladder, toward a blue ribbon and a green 4-H Club cloverleaf. Her heritage, inked on her skin.

"You should be proud."

"As should you. I know this Founding Families thing is hurtful. If there's something you need that I can help with, ask."

"Thank you."

And she was right. Founding Families *was* hurtful. How could Lana Jean dupe me into making a dress for the event—in the apartment owned by the man who beat my mother and murdered her best friend! How could she literally roll out a red carpet for those dangerous organizations? And how could Cicada be her accomplice?

As I rushed across the fairgrounds, I didn't know what I would do to the dress. Maybe I would drive it to Tangleroot and torch it in my bedroom fireplace. Maybe I would pitch it into a dumpster. Or let it float like a disembodied Ophelia, gliding down one of the rivers that laced the region, until it sank for good.

Tomorrow, that gown wouldn't see the light of day.

I hustled. The docent still stood on the sidewalk, undoubtedly wondering where Fluvie and I had rushed to together, and what I was racing toward alone. The buttons in my backpack rolled like rocks in a tumbler. Unable to stand the sound, I yanked the box from my bag.

As if seeing it for the first time, I recoiled. Because didn't Lana Jean describe where her grandmother stored the original buttons from that gown? How she'd put them in a red Miller & Rhoads jewelry box?

I open the hinged case. *Miller & Rhoads* was embossed on the satin lining. And a bevy of mother-of-pearl buttons glowed like treasure.

These were the gown's original buttons. The very same buttons that sprang from my eight-year-old great-grandmother's fingers when a grown woman slapped her. My hands shook. Two buttons rolled out. Closing the case, I searched the grass for shine.

How dare Lana Jean. How fucking dare she. Maybe she didn't know Priscilla Lavigne Harper's story of striking my great-grandmother, but she knew that woman's antique notions.

I imagined grabbing the sharpest shears I could find and going at that gown like a paper shredder.

Above Buried Silver, I hastily keyed in the apartment code. A red light flashed. I keyed again, carefully this time: *1799*. Another red light. I rummaged in my backpack. The original scribbled code was still there, crumpled and ink-stained.

Another red light.

Oh my god.

Lana Jean had locked me out.

Unsure of what to do next, I hurried down the stairs. My foot kicked a gift bag in the corner of the interior hallway. I hadn't noticed it before. Inside was *Magnolia: A Gracious History*. Ribbon-tied to the handle was a sheet of pastel stationery.

Dearest Noni,
For your exquisite and faithful rendition of Priscilla Lavigne Harper's legendary gown, I have enclosed this book to fulfill part of my commitment. It is abundant with the history of our town's founding families, and you should find it immeasurable in your studious endeavors.

Tomorrow, I shall have more documents of great interest to you in your search for the history of Tangleroot, for we require you at the pageant. I fear a ripped stitch or some other need of your skillful hands. As you may now know, this beloved tradition will take place as part of our Founding Families Celebration. By day's end, I shall remit the balance of my promise.

Best,

Lana Jean Chilton

P.S. The rhinestone buttons are beautiful. I prefer them, don't you? Though tomorrow, do bring the mother-of-pearl, which I shall return to Trianon's cache.

A shaving kit. Perfume bottles. A busted jewelry box with nothing but papers. Like Hoyt Askew and his trinkets, I took mine.

And I wept all the way back to Tangleroot.

How many times had I been so furious at my mother, so frustrated, that all I could do was fight to hold back tears? How many times had I felt I couldn't get through to her?

Now, I wanted her here. The very first time Cicada asked me to make this dress, I should have told Mom. When I wanted to back out of the deal, I should have asked my mother for help, instead of just thinking about it over and over again.

When my mother broke the news I wasn't going to Boston, I should have understood her worry that I wouldn't thrive there. If I were truly confident in my talent, I would've realized there's never only one opportunity. I could have another chance to work with a theater the following year. Instead, all I did was bang on the walls of Virginia, trying to get out.

Even when I felt so cut off by Fluvie at Town Hall—because of my own transgression—I shouldn't have colluded with Lana Jean as a way out of my own shame. And yes, I felt lonely, but only because I made myself so. I resisted making friends with the Charm girls. I made up reasons not to fully trust Will, telling myself that because he was into Mom, he couldn't be there for me. I even held Jabari at arm's length for a long time.

I should have trusted my mother—even as I chafed at her holding me back.

And maybe she did. Because maybe like firing a slingshot, she hoped to sail me forward.

CHAPTER 23

Sweetheart, are you all right? I just heard what's happening in Magnolia.

It was Mom. I wished I could tell her everything in a text back. Instead I said I was okay.

Will's keeping an eye on you. Blondell is closing Charm now through the wknd. She'll text. Hate and extremist groups are coming to Founding Families. Please Noni, stay home.

I almost smiled, because besides work and school, I never let myself go anywhere.

I'll be fine. How's DC? I asked.

Oh Noni. In just a few, I'll be sitting with Carla Hayden for lunch. She followed with an emoji of a folding fan and an avatar I'd made of her once.

Fan Girl. For the Director of the Library of Congress.

I smiled again. Oh, Mom.

A municipal celebration of a small town's history didn't usually make the national news. Our town's hit the *Washington Post*: "As a Small Town Prepares to Celebrate Its 'Founding Families,' a Referendum on Banned Books and Curriculums Takes Root."

The article recapped the names of some of the same groups Fluvie had said would be there, repeating that these organizations' members weren't known to physically harm anyone, but their social media and websites were full of "rhetoric some might consider inflammatory."

Blondell provided a quote about closing Charm. "It's not about politics. We serve folks of all political stripes all day, all week long. This is about morals. These hate groups can stay out of my barn."

The paper confirmed the governor would be there. "I'm looking forward to commemorating a quintessential Virginia town, one that represents the real American South," Clinch Hallard stated. "This is a celebration of the values our history has always upheld."

Lana Jean also dripped drivel. "Founding Families is a joyful tradition, one marking the gloried roots of Magnolia, Virginia. Our town never forgets the legacy of family."

As I read, my phone buzzed like a pissed-off bumblebee that someone tried to swat away. It kept buzzing for the next hour.

Valerie: *Baby, do you want to spend the weekend with us? Reggie and I can pick you up.*

Will: *Don't forget I'm right down the hill. Tell me if you need anything. What do you need?*

Blondell: *I'm here for you, darling. If you want to stay with us till your mama gets back, we'll come get you.*

Aunt Nichelle: *Lock all your doors and windows. Don't forget the bathroom window, that's always where the creeps look.*

Kadeem: *You good? Bc I can make it to Mongolia in four. Where's that again exactly?*

Uncle Brian: *Remember, all those African statues your mom has are heavy AF and can knock someone out.*

My dad: *Hey kiddo. Hang in there. I love you.*

I was surprised when Jabari knocked, bearing gifts of pulled pork in a crockpot. We ate like kids: sitting on the blanket-spread foyer floor, plates piled with messy sandwiches and a heap of potato chips. The junky comfort food was what I needed.

I was also grateful for him. The last time we'd talked, he had to square what he knew of me with the same person who had accosted Fluvie.

I had to do the same thing for myself. My impulse was to explain away why I tried to goad Fluvie into forgiveness, but I realized nothing needed to be said right now. I messed up, I learned, and she gave me a way to move on.

Jabari must have known that. She must have told him when she gave him the rundown of Founding Families. So when he asked what was on my mind, I told him how angry I was at what was happening the next day. And I told him I'd discovered that Weldon Golden could be my father. And simultaneously, I had to mourn his death, a man I never knew but felt kinship-close to, whether he was blood or not. Jabari nodded, as if to acknowledge he was hearing me out. But there was no sense of surprise.

"You knew," I said.

"Stories spin here for a long time."

Then I confessed about making Cicada's gown, first describing the day she ran into me outside the historical museum. His eyebrows pulled together. "She didn't 'run into' you. The docent told Lana Jean you were scheduled to be there."

"But why would she do that?"

"Because Lana Jean's conniving. She basically put an old-lady AirTag on you. She set it up for Cicada to magically find you."

I finished my story, ending with the locked apartment door. His eyebrows formed one wide V, like a bird's outstretched wings. "Lana Jean tried to play you. She tried to punk you."

"No, Jabari. I think she *did*." I took the hated book from my backpack. "This is all I got. That's *it*. Anything else, and I have to show up tomorrow."

I thumbed through the book, ferocity pulsing through my fingers. "Look at this! It's all about the senator." If I had ever hoped for any watershed stories of Sophie Dearborn, I would have been sorely disappointed. "It even talks about all the crap he owned. A whole page about his favorite cigar. And another page about some candleholder!" It was the same one I'd seen on the senator's old desk only days ago.

The only mention of Sophie was, "tragically, Sophronia Dearborn died at the tender age of eighteen, in the prime of her beauty." This, while Lana Jean acknowledged there were no known portraits of any of the Dearborns. Sophie could have looked like a barn owl, for all she knew.

Priscilla's portrait took up a full page. As I glared at her image in that magnolia dress I'd come to hate, my cheeks got so hot, I felt like someone had taken the fat and fancy candleholder painted on the table beside her and set it right under my face.

The candleholder.

I flipped backward. It was the same candleholder on the senator's desk. But where else had I seen it?

"Oh my god." I jumped up as if stung by a bee, rushing into the parlor. The dark eyes of Lacey Castine in her boudoir portrait met me. On the table beside her was the same candleholder, with blue-and-white designs scrolled all along it. Swirl for swirl those two candleholders were identical.

Priscilla's portrait was captioned: *Vermilion P. Harper was an accomplished artist, capturing his wife's alabaster beauty.*

Holy shit. Vermilion P. Harper painted his wife on a literal pedestal.

And he objectified his lover.

Pieces of a story fell together. Lacey had been broke during her first few years in Magnolia after her parents ousted her. But by the time Gramma was born, she lived comfortably: new shoes, nice dresses, warm coats, good food. This, even though she was sewing piecework.

Lacey had lied to Gramma. Maybe she did have a relationship with Calvin Fortune, but he didn't father her child. She didn't want to admit to Gramma that her father was a fire-breathing racist. Even if everyone in The Gather knew what was going on—and they must have—they weren't going to betray Lacey's secret to her daughter.

It was just like how no one betrayed Mom's secret to me. *Everything's everyone's business,* Fluvie had once said—everyone's, except the person most affected.

Lacey led Gramma to believe she was the granddaughter of Cuffee, a local icon. She even put Calvin's name on Gramma's birth certificate. And Calvin Fortune was dead by the time Gramma was born. What would he know?

That's right! Calvin *was* dead. I hurried over to my book bag in the foyer, then yanked out my laptop and found a family tree I had made as part of my capstone paper. Cuffee Fortune's son Calvin, who was supposed to be Gramma's dad, died on March 17, 1916.

But Gramma was born on December 24, 1916. That was about a nine-month difference, but I remembered Gramma's narrative: *Mama said I was a little bitty thing, just four pounds. I was born almost two months early.*

Birthdates, birth weights. That Gramma was born early meant she would've been conceived in May or June 1916, after Calvin died. Mom had overlooked it. She'd never questioned that Calvin Fortune was Gramma's father.

Not only was Sophie Dearborn my great-great-great-great-grandmother, but the senator was my great-great-great-grandfather. I was actually related to Lana Jean Chilton. To the person who duped me into toiling over a gown for her daughter in her murderer son's bedroom.

I passed Lana Jean's open book to Jabari. "Look. The candleholder in both portraits is the same."

He took a breath. "Does that mean you're . . ."

It's like he couldn't say it. I couldn't, either.

The front door pushed open. My mother swept in. "I got here as soon as I was could." She pulled me to her.

For a moment, I leaned into her, enjoying the comfort of her holding me. Then I realized the time. "Mom, you must've missed your luncheon!"

"Of course I did. I gave my apologies to Carla Hayden. She understood. I was too worried." She hugged Jabari. "Thank you for staying with Noni."

"Of course, Dr. Castine."

"I'm going to get my bags, I'll be right back."

As much as I had missed her, I was perturbed. "Your bags? Jabari, don't help her." I grabbed his arm to stop him from following her outside. "Mom, you need to get back on the road. The Courageous Curriculums announcement is tomorrow!"

"I'll give my regrets. There are members of hate groups in town. I won't leave you here alone. Neither of you."

"Oh, jeez, Mom, do you have any idea how many adults have tried to put me into their cars?"

Her hand touched her chest. "What?"

"Like Valerie. Blondell. People offering me a place to crash over the weekend." I texted Will. *Mom's back. Her big event's tomorrow! Aauugghhh.*

He responded immediately. *OMW already. Saw her car pull up, thought something was wrong.*

"You can't miss your announcement!" I tried to talk sense into her. "As far as Founding Families, look, I know—it's a clusterfuck. But I promise, I'm going to work this out."

Her mouth opened in surprise.

"Flustercluck," I corrected.

But she'd seized on something else. "Work what out, Noni? What is there for *you* to do except stay home? With me?" She knew me too well. "Or is there something else?"

Will came in through the back door. Without taking her eyes off me, my mother waved her hand toward him and Jabari. "I need to talk with my daughter."

Will and Jabari looked at each other. "Vintage video games?" Will suggested. "I got *Street Fighter* and *Mortal Kombat*."

"Let's play."

The back door closed. Mom gripped my arms and leaned down to meet my eyes. "Tell me what you did." Taking a breath, she rephrased. "Sweetheart, tell me what happened."

We sat down where Jabari and I had been, on the floor, in the foyer. And I recounted what I told him about Lana Jean and Cicada. She, too, thought Lana Jean orchestrated our supposedly chance meeting.

When I revealed that Cicada asked for a replica of Priscilla Lavigne Harper's dress, Mom stood up and paced. "Did she tell you it was for Founding Families?"

"She just told me it was for a pageant."

"Did you talk to Lana Jean?"

"A little. She confirmed what she'd pay and she gave me some specifications."

"Of course she got her daughter to do her dirty work." Mom was boiling mad. I could almost see steam peeling off her ears. Her anger wasn't at me—for now. Still, I pressed forward. While I didn't talk about the Sophie Dearborn bait that Lana Jean had wiggled before me, I was honest about the incentive of living in Boston on my own. But still, her fury radiated elsewhere. Away from me.

I even handed her Lana Jean's letter, realizing too late that it alluded to research about the Dearborns.

"'Part of her commitment'?"

"It's kind of a longer story. Research she figured the book might help with."

Mom *hmmffed*. But she didn't press. "What's this about buttons?"

"She was insistent that I sew antique buttons onto the dress. I thought she'd buy them from one of the shops here. But she found the originals from the gown. Her grandma had kept them."

Her eyes lit up. "Where are they?"

"In my backpack."

"Give them to me."

I pulled the red velvet box from my bag. Mom took them, and I followed her into the library. Together, we opened the box. The buttons glowed as if they cast their own light from within. Snapping the case closed, she slipped it into the safe under her desk.

"How long are we going to hang on to them?" I asked.

"If you have children one day, you can bequeath them. They're yours now."

"So I won't give them back at Founding Families tomorrow?"

"No, honey. You're not going."

"She promised eight thousand dollars. But only if I'm there."

"She was happy to pay far more than the value of the dress itself. It's money you'll forfeit, of course. In life, we forfeit. Sometimes greatly. It's so hard. I'm sorry." She opened the front door, walking out to the porch. The daylight was fading. We leaned against the railing, looking out at the mountains.

"Mom? Why didn't you ever tell me about Weldon?"

"I couldn't say the words." Her tone was simple, as if to tell me she couldn't find her reading glasses. But then she kissed my hair. "I tried to tell you before we moved here. And I couldn't say it. But I thought bringing you here would bring you closer to him. Even if he's not your father."

"Because my father could be Dad."

"That's what's made this so hard, Noni." Her chin quivered. I froze when I saw the sheen of tears. I had never seen my mother cry. Never, ever. I didn't know what else to do but wrap my arms around her.

"Rebel Chilton," she said, then stopped. "Rebel . . ."

Rebel had lunged at her after she stabbed his friend in the eye. Rebel had murdered Weldon Golden. After he dragged Radiance into the truck and beat her.

"Rebel," she began again.

My arms didn't seem like enough. Still, I held her, speaking softly. "I know, Mom. I know."

"Not all of it." She wept into my hair. "Not the part I've never told anyone."

Oh no. Oh no, no, no, no.

"I want to tell you but I can't say it." Her voice broke.

"You don't have to." I comforted her even as pain backed up in my chest and fury kicked up in my heart. I knew what she couldn't say. I knew what had happened to her that night in a lonely field.

"I never told a soul. Not even when the murder trial took place. I was a new mother by then. You were six months old, and your father had just started a new job, so he couldn't be with me. I had to bring you. Gramma looked after you while I was in the courtroom.

"They didn't have rooms for breastfeeding mothers back then. There had been a bear sighting in the area, but we had nowhere else to go but outside. I bundled you carefully. Then I fed you, and you napped. I looked over the gully, imagining what could become of that railroad bridge."

I pictured myself as a baby, snug in my blankets and in her arms. Blissfully sleeping and warm.

"Lana Jean stepped outside. She fumbled with a cigarette, but she must've bummed it, because she didn't seem to have a lighter. So she put it away. Then she noticed us. It occurred to me that she could have been—a grandmother."

My mother didn't say "your grandmother." I was grateful.

"We weren't supposed to talk if we saw each other in passing, per the judge's instructions. But if there was a—relationship, I felt she deserved, at least, to look at you. Even after her son did—after he did what happened." Her words faltered. She shed tears anew.

"She came over. I let her peer at you as you slept. And I let her lean in close."

Mom's voice curdled. "She said, 'My son told me everything.' And then she spat on your face."

I was horrified. "She spat on me?"

My mother wiped her thumb against my forehead as if the memory were wet paint. "If I hadn't been holding you, reminding myself how much you would always need me, I would have gone to jail that day. I might be there still."

We sat without speaking for a long while. I think the hush between us reminded Mom of her own. "I shouldn't have let this stay quiet."

"Will you ever say something?"

"I want it to be heard, but I've never been able to speak."

"Because people would know that . . ." The truth of my parentage, the truth that *could* be felt like the pressure of an unreleased breath inside my body. "What if *I* wanted it known?"

“Then it’s your story to tell.”

Silence welled around us once more. But by nine, I knew I had to get Mom back to DC. The Courageous Curriculums Initiative announcement would go on even if she weren’t there, but she had to be a counterpoint to what would happen at the courthouse. The world had to know that Magnolia, Virginia, wasn’t a town of Lana Jeans. Magnolia was people like Mom and Blondell and Jabari and Will. It was the people who tried and yet had things to learn: Like Darlie. Like Fluvie.

Like me.

Mom realized she needed to be in Washington, too. She asked if I would be all right without her after all. But her eyelids sagged. I worried.

“I’ll be fine. What about you? That’s a four-hour drive.”

Gentle knocks sounded from inside. Will and Jabari stepped out. “You ladies okay?” Jabari asked.

“Maybe.” I was honest. “Will, can you drive Mom to DC?”

“Sure thing. I’ll turn right back around and be back in the morning.” He glanced at Jabari.

“Can’t you stay with Mom tomorrow?” I didn’t want her to be alone, revisiting her loss and trauma. “I’m sure the hotel has extra rooms.”

Mom didn’t disagree. She looked up at him. “I can book you something.”

“I’ll go pack a bag if that’s okay. Noni, would you mind feeding my cat in the morning?”

“Of course not.”

“I’ll get my stuff, too,” Jabari said.

As he headed to his car, Mom told me, “I called Jabari earlier and told him he was welcome to stay in the guest room.”

Her eyes narrowed into her stern, no-nonsense college dean look.

I wondered if she would give me another Safe Sex Talk. But she didn't. "Noni, I need you to stay home tomorrow. Don't go anywhere."

"I'll be okay, Mom."

Fifteen minutes later, Jabari and I watched the car's taillights disappear into the darkness. "How were the video games?"

"We didn't end up playing. I talked to some friends, and Will caught up with someone. About tomorrow. That's where our minds were."

"Are you up for a movie?" I fought to smile through the day's emotions. "*Society Balls* is streaming. It's the rom-com about a couple that crashes fancy galas because they really like cheese and crackers." If I could laugh, that would push out the breath I'd been holding.

He surprised me by taking my hand. "We can do that. But what do you think about making our own party-crasher rom-com tomorrow?"

I glanced up at him, puzzled.

"Starring the two of us with an all-star cast of characters. At Founding Families."

"What did Valerie say when you told her you needed her soundboard?" I asked after Jabari got back into his old Kia. We were parked behind The Gather Coffee and Teahouse. Since he'd painted and done repairs, he still had keys. Her shop was closed, but I wished I had chamomile tea to dull my senses: the headache-inducing sounds of the loud crowd upon the fairgrounds, a crowd we couldn't see but could hear too well.

And the heartache of all that I spilled to Jabari last night.

Jabari only started up the engine. So I knew he hadn't asked her.

My night had been sleepless and strange. We didn't watch a movie. Mom had released me from our secrets, hers and mine, and I realized I didn't need to laugh. I needed a good, strong cry. I curled against Jabari on the sofa and did just that. And I told him. He was shocked at what had happened. And angered. I knew, because I saw his brows gravitate together and could feel the stiffness in his arms, but they softened as he held me. He asked, "Is she—is it all right that I know this?"

"She wants it to be known, Jabari. She wants the truth out. But I'm part of that truth, and I can't . . ." I shook with more tears.

In bed, I felt the presence of him lying in the room next to mine. I pressed my hand against the wall behind my headboard, knowing his pillow was only a foot away.

In the morning, Jabari took care of Will's cat while I got ready. I wore my graduation jumpsuit and fastened on the mudcloth belt I'd made at Christmastime. Dress for the job you want, my father—my father? That is what he said. I didn't want *any* job with Lana Jean. My problem was that I'd taken one. But I wanted to look VIP.

Jabari came back with groceries. "I talked to Will. He suggested I raid his fridge."

"Oh, thank you." With Mom and I being so busy, neither of us had gone shopping for an epoch. Jabari made blueberry pancakes, Fluharty farm bacon, and eggs. We watched the Courageous Curriculums announcement on my laptop. The vice president introduced Mom and her cochair Rosemary Yukawa, a history teacher from New Jersey and an author of kids' and YA books, in the White House Rose Garden. I was so proud of my mother as she spoke about what this meant to her, as a daughter of Magnolia. And yet, spying the brilliant blooms around her, I thought of that stolen dress. Because that's what it was—stolen. I hadn't meant to give it.

Now, as we idled behind Valerie's shop, Jabari told me, "Noni, I have to drop you off here."

"We're not going together?" I felt panicked.

"We can't. I have to enter through the loading dock and take the freight elevator to the fourth floor, since it's closed off to visitors today. That's the only way Fluvie's boyfriend can sneak me in. And you should go directly to the second floor, just as Lana Jean expects."

"You said rom-com, Jabari. I thought this would be some exciting caper together. I didn't expect all this!" I was scared.

"I know. And I can't give you the com part. But I've got the rom covered." He leaned close and kissed my lips, softly and deeply. Then his mouth brushed the side of my face before he kissed me again. He tilted my chin with his finger. "Keep your head up, Noni."

CHAPTER 24

I held on to his words, and the floaty feeling of his kiss, as I approached the back of the packed fairgrounds. What felt like a Taylor Swift–concert amount of people were jammed onto the green, except these were Swifties all grown up. These were mostly women, thousands and thousands of mom types. This could've been a massive PTA meeting in Suburbia, U.S.A., if PTA members shouted and screamed like mad.

The Bang Diddlies band performed on the courthouse stair landing. This wasn't the twangy, folksy music from the cow fair. This was a heavy, pulsing country rock, without a single blade of bluegrass: just sharpened steel. Reeling on a jumbotron behind them were stereotypical peaceful country scenes interspersed with dangerous things: a hay barn, then a hunting knife. A field of cows, then a stabby-looking farm tool. An old dog, followed by a shotgun. All the while, the crowd screamed.

Steel barricades separated the crowd from the sidewalk. But I didn't feel safe. My brown skin set me apart from the crowd like a stone in a bowl of grits. Some of the moms even brandished Confederate flag gear.

There was news media everywhere, with newscasters calmly speaking in front of the commotion. At least two helicopters shuttled overhead. A few anchors tried to corner me with mics—they knew I probably had a story. I just kept walking.

It grew even weirder toward the front of the fairgrounds, where tents and stanchions set the invited organizations apart. A group of fashionable, sleek-haired older ladies drank wine in a reception area complete with high-topped tables and linens. Sneering, they launched groans of disgust as I walked by. So did a bevy of pastel-attired women who snacked on finger sandwiches at a cluster of outdoor café seating. "Well, I could lose my lunch," one of them spoke up haughtily. The

Dean's Fist students were my age, but the guys had their collars turned up and the girls wore pearls. They side-eyed me as they clustered around a keg parked in their designated spot. "Good thing they outlawed affirmative action!" one of them yelled.

My skin was a tell. I didn't belong. I stiffened as I ventured past dozens of men in button-downs and khaki pants, some wearing aprons, and all shaking grilling tools at the stage as if they were torches and pitchforks. The Bake Sale Moms in their springy blouses yelled alongside them, waving sheet pans with messages like "Burn Burn Burn" emblazoned in red paint.

"Hey!" someone shouted. I turned, and something hard hit the center of my forehead. A cookie, oven-scorched and rock-hard, skidded along the sidewalk.

Near tears, I arrived at the courthouse rear entrance, taking a minute to compose myself—though I couldn't miss the marble bench facing the building, the bench where my mother would have nursed me years ago before Lana Jean spat on my face. Fresh tears sprang up. I wiped them away.

"You doing okay?" Jake, Fluvie's boyfriend, shuttled me through a metal detector and checked off my name on the list Lana Jean had supplied. He was older than us, maybe in his mid-twenties, with a reddish beard. He looked like a denim-overalls man, just like Fluvie was a denim-overalls girl.

"I'm okay," I told him. "Hey, thanks for everything."

"I planned on quitting this summer anyway. I'm going to grad school." He grinned. "Now I'll just get fired sooner."

I headed to the second floor, finding a small ballroom where servers weaved through, passing hors d'oeuvres. Arched windows overlooked the courthouse stair landing and the Bang Diddlies' act. In the back of the open area, a large mounted TV screen reflected the jumbotron's scenes: a pair of silos, then a half-open box of bullets. A tractor, and then weathered hands honing an axe. A little blond girl picking flowers. And then a meat grinder.

Cicada was perched atop a tall stool, the dress a fortress around her. The gown's petals stood out at attention, as did the bristle-brush eyelashes she wore. Her hair, tricked up with extensions and gilded with a fresh veneer of blond, was puffed and poufed into an impressive popover-muffin-like updo, with a few curled locks snaking down to her waist. Her enormous diamond necklace could have anchored a ship.

"Isn't she stunning?" Lana Jean touched my arm, but all I could feel was an imaginary wad of spit on my forehead. That she knew what her son did—that she knew! And that she treated *my* mother's child with such a disgusting and cruel action galled me. I had no memory of it. But my mother! It must have been so angering, so hurtful, so traumatic, on top of the terrible experience of giving testimony. How dare Lana Jean!

But I found a smile and I made it look real. "Isn't she."

"In part due to you. We'll make sure all is settled at the end of the day."

Make sure all is settled. Yeah, we would.

"Why don't you head to the reception, darling."

It would be hard to find a place to stand. Because Cicada was now working the room, and guests had to move out of her way as she went by. She seemed delighted with the inconvenience she imposed on others in the name of beauty.

But Mrs. Chilton cleared her throat. "Noni, your reception is on the third floor."

Fine. I liked that better anyway. My smile was tight, like a windup doll's.

The third-floor reception turned out to be sandwiches in a conference room, one that also overlooked the stair landing. Someone had left

Lana Jean's book, *Magnolia: A Gracious History*, on a side table. Plunking my sewing bag on top of its cover, I felt a new flush of anger. Lana Jean wasn't even pretending to need me here at all! She just wanted to force me to watch this terrible live racism show.

When her husband introduced their son's band, Hot Southern Glory, the feminine crowd blew up the Richter scale. I was pretty sure the shrieks unleashed a sky-high tsunami on some coastal vacation town somewhere. Drums started up, and Brigade Chilton belted out, "Chicken-fried thiiighs! Gimme them fries!" Two more lyrics in, and I knew he was talking about women, not KFC.

The music couldn't die down soon enough. Onstage, Conway Chilton teased Lana Jean's big entrance. "Y'all gonna hear an exciting announcement from my beautiful wife. But first, I want to tell y'all a little about the wonderful children we've raised."

He started with Brigade and went down the line. I seethed when he bragged about Cicada Chilton: how she was Miss this and Miss that. He could miss me with that garbage. She was gleefully complicit in her mother's racism.

"And lastly, I must highlight my eldest son." He grew somber. "An athlete and a scholar, a man who devoted his short life to keeping the values of the true South alive. That man was Rebel Chilton."

The crowd cheered in anticipation. "Now y'all know that in a few months, I'll be cutting the ribbon to that old railroad trestle. We've got a nice committee that raised money to do it up, but the town council gets to name it. And last week, we voted unanimously. It will be called . . . the Rebel V. Chilton Memorial Bridge!"

What in the fuck! My stomach turned as Rebel's head took up the monitor, with a bad graphic of an eagle soaring above him. How could Conway Chilton do this! Mom worked so hard to spearhead raising the money for that bridge. She met with engineers and landscape artists and everything! And he was naming it after her rapist and the murderer of her best friend?

Did Lana Jean really think I would listen to this? I wasn't here for a check, but even if I were, she couldn't pay me enough! Never! I jumped up, grabbed my sewing bag, and hurried down the corridor. As I pivoted to another hallway, someone shouted breathlessly, "Corner!"

It was Fluvie. "Whew, I'm not at Charm, but old habits die hard. I was hoping to find you. Jabari called me last night and asked if I could staff the event today, so I put myself on the schedule last minute." She clutched my arm. "Noni. Do you know anything about old papers? There was a whole stack of them in a manila folder. Mrs. Chilton had them on the counter in the restroom."

"No . . ."

Fluvie's eyes were wide. "They looked like old letters. And something's not sitting right."

I gasped. Cuffee's memoir. That's what nagged me in her study when Lana Jean gave me the buttons. She said he would've learned to read because he wrote a memoir. She knew details, even. But how, unless she'd read it? "Where's the folder?" I asked.

"I reckon she took it with her back to the rich-people party. I'll text Jake. He'll get you to the fourth floor with Jabari; maybe you can figure something out together."

Desperate, Gramma had sold Cuffee's memoirs to pay for Mom's hospital bills. And they must have ended up with Lana Jean's father. But why would Lana Jean bring them here? I hurried to meet Jake, though I wished I had my mother. She probably left immediately after the announcement, but even so, she would still be two hours from Magnolia—and longer if there was traffic. And in DC, she'd said, there was always traffic.

On the top floor, Jabari had set up two large monitors. "Got these from security. On this one"—he tapped a screen to his right—"we can see what the crowd's seeing. Everything on the jumbotron."

He motioned to the live stream of Conway Chilton blathering into the microphone. "And this one gives us an on-the-ground look at the stair landing. Security got me a feed."

"How'd you get access to the jumbotron video?" I asked.

"They're just streaming through a social network called Rallyround. Anyone can get access to *view* this video."

Why did he emphasize "view" the video? Jabari didn't elaborate. He set the soundboard and a laptop up on a table. "Now here's the harder part. Hacking into the Borton Brothers' Wi-Fi, so we can commandeer the sound system." He keyed frantically.

"And then we'll blast music during the pageant," I confirmed. That's what we'd planned. "Hey, I don't mean to break your concentration, but Lana Jean has some papers that I'd rather she not." I told him about Cuffee's memoir.

"Shit." He looked alarmed.

My phone buzzed. "Ugh. It's her. I'm not answering."

"Don't make her look for you. Pick up."

I did. "Noni, darling, where are you?"

I played innocent. "I'm watching Founding Families from the window."

"Cicada is about to go on. I want to make sure you see her."

"I'll be right here."

"Good," Lana Jean said. "And Noni, you do have those pearls, don't you?"

"Of course."

The box was at home, though two buttons rode in my purse from when they'd fallen at the fairgrounds. I reached in a zippered pocket and rubbed them in my fingers. They felt like good luck charms. I slipped them into my jumpsuit pocket.

"What the hell." Jabari stared at the on-the-ground monitor. It showed stagehands waiting inside the courthouse doorway with an enormous fake fireplace on a set of wheels. They pushed the structure onto the landing.

I watched from the window. Sun reflected metal, an open-sided steel box built within the fireplace well. This faux stone fireplace was meant to cradle real flames.

I tasted copper in my mouth and my blood felt thick. "Jabari. They're going to burn Cuffee's papers."

Jabari texted like mad. "No, they're not."

"No, I think that's precisely what they're gonna do."

His eyebrows furrowed. "They're going to *try*."

But even as he spoke, the mayor introduced the governor. Now Jabari had to fairly shout over the applause. "There's a change to our program."

When he told me what he wanted me to do, sweat broke out on my forehead. "But we were just supposed to blast loud music during the pageant," I reminded him.

"That's not enough, Noni. You know it's not."

On the landing, the governor spoke, his voice growing louder. My hands shook. Jabari stilled them in his. "We're going to roll our own video on the jumbotron. And we're hijacking the Rallyround network, too."

"How?"

"No idea, but Darlie knows."

"Is it legal?

"Gray area."

"What is she showing?"

He didn't answer. "Remember, security 'can't locate the key.' So bolt the door when I leave, and don't open it for anyone."

"When you leave?" My heart rate jumped. Below us, Clinch Hallard hollered.

"I've gotta hit the kill-switch for the main audio system." He placed a cordless mic on top of the speaker.

The governor matched the crowd's roar decibel for decibel. ". . . so when I hear these ACTIVIST TEACHERS AND LIBRARIANS, and these RADICAL PROFESSORS in their ivory towers! When I hear of that professor living right here in Magnolia, that invasive species from *BOSTON . . .*"

My heart hammered hard. The audience booed.

"That carpetbagger! Trying to change the name of a renowned Virginia college to the name of a slave . . . because *her* version of history means bringing down the legacy of this town's beloved senator!"

His righteous finger struck the air and his words struck a chord, sparking thousands of whoops and hollers. The frenzied audience chanted, "Burn it down! Burn it down! Burn it down!" Amid the melee of noise, three little fair-haired girls, all clad in white, ambled onto the landing, each holding bundles of papers tied with burlap string.

"Burn it down! Burn it down! Burn it down!" The cries rose up with a vengeance, like the shouters wished the old South would. It was disturbing, seeing these three girls fidget as anger brewed like a cauldron around them. I felt as helpless as they were clueless about the papers they held in their hands.

The governor smiled at the children. "These are Conway and Lana Jean Chilton's lovely granddaughters." Everyone *awww*ed, but there was a knife edge to their collective tone.

"But they're holding something hideous! Writings of a former slave who one of Magnolia's founding families treated like one of their own! Thomas Dearborn of Tangleroot Plantation even gave this slave land, free and clear. Because that's how the planters of Magnolia thought of their slaves: as family, 'our family, black and white.'"

I paced. Could I do what Jabari thought I must?

"But in 1902, this slave put pen to paper and denounced the Dearborns, as well as the other white families of this great town, in spite of all they did for him. And the rotten apple doesn't fall far from the tree. This man is a direct ancestor of that professor, the one who wants to change the name of the college; the one who wants our children to read books that make them loathe themselves! She herself has even authored hate speech!"

From the podium, he took a copy of Mom's book, thrusting it high as its cover was projected onto the jumbotron with a red circle and a slash superimposed over it. He tossed the book into the fake-but-real fireplace. The audience raved.

"She wants little girls like these—wave, little girls! Wave!"

The granddaughters happily flapped their hands, rattling their papers.

"She wants these little girls to become the oppressed!"

A chorus of jeers coursed through the crowd like blood pumping through veins.

"Radical Radiance Castine couldn't even bother joining us today because she's in Washington, DC, with *politicians*!" He popped the *p* and spat out the rest of the word as if it didn't apply to him. "But what her slave ancestor called a memoir, we call lies!"

More cries to "Burn it down!" faded into *ooh*s as Cicada Chilton strode dramatically onto the landing, her swanlike gown floating above the red sea of carpet. Cupped in her hands was the same candleholder from the senator's desk, topped with a lit candle. A video image showed Priscilla Lavigne Harper's painted portrait.

I couldn't bring myself to listen to the governor's words about the hundredth anniversary of Founding Families. But when he uttered the word "gown," I fought my way out of my own head. Cicada turned, showing off practiced beauty queen moves as she modeled the dress. "And the seamstress of this glorious, historic gown is none other than *Miss Noni Reid*!" the governor shouted my name with anger.

I couldn't breathe. I couldn't move.

"Noni is the daughter of Radical Radiance Castine! Noni, come on out here and say hello!"

My feet felt like lead. So this is what Lana Jean wanted: to drag me forward, and to drive a stake into Mom's heart.

"Noni, we know you're in there! Come on out!" the governor demanded.

I wouldn't do it. I wanted to slap Lana Jean clear across the face, the way Priscilla Harper slapped Gramma. Hard enough to send her to the ground. To strike her with the force that knocked Molly clean out of consciousness more than a century ago, that day her child was ripped away.

What would these women have done, if they could fight back with teeth?

My arms, my hands, were not the tools for this moment. Instead, I had my voice. The promise of what it could do propelled me to pick up the microphone Jabari had left for just this purpose. That promise of who it could speak for allowed me to ignore my own fear and charge ahead.

I stepped onto the balcony, three stories above the governor's head. "I'm here."

The sound Jabari connected worked. And this was not what Clinch Hallard expected. I wasn't supposed to be heard. My calm voice was like a siren call. Lana Jean forfeited her own vaunted appearance to emerge from the courthouse, gawking beside the governor and her daughter. From the crowd, there came the same kind of audible disbelief as when I had botched the speech at Mom's event a year ago.

This time, there was no hot mic, just one as cold as a fish in the governor's hands. He switched it on and off. Nothing worked.

"Cicada, you *are* wearing a historical replica." I nodded down to her dress. "But you should know its full past."

Below me, her hand froze at her lips, while the mouths of Lana Jean and the governor moved. I heard snatches of voices but no words. Lana Jean's little granddaughters continued standing there until Fluvie crouched at the side of the stair landing, beckoning to them. She collected their papers like school assignments and shepherded them to DixieStar Chilton, who seemed paralyzed with confusion.

I had everyone's attention. "When my great-grandmother was a child, a white woman slapped her when she tried to return a handkerchief. The woman slapped her so hard, she went flying to the ground. Gramma remembered this incident until she was an old woman. She even remembered that handkerchief: ivory with scalloped edges. Initials embroidered in yellow. *PLH* for Priscilla Lavigne Harper."

The mostly female audience was silent. Mrs. Chilton looked exposed and confused. She didn't know this story. No old woman ever sat her granddaughter on her knee to talk fondly of the time she slapped an eight-year-old.

"Gramma always thought that Priscilla Harper struck her just because she was Black," I said. "She was wrong. I'll tell you why. But first, I'll share the story of another white woman of Magnolia."

I briefly described stumbling onto the grave of Sophie Dearborn and her unnamed baby in the cemetery of the Tangleroot Plantation, and how it intrigued me. I ended Sophie's story with her forcing an enslaved young man to have sex with her so that she could avoid an unwanted marriage. The audience, save for the Dean's Fist students, clutched their metaphorical pearls. Those college ladies gripped real ones.

"Sophie has a place on one branch of my family tree. But another person, someone with much more recent ties to this community, has a place, too."

Knocks boomed behind me, and the doors to the lounge rumbled in their frames. I glanced back to see Town Hall security guards outside the room, arguing with two men in dark suits.

"In my home at Tangleroot, there's a portrait of Lacey Castine, my great-great-grandmother. She's not wearing much at all." The audience was transfixed. "Her picture looks strikingly like a portrait at Lana Jean's plantation, of her grandmother wearing a gown like Cicada's today. Both of the portraits even show the same decorative candle. That's because they were painted by the same person: Senator Vermilion Harper. Lacey's daughter, my great-grandmother, was the spitting image of him, freckles and all."

The knocking stopped. I glanced behind me. Fluvie's boyfriend, Jake, stood outside the door, alone like a sentry. Last night while Mom and I talked, Jabari and Jake had gotten on the phone and briefed themselves on the rules. Because I didn't pose a threat to the governor's safety, only his ego, his security detail couldn't use potentially harmful force without higher-level approval.

A wave of static pulsed on the jumbotron. A buzz of shock lifted from the audience. Darlie *had* usurped the Rallyround feed, showing the two paintings side by side. She *was* a cyber genius. She zeroed in on the same candle in both images.

"When Priscilla Harper struck my great-grandmother, it wasn't because she saw a Black girl passing her the handkerchief. It was because she saw the child of her husband. That's because my maternal great-great-grandfather was Senator Vermilion P. Harper. Not Calvin Fortune, Cuffee Fortune's son, as I believed up until just yesterday."

I swallowed. "And Clinch—" Yeah I called him that. He didn't deserve the honor of his title. "What you said about the enslaved and enslavers being one family, Black and white, also isn't true. We *did* live in intimate spheres. But let's think about the people we call family. We don't force our family to work for us, then in turn provide them crude housing, food, and clothing. We don't sell our family members. Slavery was a lifetime of trauma. The only 'family, Black and white' usually came from rape and unequal relationships."

It was as if I had posed a discussion question among the audience, like Dr. Corn would do in class. People murmured while the governor, Lana Jean, and Cicada gaped. I found myself taking the mother-of-pearl buttons from my jumpsuit pocket. They shone in my palm like two moons, each orbiting the other, each casting its own light from within. Each reflected the other's glow.

My mother would find out we were not of Cuffee's blood, and this discovery would take something beloved from her. Her whole life had been driven by her place as Cuffee Fortune's descendant. She wrote a dissertation about him. She'd bought the house he built. She became the president of his college, and was fighting to name it after him. She worked hard for his legacy to frame her life because she thought it would make up for what had happened to her, what had happened to Weldon, and what had happened to The Gather itself.

But in the end, we couldn't choose our families.

Case in point: I could be "inbred," the child of a racist rapist, *and* the great-great-granddaughter of his ancestor. The thought soured my stomach. A different family tree, one warped and ugly, grew in my imagination.

Behind me, a key turned the door latch. So the governor's security team had legally strong-armed Jake after all. I didn't give them the dignity of turning to meet their eyes. I braced myself for hands seizing me, for rough strength.

Instead, I heard my mother's voice. "Noni."

I was in trouble. "How did you . . . ?" I put down the mic.

"Will's friend flew us. He insisted we get here."

So Will had known, then. He'd schemed with Jabari. He'd been on my side.

Our side, because what I did was for Mom, too.

"I arrived just in time to see you. I'm proud of you. I always am, but especially now."

She held my hand. "Noni, if you're ready, tell them."

I clutched the mic. For a moment, the words wouldn't free themselves, but it was as if the audience held their breath. They waited. Then the words unlodged, along with tears. "Rebel Chilton did more than murder a kind, intelligent, and promising young man. He forever scarred a brilliant young woman that night—the woman who became my mother. And so, I may be part of that terrible legacy."

There must have been a thousand hands rising to hearts, to lips. They understood. And *I* understood: Mom had work to do in this snow globe of a town, this place trapped in time. But she'd needed me alongside her. I was her beloved. Her Promise.

I had looked toward Sophie Dearborn instead. It felt like she was the worst in me. And the senator, and maybe even—maybe—

It hurt too much to think about. But that worst in me, those moldy parts of my cheese, was me all the same. If I could see the grody fuzz, I could cut it away.

"I shouldn't have fought you," I told Mom.

"I shouldn't have fought *you*. I respect your talent; I always have. Maybe I've even been intimidated by it. Your mind works in ways mine never could. And I tried to make you walk in my footsteps. I should have encouraged you to plant your own." She held me. "You can be wherever you want this fall."

That was good. Because I knew where I wanted to be. And I'd said all I needed to say—almost. I spoke to Lana Jean, who stood stock-still with shock. "Your son did something reprehensible, and it scarred both of you. But it's cruel to pass that suffering on to others."

Another round of murmurs swept through the crowd. I swiveled to the monitor. There was a black-and-white video of a Black woman sitting on a bench—the same bench outside the courthouse.

"Oh my god," I whispered. It must have been footage from the wildlife cam Will and his coworkers set up almost eighteen years ago.

In the video, the woman's slim shoulders seemed tight with anxiety and hurt, even as she looked upon a baby in her arms. A blond woman appeared in the frame, stepping toward them curiously, like some long-legged animal sniffing at bait.

She leaned forward as if to peer at the child.

The reel caught her words, just as Mom described them. It caught the plosive sound of spittle launched at the baby's face. Horrified gasps leapt from the audience.

The jumbotron footage flickered to a bear cub tearing apart a snake while its mother looked on, before switching off entirely.

Below, Lana Jean's face twisted with rage. But I simply took Mom's hand. "Let's go home." Turning, we headed off the balcony.

Below us was the sudden thud of something heavy hitting the ground, followed by a chorus of frightened sounds. Startled, I spun around.

Lana Jean Chilton lay on the carpeted steps, out cold.

She had swooned. Like a tragic fucking heroine.

CHAPTER 25

The trail to the burying ground wasn't a long one, but you had to know what you were looking for.

"We're to follow this creek until it forks," Alexander Kersey said after we'd crossed the footbridge. He was a tall, broad-shouldered man with graying temples and the bearing I imagined of Cuffee Fortune. He took the lead as the six of us walked along the path beside the bank of Cane's Creek, the water shimmering beneath the August sun. No one spoke. Will lay his palm on the small of Mom's back, his wedding band glowing against tan skin. Jabari and I held hands. Trekking ahead was Yagba Golden, as that's what I'd begun calling her, after the Yoruba word *ìyá àgbà*. An honorific. Alongside her, Gertie Derry carried a carved wooden walking stick. The professor had been to Tangleroot three times to look for the cemetery. Neither she nor Mom had ever found it.

"The creek should fork about a half mile down," Alex predicted.

"It does." Will gave a confirming nod. "I've gone running down this way before." But even he had never encountered the cemetery. It seemed incredible that anyone could ever locate it, especially not Alex Kersey, who'd never been to Virginia, let alone Tangleroot. He'd flown from Arizona a day ago. Yet, he knew the path to the burial ground because it had been passed down to him by his great-grandmother.

The creek did split after we'd walked for some time. Kingfishers swooped and dove, skimming the silvery water. A pair of mallard ducks paddled along the water's edge. "We take the right-hand fork," Alex said. "Then we'll find another creek farther down, a shallow one. We cross it and follow it until it crooks."

Alexander Kersey's great-grandmother Caroline always wanted to "return home," to the place she knew her parents would choose to be laid to rest. She remembered her childhood well, never forgetting the day a white man struck her mother with all of his strength. Nor did she forget the loneliness of traveling in a rickety wagon across wilderness and swampland. Her enslavers expected her to do a grown woman's work, hauling water and fuel, sometimes for more than a mile; caring for the children; cooking over a fire; dragging linens and clothing to wash in faraway creeks. At night, she muffled her sobs with the worn hem of her patched shift. She missed her home, her parents, her siblings, and she desperately missed the comfort of her doll, Promise. She was constantly terrified—of whippings, of rattlesnakes, of violent storms, and of white men even more. The group settled on a farm near the San Antonio River, but her life did not become easier.

The 1863 Emancipation Proclamation should have freed enslaved people in Texas, but the state was vast and lawless, without a presence of Union officers to enforce federal order. At only twelve, Carrie drew upon her strength, hard-won from her forced cross-country march as a younger child. She escaped from the Mullers, and she found work at a Galveston Island hotel, living with a local Black family. Years later, she married the hotel's cook. Together, they opened a restaurant. In 1900, a massive hurricane killed thousands and leveled the island, but Carrie and her husband, Alexander, survived, stayed, and rebuilt. They eventually opened another restaurant in Houston, then another in Austin.

Finding Alexander Kersey IV, one of the only real direct descendants of Cuffee and Molly Fortune, was a project for an independent study course I took with Dr. Corn's guidance. The research was unbelievably difficult, because at first, I didn't even know Carrie's last name.

For Mom, discovering that she was not a descendant of Cuffee Fortune was a blow. In the days following the Founding Families event a year ago, Mrs. Chilton's brother in Atlanta wrote a scathing editorial in the local paper blasting me for announcing "lies about his venerable grandfather." He didn't believe my great-grandmother was the daughter of Vermilion Harper.

Mom and I both talked. In the end, she swabbed her cheek. The results made a ripple in the national news.

Knowing for sure that she was a great-grandchild of the senator and not a descendant of Cuffee Fortune was hard for my mother. And with the way online connections go, she discovered her father's name. He was in his nineties, but his mind was long gone. It was okay. She spoke on the phone with her half siblings and considered flying to California to see them, but she wasn't sure she was ready.

For the first time, I realized why she'd always been reluctant to meet her unknown family. And somehow on the other side of the coin, *I* wanted to uncover my full family tree, my yearning to know edging away my fear of an answer. Mom gave me her blessing. And when I visited my father, I tried to form the question: "Would you be okay if—how would you feel if—" I couldn't say it.

Dad and I walked a wide trail, one lush with shaggy ferns and fragrant with the scent of tall Douglas firs. "You don't need permission to find out who you are," he said.

"And besides, I already know." I snuggled under his arm. "I'm your kid, right?" He rubbed my hair like he used to when I was a little girl. Things still felt strained between us, but they were moving in a better direction. We were both working on it.

It was the same with Mom. There were so many avenues of forgiveness we needed to take together. And alone.

She made a public apology to Stonepost College—as if she had anything to apologize for. But she let the student body and faculty know she had been mistaken about her descendancy. The DNA test results came in hours before she was to announce that Stonepost College would be renamed in the fall. The resurfaced memoirs in which Cuffee described all the incidents leading to the theft of his college, which Mom could corroborate with other documents, were proof. And they were damning to the planter families of Magnolia. No wonder Lana Jean wanted them burned.

I went to Mom's address, moved along with everyone else standing there except the miffed board of directors. Later, Mom introduced me to her colleagues, a few of whom would soon be my professors. I would be attending Cuffee Fortune College in the fall, and working part-time at my yagba and baba's second coffee shop, which would be opening in Daventry.

So much was different. Magnolia was no exception. The old condemned railroad bridge that pushed our town apart from Daventry became a beautifully landscaped walking and biking trail. With local pressure, it was named for Weldon T. Golden. On the day his bridge opened, Magnolia instantly felt a little more diverse, and younger.

In ensuing months, a Stonepost graduate started a tech company and coworking space in the old candy factory. With a base of new customers, Jabari's mom opened a soul food restaurant and bar, one with the same swanky vibe as her place in Richmond.

Getting caught spitting on a baby was career-ending. Lana Jean Chilton slunk away to Dallas to live with her sister. The governor waited out his term in controversy. Cicada eloped with her brother's bandmate when she got pregnant, but he'd been cheating all along with her cousin Flouncy, and everyone knew it but her. It was all the gossip among the Charm girls, who I hung out with each month, although I stayed above *that* fray.

Meanwhile, a Chilton nephew and his husband bought out Trianon, opening a brewery on the grounds, one that hosted concerts on weekends. During their spring break from Virginia Tech, Fluvie—her hair a vibrant lilac—and Jake hung out with Jabari and me to catch a band we liked.

And a new theater in Daventry featured experimental shows and exploratory takes on classics. I watched some performances, including a feminist reimagining of *The Tempest* when Alyssa came to visit. She declared central Virginia "cool AF," asking, "Why'd you ever want to leave?"

I wished I could've worked at the new theater, but I was so busy. Will had donated his family plantation to an organization called Black Seed, founded by Andrea and Pastor Price. They held workshops and classes on beekeeping and community gardening. And there were cows. I volunteered there, weeding the garden and giving special treats to Hay Girl, their sweet-faced Jersey who won Miss Moo Magnolia. Some things hadn't changed. Nor did they need to.

But some things were gone forever. The Gather couldn't be remade, but it could be repurposed as a nature trail, one blooming with pollinator plants and songbird habitats, and marked with monuments of what was once there. All paths led to the schoolhouse, now a small museum. My yagba and baba's youngest son, one with dreams of starting a vineyard, bought out Twenty Paces. The enormous home held an extended family brimming with warmth and love—and stories of Weldon Golden. I spent many dinners at their antique table.

When I found Alex Kersey, I felt my family grow that much larger. He never knew his great-grandmother—she died long before he was born—but he'd been told stories over and over again about her life.

She'd been stolen from her parents. She wanted to be returned. Carrie recalled the acreage of her plantation home intimately, down to the exact path from the kitchen to the burying ground where she hoped to one day rest. But she had never left those grounds until she was hastily awakened one night, forced to begin a 1,500 mile march on unshod feet, her leg throbbing with pain the entire way. Texas, she later learned, was her new land of captivity. But she didn't know where she'd lived before.

Her son could only describe the burial route through a property unnamed to him, and tell his children and grandchildren. But Caroline Kersey never came home.

There wasn't a bridge or stepping stones over the second creek, so we removed our shoes, rolled up our pants, and waded. The water felt cool around my knees, and the rocks beneath my feet were slippery and sharp.

The stream bent several yards down. From there, we turned south toward a hill that Alexander said should be there. His voice was a map. The land sloped as he said it would. It was thick with brush and trees, so we walked carefully. Squirrels scattered, and birds shouted alarm calls overhead.

"The cemetery is at the top of the hill," Alex assured us as we made our way through the tangle. Branches snagged at my hair. The rise was a minefield of large rocks—I had to take care not to stumble. Finally, the woods opened to a clearing studded with spindly trees. "This is the burying ground," he announced.

"Where?" All I saw was tall grass and weeds, surrounded by knotty briar and raveled brush. I thought of the fenced-in cemetery where Sophie Dearborn was buried.

Dr. Derry stepped a few yards into the clearing and, with her walking stick, gently touched something on the ground. "Here," she said.

A large stone jutted upward from the earth like a tooth. Dr. Derry moved her walking stick to touch a smaller stone. "And here."

"How many markers might there be?" I asked.

"The only way to know is to count them."

We scattered, searching the tall grass like children in an Easter egg hunt, but Mom immediately walked toward the north end of the field. She must have noticed something there. Locating another headstone, I gripped it with my hand, feeling how firmly it was rooted into the soil. I thought of the smooth, perfect oval of Sophie Dearborn's gravestone, the story it told me.

Mom still stood beneath a willow tree, arms folded. I joined her there.

"I feel like Cuffee and Molly are here," she said. The two burial stones were placed next to each other. They were large, flattened rocks unlike the other markers. A spiny yucca plant bloomed between them. "Of course, there's no true real way to tell."

"There is. You were drawn here." My fingers rested on my mosaic pendant.

Mom's shoulders sank. "This just seemed like a direction to go. There's nothing divine or supernatural. I'm not their descendant."

"But you're family." *Kin by blood, or by belonging.* Her words resonated here. She pulled me close.

. . . there is power in the breath that invokes a name, that calls forth a story . . .

"Cuffee Fortune. Molly. Caroline Kersey." I voiced their names aloud as we stood, my mother and I.

Hoyt Askew. Lacey Castine in all her incarnations, all her faults. Fawnie Castine. Euphemia Sterling. Milliard Walker.

Weldon Golden.

And Radiance Clare Castine.

Sophronia Castine Dearborn, the girl with my name and my birthday. I'd come to understand her loneliness, her cruelty, her desperation.

Isaac, who never even had the privilege of a last name. Where was he buried?

... we are always here, abiding in the minds of our descendants ...

How do they speak to you? Professor Corn had asked.

I knew. I knew.

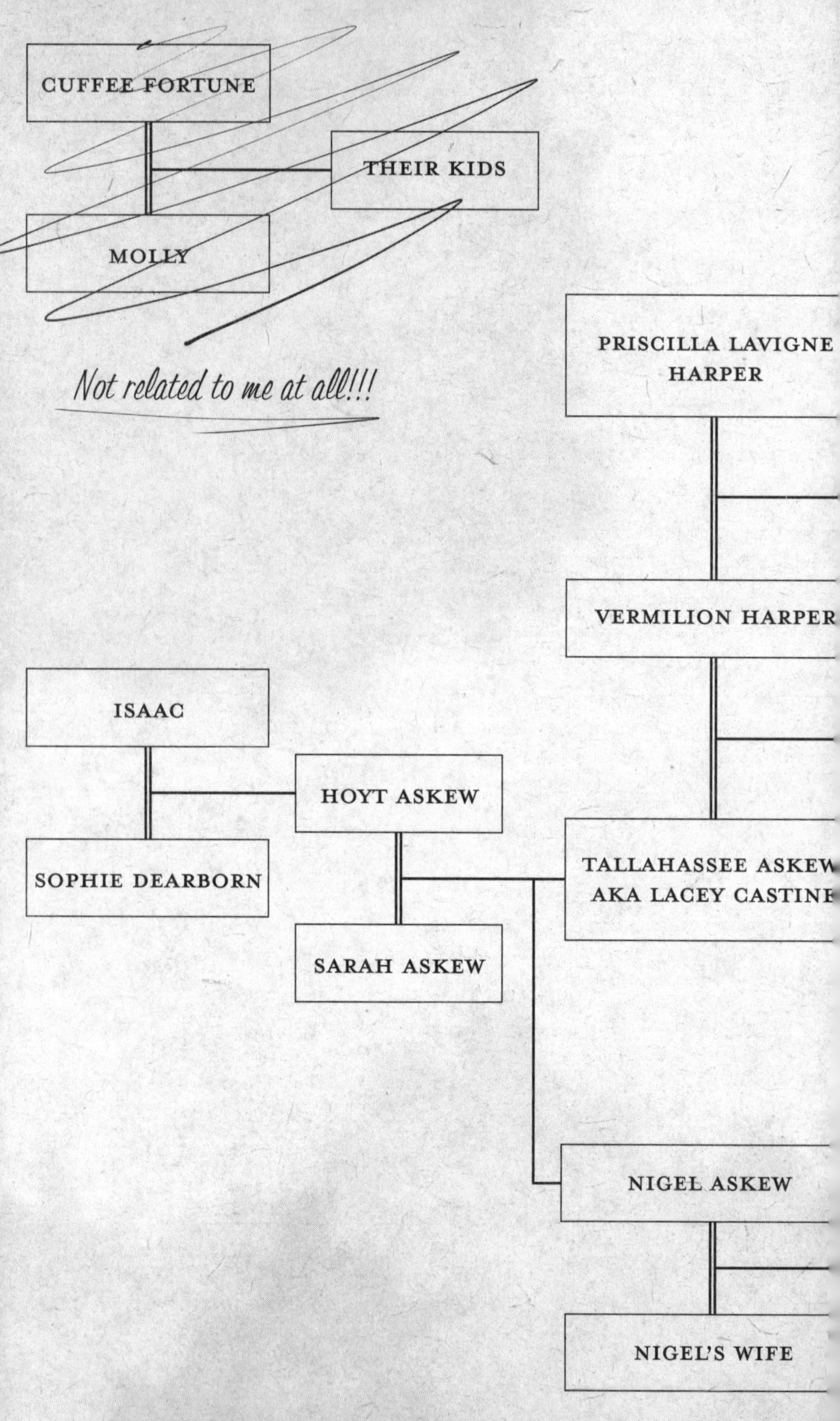
CUFFEE FORTUNE
THEIR KIDS
MOLLY
Not related to me at all!!!
PRISCILLA LAVIGNE HARPER
VERMILION HARPER
ISAAC
HOYT ASKEW
SOPHIE DEARBORN
TALLAHASSEE ASKEW AKA LACEY CASTINE
SARAH ASKEW
NIGEL ASKEW
NIGEL'S WIFE

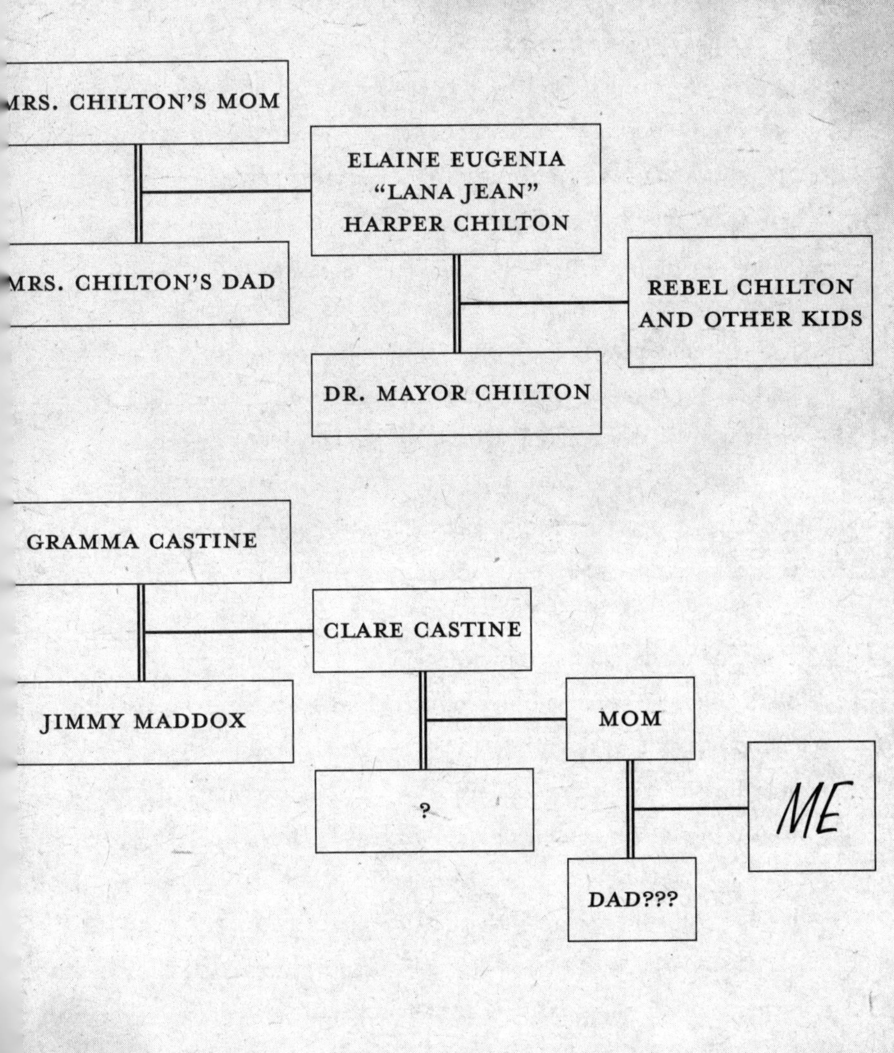
MRS. CHILTON'S MOM
ELAINE EUGENIA "LANA JEAN" HARPER CHILTON
MRS. CHILTON'S DAD
REBEL CHILTON AND OTHER KIDS
DR. MAYOR CHILTON
GRAMMA CASTINE
CLARE CASTINE
JIMMY MADDOX
MOM
?
ME
DAD???
NE OF NIGEL'S KIDS
MRS. THELMA TINSLEY

AUTHOR'S NOTE

If you are Noni's age—seventeen, eighteen—the writing of this story began before you were born.

The inspiration dates back even earlier, back to 1990s Georgia, where I grew up. One summer at 4-H camp, I took a tour of an enslaved community's burial ground nearby. After a long trek through thick woods in the afternoon heat, swatting away mosquitoes as well as problematic comments from a couple of other teens—I was the only Black kid in our group—I expected a neat lawn and rows of tombstones, just like I'd seen in other cemeteries. Instead, what we walked upon were slabs of quartz that seemed randomly placed amid an overgrowth of trees and brush. There were no dates carved on these stones. There were no names.

I had wanted to know their names, these people who had lived, involuntarily labored, and died on that land—people who were enslaved like *my* ancestors had been. But that hope evaporated like sweat.

Ten years later, I was twenty-three and living in Charlottesville, Virginia, floundering in the kind of low-paying, bottom-level, high-stress job that's the fate of many a recent-ish college graduate. My work with a nonprofit sent me driving down hidden roads throughout central Virginia. I wish I could remember exactly where I saw the grave of a young woman buried with an infant child in a small family plot, almost certainly a white family plot. Her name has been lost in my memory. But that day, a story began taking shape in my mind.

That story first appeared on paper twenty years ago. It was about a white modern-day girl trying to fit in at school, who finds the 1880s grave of a young mother. I wrote about white teens then because I didn't think a YA novel like this one, featuring a Black character, would ever get published.

I put the project down for several years, working on a different manuscript while I was in graduate school. But I returned to it in 2008, this time writing my way into two new characters, a Black teen and her mother who move into a plantation house their ancestor had built. Noni (though she had a different name then) would rediscover the grave of a young white woman and wonder about her life. And—because I never forgot that enslaved people's burial ground—she would uncover her own heritage in the process.

But what did Noni's new house look like? And what could her ancestor Cuffee's life have been like? And what about the lives of his family members at Tangleroot? And the white woman buried there . . . and . . . and . . . and . . .

The core of what novelists do is to make things up. But when we infuse history into our writing, sometimes we have to research. Tons. Think of the hardest paper you've ever written for a class. Then triple those hours you spent, and then add the square root of a gazillionpalooza. Okay, I don't do math. Obviously. But this is to say, some fiction writers spend days, weeks, and even years immersed in truth.

So I began my research. I invented Magnolia, Virginia, drawing from other towns and small cities in central Virginia. I read big historic house books, the kind people display on coffee tables. And I visited plantation homes that host tours, walking across parquet floors and gazing through Palladian windows.

With historian Dr. Lynn Rainville, I toured the enslaved people's burial ground at Sweet Briar College, also a former plantation, learning about burial traditions. I read books about the lives of enslaved people, and studied dozens and dozens of narratives, most of which were collected in the 1930s by the Works Progress Administration (WPA) Federal Writers' Project—that was basically a nationwide initiative designed to give writers jobs during the Great Depression. I created fictional

Cuffee, Molly, and Carrie, and I made up the backstory of two Harvard graduate students gathering a trove of narratives in 1889. But the short snippets that Noni reads in the hallway outside her college's student center were drawn from the harrowing experiences of real enslaved people.

I also envisioned Sophie Dearborn. She came alive for me when the owners of a central Virginia bed-and-breakfast, Rockmill Farm, showed me around their antebellum home. Pasted to a closet door were fashion magazine pages from the 1850s.

And Noni wearing out her eyeballs on a Library of Virginia microfilm machine? That was me. There, in other archives and on historical websites, I read primary sources—those are firsthand accounts of people who lived during a particular era or who experienced an event—such as family papers and letters. Historic obituaries and wills, for instance, gave me the text for Thomas Dearborn's. A letter penned by Southern poet Margaret Junkin Preston condescendingly described the wedding of an enslaved servant who she called "Rhinie," inspiring my fictional Euphemia, or "Effie."

The Gather is fictional, but the erasure and destruction of Black neighborhoods is all too real. It happened in cities like Tulsa, Oklahoma, and Wilmington, North Carolina, and in towns like Rosewood, Florida. And it happened to other Virginia communities, like Uniontown in Staunton, Gainsboro in Roanoke, and Vinegar Hill in Charlottesville.

I finished a version of *Tangleroot*—it had a different title then—in 2011. But I couldn't find an agent—and writers usually need literary agents to sell their works to notable publishers. During that time, I lost my mom. And I put the manuscript away.

After the white supremacist rally around a Robert E. Lee statue in Charlottesville, and after the murder of George Floyd, I sensed it was time to begin a total rewrite and overhaul. By then, I'd been with my partner Davey for a few years, so I pulled from his knowledge as the kid (and grandkid) of small-town Indiana hog farmers to create Fluvie.

Lacey Castine played a bit part in the first version of the manuscript. Now, I wanted her to be a bolder character—one who committed a transgression that took her to central Virginia. Davey, a playwright and actor, suggested theater, which was often considered a risqué career at the time. Then I found out that some Black folks watched and even performed in minstrel theater. That's the *kind* of theater I saw Lacey doing. A few more books and a consult with theater historian Peter Schmitz taught me more. While Lacey is fictional, as is the deplorable troupe and production she found herself in, it's right in line with troupes that existed and performances that actually happened.

I wrote Lacey's dressmaker ad by combing through digitized issues of the *Philadelphia Inquirer* and borrowing words from real-life early 1900s dressmakers. I copied the department store employment ads verbatim.

And "crazy quilts" were indeed all the rage in the late nineteenth century. But the whereabouts of surviving United States Colored Troops flags are scattered, as was explained to me by historian Marvin-Alonzo Greer. Some did end up at the US War Department, and storage did become a problem, but this is a simplified fabric trail and an adjusted timeline. I made up the story that Lacey, then Tallahassee Askew, requested these old flags.

At the Historical Society of Pennsylvania, I found an early 1900s-era handbill advertising an educator's visit to Philadelphia to raise money for a Black industrial school in Georgia. I used that wording to create Cuffee's fundraising flyer for his college, which is a fictional institution. While the Askew family is also fictional, William Still and Jacob C. White Jr. were true-life activists in Philadelphia's Black community. Both were involved with the abolitionist movement in the mid-1800s, when Still was known as "the Father of the Underground Railroad" for shuttling enslaved people to freedom. Later, they fought for civil rights in Philadelphia.

The Historical Society of Pennsylvania also holds incredible full-color theatrical posters, just like the ones Noni looks at. Again, I pulled the titles of old plays like *The Wages of Sin* verbatim and described the images as I saw them. The minstrel ephemera I sourced from the historian Peter Schmitz. McCabe & Young's was a real performing company, and I amalgamated wording from ads promoting their Black actors, as well as ads for other Black minstrel performers.

In rewriting my manuscript, I read and reread even more old letters and diaries, but I struggled to remake Euphemia's narrative and Sophie's diary pages, which had been a major weakness in my 2011 manuscript. Real diaries and letters of that period often don't have the storytelling aspect and emotive output that I needed for these women's fictional voices. There's often no "and then this happened, and then *this* happened, and these are all my feelings" quality that *you* might scribble down, if you keep a diary. When I tried to imitate real-life personal writings in addition to telling a story, the prose was clunky, stilted, and awkward, and well—just *bad*.

So in my rewrite, I poeticized both voices, but I grounded these adaptations in history. I turned to book-length autobiographies by formerly enslaved people such as Harriet Jacobs, Solomon Northup, and Frederick Douglass as I wrote Euphemia's narrative. I was also informed by poetry and fiction of nineteenth-century Black women Frances Ellen Watkins Harper and Hannah Crafts, as well as the diaries, journals, and letters of Emilie Davis, Rosetta Douglass, and Charlotte Forten Grimké, all young Black women of the Civil War era.

To fashion Sophie Dearborn, I read the writings of antebellum Southern white girls and women: Sarah Morgan Dawson, Eleanor

Agnes Lee, Mary Boykin Chesnut. Although I stylized Sophie's voice, her sentiments about race and slavery fall in step with real life. Historian Judith Giesberg gave me insight into how a young Southern woman like Sophie might have thought. These kinds of fictional re-creations are a balance between being true to history and serving the narrative needs of one's work.

In rewriting, I also dug deeper into fashion, reviewing digitized images from *Godey's Lady's Book, Peterson's Magazine,* and *Frank Leslie's Lady's Magazine,* pulling most dress descriptions verbatim. *La Mode Illustrée* was also a real fashion publication, but it didn't debut until 1860: a tiny bit late for our story. So I bent history once more because I needed something French, and I liked the title.

The doll that Cuffie's daughter Carrie once held is an example of a real kind of doll, a topsy-turvy doll or upside-down doll. They would have seen their beginnings in antebellum times and remained in toy boxes well into the twentieth century. Both Black and white girls played with them.

Carrie is fully fictional, but her story, sadly, mirrors the traumatic childhoods of so many enslaved people. So many names have been lost to history. So many people's lives will never be uncovered. But I wanted to imagine that Carrie found a way out. That she survived and thrived. That like Radiance Castine, like *my* real-life mother, and like Black mothers from time immemorial, she lavished love upon her children, making for them a way out of no way, and passing to them her stories of breathtaking resilience.

As I write this, I'm more than twenty years away from that stressful nonprofit job that took me into the Virginian hinterlands, driving hide-away roads and burning gas I couldn't afford. I have another job for a different nonprofit that also sends me all over the Commonwealth. This time, I get reimbursed for mileage. And now? I'm in a leadership role.

Okay, well technically, it's middle-management.

But it's work I love, because I create literary programs. I work with authors and readers, building avenues for books to bring us together, sharing how they create and re-create worlds, and how they nudge us toward finding out what was—and kindle that electric spark of what could be.

For a list of books and resources for further study, writing prompts, program ideas, and cheese-ball recipes, visit the author's website: kalelawilliams.com.

ACKNOWLEDGMENTS

There are people I can never thank by name, because their individual stories have been lost in the tumult of history. But I'm inexpressibly grateful for the resilience of my unknown ancestors: my zamani. The heaviness of their forgotten stories within my family tree is the trunk I lean against in times of doubt, fear, and sadness; emotions I weathered as I researched and wrote this book.

I'm grateful to my sasha, those living on in my memory. My maternal grandmother Gladys Simmons Suddeth's flinty strength and her playful joy, plus her memories of her grandmother Sophronia Bowman, gave me a deep sense of family continuity and a name to work from. My paternal grandmother Dorothy Williams's fierce industriousness, fired up by love, inspired an essence of Black mamahood I wished to bring to life in this book. My most beloved ancestor is my mother, Zeborah S. Williams. I consider her unswerving belief in me as my destiny. I wish I could see her when I say: Mum, every accomplishment I ever earn, every aspiration I ever hold, is yours—it is yours. I love you.

There are those who shaped my life, and there are others who changed it. Allison Remcheck Pernetti, like the publication of *Tangleroot* itself, you were a wish come true. I'm so thankful you saw my work for what it could be and furthered it into what it is. And to my editor Liz Szabla, I can't express my gratitude for your insight and insistence in pushing me to reimagine Noni's interior arc, in helping me reframe her journey, and in laying out a pathway to remake such crucial parts of my draft. I've grown as a writer because of you. My appreciation extends to everyone at Stimola Literary Studio, Feiwel & Friends, and elsewhere, who has been a part of this publication, especially to the sharp-eyed copyeditor, Starr Baer, and the artist, Neptune, whose haunting artistic talent has made a vision of my vision.

To Lance Cleland and the staff at Tin House, my residency with you was a pivotal point in the writing of this book. So was my friendship with Stacey Austin Egan during those memorable, productive, and fun two weeks. And thank you to the Elizabeth George Foundation for championing me as a novelist.

This book is a product of immense research, and I owe so much to the expertise of Marvin-Alonzo Greer, Dr. Judy Giesberg, Dr. Lynn Rainville, and Peter Schmitz. And to the amazing staff at the Library of Virginia, whom I turned to when I began research more than a decade ago; and my friends at the Historical Society of Pennsylvania and their stewardship of a treasured collection. I owe a special thanks to my colleagues at Virginia Humanities for those boosts of good vibes as I was mired in revisions and edits.

Thanks to Liz Rosenberg, for reviewing my original major draft—years later, the memory of your excitement over this book's potential gave me the confidence to try again. And a special thanks to my amazing friend Samantha Maldonado. My major second draft was so much stronger due to your editorial smarts and literary skill. And to Alicia Bessette and Matthew Quick: I have valued our friendship and your writerly guidance so much.

I'm thankful for an array of other friends for their encouragement, brainstorming, knowledge sharing, and advice through all these years of this novel coming to be: Adam Edmunds, Rachel Fryd, Alix Gerz, Katherine Gulick, Isaiah Harris, Andy Kahan, Autumn McClintock, Eileen Owens, Naisha Tyler, and Megan Weireter. And thank you Joanne Gabbin, Sandy Horrocks, and Tim Whitaker, for your faith in my work and efforts! To Julian Shendelman and the members of Sit & Write—those weekends were a much-needed restart to my writing life. To the fellow writers in my favorite breakfast club: my sweetheart Davey as well as Mike Anderson, Diana Black, Zan Gillies, Zach Laliberte, Carlton Melton, Lysandra Petersson, Lindsey Sitz, Chris Tucker, and Cassy Whitacre; thank you for checking in and for cheering me on. Another round of thanks goes to my entire Staunton community, for your friendship and support. I'm so lucky to have found myself back here.

Thank you to Janet and Larry White, for all the time in your home and on your farm, where I've learned so much and felt so loved. To my aunt and uncle Harmoniest and Vohn Busby: your support, your love, and your generosity have given me more than I can say. And thank you to my father, John Williams, for your ambitious nature that drives me forward, and your boisterous heart that carries me through. And—don't tell them, because they'll hold it over my head forever—but I'm so very grateful to my siblings John Williams Jr. and Anica Williams for believing in me from the time I was a bratty child (according to *their* accounts, but I recall being perfect). Speaking of great kids, Lawrence Williams, you're my brilliant light. I'm so proud to be your auntie, and to write and hope for your generation.

And of course, my love to Davey Strattan White, for everything, all of it. From cooking five-star meals to lending your storytelling genius, to inspiring me every single day as we create together, I couldn't be me without you. What a lovely, ridiculous, cat-filled, pun-studded, gutsy, artsy, nerdy, and wonderfully weird life we share. I'm so fortunate.

Finally, I have so much gratitude for you, readers of *Tangleroot*. Whether we've already met; whether we will meet one day (I hope to!); or whether I may never know your name, you mean so much. Keep reading, keep knowing, keep searching. Turn pages. Turn over stones and discover what's beneath. Turn to your sense of curiosity—hold it jealously. It is yours.

THANK YOU FOR READING THIS FEIWEL & FRIENDS BOOK. THE FRIENDS WHO MADE

TANGLEROOT

POSSIBLE ARE:

JEAN FEIWEL, PUBLISHER
LIZ SZABLA, VP, ASSOCIATE PUBLISHER
RICH DEAS, SENIOR CREATIVE DIRECTOR
ANNA ROBERTO, EXECUTIVE EDITOR
HOLLY WEST, SENIOR EDITOR
KAT BRZOZOWSKI, SENIOR EDITOR
DAWN RYAN, EXECUTIVE MANAGING EDITOR
RAYMOND ERNESTO COLÓN, DIRECTOR OF PRODUCTION
KIM WAYMER, SENIOR PRODUCTION MANAGER
FOYINSI ADEGBONMIRE, EDITOR
RACHEL DIEBEL, EDITOR
EMILY SETTLE, EDITOR
BRITTANY GROVES, ASSISTANT EDITOR
MEG SAYRE, JUNIOR DESIGNER
HELEN SEACHRIST, SENIOR PRODUCTION EDITOR